Ken McClure is an award-winning research scientist with the Medical Research Council of Great Britain. His medical thrillers have been translated into fifteen different languages and are all international bestsellers. He lives and works in Edinburgh, where he is currently at work on his sixth novel.

Acclaim for Ken McClure

`(Ken McClure) explains contagious illnesses in everyday language that makes you hold your breath in case you catch them'.
The Scotsman

`A pacy thriller from Scotland's very own Michael Crichton'.
Aberdeen Evening Express (Chameleon)

Rhodesia Bowls Club

CHAMELEON

Ken McClure

POCKET
B O O K S

LONDON · SYDNEY · NEW YORK · TOKYO · SINGAPORE · TORONTO

First published in Great Britain by Simon & Schuster Ltd, 1994
First published by Pocket Books, 1995
An imprint of Simon & Schuster Ltd
A Paramount Communications Company

Simon & Schuster Ltd
West Garden Place
Kendal Street
London W2 2AQ

Simon & Schuster of Australia Pty Ltd
Sydney

A CIP catalogue record for this book is available from the
British Library.
ISBN 0-671-85415-1

Printed by HarperCollins Manufacturing.

What man that sees the ever whirling wheel
Of change, the which all mortal things doth sway
But that thereby doth find and plainly feel
How mutability in them doth play
Her cruel sports, to many men's decay.

Edmund Spenser
(1522–99)

Prologue

Gail Spooner smoothed the front of her skirt and evened her lipstick by pursing her lips several times as she saw the car slow down. She had been expecting it, because the same Ford Orion was on its third lap of the area. It drew to a halt and she switched on her smile. Stepping out from the shadows, she walked over to the car and rested her elbow on the car's roof as she bent down to speak to the driver through the open window. 'Hello there,' she said as if he were an old friend.

The driver leaned across to open the passenger door and said, 'Get in.'

'Oh, the masterful kind,' said Gail, getting in and swinging her legs round to expose the maximum amount of stockinged thigh. 'I like a man who knows what he wants.' She turned to look at the driver and found no smile on his face. 'God, you're not the police, are you?' she asked nervously.

'No. Where do we go?'

'The car park at the back of Tesco's. It's nice and dark there and no one will bother us.'

'No, not in the car.'

'I've got a place, but it's going to cost you.'

'How much?'

'Forty-five. More if you want extras.'

'Extras?'

'You know, if I have to dress up or do anything . . .'

'What do you mean?'

Gail said, 'It's all right, I'm not criticising. You can tell

1

me what turns you on. Anything goes as long as it doesn't hurt.'

'No, nothing like that.'

'Right then, we'll have ourselves a little party, shall we? How about a drink first?'

'No drink. Where do we go?'

'My place is in Spicer's Row. It's a studio flat, an attic really, but it's cosy.'

The car crept through the dark streets and glided to a halt at the junction between Barton Road and Spicer's Row.

'We'll walk from here.'

'Please yourself.'

The couple walked down Spicer's Row and turned into a darkened doorway to wait while Gail fumbled in her handbag. The rattle of a lipstick against a powder compact continued intermittently until it gave way to a more metallic sound as she found her keys. She reached up to insert her door key in the lock with her bag held awkwardly under her arm. Curtains moved and a face looked out from a ground floor window to their left.

'Nosey old cow!' hissed Gail.

The man looked away to the right and drew his collar up. Gail thought nothing of the gesture. She was used to men being ill at ease at being seen with her; pulled-up collars and furtive looks over the shoulder were all part of the job.

Gail led the way up a flight of winding wooden stairs which creaked badly. She stopped half way up to turn and say, 'You haven't touched my bum. They all touch my bum when I climb these stairs. You've got a bit of class. I like that.'

The man just grunted in reply and they climbed to the top where Gail opened a door and clicked on the light. They entered and she switched on a fan heater which rattled intermittently and filled the room with the smell of burning dust from elements which had not been used for some time. Gail took off her jacket and threw it casually on the bed. She placed her hands on the man's shoulders and smiled up at him, saying seductively, 'Let's enjoy ourselves, shall we?'

Ignoring her, the man looked about him. A slight sneer played on his lips as he looked at the posters on the wall. They were mainly of film and pop stars but there was a large travel poster advertising the Greek islands. 'Have you been there?' he asked.

'Not yet,' Gail replied.

The man looked at her without expression for a moment before continuing with his inspection of the room.

'It's not much, but it's home,' said Gail with a small forced laugh. The man did not smile.

Interpreting the man's silence as shyness, Gail smiled and took a step backwards to begin taking off her clothes. She did it with the confidence of a woman sure of her ability to arouse men. When she was down to her underwear she turned sideways and simpered coyly, 'Perhaps you would like to help me with the rest?'

'Lie down.'

'So you are the masterful kind,' smiled Gail, spreadeagling herself on the bed and putting her hands behind her head.

There were a series of ribbons tied to the end of the bed. The man took them lightly in his hand and ran them through his fingers as if captivated by the sensation.

'So that's what you like . . . Well, why not?' Gail held up her wrists and said in a husky whisper, 'Tie me. Tie me up and then I'll be completely at your mercy. Would you like that?'

The man smiled for the first time and Gail took this as a sign of success. She simpered professionally as the man secured each wrist to a corner of the bed and then removed two more of the ribbons to start working on her ankles. Gail giggled and said, 'Don't you think you should take off my panties first?' She said it like a shy schoolgirl, but the man behaved as if he hadn't heard and finished securing her. He stood up to admire his handiwork and Gail pretended to struggle a little against her bonds. 'You've got me now,' she whispered. 'What are you going to do to me?'

Beads of sweat appeared along the man's top lip and the muscle in his left cheek quivered slightly as he muttered

3

something in what Gail thought was a foreign language. 'Here, what are you talking about?' she asked, her voice suddenly taking on a degree of uncertainty.

The man held Gail's gaze while he reached inside his jacket and pulled out a velvet cloth. He unwrapped it carefully and removed a metal object to hold it up before her. 'Do you know what this is?' he asked. There was a hoarse quality about his voice.

Gail's eyes were wide with fear. 'It's a knife,' she stammered. 'It's one of those knives doctors use . . .' Terror had tightened her throat and made her voice sound strained. She watched helplessly as the man brought the blade down slowly towards her skin. He paused and then cut away her bra straps cleanly. He removed the material then traced the flat of the blade gently to and fro down and across her stomach before cutting away the rest of her underwear.

A distant smile appeared on the man's face and Gail found her voice. 'Steady on, they cost me a fortune,' she joked nervously. 'They're French.'

The man looked at her as if lost in a dream, but then suddenly his eyes hardened. Gail's fear turned to terror. She opened her mouth to scream, but the man covered it with his hand and brought his face down close to hers. 'You're right,' he whispered. 'It's a knife that doctors use . . .'

1

'How do you feel?' Sue Jamieson asked her husband.

Scott Jamieson looked up at the pretty girl who was smiling down at him, her head slightly to one side. 'Amorous,' he said.

'Be serious.'

'I am serious.'

'You're not on,' laughed Sue.

'Come back to bed.'

'There isn't time. You can't be late for your interview.' she said, sitting down on the edge of the bed and ruffling her husband's dark hair.

'Of course there's time,' said Scott Jamieson. He circled his arm round Sue and pulled her down on top of him, but she remained adamant. 'There isn't!' she said, putting both hands against his chest to fend him off.

Jamieson relaxed his grip and smiled. 'I love you,' he said softly.

'I know you do and I love you,' said Sue. 'But right now . . . shower!'

'You win,' conceded Jamieson, swinging his legs over the side of the bed. Sue looked at the scars on his body as he sat up and kissed his shoulder on impulse. 'Change your mind?' he asked.

'Get on with you,' she said. 'I'll get breakfast.'

Jamieson turned on the shower with his right hand and felt a sudden, sharp twinge of pain in his fingers that made him draw back with a soft curse. He stretched his fingers out and examined them as he had done a thousand times before in the recent past, but there was nothing untoward to see, no disfigurement, no indication of misalignment, no obvious reason why he should not hold a scalpel again, if it were not for a residual stiffness that prevented him keeping perfect control of it. Give it time, Jamieson, he reminded himself and immediately felt pleased at his new-found philosophical attitude.

It was a view he could not have expressed in the early months of his recovery when a mixture of frustration, self-pity and blind anger had ruled his head and made him almost insufferable to live with. But Sue had never wavered. From the time of the accident she had been a tower of strength, nursing him through the physical pain and then the mental anguish that followed. She had made him face up to the obvious – that he should at least think about changing specialties, an idea he had found abhorrent at first but had eventually come to accept.

Pathology had been a possibility, but a career among cadavers and the sweet, sickly smell of formaldehyde had held little attraction. Too many of the pathologists he knew were well on the way to alcoholism and he could understand why. For him, medicine was about saving lives, not finding out why they had failed. He knew that this was a ridiculously simplistic view, but white tiles and the stench of death were not for him.

That had left radiology and the lab specialties – haematology, biochemistry and microbiology. In all, Jamieson had spent eighteen months trying to find a new niche in medicine, but in the end he had admitted defeat. His academic performance in refresher and re-training courses had been beyond reproach, but once the challenge of learning something new had receded he had been left with an undeniable feeling of restlessness that he suspected the laboratory specialties could never satisfy. He was temperamentally unsuited to them, having known the excitement and challenge of surgery too well.

Jamieson had been about to leave medicine altogether and join his father's business, when one of the consultants on his last re-training course had persuaded him to let him put his name forward for a job he thought Jamieson well-suited for. He could not be inveigled into saying exactly what the job would be, only that it would not be ordinary and that it would not be a desk job. Agreeing finally that he had nothing to lose by applying, Jamieson was invited to attend an interview at the Home Office.

Scott Jamieson was thirty-three, eight years older than his wife Sue. He had been brought up in the Scottish border town of Galashiels, a mill town that nestled on the banks of the River Tweed in soft, rolling countryside. The eldest son of a successful mill owner, Jamieson had been educated at Merchiston Castle School in Edinburgh, like his father before him. Blessed with an easy charm and both physical and scholastic ability, he had sailed through his school years and, in the process, acquired the confidence of someone who had never known anything but success.

A down-to-earth father and the level headedness of the border folk who were his friends and neighbours had prevented this confidence from turning into arrogance. It was one thing to be captain of rugby at school, quite another to take the field with the rugby-mad border teams on a Saturday afternoon. Self-conceit had a habit of coming to grief in border mud.

From school Jamieson had gone on to Glasgow University to study medicine after taking a year out to work in his father's mill. Although he had enjoyed the experience of working in the mill, he knew that the life was not for him and had been relieved when his father had not seemed too disappointed when he told him as much. The fact that he had two younger brothers probably helped.

At university, he made the first mistake of his young life when he underestimated the demands of first-year medicine and spent too much time socialising when he should have been studying. He had come close to failing the exams, but scraped through and was careful not to make the same mistake again. He eventually graduated in the top one third of his class. An elective at a Boston teaching hospital in the United States had been followed by residencies at two London hospitals and a decision to become a surgeon.

He had met Sue, who was then a student nurse, during his appointment as surgical registrar at Addenbrooke's Hospital in Cambridge and, like so many men who had had a string of girl friends, Jamieson had fallen head over heels in love when the real thing happened. He had known at once that Sue was the girl he must marry and eight months later he did.

Sue's father, a Surrey stockbroker, had given them a splendid wedding in the village where Sue had been brought up. They were married in the Norman village church on a beautiful sunny day with Scott and his brothers adding colour to the gentle green of English grass by wearing full Highland dress. Tartan had mingled easily with taffeta and champagne had sparkled in glasses shaded by floppy hats as both families and a host of friends celebrated the wedding of a golden couple whose horizons seemed limitless.

Ironically, it was Jamieson's unfamiliarity with any kind of failure that left him unable to cope after the car accident. He was unconscious for nearly a fortnight and very weak when he finally did come round, but as soon as his strength started to return he felt sure that it would be only a short time before his life returned to normal. He would start operating again and resume his climb to the top of his profession. When it finally dawned on him that recovery was going to be a long, slow process and there was still a question mark over how complete it would be, he had started to behave with a petulance and ill temper that he had never displayed before.

His general rudeness to the hospital staff and in particular to the people who cared about him most had been compounded with long periods of relentless self-pity, with suicide as its main theme. Throughout, Sue had shown a maturity beyond her years and she had brought him through the darkest period of his life to accept what lay before him. Before *them*, as she had never tired of pointing out. She eventually succeeded in restoring Jamieson to a stage where he became thoroughly ashamed of his insufferable behaviour. From then on he had improved day by day until now when, although there was still a large question mark over his future as a surgeon, he was definitely restored to her as her husband, the old Scott Jamieson.

'Good luck,' Sue said now as Jamieson turned at the door and kissed her on the cheek.

'If they want me to catalogue bedpans, I'm not taking the job. Is that understood?' said Jamieson.

'Understood,' said Sue with a smile. 'But I'll get something special in for dinner just in case.' She stood in the road waving until the car had disappeared round the corner at the end of the lane.

Scott Jamieson always had to steel himself to leave the peaceful Kent village where he and Sue lived to go into central London in July or August. The crowds and the oppressive heat on sunny days invariably made him short-tempered. Today it was muggy and a dull greyness gave the buildings in the city a blanket anonymity as he drove to an underground car park behind Trafalgar Square and collected his ticket at the barrier. It was a slow, five-minute spiral before he found a place being vacated by an elderly man. The man was having difficulty reversing owing to an inability to turn his head properly. Each attempt was accompanied by a corresponding increase in engine revs until, when he finally succeeded, the entire parking level was filled with drifting blue smoke.

Jamieson locked up his car and sprinted up the stairs to begin his walk to Whitehall, weaving in and out of groups of tourists who were moving along aimlessly and seldom looking in the direction in which they were travelling. He had to halt and make three attempts to pass a Japanese man, Nikon held to his face, moving synchronously with him each time he decided to change direction. The man's wife laid a hand on her husband's forearm and the impasse was resolved with an oriental bow and an occidental smile.

A uniformed man stopped Jamieson at the entrance to the Home Office and Jamieson produced his letter. He waited patiently while the man read it and then announced that he would have to check. He made a phone call on the internal system and then said, 'Miss Roberts will be down presently.' He invited Jamieson to take a seat and indicated a bench in the hallway.

Jamieson sat down and idly watched the pedestrian traffic. A serious young man, wearing glasses that threatened to fall off his nose, shuffled along the corridor while sifting through a sheaf of papers. The man had feet which pointed outwards, giving him the air of a silent-film comedian. His inattention to direction caused him to collide with two girls carrying tea cups. The tea slopped on to the floor as the girls tottered backwards holding their cups at arms' length. The man looked up from his papers oblivious of the fact that he had been the cause of the bother. He smiled briefly and walked on, leaving the typists looking daggers after him. Jamieson smiled sympathetically and one of the girls shook her head.

Two men, wearing conservatively dark suits, approached from the other direction, speaking in loud voices and moving slowly. Jamieson noticed that the uniformed men stiffened at their approach.

'Absolutely,' said one of the men as they passed Jamieson without apparently noticing he was there. 'That kind of authorisation can only come from the Minister himself.'

Jamieson watched their backs as they passed the uniformed men without a glance, totally engrossed in what they were saying. God save me from office society, he thought.

A woman wearing a mauve suit emerged from one of the lifts and walked purposefully towards him; she was carrying a clip-board. 'Dr Jamieson?' she enquired. Jamieson agreed and the woman made a tick on her clip-board before saying, 'I'm Miss Roberts. If you would like to come this way, please.'

Jamieson and the woman exchanged a brief smile as their eyes met in the lift and then the woman studied her feet for the remainder of the journey while Jamieson looked intently at the floor indicator. He was trying to remember the name of the perfume the woman was wearing. In the confines of the lift it was strong and for some reason, quite haunting. Femme! he decided just before the lift doors opened. He now remembered why it was haunting. In his teens he had had a holiday romance with a girl who subsequently drenched her letters in the stuff.

The doors slid back and the woman led them along a corridor to stop outside a room marked 'Suite 4'. Jamieson was left alone for a moment in a small ante room before the woman returned and said, 'The committee will see you now.'

Miss Roberts held the door and Jamieson walked into a large room which would have been sunny had not the sky been so overcast. He found three men there. The middle one made the introductions. 'Dr Armour,' he said, indicating on his left a small, grey-haired man sporting a polka-dotted bow-tie, 'and Dr Foreman,' he said, turning to his right. A thick-set man with coarse, Brylcreemed hair which came to a widow's peak on his narrow forehead gave a cursory nod. 'My name is Macmillan,' said the man in the middle, turning his gaze back to Jamieson. There was nothing rude in his stare but Jamieson was aware of being appraised. Macmillan was in his fifties, tall, slim, and his complexion bore the smooth tan that Jamieson associated with good living. His silver hair swept back from his forehead to sit comfortably on the collar of his blue, Bengal-striped shirt.

'Let me explain,' said Macmillan. 'We represent the medical section of the Sci-Med Monitor.'

Jamieson looked blank and Macmillan continued. 'We are a relatively small body; we have a staff of twenty and we investigate and, if feasible, deal with problems arising specifically within the areas of science and medicine in this country.'

'I'm sorry. I don't follow?' said Jamieson.

Macmillan said, 'Frankly, it's hard to be more specific. Our brief is so wide and varied.'

'You said "problems",' said Jamieson. 'What sort of problems?'

Macmillan touched his finger tips together and then moved his hands apart in a deliberate gesture of vagueness. 'Matters of medical practice, matters of ethics, matters of circumstance and occasionally matters of criminality.'

11

'I'm still lost,' confessed Jamieson looking at Foreman. 'Surely the police handle anything of a criminal nature?'

'Indeed,' said Foreman. 'But only once it is established that a criminal offence has taken place, and that's where the difficulty can sometimes lie. There are occasions when the police simply do not have the expertise to operate. They have specialist officers, of course, as in the case of the Fraud Squad, but when it comes to science and medicine they need expert help.'

'What about the forensic science service?' Jamieson querried.

'True, but they are back-room boys, both by inclination and by training. They are largely for after the event. Occasionally we need people up front and that's where the Sci-Med Monitor comes in. Let me give you an example. Quite recently, drug-related offences suddenly started to rocket in a certain northern university town. The police had no success in finding out where the stuff was coming from until we put one of our people in on the ground. Three weeks later we had our answer. Four post-graduate students in the science faculty were manufacturing the stuff. They had all but cornered the market in hallucigenic agents. They all worked in different departments and each was responsible for obtaining a few of the chemicals needed for the manufacturing process. Because the materials were being spread out over four different order lists, suspicion was not aroused until our man, who had access to all the paper work and the time to peruse it, spotted what was going on.'

'I see,' said Jamieson. 'I wouldn't have. I have no idea how to make LSD.'

'We wouldn't expect you to,' said Armour. 'Our chap in that instance was a biochemist. Because, as Macmillan said, our brief is so wide, we have to fit our person to the job. Let me give you another example. One of our biggest pharmaceutical companies was being embarrassed by rumours of success which had no basis in fact. One of our people traced the problem to a scientist working in a prestigious biotechnology unit located in one of our top universities. The individual in question had invested every last penny he had in the drug company's shares and then "leaked" a false story to the newspapers about the unit having come up with an effective vaccine against AIDS and how the pharmaceutical company had been given the right to manufacture it. Because the leak had originated in such an eminent establishment the press swallowed it and printed the story. The company's shares shot up, of course, and the man made a killing.'

'I didn't even buy shares in British Gas,' confessed Jamieson.

'Again we recognise that this is not your area of expertise,' said Macmillan.

'Then what is?' asked Jamieson.

'You are a surgeon and you also have considerable knowledge of other medical specialties thanks to the auxiliary training you did after your unfortunate accident. We think that this would make you a valuable asset to Sci-Med.'

'You said that you tend to fit people to the job in hand. Have you a specific job in mind for me?' asked Jamieson.

'As a matter of fact we have,' said Macmillan. 'The problem is surgical, not criminal, and that's largely why we think you are the man for the job.'

'I'm all ears,' said Jamieson. For the first time in many months he was interested and intrigued at the prospect of a job.

Macmillan opened a file in front of him and removed something from the top of the pile. It was a single page report, typed on blue paper. He handed it to Jamieson.

Jamieson read the document in silence, trying to concentrate under the stares of the three men. He learned that two women had died recently after undergoing surgery in the gynaecology unit at Kerr Memorial Hospital in Leeds. Both had contracted post-operative infections which had not responded to treatment.

'What's the problem?' asked Jamieson.

'The women, both in for fairly minor surgery, contracted a *Pseudomonas* infection after their operations and treatment proved ineffectual,' said Macmillan.

'Do you know why?'

'The strain turned out to be antibiotic resistant.'

'The usual problem with *Pseudomonas*,' said Jamieson.

'Quite so,' said Armour, 'but this one was particularly bad. Even the specialised drugs wouldn't touch it.'

'Nasty,' said Jamieson. 'Did they manage to trace the source of the infection?'

'No, and that's the real crux of the problem,' said Macmillan. 'Despite intensive investigation by the staff of the microbiology lab at the hospital and a flurry of disinfection after the second death, the problem has persisted; three days ago a third woman contracted the infection. She's very ill.'

'That's all a bit odd,' said Jamieson. 'Surely with a bit of co-operation between the labs and the surgical teams it should have been possible to identify the source of the outbreak and clear it up?'

'You put your finger on the problem when you said "co-operation",' said Armour. 'The head of surgery at Kerr Memorial is rather a difficult man. Thelwell's his name. He is currently blaming the lab for failing to identify the source of the infection. Richardson, the consultant bacteriologist, is naturally having none of it. He maintains that if the wards and theatres are clean then the fault must lie somewhere within the surgical team itself.'

'Both sides have become entrenched,' added Macmillan.

'That makes things awkward,' agreed Jamieson.

'The local press haven't got on to the staff disharmony angle as yet but it can only be a matter of time. They're already showing signs of latching on to the problem as a political football. You know the sort of thing, cut-backs equal dirty hospitals, understaffing means danger for the patients.'

'And where exactly do I fit in?' asked Jamieson tentatively.

'You are a surgeon, you can tell good practice from bad. You have also spent enough time in microbiology labs to be familiar with their side of things. We would like you, if you decide to join us, to go up there and take a good look at the situation. Try to find out where the problem lies and if possible sort it out.'

'My presence will be resented,' said Jamieson.

'Indeed it will,' agreed Armour. 'What people see as outside interference is never welcome in any profession, perhaps least of all in ours.'

Jamieson nodded and asked, 'What if they should refuse to co-operate?'

'They can't,' said Macmillan. 'You will have the full authorisation of Her Majesty's Government to make any enquiry you wish. We would prefer you not to stand on too many toes, but on the other hand when it comes to playing silly buggers with peoples' lives personal dignity comes second.'

'I see.'

'You can have until tomorrow lunch-time to decide whether you want to join us or not,' said Macmillan. 'We must know by then.'

'If it's not a rude question . . .' began Jamieson tentatively.

'You'll be paid a salary equivalent to that of a senior registrar,' said Macmillan.

'Time won't be necessary,' said Jamieson firmly. 'I've already decided. You can count me in.'

'Excellent,' said Macmillan. He got up and shook Jamieson's hand. Armour and Foreman did the same. 'Miss Roberts will give you details on the way out. The sooner you get started the sooner this business will be cleared up.'

'I'll travel up tomorrow if that's all right,' said Jamieson.

'You'd better take this,' said Macmillan, handing Jamieson the file on Kerr Memorial that lay in front of him. 'You will find information on the senior staff in here. It's as well to know something about the place before you arrive.'

Jamieson left the room and gave Miss Roberts the information necessary for her to complete the paperwork for his appointment. In turn, she provided him with documents of authorisation and two credit cards. A booklet on allowable expenses was included. He was asked if it would be convenient to have his photograph taken and undergo a routine medical examination that same afternoon. Jamieson said that he would have some lunch and come straight back.

Jamieson left the building feeling better than he had for a long time. He had found himself a real job, not just a place on a refresher or re-training course, and, what was more, it sounded interesting. He phoned Sue from the first call box he came to and told her the news.

'That's marvellous,' said Sue. 'What is it exactly?'

'I'll tell you when I get home, but it's something useful and I feel good about it.'

'I can hear that,' laughed Sue. 'When do you start?'

'Tomorrow.'

'That was quick!'

'In Leeds.'

'Leeds!' exclaimed Sue with dismay in her voice. 'Does this mean we have to move to . . .'

'No, it doesn't,' interrupted Jamieson. 'We stay where we are but if the job works out I may be away from home quite a bit. We can talk about it when I get back.'

'What time will you be home?'

'Early evening.'

'Bring some wine in with you,' said Sue.

It started to rain as Jamieson drove back along the A2 towards Canterbury. By the time he had passed through the town and was travelling along the lanes flanked by fruit farms he could tell from the heaviness of the sky that there was a lot more to come.

Water streamed down the windows of the cottage as Sue served up dinner and Jamieson told her about his job.

'Sounds like you are going to be some kind of medical detective,' said Sue.

'Not really. I think it's more a case of an outsider being able to see something that people who are too involved might miss.'

'The wood for the trees,' said Sue.

'That sort of thing.'

'More wine?'

'I have to work,' said Jamieson.

'On our last evening together?'

'I have to read through some papers about the hospital. I'm sorry, but it is important . . .'

Sue smiled at Jamieson's discomfort and kissed him on the forehead. 'Go on with you then,' she said. 'I'll clear up.'

Jamieson took the file he had brought home upstairs to the small room he used as a study and turned on the desk lamp. The desk was directly beneath the window and he watched the rain beat against it briefly before adjusting the angle of the lamp and starting to work his way through the papers. He left the main light off, preferring instead to use the circular pool of light from the desk lamp as an island of concentration.

Two hours later, Jamieson felt satisfied that he had assimilated all the information necessary to give him a head start at the Kerr Memorial. He had familiarised himself with the names and backgrounds of half a dozen of the senior staff and how they related to each other in the hierarchy of hospital life. He flipped the folder shut and leaned back in his chair to stretch up his arms into the darkness outside the scope of the lamp.

Sue entered the room and came up behind him to wrap her arms around his shoulders and rest her cheek against the top of his head.

'We have some unfinished business,' she said.

'We have?'

'This morning . . .'

They paused on the landing outside the study door and Sue said, 'Sssh! Listen!' They listened together to the sound of the rain on the roof and of the larger drops falling from the branches of the willow tree outside. 'I love this place,' said Sue.

Jamieson kissed her hair and said, 'I know, so do I. I'd like us to grow old here. I'd like to sit out there on a summer's evening watching our grandchildren playing round a house that stood here a hundred years before Bonnie Prince Charlie marched south.'

'Who's a sentimental old softy then?' said Sue.

'Me,' said Jamieson. 'Until tomorrow.'

Sue turned her face up to Jamieson and said softly, 'At least I've got you until then.' She pulled his mouth down on to hers.

*   *   *

17

Jamieson was up first in the morning. He was in the bath when he heard Sue get up and go downstairs. The sounds from the radio drifted upstairs as he towelled himself dry and looked out to see that it was still raining. He cursed softly at the thought of having to travel north on a wet motorway with spray from heavy lorries obscuring his vision. He looked up at the sky in both directions, hoping to find a break in the clouds, but found none. With a grimace, he padded back to the bedroom to begin dressing.

Jamieson came downstairs wearing a dark blue suit and adjusting his tie as if it were too tight. 'Do I look like a detective?' he asked.

'No, you look like a doctor.'

'Is that bad?'

Sue smiled and said, 'No, that's just fine.'

'Maybe I should wear a dirty raincoat and scratch my head a lot?'

'The nurses would probably give you a bath,' said Sue.

'All right,' conceded Jamieson.

'A prostitute was found murdered in Leeds yesterday. I heard it on the radio,' said Sue, pouring the coffee.

'Not the safest of professions.'

'I'll bear that in mind in case you don't take to your new job.'

Jamieson smiled and Sue said, 'You're nervous. I can tell.'

'A bit,' confessed Jamieson. 'I'll be glad when today is over and I've made a start.'

'I can understand that,' said Sue. 'You will try and call me this evening?'

'Of course,' said Jamieson. 'With a bit of luck this really shouldn't take too long.'

'This bug that's causing all the problems up there, what exactly is it?' asked Sue.

'It's called *Pseudomonas*. It's a fairly common bug that likes to live anywhere where there's moisture. You often find it in flower vases and the like in hospitals, but it becomes a problem when it gets in to open wounds and sets up an infection, because it's difficult to treat. This one seems particularly bad.'

'It must be an absolute nightmare to go into hospital for something fairly simple and catch something much worse while you're there,' said Sue.

Jamieson nodded and said, 'It can happen all too easily and it's the sort of thing that erodes public confidence. That's why the Ministry are eager to see an end to it.' Jamieson picked up his bag and put his free arm round Sue. 'I'll call you tonight,' he said.

'Take care,' said Sue.

2

Gordon Thomas Thelwell was a product of his upbringing. Whatever warmth of feeling he might once have had, had been purged by a public school obsessed with self-discipline and a lifetime's unquestioning adherence to upper-middle class notions of respectability and correct behaviour. His thin lips rarely smiled and, on the odd occasions when they did, bestowed on him the uneasy look of a man performing an unnatural act. When he spoke, his voice followed a level monotone as sombre as the suits he favoured. The starched rigidity of his shirt collars seemed to have been specifically designed to afford him the maximum discomfort, always an essential element in the dress favoured by lay preachers.

Although eloquent enough when passing on the views of others, be they medical when instructing junior doctors or religious when reading the Sunday lesson, unscripted communication with his fellows had always been a bit of a problem for Thelwell. Small talk was uncharted territory. Humour lay in the province of the vulgar. Anger was displayed by a slight clipping of the vowels when he spoke and he had a penchant for biting sarcasm that showed scant regard for the sensibilities of others. Satisfaction, on the other hand, would be indicated by a cursory nod and a momentary puckering of the lips. In short, G.T. Thelwell was not going to win any popularity contest among the staff at Kerr Memorial Hospital, but he was respected as a competent if unapproachable consultant surgeon and a pillar of the local community.

The fact that Thelwell was the father of two girls was the subject of some disrespectful comment among the more junior nurses at the hospital who could not, or preferred not to, imagine Thelwell ever making love to anyone. Those who knew his wife, Marion, recognised that she was the exact female counterpart of Thelwell, but whereas he seldom smiled, Marion wore a permanent dutiful smile of the kind adopted by royalty when opening biscuit factories and having to greet the entire production staff.

Marion, when not dealing with the day-to-day problems of 'Les girls', as she habitually referred to her daughters, immersed herself in charity work. Her particular interests were dumb animals and underprivileged children, although lately she had taken to organising fund-raising ventures associated with the buying of new equipment for the hospital. As chairperson of the Friends of Kerr Memorial, she had recently handed over two new incubator units to the hospital in a small ceremony reported in the local paper. A print of the photograph accompanying the article had been framed and now stood on her dressing table.

Like her husband, Marion Thelwell saw humour and passion as the enemy of duty. In another age she and her husband might well have found their true niche in India or some other far-flung corner of Empire, where Thelwell would have been an authoritarian District Commissioner and Marion would have played her full and supporting role in whipping the natives into order.

The alarm went off in the Thelwells' bedroom at seven and Marion rose first as she always did to wrap her gown loosely about her before going to the kitchen to switch on the kettle. On the way back she checked that the girls were awake before returning to the bedroom to open the curtains. 'Oh dear,' she tutted. 'More rain.'

'Really,' replied her husband automatically.

'Do you have much on today, dear?'

'Two exploratories and a hysterectomy and that damned man is coming up from the Ministry.'

'Man, dear?'

'Some interfering busybody from the Department of Health is coming up from London to "take a look at our problem" as they put it.'

'I'm sure they're only trying to help, dear. Do you think you will be back by four?'

'Seems unlikely. I am informed by our illustrious medical superintendent that I must humour this nosey parker, give him every assistance.' Thelwell's voice was heavy with vitriol. 'Why do you ask?'

'I have a committee meeting at four. I wondered whether I should ask Mrs Rivers to look after the girls?'

'It would be as well. I'll call you later when I've dealt with Mr Nosey Parker.'

'Aren't you being a bit hard on this man?' put in Marion. 'Surely the sooner this infection business is cleared up, the better for everyone?'

Thelwell gave his wife a look that suggested she was questioning holy writ and said, 'It's not a man from London we need at Kerr Memorial, Marion, it's a competent microbiology department. If we had a laboratory that could do its job properly and find the source of this damned bug we wouldn't need outside interference. I thought you understood that?'

'Yes, dear.'

'Good morning, Daddy.' A girl of eleven came into the room, her face pink from washing.

'Good morning, Nicola.'

'Good morning, Daddy.' A second girl, slightly taller than her sister but with the same scrubbed complexion, came into the room and stood beside Nicola.

'Good morning, Patricia.'

The ritual over, both girls were ushered out by their mother, leaving G.T. Thelwell to rise and face the day.

'The police found a murdered woman in the city last night,' Marion told him shortly afterwards as she served Thelwell's breakfast of two boiled eggs. (Three minutes, fifteen seconds.) 'A prostitute.'

Thelwell gave a quiet grunt of disapproval as he looked around for the salt cellar. His exaggerated movement alerted Marion to the problem and she handed it to him. 'Considering the lives they lead, I'm surprised there aren't many more,' he said. He sliced the top off his first egg with a decisive sweep of his knife.

John Richardson, consultant bacteriologist at Kerr Memorial, yawned and scratched at the stubble on his chin. He grimaced as he saw the rain outside and murmured, 'Ye gods, another day nearer the grave.'

'I think that's why I married you,' said a woman's voice from under the covers. 'Your infectious sense of optimism.'

'I think you have just talked yourself out of a cup of tea,' said Richardson.

'I take it back,' said the voice lazily.

Richardson smiled. 'You should have been a politician with such limpet-like adherence to principle,' he said. 'Tea or coffee?'

'Tea. You're up early.'

'I've got a lot on and that chap from London is coming today, you know, the one I told you about,' said Richardson still looking out at the rain.

'The government investigator,' said Claire Richardson with mock solemnity.

'That's the one.'

'What is he exactly? A bureaucrat?'

'No, I understand he's medically qualified. He's from some body called the Sci-Med Monitor.'

'Do you think he's going to make any difference?'

Richardson shrugged and rubbed his chin again. 'Normally, I would have said no, but who knows? Right now I'm willing to agree to anything before someone else dies needlessly. We've tried everything we can think of to find the source of the infection but we keep coming up with blanks.'

'Frustrating.'

'And embarrassing,' added Richardson. 'It's making me look a complete fool, as Thelwell never fails to point out.'

'They can't blame you,' said Claire. 'You've covered every test in the book and you're one of the most experienced bacteriologists in the region.'

'Counts for nothing when women start dying and I can't tell them why.'

'You've still no notion at all where the infection might be coming from?'

'None.'

'Isn't that a bit odd?'

Richardson gave a bitter laugh and said, 'You're beginning to sound like Thelwell.'

'I'm sorry, I didn't mean it that way. It just seems strange that you haven't managed to find the source when you said yourself that it was an everyday sort of bug and there's such a lot known about it.'

Richardson looked at his wife's worried face and smiled. He said gently, 'I know you didn't and you're right, it is strange. That's what makes me feel that we haven't missed anything in the tests. The bug isn't hiding somewhere in the hospital, it's being carried by a member of staff.'

'But surely you've tested all the staff?'

'Of course,' agreed Richardson. 'And they were all negative.'

'Back to square one.'

Richardson nodded and turned away as a loud click from the kitchen told him that the kettle had boiled.

'How is your new assistant settling in?' Claire called through to him.

'Evans? He's first class,'

Claire Richardson smiled affectionately at her husband as he returned carrying a tray with her tea and biscuits on it. She said, 'You say that about all your staff. You're a big softie, John Richardson.'

'Nonsense,' said Richardson gruffly. 'He's an excellent microbiologist and he has certainly taken a weight off my shoulders.'

Claire Richardson smiled at the unease her husband always displayed at any suggestion of a compliment. There was a definite mannerism associated with it. He would reach up his left hand to rub his neck as if he had an itch there. She had never mentioned this to him. 'If I were thirty years younger I could fall in love with you all over again.' she said.

'What some women will say to get tea in bed,' muttered Richardson shuffling out of the room.

Jamieson swung the car in through the gates of Kerr Memorial and was waved to a halt by a uniformed man. He had to sit still while the man made a detailed inspection of his windscreen and then indicated that he should wind down his window.

'No permit,' said the man as if it were a death sentence.

Jamieson reached into his inside pocket and produced the ID card that he had been provided with by Whitehall. The man looked at the photograph and then at Jamieson. He repeated this operation three times before committing himself to reading what was on the card. This he did with a thoroughness that Jamieson felt sure would have been a credit to an accountant at the Bank of England. The man handed him the card back and stretched himself to his full height. 'Not in my instructions,' he said, putting his hands behind his back and standing tall like a human wall.

'I beg your pardon,' said Jamieson when he felt that no more was forthcoming.

'My instructions are clear,' said the man. 'No one comes through these gates without a permit authorised and signed by the hospital secretary. You'll have to leave.'

Jamieson looked at the man and the man diverted his eyes to stare into the middle distance which officialdom always finds so compelling. Jamieson bit his tongue and reversed the car out through the gates. The rain on the rear screen made it more difficult than it might otherwise have been and did nothing to improve his temper. 'What a start,' he muttered. The 'full authorisation of Her Majesty's Government' and I can't get through the bloody gates . . .'

He found a parking place after a five-minute hunt through the streets and switched off the engine with a sigh. He gave

himself a couple of minutes to see if the rain might ease off
before starting on the the half-mile walk back to the hospital,
but the slight lightening in the sky he thought he detected
had disappeared. The rain got heavier and Richardson's mood
grew blacker as his hair got wetter. He entertained the paranoid
thought that the man on the gate had been primed to make
things awkward for him, part of the obstructiveness he was
prepared for, but then he dismissed the thought. That would
be just too childish. Wouldn't it? He avoided looking at the
man on the gate as he passed through on foot, feeling like a
captured soldier being forced to parade through the streets of his
conqueror. He started to follow the signs for 'Administration'.

'Do you have an appointment?' asked the woman in response to
Jamieson's request to see the hospital secretary. She spoke with
a nasal whine that made her even less attractive than the fact that
she was decidedly round shouldered and had parchment dry
skin. Her hair was tied up in a tight, grey bun and her spectacles
hung from a gold chain.

'Not exactly, but I think you will find he is expecting me.'

The woman gave a humourless smirk as if she had caught
Jamieson out in a lie and said, 'Mr Crichton does not see anyone
without an appointment.'

Jamieson, his hair still wet from the walk and his temper
barely in check, took out his ID card and put it down with slow
deliberation on the desk in front of the woman. Struggling to
keep rein on his tongue, he said, 'Just tell him I'm here . . .
please.'

The complacent smugness of a minor official began to waver.
'I'll have to check,' she stammered and then turned on her heel
to disappear through another door, still clutching Jamieson's
card. She returned a few moments later with a short man trailing
behind her. He was holding Jamieson's card in his left hand
while pressing a large white handkerchief to his nose with the
other. Jamieson had to wait until the man had finished wiping
his nose before he spoke. 'Perhaps I can help?' said the man.

'Are you the hospital secretary?'

The man gave a self-deprecating little smile and said, 'Actually no, I'm Mr Cartwright. I'm afraid Mr Crichton does not see anyone without an appointment.'

Jamieson's frustration got the better of him as a small pool of rain-water built up around his feet. He leaned on the desk counter and said solicitously, 'Mr Cartwright, will you please inform Mr Crichton that I am here and do it now!'

Cartwright's manner changed to one of barely suppressed outrage. His authority had been challenged and he bristled with indignation.

Jamieson saw the woman stiffen in preparation to support her colleague in a fresh campaign of obstruction and decided to attack first. 'The Home Office, in conjunction with the Department of Health, have sent me all the way up here to see your hospital secretary and you two have apparently decided to stop me. In the interests of what I might say about this in my report, I suggest that you . . . re-consider?'

For a moment it looked as if Cartwright was prepared to argue the point, but then he capitulated and left the room. The woman avoided Jamieson's eyes and returned to her typing.

Within minutes a painfully thin man, well over six feet tall with a large, almost totally bald head, and wearing glasses that seemed too small for him, entered the room and handed Jamieson back his card. He smiled and held out his hand. 'Dr Jamieson? I'm Hugh Crichton. I've been expecting you. You look soaked.'

Crichton took Jamieson into his office and offered him whisky, an offer that Jamieson felt inclined to accept but decided not to at four in the afternoon. He noticed that Crichton's complexion had a distinctly yellow tinge to it and wondered if alcohol had played a part in that.

'Something else perhaps?'

'A parking permit would be nice.'

Crichton threw back his head and laughed. 'Oh, I see. You've had a brush with our Mr Norris. I'm sorry, I should have foreseen that. We'll fix that right away.' Crichton pressed a button on his intercom and asked the woman at the end of it to make out a permit for Jamieson. He kept his finger down on the button and asked Jamieson, 'Tea? Coffee?'

'Tea, please.'

While they waited for the tea to arrive Crichton asked Jamieson what he would require in the way of facilities at the hospital.

'A room, a telephone, access to medical records, possibly lab space.'

Crichton nodded and said, 'Well, I think I anticipated most of these. I've arranged for you to have an office in the administration block and Dr Carew, our medical superintendent, has requested that individual consultants co-operate with you in providing suitable space for you in their domains should you require it. I've also taken the liberty of having the housekeeper prepare a room for you in the doctors' residency. I didn't know if you would want to stay in the hospital or not?'

'I do,' agreed Jamieson. 'I'm grateful.'

'Not at all. Perhaps you would like to go there now and dry off before getting started?'

Jamieson agreed and finished his tea.

'And then what?' asked Crichton. 'Where would you like to start?'

'I'd like to have a word with Dr Carew first, if that's convenient.'

'I anticipated that too,' smiled Crichton. 'Dr Carew has pencilled you in for five.'

It was Jamieson's turn to smile. He said, 'Perhaps you should just tell me what else you anticipated and we can work from there.'

'I thought you might want to have a word with the consultants, Thelwell and Richardson, so I've organised a little get-together here in my office at six. You can get to meet people informally over a sherry and make your own arrangements for tomorrow.'

'Fine,' said Jamieson.

Crichton pressed the button on his intercom and leaned towards it to say, 'Dr Jamieson will be staying in the residency.

Will you inform the housekeeper and ask Miss Dotrice if she would be so kind as to show Dr Jamieson the way.'

Jamieson thanked the girl who had accompanied him to the residency. He closed the door behind him and breathed a long sigh. The room was depressingly spartan, but it had all he needed. A bed, a table, a chair, a telephone, a reading lamp – Jamieson switched it on to relieve the gloom – and a small bathroom that had obviously been added fairly recently. It had been made by simply partitioning off a corner of the room. Jamieson ran himself a bath and took off his clothes. He felt the old, iron radiator and found it cold, the towel rail was equally arctic. There was a solitary wall heater above the bath and he pulled the cord to switch it on. He was mildly surprised when the slight groaning noise it made indicated that it was in working order.

Jamieson put his foot into the water and savoured the warmth for a moment before stepping into the tub and immersing himself, so that only his face and the tops of his knees were above the water. He let out a sigh of satisfaction and, unwilling to move lest he destroy the moment, lay still and watched the steam drift upwards to the high, cracked ceiling. The strain of the motorway journey and the hassle of petty officialdom started to drift away.

The hypnotic silence was broken by the shrill ring of the telephone and Jamieson closed his eyes in disbelief. He considered ignoring it for a moment, but there was always the possibility that it was Sue calling to see if he had arrived safely. He stretched out his right hand and grabbed the chrome handle at the back of the bath to pull himself to his feet.

He had almost reached the vertical when the handle suddenly came out of the wall and he fell heavily backwards to splash down into the water. He jarred the base of his spine and hit his left elbow hard against the side of the tub. The curse that sprang to his lips was suddenly frozen as he saw what was happening above him. A wave of fear swept over him. Five feet up on the wall, the heater had come away from its mounting and was hanging perilously by what Jamieson reckoned could not be more than a millimetre of screwnail on either side. The bar that had come away in his hand had opened up the entire wiring channel in the wall and destroyed the plaster behind the heater.

Even as Jamieson stared up at the glowing element, almost afraid to breathe in case it fell into the water and electrocuted him, he saw it move a fraction. In the background the telephone still rang. A feeling of panic urged him to pull himself up and over the side of the bath, but he realised that this would be entirely the wrong thing to do. It would almost certainly be fatal. The heater was balanced so finely that the slightest vibration would cause it to fall.

The water! thought Jamieson. He must get rid of the water in the bath! If he could do that before the heater fell on him then perhaps he could escape the short circuit that would kill him.

Cautiously he felt with his big toe under the water for the bath plug while his eyes remained glued to the red bar above him. He found the retaining chain and manipulated it between his toes to apply pressure. He felt the links bite into the soft skin between his toes as the plug refused to budge at first, but pain had become a secondary consideration. He continued increasing the pressure until he felt the plug give and heard the water start to gurgle away down the drain.

Again, he had to fight his instinct. If he jerked the plug out suddenly an air lock in the drain might cause enough vibration to bring the heater down. He steeled himself to maintain a slight opening of the plug, while water drained away in a steady trickle.

Half the bath had emptied when Jamieson heard a key being inserted in the lock next door. Terror was re-born inside his head. For God's sake, don't slam the door! he prayed as he heard the door open. A few seconds of limbo passed with the slowness of eternity before the door slammed and the heater left its mounting.

In a series of events that appeared to Jamieson to occur in agonising slow motion he ripped out the bath plug completely with his foot, flung away the chrome bar that he was still holding and raised his hands to meet the heater. It seared his palms and the smell of burning flesh filled his nostrils as he turned violently to wrench hard.

Mains voltage shot through him, locking his jaw and throwing his entire body into spasm but Jamieson's desperate gamble had paid off. The momentum of his body in the turn had been sufficient to tear the heater from its wiring and interrupt the current.

The fear of permanent damage or disfigurement to his hands made Jamieson ignore the pain and the fact that the heater, although now disconnected, was setting the bathroom carpet alight. He tore at the handle of the cold tap and held his hands under the flow, his body juddering violently from the combined effects of shock and pain.

There was a knock at the door, but Jamieson continued to sit in the bath holding his hands under the torrent of cold water.

'Are you all right in there?' a muffled voice enquired.

Jamieson could not reply for his teeth were chattering while his whole body continued to shake.

The knocking grew louder as did the voice. 'I say! There's a smell of burning. Are you all right in there?'

Jamieson tried to force his lips into the right shape to speak. He managed a croak but then improved on it with agonising difficulty and uttered a weak cry for help.

The door flew open and a thin man with red hair looked in on the scene in the bathroom. 'Good God!' he exclaimed, as his eyes took in the wiring hanging out of the wall and the smouldering carpet. The man used a towel to protect his hands and lifted the heater up to dump it safely in the hand basin. He quickly trampled out the smouldering carpet and came to Jamieson's aid. 'How bad is it?' he asked, trying to get a better look at Jamieson's hands.

Jamieson shook his head as if to indicate that he did not know.

'Let me see,' said the man.

Jamieson withdrew his hands slowly from the flow and the

31

man turned off the taps. Jamieson prepared himself mentally for the surge of pain he felt sure would return to his burns as they were exposed to the air, but was mildly surprised when it was not too bad. It was painful but certainly not the agony of second degree burns or worse.

'I think you've got away with it,' said the red-haired man examining Jamieson's hands gently. Jamieson, still in partial shock, found himself concentrating on the man's profile. A hawk-like nose, hollow cheeks and the very fair skin that invariably went with red hair. In this case the residual scars of a bad teenage acne compounded the problem.

'Mainly superficial, you must have got your hands under the cold water in time,' said the man.

Jamieson nodded. He had an instant memory from childhood when he was playing on a rope swing by the river. At one point he had slightly lost grip and slid down the entire length of the rope, using his hands as a brake. The rope burns on his hands might have been serious had it not been for the fact that his fall had ended in the river and the sudden immersion in cold water had saved him from lasting damage. It was a lesson about burns treatment that he had never forgotten.

Jamieson closed his eyes in relief as a sudden wave of tiredness hit him. The red-haired man saw the signs and said, 'I think we'd better get you over to the hospital, old son. You've had a bit of a shock . . . if you'll excuse the pun.' He picked up the towel that was lying on the floor beside him and put it around Jamieson's shoulders before helping him up.

At this point both men had overlooked the fact that, although the heater had been disconnected from the wall, the wires that serviced it were still live and protruding from the conduit channel at the back of the bath. As the red-haired man helped Jamieson to his feet, Jamieson's thigh brushed against them and, once more, mains voltage shot through his body to throw him violently over the side of the bath. He landed in a heap on the still-smoking carpet. The red-haired man, protected by the dry towel he had been holding between himself and Jamieson, fell to his knees beside Jamieson and between profuse apologies cursed his own stupidity.

The knowledge that his hands were going to be all right had removed a great deal of the worry from Jamieson's mind; in fact, so much so that, as he lay on the floor looking up at the look of anguish on the other's face, he managed a wry smile.

'Are you all right?' asked the man, fearing that Jamieson's smile might have been an indication of some kind of mental aberration.

Jamieson replied hoarsely, 'Frankly . . . I've had better days.'

The man smiled and said, 'I'm Clive Evans.'

'Scott Jamieson. You will excuse me if I don't shake hands.'

Jamieson's bed was surrounded by visitors. The thin, stick-insect like figure of the hospital secretary had been joined by a smaller, more dapper man with silver hair and a clipped, white moustache who introduced himself as Norman Carew, the medical superintendent of Kerr Memorial. A third man, grizzled and thickset, was introduced as John Richardson, consultant bacteriologist.

'My dear Doctor, what can we say, this is absolutely awful,' began Crichton, the hospital secretary. 'What a thing to have happened. I just don't know what to say.'

'It was just one of those things,' replied Jamieson, wishing that Crichton would stop being so effusive in his apologies. For some reason it was making his injuries seem worse than they were and this was irking him. Carew started making the same kind of noises and Jamieson had to insist again that it was a totally unforeseen accident that could have happened anywhere and that, apart from a few superficial, albeit painful burns, no real damage had been done.

'And I was looking forward to my sherry too,' said Richardson, immediately lightening the atmosphere. Jamieson smiled and so did the others.

Crichton glanced sideways at Carew and then said, slightly uncomfortably Jamieson thought, 'Mr Thelwell regrets that he couldn't manage to get here this evening. He asked me to convey his sympathy and say that he looks forward to meeting you when you are up and about again.'

Jamieson recalled that Thelwell was the one who had been described as being 'difficult'. He was happy to have their meeting delayed. He had had enough 'difficulty' for one day. The sooner today was consigned to the past the better.

'Is there anything we can get you?' asked Crichton as the three prepared to leave.

'I'd like to call my wife,' said Jamieson.

'Of course. Nurse will bring in the phone trolley. We'll say good night.'

Jamieson watched their backs disappear out the door. A few moments later a nurse wheeled in the phone and Jamieson called Sue.

'Scott! Where are you calling from?' asked Sue's delighted voice.

'Actually I'm in bed.'

'At this time?

'I've had a bit of an accident.'

Jamieson gave Sue a suitably understated account of what had happened but she was still very alarmed. 'But you could have been killed!' she protested.

'But I wasn't and everything is all right,' soothed Jamieson.

'But your hands, you said . . .'

'Superficial burns, that's all,' interrupted Jamieson.

'I'll come up to Leeds right away,' she insisted.

'No you won't,' he replied. 'I'm perfectly all right and I want to get on with the job as soon as possible. I don't want this silly little affair to build up into anything more than it actually was, so stay there and I'll see you when I come home at the weekend or whenever. Okay?'

There was a long pause before Sue agreed. 'I miss you already,' she said.

'I feel the same,' said Jamieson.

Jamieson had just put down the phone when there was a knock on the door and Clive Evans appeared.

'I thought I'd pop in to see how you are,' said Evans.

'That was good of you,' smiled Jamieson, now more able to take a good look at his visitor. He was of average height, somewhere in his early thirties, and Jamieson thought he detected a faint Welsh accent in his voice.

'I didn't explain,' said Evans. 'I have the room next to yours in the residency. That's how I smelt the burning.'

'I see, so you're on the staff?'

'I'm the assistant bacteriologist in the microbiology department.'

'Dr Richardson's department?'

'That's right.'

'Been here long?'

'Nearly two months.'

Jamieson smiled. He was pleased to have found someone outside of the hospital hierarchy to talk to. 'You must be very much involved in the investigation of the infection problem then?' he asked.

Evans nodded. 'We're doing everything we can, but we're not having any success and we're getting the blame for not finding out the cause.'

'Any ideas of your own?' asked Jamieson.

'It's a complete mystery,' said Evans. 'All the swabs we've taken from the surgical wards and theatres – and we've done hundreds – have been negative, but Mr Thelwell won't accept this. He thinks we are incompetent and doesn't try to hide it.'

'And what do you think?'

Dr Richardson is one of the best.'

'And Mr Thelwell?'

'It's not for me to pass comment on a surgeon, not my field, I'm afraid.'

Jamieson nodded, pleased at the loyalty and common sense of his visitor.

'When do you think you will be up and about then?' asked Evans.

'Tomorrow,' said Jamieson firmly. 'I'll get the dressings changed in the morning and then I'll get started.'

'Then I'll probably be seeing you tomorrow,' said Evans. He

held out his hand to shake Jamieson's and suddenly realised that it still might not be a very good idea. Both men laughed and Jamieson noticed that Evans had what looked like a red burn mark on the back of his right wrist. 'You must have got that from the heater in the bathroom,' he said with concern.

'It's nothing,' Evans assured him, pulling down his sleeve and getting up from the chair.

'But you should have it seen to,' insisted Jamieson. 'Burns get infected so easily. You must ask one of the nurses to dress it properly.'

'Really, it's nothing to worry about,' Evans assured him. 'It hardly broke the skin.'

Jamieson looked at him doubtfully and said, 'I'm very grateful to you for your help.'

'Don't mention it,' said Evans. 'I'd best be going. I'm on call tonight.'

As the door closed behind Evans, Jamieson lay back on the pillow and looked at his bandaged hands. He reflected on the day. 'What a start,' he murmured. 'What a bloody awful start.'

3

Outside in the courtyard, between the block where Jamieson was sleeping and the old stone building that housed the obstetrics and gynaecology department, the rain continued to fall. Sally Jenkins heard it pattering down on the cobblestones. She had been unable to get to sleep for the pain in her stomach. 'Perfectly natural after any operation,' the nurse had assured her. They would give her a pill and she would feel much better in the morning.

Keith, her husband, had been equally reassuring. He had spoken to Mr Thelwell and everything had gone well in theatre. The surgeon had located a blockage in her fallopian tubes that had been preventing her from falling pregnant. The big fear that her tubes might have been too damaged to be repaired had been shown to be groundless. Mr Thelwell had successfully cleared away the obstruction and now there was no reason why she should not have children.

She would have a son for Keith, a boy he could take fishing on the canal on Saturdays, while she and their daughter – yes, she would like a daughter too – while she and Alice would have a nice day at home. They would call her Alice after Keith's mother. Keith's mother would like that. There had always been a frostiness between them, nothing serious, but Sally knew that old Alice blamed her for the fact that she still did not have any grandchildren after five years of marriage.

Alice would have preferred Keith to have married Stella Gorman, the girl he had been going out with when Sally had first met him. Stella Gorman's father owned a garage business in Trafalgar Street and Alice had already started to make plans for Keith's future, when it had all gone wrong. Keith had married Sally, not Stella and as her father did not own a garage business, or any other kind for that matter, Keith was still working as a mechanic in the council bus depot.

Sally managed a smile in the darkness, despite the fact that her pain seemed to be getting worse not better. She did not want to bother the nurses again but it was becoming really bad. Perhaps if she thought some more about children, or maybe even if she concentrated on the sound of the rain outside, it would take her mind off the pain.

Sally liked the sound of rain. For some reason it always made her think of a time many years ago when she had gone camping with the Girl Guides. They had gone to the Forest of Dean and it had rained non stop for the entire week. They had spent hour after hour lying in their tents just listening to the sound of the rain on the canvas while their leader thought up endless variations on word games to keep them amused.

Sally had been glad to escape the games by being sent each morning to collect fresh milk from the nearby farm. Her Wellingtons had squelched through the mud and the rain had pattered on the hood of her anorak, just like it was pattering on the awning below her window.

A new stab of pain shot through her and wiped out all thoughts of rain and children. It made her gasp and reach out for the buzzer. Her fingers closed round it like a claw as the pain seemed to seek out the most sensitive nerve ending in her body. Her back arched in a subconscious attempt to escape it, but this only put unfair pressure on the stitches in her lower abdomen. Sally Jenkins added to the call of the buzzer with a scream.

The night staff nurse in charge of Princess Mary ward called out the duty houseman who was initially reluctant to come for what he felt sure was normal post-operative discomfort, but the nurse insisted. She won with a veiled threat to call Mr Thelwell directly. 'I think it might be another problem case,' she said.

'But it can't be,' insisted the houseman. 'Mr Thelwell used one of the orthopaedic theatres today. There's never been any trouble with infection in orthopaedics.'

'Well, maybe there is now,' said the nurse, putting down the phone as another scream tore the air and wakened the rest of the ward. Sleepy voices were seeking reassurance as she hurried to Sally Jenkins' assistance. 'Nothing to worry about, Mrs Elms . . . It's all right, Mrs Cartwright, we're dealing with it . . . Go back to sleep, Mrs Brown, Nothing to worry about . . .'

The houseman, white coat pulled on over a hastily donned shirt which still had three buttons undone, arrived within five minutes and ran his fingers through unkempt hair while the nurse briefed him. A cursory examination established that Sally Jenkins' temperature was touching one hundred and two and she was showing all the classic signs of bacterial septicaemia. If this had been an isolated incident, he might have prescribed the normal front-line antibiotics and felt confident of their efficacy, but with the current problem-infection in the unit he was reluctant to do this.

If there was a chance that the *Pseudomonas* was responsible for the infection then penicillin, always the safest drug to prescribe because of its lack of side-effects, would have no impact. On the other hand, none of the other drugs at his disposal had had much effect on the bug in the previous cases. The houseman hesitated for a moment, weighing up the pros and cons of seeking assistance. It was now after midnight but the desire to pass the buck on this one was overwhelming. He called Thelwell at home. Thelwell's wife answered.

'I'm sorry to disturb you at this hour, Mrs Thelwell, but could I possibly speak to your husband? It's Graham Dean at the hospital. I've got a bit of a problem.'

'I'm sorry, Graham, Gordon isn't home yet. He's been attending a dinner this evening. Would you like me to give him a message?'

Dean gave Marion Thelwell a brief outline of Sally Jenkins' condition to relay to her husband when he came home and said that he would try to contact Thelwell's number two. After reading the number from the chart on the wall behind the phone, Dean called Thelwell's senior registrar, Phillip Morton, and had more luck. He explained the situation to Morton who said that he would be there within fifteen minutes. In the meantime, Dean was instructed to start antibiotic therapy immediately on the assumption that it was a *Pseudomonas* infection like the others. 'Start her on Pyopen.'

'And the pain?' asked the houseman.

'Omnipon, usual dose,' said Morton.

The door to the basement apartment opened and heavy curtains were drawn across rain-splashed windows before it was closed again and locked twice from the inside. The man inside stood still for a moment in the darkness with his back against the door, listening to the sound of his own breathing and feeling the cold and damp surround him. A slight smile crossed his face, for to him it felt good, it felt right. He clicked on the light, not that a forty watt bulb made much inroads into the gloom, and walked slowly through to the bathroom where a rubber apron hung over the bath and a row of surgical instruments were lined up along the back of the sink where he had left them. They were clean and dry and ready for use.

He took down the apron and folded it neatly before packing it into a briefcase. The inside of the case was protected by a polythene lining, because the man prided himself on detail. There were to be no tell-tale blood stains, no blood anywhere there did not have to be.

In a separate compartment in the case he had a number of plastic bags. He counted them and decided to add a few more. There was still plenty of adhesive tape. He put down the case for a moment and went to the fridge in the kitchen to open the door. There, lying in two plastic bags, were what he had removed from the Spooner woman. The man gave a satisfied grunt. There was one less bitch to spread her filth, one less to snare and entrap the unwary with her silks and perfumes. What fools men were not to realise what vile creatures lay hidden behind the smiling faces and the pretty clothes. But they were not entirely to blame. Nature had equipped the bitches well. It was so easy to succumb to their wiles. He knew that only too well.

The man closed his eyes and shook as he relived a private agony. His mother, God bless her, had always brought him up to be aware of the deceit and artfulness of women and he in turn had always believed her, but on that one night in the town when the bitch had come out at him from the doorway he had suddenly become weak. He had wanted to push her away, but something inside had prevented him. He remembered standing there, breathing in her sweet scent, feeling her body brush against him, feeling the hardness start and the yearning to squeeze the breasts that were thrusting up at him from the half-open blouse.

The bitch had taken him by the hand, giggling and smiling, and pulled him into the darkness of the alley, where she had gripped him between the legs and complimented him on what she felt there. 'You want me, don't you?' she had crooned and the more she spoke the more he had wanted her.

He had paid her what she had asked and she had taken him to a filthy room in a crumbling tenement where the bed had smelled of sweat and the sheets had hard stains on them. But at the time it hadn't mattered. Nothing had mattered. In the midst of all that squalor, he had still wanted her. He had been on fire. He had lost all self-control in the desire to possess her. The whore had egged him on until he had taken her quickly and urgently like an animal in heat.

Afterwards, he had lain there, with her laughter ringing in his ears. With passion spent, he had been able to see clearly that the bitch had trapped him. She had tricked him into doing something entirely against his will. All at once he had been able to see everything with crystal clarity. He had felt ashamed, dirty and very very angry.

He had beaten up the whore. He felt he had a duty to. He had smashed her face with his fists and kicked her senseless. It would be a long time before she trapped anyone else with her looks. But, for him, it had all been too late. The whore had given him an infection. She had given him a terrible infection.

At first it was just a burning pain when he urinated. He couldn't bring himself to believe that it was anything more than a slight urethritis, but then the chancre appeared. It had disappeared on its own but he knew that this was just one of the symptoms, one of *Treponema pallidum's* tricks, for it would be sure to come back and next time it would bring the secondary phase of the disease, the rash, the invasion of his entire system, lesions in his bones, his joints, maybe even his central nervous system. He would go blind and maybe mad. The whore had given him syphilis.

Modern antibiotic treatment should have dealt with the problem. God knows, it was embarrassing enough to be on the treatment at all and to have to attend that damned awful clinic where you were given numbers in a pathetic attempt to preserve anonymity, but fate had something else in store for him. The strain of syphilis he had succumbed to proved not to be amenable to such treatment. It stubbornly refused to die. There was a war going on inside his body and *Treponema* was winning. The clinic staff kept up an unending stream of platitudes and reassuring pap in order to convince him that things were under control, but he knew better. They were doing their best to treat him, but they were failing. His condition was untreatable.

People have a mental threshold that decrees how much pain and anguish they can endure before they lose control and mentally start to disintegrate. Fortunately, in times of peace, few of us ever approach this borderline. But for a man who had been a loner all his life, the oddball at school, the one the girls laughed at and the boys taunted, the one who had been unable to risk leaving the security of his mother's love, the disease within him was the last straw.

He had first approached the threshold when his mother collapsed and died just over a year before. There had been no warning, no time for him to prepare. He had simply gone into her bedroom one morning and found her lying there, icy cold and with her eyes open. He had felt so betrayed and alone that he had been unable to speak for weeks. They had taken him to the clinic on the hill where he had sat in a wickerwork chair and stared at the wall for days on end, totally withdrawn and unwilling to communicate with the world for fear of what else life might have in store for him.

He had been given pills which allowed him to sleep and others which took the edge off reality during the day. He was artificially released from stress until, in time, he recovered enough to give life one more chance. He saw the disease as the result of his misplaced trust.

This time he did not lapse into a trance. He did not capitulate to the overwhelming forces of fate and bow his head in anguished acceptance. There was no flirtation at the threshold between reality and madness. He sailed way over it and there was no going back. This time he was filled with anger. A deep, burning anger that knew no bounds. What he wanted now was not pills or kind words. It was revenge.

He would have to protect himself against the evil charms of the whores, for he was not yet immune. He had known this last time when the bitch had been tied up and he had felt the hardness come on. The hardness was even coming on now when he thought about it. He pulled down his fly and reached inside his trousers to grip himself while he thought about the wiles the bitch would use. The stockings, the underwear, the perfume, the laughing red lips. He had to protect himself. He turned out the light and in the darkness of the basement he relieved himself of the desire that would be such a weakness in the task ahead of him.

With the surgical instruments wrapped in cloth so that they would not rattle and the blades in foil sheaths so that they would not be dulled, he snapped shut the case and put out the light before opening the door. He paused in the basement area for a moment to listen for footsteps but all was quiet. The rain was still falling. That was good. There would not be many people on the streets. But the whores would be there. They were always there, whatever the weather, and he would be watching.

*   *   *

Gordon Thelwell called the hospital at a quarter to one to say that he had just arrived home and understood that his houseman, Dean, had been trying to contact him earlier in the evening. He spoke to the night staff nurse in charge of the ward where Sally Jenkins lay and was given a report on her current condition and an outline of the treatment prescribed for her by Phillip Morton.

'Appalling!' exclaimed Thelwell. 'This whole hospital is a cesspit of infection.'

The nurse remained silent and waited for Thelwell to continue. He asked her what specimens had been sent to the lab and she told him after referring to the ward lab records book.

'I hope they're not just lying in the collection basket,' said Thelwell.

'They were marked urgent and the duty microbiologist was called out to deal with them, sir,' replied the nurse.

Thelwell grunted and asked if Dean was still in the ward.

'No, sir,' replied the nurse. 'Mrs Jenkins seems to be stable at the moment, sir. Dr Dean left about fifteen minutes ago.'

Thelwell grunted and asked to be informed if there was any change in the patient's condition.

'Of course, sir,' said the nurse.

'We'll see how she is in the morning.'

'Yes, sir.'

'Trouble, dear?' asked Marion Thelwell, sitting up in bed and blinking against the light which her husband had switched on.

'One of my patients. She may have a wound site infection,' replied Thelwell distantly.

Marion Thelwell stopped blinking and looked concerned. 'Not another problem case,' she sighed. 'I thought you were going to use the orthopaedic theatre today? she said.

'I did use the orthopaedic theatre,' snapped Thelwell.

'Yes, dear.'

Thelwell regretted his sharpness and apologised. 'I'm afraid I'm a bit on edge. This business is getting me down.'

'I understand, dear. Come to bed.'

'Later.'
'Yes, dear.'

Scott Jamieson woke at three in the morning. He usually did when something was troubling him. It was no comfort to know that he was one of thousands in the country who woke regularly at this time. Nature had decreed that three in the morning was the hour when people with problems ranging from the unmanageable size of their mortgage to true manic depression would wake to face their personal hell. Optimism required daylight. Despair thrived in the dark.

He felt alone as he lay in the subdued night-light of the strange ward listening to the sounds of the night. He missed not having Sue next to him. He missed not being able to stretch his arm over her sleeping body to cuddle in to her. He resolved to oppose any possible suggestion in the years to come that they change to single beds. It irked him that he had got off to such a bad start in his new job. Almost subconsciously he flexed the fingers of both hands beneath the bandages to assess how painful they were. It was academic, really, for he had already decided to start his investigation in the morning however badly he felt. As it happened, they did not feel too bad at all.

His impatience to get on with the investigation was not entirely due to his inability to come to terms with imposed idleness. It was reinforced by the belief that Sci-Med might otherwise feel obliged to send in someone else and that would mean that he had failed, a completely unacceptable state of affairs for Scott Jamieson, whatever extenuating circumstances there might be.

As Jamieson closed his eyes and tried to get back to sleep in the ward, the telephone rang beside John Richardson's bed and woke him from a deep sleep. He took a few moments to clear his head and then held the receiver to his ear.

'I'm sorry to wake you,' said Clive Evans' voice, 'but I was called out a couple of hours ago for a patient in post-op, one of

Mr Thelwell's patients, a Mrs Sally Jenkins. She's been showing signs of wound infection and Mr Thelwell's registrar took swabs for testing.'

'And?'

'Gram-negative bacilli and a positive oxidase test. It looks like it's the *Pseudomonas* again. I thought you would want to know.'

'Yes, thank you,' said Richardson, putting down the phone. His wife, who had been woken by the call, asked what the problem was.

'Another post-operative infection in gynaecology.'

'But I thought Thelwell had closed the gynae theatre?'

'He did,' replied Richardson thoughtfully. 'He insisted on moving his scheduled operations to the orthopaedic suite until we had traced the source of the outbreak.'

'Then it looks like he took the infection with him.'

Richardson looked at his wife and said, 'This is exactly what I have been saying all along. If we can't find the source of infection in the theatre itself then the fault must lie with the staff. It's time we swabbed the whole surgical team again; we must have a carrier among them. It's the only logical explanation. For some unknown reason we must have missed him . . .'

'Or her.'

'Or her, the first time around.'

Jamieson could hear two nurses talking. They were standing in the doorway of his room, one with her hand on the door knob and the other standing in the corridor outside with a steel tray in her hand. As he became fully awake Jamieson could make out some of their conversation.

'They say he cut her to pieces,' said one of the girls.

'That's what I heard too,' agreed the other. 'I don't understand how no one heard her screams.'

'Maybe they did,' said the other girl. 'They just pretended not to, a sign of the times, I'm afraid. People just don't want to get involved.'

The nurse with her hand on the door handle noticed that Jamieson was awake and cut short the conversation to come into the room and close the door behind her.

'What was that all about?' asked Jamieson.

'The prostitute who was found murdered in the city a few days ago,' replied the girl.

'My wife told me about that,' said Jamieson. 'She heard the report on the radio.'

'She wasn't just murdered,' said the girl. 'The story is, she was mutilated, cut to pieces.'

Jamieson grimaced.

'Just like Jack the Ripper, they're saying.'

Jamieson guessed that 'they' would be the tabloid papers.

'How are you feeling?'

'Right as rain. I want to leave as soon as I can get the dressings changed.'

'I think you should wait till Dr Carew has seen you. You're an important patient.'

Jamieson smiled at the girl's frankness and said, 'I'll take the responsibility.'

'If you say so, Doctor.'

Jamieson was back in his room in the doctors' residency shortly after breakfast and was pleased to see that the wall behind the bath had been repaired and the heater was back on its mounting. All the same, he could not see himself using it again, however cold the room might feel. He telephoned the hospital secretary's office and informed him that he was ready to start talking to people.

Crichton was surprised that Jamieson was back in action again and expressed concern over the wisdom of leaving the ward so soon. Jamieson bore it patiently then asked for help in organising his day.

'Fate has taken a hand, Doctor,' said Crichton. 'A patient that Mr Thelwell operated on yesterday has developed an infection, despite the fact that the operation was carried out in a different theatre in a different part of the hospital. We are holding a meeting at ten to discuss the situation. Perhaps you would like to attend?'

'I would indeed,' agreed Jamieson. 'Just one question. Where was the patient taken after her operation?'

'The post-operative ward in gynaecology.'

'Thank you,' said Jamieson and put down the phone. So they had changed the theatres and that had made no difference, thought Jamieson. That left the theatre staff themselves as a possible source of infection, or possibly the post-op ward in gynae. The patient had been brought back there after her operation. Jamieson made a mental list of the questions he wanted to ask at the meeting.

There was a general air of gloom about the men who had assembled in Hugh Crichton's office to discuss the latest problem case. Crichton turned to a serious looking, thin-lipped man, 'I don't think you have met Dr Jamieson yet, have you? Dr Jamieson, this is Mr Thelwell, consultant surgeon in gynaecology.'

Jamieson smiled across the table and Thelwell gave a barely perceptible nod in reply. Jamieson was introduced to Phillip Morton, Thelwell's registrar, and then to Clive Evans, whom he admitted he had already met.

'First of all, gentlemen, how is the patient this morning?' asked Crichton.

'She's very ill,' said Thelwell. 'Antibiotics are having no effect.'

'So it's the same strain as the others?'

'Looks like it,' said John Richardson. 'We'll know for sure when the antibiogram is ready.'

'Has there been any progress in determining the source of the outbreak?' asked Carew.

Richardson shook his head and Thelwell gave an audible snort which caused the others to move uncomfortably in their seats. Richardson carried on as if he had not heard. 'All the swabs we took from the theatres and the recovery wards were negative for the organism in question. In fact the standard of cleanliness was rather high.' Thelwell gave another snort and Carew shot him an angry glance but still said nothing.

'Where were the swabs taken from?' asked Jamieson.

'All flat surfaces including the walls. All wet areas including sink and sluice drains and flower vases in the wards,' replied Richardson.

'And no *Pseudomonas*?'

'We found *Pseudomonas* all right, but not the strain in question,' said Clive Evans. Jamieson noted that the acne scarring on Evans' face became more livid when he was under stress.

'How about air sampling?'

'We've done that too,' said Richardson. 'Negative for *Pseudomonas* in all tests.'

'Am I right in thinking that the fact that this latest case was operated on in orthopaedics means that the theatres in gynaecology are now cleared of suspicion?' asked Hugh Crichton.

'I think we can assume that,' replied Richardson.

'So what does that leave us with?'

'Nursing and medical staff as possible carriers or something in the recovery wards that we haven't thought of.'

'Presumably you have already swabbed the staff?' asked Jamieson.

Richardson nodded. 'All of them. Nasal and axillary swabs in duplicate on two separate days. We found one nurse carrying *haemolytic streptococci* but no *Pseudomonas* carrier.'

'What about instruments and dressings?'

'They are sterilised in our central sterile supply department and taken directly to theatres in sterile packs.'

'How often are the sterilisers checked?'

'The autoclaves are fitted with a wide range of safeguards against malfunction.'

'Anything else?' asked Jamieson.

'Dr Evans is in charge of bio-safety in the CSSD,' said Richardson, looking towards his junior colleague.

'The main steriliser is thermo-couple tested every week,' said Evans. 'I personally carry out the test. It's in perfect condition.

Someone from microbiology, usually myself, checks the chart recorders on the others every day. We have the records of every single autoclave run. They're kept in the lab office if you would like to examine them.'

'I think at this stage I would like to see everything, including the air sampling reports and the swab results,' said Jamieson.

Evans looked a little surprised but Richardson simply said, 'Of course. When would you like to come?'

'Immediately after this meeting if that's convenient?'

'Of course.'

Carew cleared his throat and said, 'Now, gentlemen, we come to the big question. Can we allow surgery to continue in Kerr Memorial's gynaecology department?'

Gordon Thelwell looked as if there had never been any possibility of doing otherwise. 'We have to,' he said firmly. 'My waiting list is already as long as a bank holiday traffic jam. Any suspension would only make matters worse.'

'We have to consider that two women have died after surgery and a third is seriously ill,' said Carew.

'The number has to be viewed in the context of the number of surgical cases passing through my department,' replied Thelwell.

The coldness of Thelwell's statement made Jamieson a little uneasy and he saw that it had much the same effect on the others.

'The dead women's husbands don't view the deaths in the context of any numbers,' snapped Richardson.

Thelwell, wasp-like in his response, snapped back, 'Then perhaps, Doctor, if your department did its job we would not be faced with the problem and neither would they.'

Richardson leaned forward angrily in his chair but managed to control his temper in time. He took a deep breath and said, 'We are doing everything humanly possible to identify the source of the infection and will continue to do so, starting with another swab check of the surgical team and the nurses in the post-op wards.'

'Maybe we should send the swabs directly to the Public Health

Laboratory Service this time,' said Thelwell. 'Perhaps they can find this damned bug.'

Jamieson saw the flash of anger in Richardson's eyes and noted Carew's impotence in intervening in the hostilities. He himself interrupted. 'They will go to the hospital lab in the usual manner.'

Thelwell reacted as if Jamieson had struck him. He said slowly, 'And who, might I ask, are you to make that sort of decision?'

Jamieson replied evenly, 'I think you will find that I have the authority.' He looked to Crichton and Carew.

Crichton said, 'Dr Jamieson does have the authority, Mr Thelwell.'

Thelwell's smile was dipped in sarcasm. He said, 'So a civil servant is now in charge of surgery at Kerr Memorial.'

'Actually I'm a surgeon,' said Jamieson. 'And my involvement with Kerr Memorial will cease the moment people stop dying unnecessarily in your department. And talking of your department, Mr Thelwell, I would like to be shown round it today.'

Jamieson held Thelwell's gaze without flinching. It was Thelwell who broke eye contact first. He said, 'I'll have Mr Morton accompany you.'

'I'd rather you did it personally,' said Jamieson, determined to establish his authority at the beginning in the hope that it would not be necessary to do it again.

Once again Thelwell hovered on the brink of argument and Jamieson could see the anger in his eyes as he considered his reply. The thin lips quivered before they said curtly and to everyone's relief, 'Very well. Contact my secretary and she will fit you in to my schedule.'

Carew reminded them, 'We have still not decided what to do about the surgical lists.'

'I thought we had,' said Thelwell coldly.

'You expressed an opinion, Mr Thelwell,' said Carew. 'But we did not decide. We must consider the options.'

'Which are?'

51

'Basically, there are three. One, we suspend surgery tempo-rarily. Two, we start diverting patients to other hospitals. Three, we continue operating in the hope that, with extra vigilance on all our parts, the problem will not reccur.'

'The second option is a non-starter, I'm afraid,' said Crichton. 'I've been in touch with all the other hospitals and there is no possibility of their accepting any of our patients outside of dire emergency cases. Their lists are just as long as ours.'

'So we suspend or carry on with greater care.'

'I resent the implications of that remark, Carew,' said Thelwell icily.

'There was no personal element in what I said, Thelwell. If we decide that surgery is to continue in gynaecology, aseptic procedure must be tightened up in all areas.'

It was unanimously decided that, for the present, surgery would continue in gynaecology at Kerr Memorial.

'There is one change that I would like to see,' said Jamieson.

'Yes, Doctor?' asked Carew.

'You are still using the same recovery ward for gynaecology patients. I think it would be a good idea to change to another one for the time being. Is that possible?'

After some deliberation, Crichton confirmed that it was. Alexandra ward had been closed for some months owing to shortage of nurses or, more correctly, to shortage of money to pay for them. It could be re-opened and used for post-operative cases after suitable cleaning and preparation.

'How long?' asked Jamieson.

'Two days,' said Crichton.

'Then I suggest that surgery recommences when the new ward is ready.'

There were nods of agreement round the table.

'We'll see to the fumigation of the old ward once it's empty,' said Richardson.

'Good,' said Crichton.

'If there is nothing else, gentlemen?' Carew looked around him. No one spoke. 'Very well, then. Shall we be about our business?'

4

When they left the meeting, Jamieson told Clive Evans that he wanted to call in at the residency to pick up his briefcase before going on down to microbiology. Evans said that he would accompany him and then show him the way.

'I've never seen anyone stand up to Mr Thelwell that way before,' Evans confided seriously as they crossed the cobbled yard to the blackened, stone building that served as the doctors' residency. Jamieson had not relished his first meeting with Thelwell. He had to admit that it had turned out to be even worse than he had feared, but he was reluctant to enter into any conversation about Thelwell with another member of staff. He chose to ignore the comment, and looked up at a series of stone busts on ledges at the side of the entrance to the residency. Corrosion of the sandstone had eaten away at the cornice of the ledges and also at some of the lettering. It made the names and dates difficult to read but he managed to make out the citation to the main one. It said, John Thurlow Kerr, Professor of Medicine, 1881–88.

'Our founder's bid for immortality,' said Evans.

Jamieson wondered for a moment why all busts and statues looked pretty much the same to him. What was the point of it all? What was he meant to think when he looked at a crumbling stone bust? He supposed that Evans had hit the nail on the head with his 'bid for immortality' comment. Pathetic, really.

He considered what the hospital must have been like in 1881 and how much pain and suffering these walls had seen and heard, how much human misery they had been witness to. If only they could talk, but maybe it was best not to hear. Had the public of the day had the same faith in their healers as they did today? The same blind faith? Had people looked on trustingly while leeches were applied to suck their blood under the 'learned' gaze of frock-coated sages, the medical gentlemen, the Thelwells of another age, men for whom self-doubt was an alien concept.

Jamieson reflected on the history of his profession with little pleasure. Was there any other professional body so conservative in its outlook, so fiercely insular, so determined that outsiders be kept at bay? he wondered. He doubted it and took little pride in the conclusion.

Jamieson looked at the stern, bearded face of John Thurlow Kerr and considered the state of medicine in the late nineteenth century. Surgery had meant the screams of the unanaesthetised and the near certainty of suppurating wound infection to follow. Childbirth had meant childbirth fever for so many women, a disease caused almost entirely by the doctors themselves who, in the ignorance of their age, arrogantly strode between the post-mortem room and the maternity ward unwittingly spreading the infections that they subsequently sought to cure.

How many doctors of a later day acknowledged that fact when the role of bacteria in infection was finally understood? Not many, he concluded. Humility was not an outstanding characteristic of medical practitioners. This was true the world over, whether they be Harley Street physicians or African witch doctors. In their own way both sought to keep their patients in ignorance of their own bodies and determined to keep it that way in their own interests. Both peddled pills and potions and did so with a mystique cultivated to preserve their position in society. 'What will the penicillin do, Doctor?' 'Fight the infection Mrs Brown.' But how many GPs knew what penicillin really did do? At a rough guess none out of a hundred. Jamieson knew because Jamieson wanted to know. That was his nature and that was why he had been recommended to Sci-Med in the first place.

'Shan't be a moment,' Jamieson said to Evans and ran upstairs to collect his briefcase. He paused in the room for a moment to adjust the bandage on his left hand which was threatening to come adrift. As he re-tied it he reflected on what he had learned at the meeting. 'Difficult' wasn't the word for a man like Thelwell. He was a twenty-four carat son of a bitch with no saving grace that he could determine.

Carew was too weak to be effective as medical superintendent. He was fine when it came to opening hospital fêtes and talking to the ladies' luncheon club, but useless at dealing with people like Thelwell. Crichton seemed to be a good man but, of course, as a pure administrator, he could not involve himself in matters medical. Phillip Morton seemed all right from what little he had said and Jamieson did not envy him his job under Thelwell. Richardson, too, seemed a good man. Jamieson admired the way he had kept his temper under extreme provocation from Thelwell, but was forced to wonder whether or not it was a case of real self-control or perhaps a lack of stomach for a fight due to advancing years. Clive Evans seemed competent, loyal to Richardson and keen to help in any way he could. What was more, he was waiting downstairs.

Jamieson followed Evans along a narrow lane between signs pointing to the skin clinic in one direction and the hospital laundry in the other. He was hoping for a modern microbiology department but when Evans took a left turn down some stone steps he feared the worst and was duly rewarded. It was located on the ground floor and in the basement of one of the oldest buildings in the hospital.

'Dr Richardson's office is just along here,' said Evans, still leading the way. A girl technician at specimen reception looked up as Jamieson passed and smiled. Jamieson smiled back. Smiles were important when you were on your own. They were reassuring, like the sight of a navigational buoy to a mariner in strange oceans.

Jamieson felt claustrophobia closing in on him as they progressed along a long corridor between rows of small laboratories, each scarcely big enough to warrant the term 'room'. They were little more than cubicles. The corridor narrowed in places to almost less than the width of a human body, where lack of space had forced refrigerators and other large items of equipment out into the hallway.

Although Richardson's room was bigger and had a large window, Jamieson could see that it would never receive enough daylight to warrant turning off the artificial lighting. The building across the way was less than five feet away.

'I've arranged for you to have a room downstairs,' said Richardson. 'It's not much, I'm afraid, but as you see we are a bit cramped.'

'I'm sure it will be fine,' said Jamieson.

'If there's anything you need you only have to ask.'

Clive Evans took off his jacket and donned a white lab coat. As he rolled back the cuffs of his shirt sleeves Jamieson again noticed the red burn marks on the back of his wrist and asked him about them.

'Oh, it's absolutely nothing,' insisted Evans, 'No problem at all.'

'What happened?' asked Richardson.

'Dr Evans burned himself while helping me escape electrocution yesterday,' Jamieson explained.

'Really?' exclaimed Richardson, obviously concerned at his colleague's injury. 'Have you seen about it, Clive?' he asked. 'Maybe you should have a dressing on that.' He leaned forward to examine it more closely but Evans again insisted that it was nothing and pulled down his sleeve. He turned to Jamieson and said, 'If you like, I'll show you round the lab.'

Jamieson followed Evans round the cubicles of the first floor while Evans explained what happened in each of them, then he led the way downstairs to the cold, fluorescent light of the basement and a long low room. 'This is the preparation room,' he said. 'All our glassware and equipment is cleaned and sterilised here.'

There were three women working at large stainless steel sinks and Jamieson noted the steam steriliser that was currently on an operating cycle. A relay clicked to allow more steam to enter and maintain its temperature.

'As you see, we have one large autoclave, working on the hospital's direct steam supply. We use that to sterilise all specimens once we've finished with them. In addition we have three hot air ovens and several small pressure cookers for individuals to use if they have to sterilise something in a hurry.'

'Do you sterilise anything for other wards or departments?' Jamieson asked.

'No. All general sterilising is done down in the central facility at CSSD.'

'I see,' said Jamieson. He noticed that the sweat was running off the women as they worked at their sinks and looked up at the ceiling for an extractor fan.

Evans read his mind and said, 'I'm afraid there's no air conditioning. Dr Richardson has been asking for it for a long time, I understand, but with no success. Too many other priorities. It's not so bad when the steriliser isn't running.'

'But pretty awful when it is,' added Jamieson.

The two men moved on through the basement corridor with Jamieson having to duck his head to avoid hitting it on an array of pipes that ran along the underside of the low ceiling. Evans, a couple of inches shorter than Jamieson, did not have the same problem.

'This is my lab,' said Evans, opening a door to a square room that was slightly bigger than any of the others Jamieson had seen, with the exception of Richardson's room. 'And this, I'm afraid, is yours for the duration.' Evans opened a door on the other side of the corridor and Jamieson looked in to a small, narrow room that reminded him of a walk-in wardrobe. It had a desk, a telephone and an anglepoise lamp. There was no room for anything else. There were two cardboard folders lying on the desk.

'These files contain the information you asked for,' said Evans. 'If there's anything else, I'm just across the corridor.'

Jamieson thanked him and took off his jacket to hang it over the back of his chair. He sat down and looked at the walls that enclosed him. If he reached out he could touch all of them. Above him there was a thick glass grating that allowed the merest suspicion of daylight to enter, slightly less than the greyest of dawns, Jamieson reckoned. 'One hundred and five North Tower,' he whispered, switching on the anglepoise lamp. He opened the folders and got to work.

After a good two hours' study, Jamieson could find no fault in the procedures followed by the microbiology department in trying to trace the source of the infection. According to the records, all recommended, standard procedures had been followed with meticulous care and all tests appeared to have been carried out more than once, often three or four times. But the result had always been the same. No sign of the bug that was plaguing the practice of surgery in the gynaecology department.

Jamieson went through the results of the staff tests again, just looking for anything at all out of the ordinary. His finger stopped moving as he found something. One nurse and one member of the surgical team had proved to be completely negative on each of the two separate occasions they had been tested. He found that puzzling. Most people carried bacteria of some sort in their nose and throat and on their skin. Usually it comprised a variety of harmless bugs, but in a few cases people carried organisms which could cause disease in others in certain circumstances. It was naturally unwise for these members of staff to be near patients with open wounds.

There were a number of possible explanations for a completely negative test and Jamieson considered them in turn. If the person was on some kind of anti-bacterial treatment then the normal bacterial flora of the body might have been destroyed. Alternatively, antiseptic creams might have been applied to the areas to be swabbed before the test but that would demand some explanation. Jamieson made a note of the two reference numbers from the result sheet and resolved to pursue the matter further when he had finished reading the paperwork.

He finished going through the staff reports and changed to reading the lab report on the infecting organism.

The cultural characteristics of the bug were recorded and its identity had been established beyond doubt. It was only when he saw the results of the antibiotic tests against it that he saw where the real trouble lay. The organism seemed to be immune to every known antibiotic on the standard treatment list. There was simply no way of treating such an infection. 'No wonder they died,' he said quietly.

For bacteria to become resistant to antibiotics was nothing new. It happened all the time and, perversely, especially in hospitals. With so many drugs around it was merely a case of natural selection at work. Spontaneous mutations arose all the time in bacterial populations, so that when an antibiotic was injected into a patient the occasional mutant able to resist its action would survive and multiply. It would become the dominant form of the infection and if not detected and destroyed might survive long enough to affect other patients.

The *Pseudomonas* bug that was causing all the trouble started out with the advantage of being naturally immune to many antibiotics. The acquisition of further immunity through living in a hospital environment could make it a very dangerous customer indeed. Despite that, Jamieson still found the virulence of the Kerr strain surprising.

Clive Evans put his head round the door and asked how things were going.

'I know a bit more now than I did earlier on,' replied Jamieson.

'Good. Can I show you where the staff restaurant is?'

Jamieson looked at his watch and was surprised to see that it was after one o'clock. He said. 'Can I ask a couple of questions first?'

'Of course.'

'There are two members of the surgical team who had two successive negative results from their swab tests. Was this followed up?'

'No, I don't think I noticed that,' confessed Evans.

'It might be an idea to check them out.'

'We've just done another swabbing this morning but you are right, we should have caught on to that. Who were the two?'

'I can't give you names. They were only numbers on the sheet you gave me. These ones.' Jamieson handed Evans a sheet of paper with the reference numbers on it. Evans put it in his pocket and said he would check. 'What was the other question?' he asked.

'Have you had the *Pseudomonas* checked for the presence of resistance transfer factors?'

'No we haven't,' replied Evans. 'Dr Richardson didn't think there was much point in it. If the bug is resistant to antibiotic treatment it's resistant. It was his view that it doesn't matter much to the patient why it's resistant.' Evans saw the look on Jamieson's face and quickly added, 'Well, that's what Dr Richardson said.'

Jamieson said flatly, 'It might help in establishing where the bug came from in the first place.'

'I see,' said Evans sheepishly. 'I suppose we didn't consider that. We've been concentrating on trying to find synergistic action between the antibiotics available to us. Dr Richardson thought that we might be able to find some combination of antibiotics which would be effective against the bug.'

'The one plus one equals three effect,' smiled Jamieson. 'A good thought. Have you had any success?'

'Not yet, but we're still trying.'

'Maybe the London people could help with that too,' said Jamieson.

'Where would you like me to send the strain?'

'Send it to the Sci-Med labs in London and mark it Priority E,' said Jamieson, using the code he had been given in order to attract quick and expert scientific help. He gave Evans the address of the labs.

'Anything else?' asked Evans.

'You said something about lunch?'

After a forgettable lunch in the hospital staff restaurant Jamieson

60

returned to his 'cupboard' in microbiology and telephoned Thelwell's secretary to arrange a suitable time to visit. He was told that four o'clock would be best for the surgeon. Jamieson said he would be there. He put down the phone and Evans came in to hand him a sheet of paper. 'The names of the two double negatives in the swab tests. I wish I'd noticed it earlier.'

Jamieson read the names out loud. 'Staff Nurse Laura Fantes and . . . Mr Gordon Thomas Thelwell. Thank you,' he said, trying to keep emotion out of his voice. 'I'll mention this when I go up there later on.'

'Very good,' said Evans with just a trace of a smile in his voice.

'Is there anything else I can do for you?'

'I'd like some lab space,' said Jamieson.

'Lab space?' echoed Evans.

'Yes, lab space and a culture of the *Pseudomonas*. I want to see the thing for myself, do some of my own tests.'

The request seemed to trouble Evans for a moment. 'Actually, we are a bit short of room as you probably noticed. I can't think where . . . Unless, of course, you wouldn't mind sharing my lab?'

'That's very good of you,' smiled Jamieson. 'Any bit of bench will do.'

Evans took Jamieson across the corridor into his lab and introduced him to a serious looking girl. This impression was created in part by the fact that the girl's dark hair was tied back in a neat bun and she was wearing large spectacles. She seemed intent on what she was doing and did not look up at first.

'This is Moira Lippman, one of our senior technicians,' said Evans. 'I'm sure she will help you with anything you want in the way of equipment and advice.'

The girl finally looked up and smiled. She held up her gloved hands to excuse herself from shaking Jamieson's hand.

'Of course,' said Jamieson, returning the smile.

'Moira, Dr Jamieson would like a culture of the *Pseudomonas*. Perhaps you could get him one as soon as you have a moment?'

The girl finished what she was doing and then walked over

to a sink where she stripped off her contaminated gloves and dropped them into the open maw of a pedal bin before elbowing on the taps and washing her hands. As she dried them again she walked towards Jamieson and pointed to a row of cardboard boxes above the bench. 'You'll find gloves and masks up there,' she said, 'Surgical gloves are not going to be any good for you with those bandages on your hands. You can use the large plastic inspection type; there's a box by the door. I'll try to find a lab coat for you.'

With Jamieson kitted out in mask, gloves, lab coat and plastic apron Moira said, 'We keep all the dangerous bacteria in the fridge with the red tape across the door.'

'I get the picture,' said Jamieson, noting the skull and cross bones in the middle of the red band.

'Normally we would not classify *Pseudomonas* as deadly, but this particular strain has made it on merit.' Moira opened the locked fridge with a key she took from a pin on the back of her lapel and took out a plastic dish containing a straw-coloured jelly. The surface of the jelly was pock-marked with colonies of the organism and tinged with a slight blue-green colour. 'You can't mistake it,' said Moira. 'The pigment gives it away every time.'

'*Pyocyanin*,' said Jamieson.

'You've been doing your homework,' smiled the girl. 'Someone told me you were a surgeon?'

Jamieson smiled and said, 'Jack of all trades at the moment.' He looked down at the culture dish and detected the vague smell of new-mown grass that he associated with *Pseudomonas* from his time in microbiology. It seemed so innocuous when confined to the culture dish. The pigment was even a pretty colour. Its name, *Pyocyanin*, sounded mellifluous until you thought about the meaning: blue pus producer.

Sally Jenkins' insides knew the reality of the *Pseudomonas* bug. She was dying of an infection that had turned her peritoneal cavity into a suppurating, festering mess. The organism had invaded her tissues at will, starting from her operation scars and spreading into the surrounding area with complete immunity to the drugs that were pumped into her. It had now invaded her blood stream, sending her into a delirium that separated her from her husband who sat by her bedside in his own private hell of helplessness. 'Is there nothing you can do?' he whispered hoarsely. 'God damn it, there must be something!'

Phillip Morton shook his head and swallowed his emotion. 'I'm sorry,' he said simply. 'Perhaps it would be better if you waited outside for a while?'

'No,' insisted Jenkins, taking a new grip on his wife's hand. 'I want to be with her. I'm not leaving. Sally! Can you hear me?'

Morton exchanged glances with the ward sister. Both felt impotent in the circumstances. There was nothing worse than knowing a case was hopeless in the presence of relations who expected better.

Sally threw her head from side to side, making it difficult for the nurse beside her to wipe away the sweat from her face. Her breathing was rapid and laboured and her fingers moved constantly and restlessly as if searching for an escape from pain. No one from the outside world could reach her across the intellectual deserts of delirium.

Quite suddenly she stopped moving. Her neck went rigid. For a brief moment she was absolutely silent, then a long, gurgling sigh erupted from her throat and her body relaxed slowly into death.

The death restored a sense of order to Morton and the nurses but Jenkins' agony was just beginning. He flung himself across his wife's body and sobbed in long uneven spasms. His lips sought her dead fingers to kiss them as if in some desperate attempt to communicate with her and call her back. 'Don't leave me!' he sobbed. 'Don't leave me, Sal!'

Morton ushered the nurses to the door and said softly to them, 'Give him a moment.'

Moira Lippman watched Jamieson sit down to inoculate a fresh culture dish with the *Pseudomonas* she had taken from the fridge. He flamed the inoculation wire to red heat in the bunsen burner and allowed it to cool for a moment before touching it to the donor culture and then streaking the charged wire sequentially across the surface of the new culture.

'You can tell a lot about people from the way they do that,' said Moira.

'Really?' asked Jamieson, mildly amused at the thought.

'It's a bit like handwriting. Quiet, timid people do lots of thin lines very close together. Extroverts make a few large streaks and finish the last one with a flourish, just as if they were making their signature.'

'How did I come out of it?' asked Jamieson.

Moira took the new culture and looked at the surface through the lid. 'Lines perfectly parallel, neat, well proportioned and perfectly angled. I would say a meticulous worker who shows great attention to detail.'

'I'm happy to settle for that,' smiled Jamieson.

Moira put the culture plate into the incubator and asked, 'What exactly is it that you want to do with the bug?'

'I want to do some routine biochemical tests, get a feel for the beast if you like. At the moment it's just a collection of facts and figures on paper. If I actually do the things myself I think I might have a better notion of what it's all about.'

'Standard range of tests?'

'Full range.'

'You won't be able to do them until your culture has grown up overnight. Would you like me to prepare the tubes for you in the morning?'

'That would be a big help,' agreed Jamieson. 'But I don't want to interfere with your other work.'

'No problem,' said Moira. 'I'll show where to find them in case I have to go up to the wards in the morning.

Jamieson called in at the administration block to enquire about Staff Nurse Laura Fantes, only to be told told that, according to the ward records, she was off duty until seven forty-five the following morning. He was resigning himself to having to wait to talk to the nurse when the clerk added that she lived in the nurses' home in the hospital. There was a chance that she might be there. Jamieson thanked the man and asked where the home was situated. He followed the directions he was given and found himself in a square outside a broody, dark, three-storey building that stood next to the hospital kitchens.

A sign announced The Thelma Morrison Home for Nurses, and a stained-glass window on the front of the building above the doorway depicted a nurse tending to the wounded of the Crimea. Was having a 'heritage' all that big a deal? he wondered. The whole damned business seemed to him to consist of constant allusions to a history filled with the killing and maiming of others. A glorification of them, not a derogation. Sometimes he thought it might actually be quite nice to live in a country with very little 'heritage'. Somewhere where there was no bullshit. Somewhere where the buildings were new and everything worked. Was there such a place?

The square was noisy. It was filled with the clanging of food trolleys and hissing of steam from the kitchens whose three loading bays opened out on to a yard. A porter was singing an operatic aria badly as he manhandled a heavy container in opposition to the will of its castors on the cobbles. Jamieson thought the man might be hoping for 'discovery'. Someone from a television talent show would step out from behind one of the bins and lead him to overnight stardom. He had that air of ingenuous awfulness about him. He pitied the night nurses that had to sleep through the racket during the day.

He entered the nurses' home and saw a staircase in front of him and corridors running to both sides, but no indication of who lived there or of any room plan. There was a desk, but it was unmanned and there seemed to be no one about. Jamieson found the place strange. It had the aura of a church, a property conferred on it by the light coming through the stained-glass window which, as Jamieson could now see, filled the entire wall of the first landing on the stairs.

The dull, red carpet deadened his footsteps as he moved along the corridor to explore further. The air was still and musty and had a cold edge to it that only stone-built buildings can impart to their interiors. He was looking at a perfectly formed spider's web on the reel of a fire hose when he heard the front door open and saw a man in an ill-fitting navy-blue uniform shuffle across the corridor with a cup and saucer in his hand. He settled himself behind the desk and reached underneath it for a newspaper. He had not seen Jamieson and so was startled when Jamieson walked towards him and coughed to attract his attention.

"'Ere! What's your game?' exclaimed the man, obviously startled. 'You shouldn't be in here!'

'I'm looking for Staff Nurse Fantes,' said Jamieson.

'Well, you're supposed to ask at the desk, not wander about the bleedin' corridors.'

'You weren't at the desk,' said Jamieson evenly, eyeing the cup and saucer.

The man imagined he caught a whiff of management about Jamieson and decided to play safe. He changed his tone to a more ingratiating one and asked, 'And who might I enquire is wanting her?'

'Dr Jamieson, and it's official not personal,' added Jamieson, anticipating the next question.

'I'll just see if she's in, Doctor,' said the man with what he imagined was a friendly grin, but which made him look like a dachshund with tooth-ache. He put on a pair of spectacles one handedly and traced his finger down a list of residents before picking up an internal phone and tapping three digits. He shot Jamieson another grin while he waited for a response and seemed disappointed not to get one in return, but his call was answered and he gave the message to the person at the other end.

'She'll be down in a moment, Doctor,' he concluded, putting down the phone and missing the rest at the first attempt. 'You can wait in the day room. It's along here.'

Jamieson followed the hunched figure along the bottom corridor and was shown into a large, high-ceilinged room to wait for the nurse. There was a tall, elegant fireplace at one end with an embroidered fire screen standing in front of it and a brass log box beside it. Cold rooms and empty fireplaces, thought

Jamieson. There was something very British about it. Faded oil paintings of English rural scenes hung on the white walls at regular intervals and a number of assorted arm chairs that had seen better days were dotted about the lino-covered floor. Copies of *Nursing Standard* and various women's magazines were stacked in neat piles on a small black table.

Jamieson checked his watch; it was three-fifteen. The door opened and a small dark girl in her late twenties, thin at the shoulder but broad at the hips, came into the room and closed the door quietly behind her before announcing herself as Laura Fantes.

Jamieson introduced himself and explained why he had come to Kerr Memorial.

'I see,' said the girl, but her eyes betrayed the fact that she was trying to work out why Jamieson had come to see her.

'It's about the swabs that were taken as part of the surgical team screening,' said Jamieson.

'But they were negative,' said the girl quickly.

'Indeed, that's why I'm here.'

'I don't understand,' said the girl.

'They were too negative.'

The girl shook her head slightly in bewilderment. 'Too negative?'

'No bacteria at all,' said Jamieson.

'Is that bad?' asked the girl, obviously feeling that it wasn't.

'Not bad,' said Jamieson quietly. 'It's unusual, unless of course you were on treatment involving anti-bacterial drugs . . . but there is no mention of that on your medical record.'

The girl held Jamieson's gaze for a moment, then dropped her head and looked at the floor. Her shoulders visibly drooped forward. 'What a fool,' she said softly. 'I should have thought of that. What a fool!'

Jamieson waited quietly until the girl had recovered her composure. Somewhere in the building a door slammed and the noise reverberated round the room, challenging the length of the silence.

'You are quite right,' Laura Fantes said softly. 'I am on treatment.'

'What's the problem?'

'Cystitis. I'm taking ampicillin.'

For a moment Jamieson could not see what the girl was so upset about. Cystitis was a common enough complaint in young women, perhaps correlated with sexual activity and often attracting the adjective 'honeymoon', but it was hardly a matter for either secrecy or embarrassment. Then he realised what the problem must be. 'You didn't go to your doctor?' he said.

The girl shook her head.

'You took the drugs off the ward?'

Laura Fantes nodded.

Jamieson let out his breath in a long sigh, then he said, 'You do realise that taking any drugs off the ward is an offence that renders you subject to instant dismissal?'

The girl nodded and said, 'Of course. It was a stupid thing to do. I suppose I just didn't think at the time. I quite often get cystitis and my doctor always gives me ampicillin. I suppose I just thought that this time wouldn't have been any different, so I didn't bother with the trip across town and the forty-minute wait in the waiting room. It's so depressing.'

'How long have you been a nurse?' asked Jamieson.

'Nine years.'

'Any thoughts of marriage?'

The girl gave a bitter laugh and said, 'It's ironic really. I got the cystitis after a week's holiday with my boyfriend in the Lake District. At the end of it we broke up for good and now this.' She looked at Jamieson with an air of resignation and asked, 'What happens now?'

Jamieson looked at the sorry figure in front of him and considered his options. The official line was easy to take. He should report the girl and she would be dismissed. End of matter. But there were other considerations. The girl was nearly thirty. She had lost her boyfriend and she wasn't the most attractive girl he had ever seen. What would happen to her if she lost her job as well – not only her job, but her career? He could see the threat of embittered spinsterhood looming large on her horizon. Her record said that she was an excellent nurse. Was it really right to destroy all that? The rules said that it didn't matter what drug was stolen or for whatever purpose.

Jamieson decided to disagree. Any girl who had spent nine years of her life working in institutions like Kerr Memorial and living in places like the Thelma Morrison Home for Nurses deserved personal consideration and it wasn't morphine she had taken, just ampicillin, an antibiotic that graced half the bathroom cabinets in the land. Jamieson took a deep breath and said, 'Nothing.'

'I don't understand,' said Laura looking puzzled.

'Tonight you take a trip across town and you wait for forty minutes in the waiting room along with the screaming kids and the coughing bronchitics. You read old copies of *Punch* and *What Car* until the buzzer sounds for you and then you tell your GP that you've got cystitis. That is the way – the only way – you get ampicillin in future. You never ever take anything from the ward again. Understood?'

Laura Fantes looked as if she could not believe her ears. Her face lit up like a sunrise as she fought for words to express her gratitude. 'I'll never be able to thank you enough,' she said.

'Hop it,' said Jamieson. He looked at his watch again. It was time to go and see Thelwell. He wasn't looking forward to that. As he left the nurses' home, the singing porter was aiming for the top note of *Nessun Dorma*. He missed.

5

Jamieson entered the gynaecology department through a side door but found the narrow passage leading to the stairs barred by a number of large cartons. Two orderlies stood in front of the boxes waiting for a service lift to descend.

'Won't be a minute,' said one of the men when he saw Jamieson come in. Jamieson nodded and waited. The lift was the old-fashioned type, completely open to view on all sides, more like an iron cage than a modern elevator. Jamieson saw its floor platform appear in the ceiling and then slowly brake to a halt at floor level. One of the men dragged back the concertina doors and the other slid the boxes across the floor for him to stack inside. His way now clear, Jamieson climbed the stairs and followed the signs to Thelwell's office. He knocked once and entered.

'Dr Jamieson?' asked the woman sitting behind a typewriter. 'Mr Thelwell is expecting you. Go right in.' She pointed to one of the two dark wooden doors behind her. 'G.T. Thelwell' said the brass plaque which confronted Jamieson at eye level.

Jamieson entered to find Thelwell in conversation with Phillip Morton. Thelwell acknowledged Jamieson's arrival with a curt nod and moved in his chair as if to suggest to Morton that their chat was at an end. Morton took his cue and got to his feet. He smiled at Jamieson on his way out. 'How are the hands?' he asked.

'A lot better,' replied Jamieson.

'Take a seat,' said Thelwell.

Jamieson sat down.

'I am afraid our patient, Mrs Jenkins, died this afternoon,' said Thelwell when the door closed behind Morton.

'I'm sorry,' said Jamieson. 'She must have gone downhill very fast.'

'What do you mean?'

'A little over a day from the onset of infection,' said Jamieson. 'Seems uncommonly quick.'

'What are you suggesting?' demanded Thelwell.

Jamieson could practically see the hackles rise on the man as he imagined some slur against his department. He kept calm and said, 'I am suggesting that the infecting organism is not only difficult to treat but is also unusually virulent.'

Thelwell realised he had been too quick to condemn and grunted. 'I thought you knew that. In all three cases infection has been followed by generalised septicaemia within twelve hours.

'I see,' said Jamieson.

'Well, what is it you want me to show you exactly?' asked Thelwell.

'Everything. The wards, the theatre, the recovery rooms, the scrub areas . . . everything.'

Thelwell looked as if he might object but the moment passed. He simply got up from his chair and said, 'We'd best get started then.'

As the tour progressed, Jamieson knew he was finding what he had expected to find, a well-run, snappily efficient department, as good as any other in the National Health Service, certainly as clean and modern as its budget and the constraints of an old building would permit. He could see no obvious fault at all, either in terms of substance or procedure.

Thelwell outlined the departmental routine as he showed Jamieson around and Jamieson made notes, but there was nothing out of the ordinary about anything he observed.

'Where do you store surgical instruments?' he asked as Thelwell finished showing him the gynaecology operating theatre.

Thelwell moved across the floor to a steel cupboard and opened it. There were three instrument packs, each with a CSSD label on it to indicate that they had been through the steriliser. Each one was date-stamped and initialled by the operator in CSSD who had checked them. There was a broad band of autoclave tape on each, its heat-stripe marker turned black, indicating that it had been held at the required temperature in the steriliser for a set length of time.

Jamieson nodded in satisfaction and Thelwell closed the door again. 'When are you operating again?' he asked.

'Tomorrow,' replied Thelwell.

Jamieson was surprised. He said, 'I thought we had agreed that surgery wouldn't recommence until the new recovery ward was made ready?'

'It's an emergency,' said Thelwell. 'But we have taken your wishes into consideration and arranged a side room downstairs as a personal recovery room for the patient.'

'And the case?'

'Ovarian tumour. It won't wait.'

'Orthopaedic theatre again?' asked Jamieson.

Thelwell shook his head and said, 'No, we know the infection has nothing to do with the theatre so I'm moving back in here, but tonight this theatre is going to be disinfected from top to bottom, including the ceiling, just to make sure. All the surgical team were swabbed again today to make certain that no one is carrying the damned organism. After the operation the patient will be taken directly to the room I've just mentioned and specially nursed until she has recovered. The room, like the theatre, will be cleaned and disinfected from top to bottom.'

'Well, I can't fault anything there,' said Jamieson.

'How kind of you to approve,' said Thelwell.

Jamieson ignored the jibe and said, 'I would like to attend the operation tomorrow.' He sensed Thelwell's resentment but the thin lips remained tightly closed and the face, apart from the eyes, betrayed nothing for fully ten seconds before he said, 'To what end, might I ask?' He enunciated every syllable with meticulous care.

'Just to observe,' said Jamieson. His calmness seemed to infuriate Thelwell.

'You haven't been swabbed,' said Thelwell.

'Yes, I have,' replied Jamieson. 'I had myself tested in microbiology before I came over here.'

Thelwell swallowed hard and conceded defeat. 'Very well,' he said. 'Be in scrub at ten, assuming your swab is clear.'

'Thank you.'

Thelwell looked at his watch and said, 'Now, if there's nothing else, I have a choir practice this evening.'

'Actually there is,' said Jamieson, making Thelwell stop in his tracks. 'I want to discuss your own swabs. I want you to explain two completely negative nasal swabs in the last two staff screenings.'

'I don't understand,' stammered Thelwell, but Jamieson could sense that he did. He waited for something more and Thelwell gave in. He said, 'I always make a practice of using Naseptin cream in the interests of my patients. That's why my swabs were completely clear. It's a hard habit to break and I must have forgotten not to use it on the days swabs were taken.'

Jamieson let Thelwell dangle on the hook for a moment before stating the obvious. 'But the object of the staff screening exercise was to establish whether any of the staff are carrying organisms that are dangerous to the patients. If everyone sterilised their nasal passages before the test there would be no point in doing them . . .' Jamieson knew that Thelwell was writhing in discomfort behind the apparently bland exterior.

'As I said,' said Thelwell, 'I must have forgotten to stop the cream on the days of the tests. I have a lot on my mind at the moment.'

Jamieson continued to stare at Thelwell, wondering if there was any more to come. His silence bore fruit. Thelwell said, 'All right, if you must know, I did not want to give that idiot, Richardson, any opportunity to embarrass me with his incompetence. That man would probably say he found typhoid in my naso-pharynx.'

Jamieson found it hard to maintain his composure. Was this a hospital or a lunatic asylum? he wondered. Thelwell's paranoia must be bordering on the clinical, but for the moment he had to keep things in perspective. He had to consider that Thelwell might be telling the truth about using the cream routinely. He said, 'Perhaps after tomorrow you might submit another screening swab to the lab?'

'Of course,' murmured Thelwell, embarrassed and anxious that this line of conversation should end.

'Enjoy your practice,' said Jamieson. 'A local choir?'

'Yes . . . yes,' stammered Thelwell, uneasy with the change to social chit chat. 'St Serf's Church. We are doing the *Te Deum*.'

'Nice,' said Jamieson inappropriately.

The man stood in the shadows of a shop door and watched what was happening down the road. The sluts were still there, flitting in and out of the darkness in their imitation leopard skin and leather, but they didn't fool him. Half of them had warrant cards in their handbags and the Ford Sierra that was parked in Clarion Street might just as well have a blue light on its roof instead of two clods eating sandwiches and looking at their watches. Did they think he was a complete idiot? Did they really think that he would try exactly the same line of attack? Walk into their puny little trap like some mental defective? There was no anger in his thinking. He was just surprised that they could be so stupid. Talk about bolting the stable door . . .

A bus loomed up from his right and pulled to a halt in front of him. He pulled up his collar and got on board. He would concentrate on other things this evening and the fact that the police would be out all night in the cold made the prospect all the more pleasant. Anyone who protected these filthy creatures deserved all the discomfort that was coming to them.

The bus stopped on the far side of the circle and the man got off, carrying his briefcase and pressing his hat a little more firmly on to his head. It had started to rain but it was only a short walk back to the basement flat and then he could get on with the evening's work. He turned into the lane that separated the main road from the street where the flat was situated and passed along it, carefully avoiding the piles of cartons and waste paper that had been bundled out for collection on the following morning.

The location of the flat was ideal for his purpose because all the surrounding buildings were in use as offices. At night there was rarely anyone about. The windows of the entire street were in darkness save for one upstairs light in the surveyor's office across the road from the flat. This was so unusual that it made him stop briefly in the shadows at the end of the lane and look up at it. He was curious. No one had ever worked late there before. His natural caution made him consider all possible implications.

As he watched, a young woman appeared at the window. She was laughing and, as she reached up to the cord for the blinds, a man came up behind her and slid his arm round her waist. The man in the shadows watched as the man in the window slid his hands up on to the woman's breasts and buried his face against the side of her neck. 'Fool!' he hissed, his eyes burning with anger as he watched the woman laugh again and reach up her hand to stroke her companion's hair. 'Can't you see she's trying to trap you!'

The venetian blinds snapped shut and the two figures were eclipsed, leaving the man at the corner of the lane still staring up at the window. He swallowed twice and regained his composure. There was work to be done. He descended the basement steps and opened the door extra quietly. He did not want to give the couple across the street any occasion to look out of the window, not that that was likely. That poor fool would have other things on his mind. But, as ever, caution was of the essence . . .

He closed the door silently and pulled the curtains across the window before switching on the light. A spider scuttled up the lifeline of its web, having been exposed against the whitewash of the walls, but the man ignored it. He opened the door of a small metal cupboard and examined what was inside. Excellent, he thought, it was all going well. When the time came for a change he would be ready and it could begin all over again.

He closed the door of the cupboard and went through to the kitchen to switch on a small spotlight that sat in the middle of the kitchen table. A dull, purple glow came from the lamp at first, but it grew brighter as the minutes passed. The man returned from the bedroom wearing white overalls and a full plastic face visor. He checked that his gloves were fitting properly, that the cuffs of his overalls overlapped them and the tunic was fastened up to his neck. There were to be no more slip-ups. After more checking and preening he seemed satisfied with the state of his protection and got to work.

Two hours passed before he decided that he had done enough for one evening. He switched off the lamp and removed his visor. The cold air of the basement felt damp against the thin film of sweat on his forehead and made him shiver slightly as he got to his feet and started clearing up. With everything safely away inside the metal cupboard he sighed in satisfaction and looked at his watch. A last check on the thermometer protruding from the top of the cupboard and there was no more to be done this evening.

As he switched off the room light before opening the outside door he became aware of voices in the street above and stopped in the darkness to listen. A man and a woman were talking but he could not make out what was being said. As the minutes passed he became more and more impatient. Standing motionless was making him acutely aware of the cold and damp. Very slowly he turned the Yale lock on the back of the door, keeping his full weight against it in case it should move against the jamb and make a noise. With painful slowness he inched the door open until he could hear what was being said.

As he listened, he came to realise that the voices belonged to the man and woman he had seen in the window across the street. Their illicit liaison in the office was over and they were now leaving. Where had they done it in the office? he wondered. Across a desk? Writhing on the floor like animals? Against a wall, perhaps, with the bitch egging him on? There was no limit to the ingenuity of the sluts. That was why he himself had to be equally devious if he were to redress the balance.

The woman was insisting that there was no need for the man to run her home. He was late already and that would only cause more trouble at home. She was quite happy to get the bus; the stop was only round the corner and she would be home in fifteen minutes.

'If you're sure,' said the man.

'Absolutely,' said the woman.

There was a long silence and the man in the basement deduced that the pair must be embracing. A look of disgust crossed his face in the dim yellow light that filtered down from the street.

There were a few whispered good nights and then the click of high heeled shoes on the pavement that said they had parted. A car moving off a few seconds later said that it was now safe for him to leave. But the seeds of an idea had been planted inside his head. He had not planned it, but could he turn a chance like this down?

Care! He must take care! There was always danger in unplanned action. Spontaneity could spell disaster, but on the other hand he must not turn down the chance of ridding society of another of these creatures. He closed the door again and once more shut the curtains before switching on the light. He went to the bathroom and took down the rubber apron from the line across the bath and folded it quickly before stuffing it into his briefcase. The instruments were ready on the side of the sink. He wrapped them up quickly in the velvet cloth.

This would be a test, he thought, as he closed the basement door quietly behind him. If the bitch was standing at the bus stop when he got there it would be a sign that fate was on his side. If she was not, he would return to the flat and abandon the entire notion.

He caught his foot against the edge of a cardboard box in the lane as he hurried along it and almost went sprawling, but recovered his balance in time to remind himself to take more care. He paused at the end of the lane to compose himself, smoothing the front of his coat and adjusting the angle of his hat, before rounding the corner to approach the bus stop.

She was still there! The bitch was standing there, her skirt hugging the line of her buttocks, the slit in the back revealing a triangle of white underskirt, the line of her jacket designed specifically to enhance the curve of her breasts. She turned to look at him as he joined her at the stop, but her face registered nothing. That was the way the bitches always looked at him, as if he weren't there. He stared at the back of her neck and then at the slight haughtiness of her profile as she turned slightly. Who did she think she was kidding with her air of respectability? Did she really imagine that he could not see through the sham? Through to the dirt and the evil!

The bus arrived and the woman climbed aboard. She had difficulty in mounting the high step due to the tightness of her skirt and had to reach down to hitch it up a few inches. Behind her the man felt the pressure behind his eyes increase as he realised that this must be for his benefit. She was trying to distract him from his task by flaunting her evil charms. She was using the very weapons that had caught him out before! He felt the hardness stir and tiny beads of perspiration broke out along his upper lip. He fought the feeling. He must not be swayed.

The woman asked for a fifty pence fare and the man, after a suitable delay while he pretended to search for change in his pocket, asked for the same. He collected his ticket from the dispenser but, as he did so, he banged his briefcase against the base of the machine and the instruments inside rattled free from their wrapping.

'What you got in there, mate?' asked the driver. 'The Crown Jewels?'

The man managed a smile, but it was strained and unnatural. With an outward air of calm he moved into a seat at the back of the bus. There, he would be free from curious eyes. He was four rows behind the woman and inside his head he was furious with himself. He had thrown away his chance! He could not now go ahead with the plan. The driver would remember him getting on the bus at the same time as the deceased. The incident with the instruments rattling free would ensure that he wasn't forgotten. Why hadn't he taken the time to pack the instruments properly!

The bus turned into a brightly lit street where the local pubs were turning out their clientele in compliance with the law. It was noisy and disorderly and the man grimaced involuntarily as he saw a crowd of youths respond to the sight of the bus by running towards the stop. The doors slid open and two of them had an argument in the doorway as they both tried to board first. The driver remonstrated with them and received a torrent of abuse in return. He said no more as they dropped their money into the tray and continued to push and shove each other.

There were five in all. They lifted the hat off an old man as they moved inside the bus and let it fall again so that it dropped over his eyes. His protests were met with loud derision.

'What's wrong, Grandad? Gone blind?'

They turned their attention to a teenage girl who flushed in embarrassment as they started to discuss her appearance.

'Nice tits, shame about the face!' hooted one of the yobs to the loud amusement of the others.

'Nice little bum as well. Bet she could give you a fair bang.'

'Think we should give it a try?' asked another and there was a moment's pause in the noise.

'Yeah . . . let's,' growled one of the yobs ogling the girl's legs.

The young girl sprang to her feet and rushed towards the front of the bus demanding to be let off and the police be called. The driver was reluctant to do anything, but at the protests of another passenger, an old woman sitting near the front, he lifted his radio handset.

'Touch that and you're for the fucking hospital!' warned the leader of the yobs moving down the aisle towards the driver.

The driver smiled apologetically at the girl and replaced the handset. He opened the doors of the bus and said, 'Run along home, love. It's for the best.'

The girl left the bus and the yob returned to his friends to shout filth at the girl from the window. Their comments were reinforced with hand gestures indicating what they wanted to do to her.

They now turned their attention to the woman in the tight skirt.

'What have we here then?' asked one as he moved into the seat across the aisle from the woman. The others moved up to join him.

'Just look at this . . .'

The woman maintained a dignified silence and ignored the youths to look out of the window.

'The older ones are always the best,' confided the leader of the yobs. 'They know what it's all about.' He turned to the woman and said, 'Don't you, darlin'?'

The woman continued to ignore them.

The leader moved into the seat beside the woman and sidled up close to her. 'You know what it's for, don't you darlin'! You've had a few in your time, haven't you? Of course you have. I bet you're a real goer when you get started . . .'

One of the yobs leapt into the aisle and started moving his hips back and forth rapidly to the delight of the others.

The woman's composure was broken. She turned from the window and hissed angrily, 'Animals!'

The comment provoked nothing but loud laughter from the yobs who fell about. One passenger, a middle-aged man wearing an anorak, could stand it no longer. 'Why don't you shut your filthy mouths!' he demanded, red in the face with a mixture of anger and embarrassment. The yobs turned and exchanged amused glances before moving towards him.

'Well, what have we here then?' hissed the leader.

'Looks like a real dick-head to me,' said one of the others.

'Bet he works in a bank, looks like the kind of wanker who works in a bank,' said the leader.

'Yes sir, no sir, three bags full sir,' mimicked one of the others.

'Well, do you then?' demanded the leader, putting his face down close to the man.

'Just shut up and go away,' said the man.

'Are you going to make us, like?' said the leader with quiet menace and a grin that held no humour in it.

'Don't you have any decency in you?' spluttered the man. 'Don't you have parents or are they like you? Trash!'

The yob leader let the grin slowly fade from his face before he turned to the others and said, 'He's talkin' about my mum. Did you hear what he said about my mum?'

'Old bastard!'

'Give him one!'

'For God's sake, stop it! Leave him alone!' pleaded the woman whose plight had prompted the outburst.

'Shut up! We're comin' to you, darlin'!' said the yob leader without taking his eyes off the man who was his current target. 'Nobody talks like that about my mum, nobody . . . understand?'

The man was given no chance to say anything before the yob smashed his forehead down on the bridge of the man's nose and split it wide open. The man's spectacles shattered and blood showered down on to the seat in front of him as he collapsed with a gasp.

'For God's sake, stop it!' screamed a woman at the front and others joined in demands to the driver.

The feeling that the passengers, who had up until now been an assortment of ineffectual individuals, were beginning to gel into a cohesive opposition began to tell on the yob leader. 'You heard what he said about my mum!' he appealed, obviously feeling that now he had been given a valid reason for behaving in the way he always did anyway. 'You heard him! Old bastard. Deserved all he got, he did.' The other yobs agreed, but their support was subdued as they too felt the pressure of public opinion mount against them and looked at the sorry figure of the man holding his face while blood ran down his wrists to disappear into his cuffs.

The woman in the tight skirt slipped out of her seat and pressed the emergency door release button. The doors hissed back and she stepped out into the night and was quickly on her way.

81

The yobs were still uncertain of their position as they looked about them. The driver, too, was beginning to gain confidence; his fingers were considering a move towards the handset.

'Oh, fuck them!' snarled the leader. 'Bunch of wankers! Let's get the fuck out of here!' The yobs poured out of the open door and ran off into the night. 'Let's get the tart!' was the last comment the bus passengers were to hear.

'For God's sake, drive on!' demanded one of the passengers. 'Before they change their mind and come back!'

What a piece of luck, thought the man at the back. He had been restored to anonymity by the behaviour of a bunch of human trash, the sweepings of the municipal streets, the lager-swilling bottom of the social heap. He got up from his seat and pressed the bell. The driver avoided meeting his eyes in the mirror and the man was pleased at being proved right. The driver would no longer remember anything about him. The incident with the rattling instruments would be forgotten. The driver would have only one memory of this night, his run-in with the yobs and how they had terrorised his passengers while he had sat there too scared to do anything.

As the man was leaving the bus, people were flocking round the injured passenger and discussing whether it was best to drive straight to the hospital or whether they should stop and wait for the police to arrive. The man heard the hospital option win as he stepped down on to the kerb to wait until the bus had moved off into the night before starting to retrace the route to where the woman and the yobs had alighted.

It was only three hundred metres to the spot but when the man got there, all was quiet. He stood still for a moment and looked about him like an animal sniffing the night. It was a quiet area. The road was broad. Trees lined both sides and a wide grass verge on one side separated a housing estate from the road. On the other side, the side where he stood, there were railings between him and what he thought might be a park, although he didn't know the area at all. It was difficult to tell because of the dense shrubbery on the other side of the railings. It could be a bowling green, tennis courts or even a boating pond.

He imagined he heard a distant laugh and trained his ears in the direction he thought it had come from. There it was again. He was sure this time. It had come from the shrubbery another hundred metres or so down the road. The man looked about him and saw that he was still alone in the road. He walked on with deliberate slowness, taking great care not to make a sound. He moved towards the spot where the noise was coming from.

It was them! And they had the woman! They were enjoying the woman and he could hear them arguing in stage whispers over whose turn it was next.

'Keep your hand over her mouth!' hissed one.

'For Christ's sake, hold her legs apart!' demanded another.

'Scared she'll snap it off?' giggled another in the darkness.

'Get on with it!'

Scum! thought the man. An ignorant rabble who deserved all they got from the bitch, but tonight they would serve their purpose for him. Tomorrow the bus passengers would conveniently remember that the scum had got off behind the woman and that the last words of their leader had been, 'Let's get the tart.'

Time was getting on. The road would not stay quiet for ever.

The man moved another thirty metres along the pavement and hoisted himself over the railings. He dropped to his knees and paused for a moment before moving silently into the bushes. He circled around the area where he knew the yobs were located. When he was in the position he wanted to be in he called out sharply, 'Police! Come out of there!'

The air was suddenly full of curses and the sound of breaking twigs and branches as the yobs scattered through the undergrowth in panic. The man stood perfectly still until the sounds had faded into the distance, then he moved towards the sound of sobbing.

He found the woman lying on the ground supporting herself weakly on one elbow and weeping. The bottom half of her body was naked and the clothes on her top half were in tatters. 'Thank God,' she whispered weakly. 'Thank God you've come.'

The man looked down at her, earth in her hair and blood on her face where she had been beaten. He looked at her breasts hanging down on her stomach and the pathetic way she tried to cover her crotch with one hand. The whore was still at work. He felt the hardness begin and was angry with himself.

'You will not trap me, you whore!' he hissed, undoing his trousers and taking out his erect penis.

Fear filled the woman's eyes as her nightmare soared to new heights. For a moment her mind refused to believe what was happening, then she opened her mouth to scream. The man lashed the back of his hand across her face and sent her sprawling before any sound got out. He masturbated furiously over her while staring down at the curves of her body and the smoothness of her thighs. He climaxed over her prostrate body and gasped, 'I don't need you, you bitch. You can't trap me!'

The woman whimpered and scratched at the earth as terror and shock threatened to deprive her of her reason. She did not see the man open his case and take out the rubber apron. She was oblivious of the glint of the surgical instruments as he laid them out on the plastic sheet.

The man finished with the woman. He had cut away the evil from another of these creatures. But there was more to do if the yobs were to get the blame. Complete disfigurement was called for. The knife cut and hacked its way down the corpse.

The man stepped back from the scene and took off the apron. He laid it on the ground and folded it inwards so that the blood was to the inside, then he placed it inside a plastic bag and returned it to the briefcase. The instruments were wrapped and placed in another plastic bag. Gloves were placed in yet another and the case was closed.

Without looking back at the body, the man moved off through the shrubbery, but only to freeze at the suggestion of a flashing light somewhere through the trees. He crouched down in the long grass near the railings and waited as the light grew brighter and nearer. It was blue.

A Police Panda car cruised slowly down the road with its two occupants looking impassively out of its windows. The man knew that they were looking for the yobs. The driver of the bus or the hospital where they had taken the injured passenger would have reported the incident. The police would cruise around the streets, advertising their presence, but nothing would happen until the woman was found. Then all hell would break loose.

When all was quiet again and the car had turned the corner at the end of the road, the man climbed quickly over the railings and resumed the confident, purposeful gait normally expected of a man who carried a briefcase.

6

Jamieson returned to his room in the residency at nine. He had gone into the city to eat, feeling that he needed to get away from the hospital for a while. He had found an Italian restaurant with enough atmosphere to divert his attention briefly from the rain outside thanks to canned music and sunny travel posters, but now he was back in the cloistered confines of Victorian stone and inadequate heating. He felt the radiator under the window through the light bandaging on his hands and decided that it was on – although he would have been loath to put money on it. He even considered that his hands might be heating it rather than the other way around. He checked the pipes leading into the radiator and was reassured to find that the inlet was marginally warmer than the outlet.

Why was it such a big deal in this country, he wondered, to have a heating system that worked? Was this something the British had missed out on while they had been inventing the steam engine and television, anaesthetics and radar? Or was it the result of some innate belief that discomfort was good for the soul? A legacy of the Reformation, perhaps? Hard work, cold showers, and cross-country runs had all played their part in his own formative years at school and he had been brought up to believe that medicine always had to taste nasty before it could do any good. Had this all been part of a planned preparation for life in a country where houses were perpetually cold and damp and hotels always had 'a problem with the hot water'? Or was being on his own in a strange city looking out at the rain getting to him more than he cared to admit?

Jamieson had rung Sue earlier in the evening, and felt that he could not call her again so soon. But what he would do, he decided, was go home at the weekend.

The telephone rang and startled him. He lifted it to hear Carew's voice.

'They are carrying out the post-mortem on Mrs Jenkins this evening. I thought you might want to attend?'

Jamieson looked at his watch and saw that it was half past nine. 'This is a bit unusual, isn't it?' he asked.

'We thought it best to make absolutely sure that it was the *Pseudomonas* that was responsible for her death as quickly as possible.'

Jamieson said that he wanted to be there.

'The PM room is attached to the mortuary,' said Carew.

'Where's that?'

'Near the east gate. There's a clump of trees to your left as you approach the gate. The mortuary is behind them.'

The rain had stopped as Jamieson left the residency but an unpleasant wind had taken its place. It blew directly into his face as he walked the three hundred metres or so to the east gate. He was showered with water as he passed under the clump of trees when a particularly strong gust of wind caught their branches. The trees were there to shield the mortuary from public view.

As he brushed the water from his shoulders, Jamieson reflected on just how important a role psychology played in the treatment of illness. Trust and confidence were essential ingredients in the formula. If a patient entered hospital feeling that he or she were in the best place for their treatment and that success was almost guaranteed then half the battle had already been fought and won. There could be no more poignant reminder that failure was an ever present possibility in hospitals than the silent, forbidding presence of a mortuary

Jamieson tried the front door and found it locked. He walked round the outside of the building in a clockwise direction until he found a small, blue door at the back which was unlocked.

He entered to find himself alone in a sparsely furnished room with a row of coat pegs hung with gowns and aprons and an assortment of Wellington boots lined up under a wooden bench below. Assuming that the PM was already under way, he took off his jacket and hung it up on a vacant peg. He found a pair of boots his size and helped himself to gown and apron. He couldn't fasten all the gown ties himself because they were at the back, but for this purpose it was not going to matter. He did the best he could, then opened the door to the interior to find himself in a hallway.

There were three doors leading off it but light was coming from under only one. He knocked and entered. It was the post-mortem room. There were three pedestal tables arranged side by side in the room, but only one was in use. Two powerful lamps above it augmented the strip lighting on the ceiling and an instrument trolley serviced the needs of the pathologist who was working alone. He looked up from the table and said, 'You must be Jamieson. They told me you might come along. I'm Vogel.'

Jamieson estimated that Vogel was in his late fifties, grey haired and bespectacled and with a moustache that drooped at the corners. His gown was tied tightly enough to emphasise the size of his paunch and his sleeves were rolled up far enough to reveal powerful arms with thick wrists. His left one carried a large, stainless steel wrist watch.

Jamieson joined Vogel at the table and saw that the pathologist had already opened up the body of Sally Jenkins. He was removing some of her internal organs. 'Look at that,' said Vogel, holding up a handful of tissue which Jamieson could not recognise out of context. 'What a mess.'

'Was it a *Pseudomonas* infection?' asked Jamieson.

'No doubt about it. You can smell it.'

Jamieson saw that Vogel was serious and moved closer still until he noticed the same smell of new-mown grass that had come from the culture dish in the lab. 'So you can,' he said.

'Just look at the damage here,' said Vogel. He held up the diseased tissue and invited Jamieson to examine it. Jamieson was reluctant to add to the already overpowering assault on his senses of sight and smell. He had never liked pathology. He nodded and looked down at the marble white face lying on the table as Vogel sluiced some of the mess down the drain channels with the aid of a hand-held hose which he removed from a holster at the head of the table. She seemed so young.

'There are half a dozen infections I can tell by smell,' said Vogel. '*Pseudomonas* is one of the easiest.'

'You've come across it a lot then?' asked Jamieson.

'Thirty years ago and before I became a pathologist, I worked in a burns unit. *Pseudomonas* was the scourge of burns cases at the time. Once it got into the wounds there was practically nothing we could do. A lot of people died in a lot of pain because of this damned organism. Nowadays we have the drugs to deal with it. We don't often see something like this.'

Jamieson looked at Vogel but then looked away sharply for fear of revealing in his eyes what he felt about the pathologist's expression. He was thinking that already in Vogel's mind, Sally Jenkins had become 'something like this'. He cautioned himself not to be too critical of his colleague because, in a way, Vogel was right. The figure on the table was just another cadaver, another medical problem to be solved and reported on, but for him Sally Jenkins was still a patient and her death at such an age was an absolute tragedy.

'The degree of tissue invasion in this particular case is quite remarkable,' continued Vogel. 'To have caused so much internal damage in such a short time is phenomenal. Look at that.'

Jamieson followed the line of Vogel's knife and saw the festering, deformed tissue that had been a healthy uterus only two days before.

'We'll get this to the lab,' said Vogel. 'But there is no doubt in my mind. The *Pseudomonas* killed her.'

Jamieson left to return to the residency and this time he did not object to the strength of the wind. It would aerate his clothing. He always felt unclean after being in pathology for he knew that the smell of formaldehyde and the hideous odours from the exposed cadavers could cling tenaciously to clothes. He remembered that a long time ago a local cinema back home had started to use the same air freshener as was used in the hospital mortuary. He had stopped going to see films after that. The heavy scent had made him see something quite different on the screen from what was actually up there.

He took a warm relaxing bath and then made himself some coffee, using the electric kettle that was provided in his room and a sachet of the instant sort he had bought down in the town. He planned to have an early night because tomorrow he would be back in theatre for the first time since the accident. He would not be doing anything other than observe, but just being there was going to mean a lot.

As he lay in bed, he thought back to his accident and relived it. On that morning he had been driving in the outside lane of the M6 when a van coming in the opposite direction had swung violently to the right after a tyre had blown. It had mounted the central reservation and flipped over on to its side to tumble right into the path of his car. There was nothing he could have done. He had careered headlong into it.

For a long time after the impact Jamieson was unconscious, but when he did come round he started to remember little details about the moments leading up to the collision. Not all at once because, at first, his mind had been a total blank, but gradually and usually when he was least expecting it, latent memory would restore to him a jigsaw piece of the event.

One evening, he suddenly found that he could remember the face of the van driver. It must have been seconds before his own car had ploughed into the overturned vehicle and the vision could only have occupied the merest fraction of a second, but Jamieson could remember seeing fear on the man's face.

The vanman's passenger, a boy in his teens, had time enough only to register surprise before death overtook him. The bumper of Jamieson's car had caught him in the midriff and crushed him against the rear stanchion of the cab. His arms and legs were flung out as if he were executing a difficult vault in a school gymnasium. This was another memory that could have occupied only the merest fraction of time, but it had been stored in his subconscious as an indelible part of the record of that awful day. These particular visions returned to haunt him regularly.

Knowing that he had to be in scrub by ten, Jamieson got into the microbiology lab dead on nine to check that his nasal swab was clear of potential pathogens and also to see if the *Pseudomonas* cultures he had inoculated on the previous day had grown. He was satisfied on both counts and Moira Lippman told him that she would be happy to prepare the biochemical reagents for the tests he wanted to do while he was in theatre. It was an offer that Jamieson was glad to accept, but once again he reminded Moira that he did not want to interfere with her routine lab work.

'No problem,' smiled the girl. 'I can fit it in. Besides,' she added, 'I have a vested interest in seeing an end to this infection.'

'Tell me,' said Jamieson.

'My sister-in-law is due to come into Kerr Memorial next week for an op.'

'I see,' said Jamieson.

The nurses in the scrub area for the gynaecology theatre had to make special arrangements for Jamieson. The bandages on his hands could not be removed to permit washing, so they added more sterile dressings to them and sealed them inside sterile inspection gloves. They sealed the cuffs with sterile tape. One of them helped him adjust his mask to sit more comfortably over his face and he was ready to enter theatre.

'Good morning,' said Jamieson as he entered.

Thelwell, watching the preparation of the patient, looked up at him but did not reply. Phillip Morton, who had been detailed to assist, bid him good morning as did the theatre sister.

A nurse asked, 'Music, sir?'

'Mozart, I think,' replied Thelwell. 'Unless anyone objects?'

No one objected. Heaven help them if they had, thought Jamieson.

The strains of *Eine Kleine Nachtmusik* began to fill the theatre, affording it the ambience of an aircraft during boarding.

Phillip Morton supervised a junior houseman in the final preparation of the area where the first incision would be made. The green sheets were re-adjusted to display only the operating site and Morton said, 'Ready here, sir.'

Thelwell looked to the anaesthetist and said, 'Well, Dr Singh. Is she sleeping comfortably?'

'Like a baby, sir,' replied the Indian.

Thelwell began with a preamble for the benefit of the junior houseman and two medical students who had been permitted to attend. A nurse turned down the music a little and Thelwell spoke to punctuating beeps from the monitor.

'Mrs Edelman is twenty-nine years old. She is the wife of a German engineer who is based here in Britain with the car company he works for.'

'BMW,' said Phillip Morton, but Thelwell just frowned and continued. 'Mrs Edelman has one child, a boy of three years, but a later pregnancy was miscarried at eighteen weeks. She had a second miscarriage last year, again at around eighteen weeks, and she and her husband decided not to try again. A few weeks ago she developed severe pain in her lower stomach and was referred to us by her GP. The scans we did show a sizeable growth on her right ovary. We fear it may be malignant. Today we are going to have a look and decide with the aid of the pathology department just what to do.'

Jamieson had been watching the theatre sister lay out the instruments in order. She knew what Thelwell would ask for first and held it in readiness, while a more junior nurse waited behind her ready to replace instruments as they were used.

Once again Jamieson saw what he expected to see. Thelwell was a competent surgeon. He could not be faulted on anything as he performed what was a delicate though fairly routine operation. The discipline in the theatre was excellent and the team functioned with the efficiency of a group who knew each other well.

'How is she?' Thelwell asked the anaesthetist as the entire

theatre waited for the pathology lab's verdict on the tissue that Thelwell had removed from the woman's ovary.

'Quite stable. No problems,' answered the man sitting at the head of the patient.

Thelwell looked at the clock again and tutted. 'They seem to take longer each time,' he muttered.

No one spoke for they knew that Thelwell always said that at this point in the proceedings. It was never true. The pathology lab were always efficient when it came to emergency sections.

The swing doors opened and a green-clad figure came in to join them. 'I'm sorry, it's malignant,' she said.

'Thank you,' said Thelwell matter of factly before turning to the anaesthetist. 'Is she still all right?'

'No problems.'

'Might as well get on with it then.'

Thelwell detailed the extent of the tissue he would have to cut away for the benefit of the houseman and students and then proceeded to do it while Phillip Morton assisted. Jamieson admired the business-like way Thelwell went about the remainder of the operation. There was no hesitation, no pause for second thoughts or discussion of alternatives. He made his decisions as soon as they were required and then acted on them. The operation was over with laudable speed and Phillip Morton was left to carry out the final stages before the patient was allowed to begin a controlled ascent to consciousness.

'Thank you, everyone,' said Thelwell, stripping off his gloves as he left the theatre. Jamieson joined him outside for gown and mask removal.

'Well, what did you see, Jamieson?' asked Thelwell.

'I saw an excellent surgeon doing his job assisted by a first-class theatre team,' replied Jamieson.

Thelwell grunted and Jamieson sensed that the man was suspicious of compliments. His paranoia demanded it. 'How kind of you to say so, Doctor,' he said sarcastically.

For the moment Jamieson could not think of the right word to describe Thelwell. He decided that 'shit' would have to do.

'And have you solved our infection problem?' asked Thelwell with an air of amused superiority.

'Not yet,' replied Jamieson, keeping his temper. 'But I will.' He turned to face Thelwell and look directly at him. He knew that it was a challenging gesture that Thelwell would not experience too often in this little world where he was king and no one dared cross him. A flicker of uncertainty appeared in Thelwell's eyes and Jamieson was satisfied. That was what he had hoped for. 'You will remember to submit a nasal swab to the lab, won't you?' he said as he put on his jacket to leave. 'One without the antiseptic.' Thelwell turned crimson and Jamieson said, 'Good day, Mr Thelwell.'

Jamieson walked back to microbiology and met Clive Evans en route; he was on his way to a late lunch at the hospital restaurant. Jamieson said that he would join him. It was nearly two o'clock and what was left in the heated metal trays at the food counter looked even less appetising than usual. Jamieson examined the congealed stodge and opted for a salad. Evans risked the steak pie. They found a clean table but it was hard to talk over the noise of the domestic staff who were clearing other tables nearby and scraping waste food from plates into large metal receptacles.

'How did the op go this morning?' asked Evans.

'Smoothly, but the woman's tumour turned out to be malignant as they had feared.'

'Bad luck,' said Evans.

'By the way, I asked Mr Thelwell to submit another nasal swab to the lab when he has a moment. He was using antiseptic cream at the time of the last test.'

'Was he now?' said Evans raising his eyebrows.

Jamieson wondered what was going through Evans' mind but when the microbiologist realised that Jamieson was watching him he quickly snapped out of his preoccupation and asked, 'Was that the case with the nurse too?'

'No,' replied Jamieson. 'She was being treated with antibiotics.'

'Moira tells me you want to run some of your own tests on the *Pseudomonas*?'

'Just a case of "know your enemy". I need to have a feel for the bug. If you are objecting to me diverting Miss Lippman from other work, I can carry out the tests myself.'

'Moira tells me she can fit your stuff in with her routine work, so there's no problem.'

'Good. I like Miss Lippman. She seems very knowledgeable and efficient.'

'She is,' agreed Evans.

Jamieson became aware of the kitchen staff looking at their watches and exchanging muttered comments behind the food counter. He said to Evans, 'I think we've outstayed our welcome.'

Evans looked round balefully then shrugged. He got to his feet and said, 'We'd better go.'

Jamieson finished setting up his biochemical tests on the *Pseudomonas* by four o'clock and called in on John Richardson to discuss the results of the latest staff screening tests.

'They were all negative for what we are looking for,' confessed Richardson with a weary sigh.

'And the theatre and recovery room tests before the disinfection last night?'

'Negative.'

'So you are no further forward,' said Jamieson.

"Fraid not. Evans tells me you sent the bug to your labs for special tests?'

'I want to know why it's so resistant to antibiotic therapy.'

'Will that help?'

Jamieson took the point that Richardson was making. It would not help the patients to know *why* the bug was immune to so many antibiotics. 'I agree, it's academic,' he said. 'But it might give us some insight into the environment that spawned the bug in the first place. I particularly want to know how much of the problem is chromosomal and how much is due to the bug having picked up extra plasmid DNA.'

Richardson rubbed his eyes as if he were very tired and asked, 'Supposing the damned thing is not carrying extra plasmid DNA, what could you conclude?'

'I would be very surprised. It would mean that the bug was resistant to all these drugs in its own right,' said Jamieson. 'It would have to have undergone multiple mutations.'

'It could have acquired the resistances one at a time,' said Richardson.

'It could,' agreed Jamieson. 'But it would have to have been over a very long course of time and the chances are that it would have caused trouble before now.'

'I suppose it would,' agreed Richardson, 'But somehow I'd go for that, or something like that . . .'

'I don't quite understand . . .' said Jamieson. He could sense that Richardson was holding something back.

Richardson looked troubled and shook his head slightly as if to dismiss a thought as being of no importance. He said, 'Evans tells me that you were carrying out some tests of your own?'

'Routine biochemistry,' said Jamieson. 'I'm a great believer in accumulating as much information about a problem as possible and then stepping back to take a look at it all.'

Richardson nodded and asked, 'Are you running tests for carbon source utilisation?'

'Yes. Why do you ask?'

Richardson remained silent for a moment as though deep in thought again and then shrugged. He made a dismissive gesture with his right hand and said, 'I'd be interested to hear your results, that's all.'

Jamieson was intrigued by Richardson's preoccupied manner. He said, 'Doctor, I wish you would tell me exactly what's on your mind.'

'Not yet,' said Richardson. 'It's too soon. It may be nothing.'

The lab receptionist put her head round the door and said to Richardson. 'Mr Thelwell has sent down his nasal swab for analysis as requested.'

Richardson looked puzzled and Jamieson intervened to clear

up the mystery. 'I requested it,' he said. 'Mr Thelwell was using Naseptin at the time of his last screen.'

'Very well. Ask Dr Evans to deal with it,' said Richardson. 'And say I'd like to see the result in the morning. In fact, tell him to put the culture in my incubator.'

'Yes, Doctor.'

Jamieson returned to his room after picking up a copy of the local evening paper from a trolley doing ward rounds. He made himself some coffee and sat down to glance at the front page while he ran a bath. Another woman had been found murdered in the city. Her picture was on the front page, looking totally incongruous in a swimming costume and holding an ice cream cone on some foreign beach. Jamieson supposed that this was the best the woman's family had been able to come up with at the request of the paper.

Sheila Stubbs had been a respectable secretary with a firm of Chartered Surveyors. She had been working late, the paper reported. Police were refusing to speculate at this stage as to whether the murder was connected with the other deaths in the city. At the moment they were actively seeking a gang of youths who had been travelling on the same bus as the woman. Witnesses were urged to come forward. There was a rough map of the area where Sheila Stubbs' body had been found and an 'X' marked the spot.

Jamieson took his bath and then rang Sue. She asked how he was getting on.

'Slowly,' replied Jamieson.

'What does that mean?'

'It means that this damned bug seems to appear out of fresh air; it kills a patient and then disappears again.'

'So it's going to take longer than you thought to trace the source?' asked Sue.

'It's beginning to look that way,' agreed Jamieson.

'You sound very down,' said Sue sympathetically.

'I'm okay.'

'Will you make it home this weekend?'

97

'I'll be home,' said Jamieson.

'How are your hands?'

'They're fine. I've changed to light dressings and I'll be able to take them off in a couple of days.'

'Good. I wish I could cheer you up,' said Sue. 'If the job had been that easy they wouldn't have sent you up there in the first place. Maybe you underestimated it?'

'Maybe,' agreed Jamieson. Anyway, I'll see you tomorrow night.'

'I look forward to it,' said Sue gently.

'Me, too.'

Jamieson got into the microbiology lab in the morning to find people whispering in corners. He looked in on Clive Evans' lab to find Moira Lippman alone. 'What's going on?' he asked.

'I think you'd better hear it from Dr Richardson or Dr Evans,' she replied.

Jamieson shrugged his shoulders and asked, 'Where do I find them?'

'They're both in Dr Richardson's office.'

Jamieson retraced his steps through the lab and knocked on Richardson's door.

'Come in,' said Richardson, 'You've come at just the right moment.' Jamieson entered and closed the door behind him.

'In what way?'

Evans handed Jamieson a small, round, plastic dish and said, 'This is the culture from Thelwell's nasal swab.'

Jamieson looked at the spreading bacterial growth on the plate and removed the lid of the culture dish to smell it. It smelt of cut grass. 'Good God,' he said quietly. *'The Pseudomonas.'*

'A Pseudomonas,' insisted Richardson. 'The question now is, is it the one that has been causing all the trouble?'

'When will you know?'

'Moira is putting up the antibiotic tests now,' said Evans.

Jamieson was full of conflicting emotions. If Thelwell proved to be a carrier of the killer strain it would mean that, in all probability, he had been responsible for the recent surgery deaths at Kerr Memorial. How could the man live with himself after that? he wondered. On the positive side it would mean that at least the cause of the outbreak would have been identified and the problem would now be over. His job would be complete and he could report an end to the affair to Sci-Med.

Jamieson wondered how the staff would react to such news. Sympathy and understanding would not readily be forthcoming for such an objectionable character as Thelwell. At the moment, Evans appeared to be neutral, but Richardson was showing distinct signs of gloating. Jamieson could not honestly say that he blamed him after the way he had been treated by Thelwell.

Jamieson had an unpleasant thought. He asked, 'How is the patient he operated on yesterday?'

It was obvious from their faces that neither Richardson nor Evans had thought to enquire. 'I'll ring now,' said Richardson.

Evans and Jamieson sat patiently while Richardson listened to what was being said on the other end of the telephone. They had to wait again when Richardson put the phone down slowly and took a moment to gather his thoughts. 'She has a temperature this morning,' he said finally. 'And she's in some pain.'

Jamieson noted that any suggestion of gloating had disappeared from Richardson entirely. He had just been reminded of the awful human cost involved in the affair.

'Will you speak to Mr Thelwell?' Evans asked Richardson.

Richardson hesitated and Jamieson said, 'I think under the circumstances I had best do that,' said Jamieson.

'I would be grateful,' said Richardson. 'It would not come well from me.'

Jamieson returned to his tiny room to call Thelwell's secretary. There was an envelope lying on his desk; he opened it before dialling. It was the report from the Sci-Med lab on the *Pseudomonas*. Their analysis had failed to uncover the presence of any extraneous plasmid DNA. Jamieson frowned. He had been wrong. The bug had not been invaded by outside elements to make it resistant to antibiotics; it was a killer in its own right.

This was a surprise. At least it was a surprise to him.

Something told him that it would not come as such a surprise to John Richardson. The last time they had spoken Richardson had seemed to hint at this being a possibility. He had asked to be informed about routine carbon source tests. Why? he wondered. What did Richardson suspect?

'Mr Thelwell's secretary,' said the voice in the ear-piece.

'This is Dr Jamieson. I wonder if I might have a word with Mr Thelwell?'

'Is it important?'

'Very.'

Richardson was no longer in his office when Jamieson called in on his way out of the lab so he left the report he had just received from Sci-Med on the consultant's desk along with a little note saying, 'You were right. How did you know?'

Jamieson knew that it was going to be difficult to tell Thelwell the unpleasant truth. It seemed to grow more difficult with each step he took up the stairs until he found himself even hesitating to knock on the door outside the surgeon's office.

'Mr Thelwell can give you five minutes,' said the secretary when Jamieson finally entered. 'He has a busy schedule.'

Had, thought Jamieson. His life is not ever going to be quite the same again.

Thelwell frowned when he saw Jamieson. 'Yes?' he said with an exasperated sigh. 'What now?'

'I've come about your nasal swab test,' said Jamieson.

'What about it? I didn't use cream this time.'

'I know. The lab grew *Pseudomonas* from it.'

Thelwell looked as if he had been struck by a thunderbolt. His face clouded then his eyes flashed. 'No!' he rasped. 'I will not have it. This is something dreamed up by Richardson! I do not believe it! I just do not believe it!'

'I've seen the culture, Mr Thelwell. It's *Pseudomonas* all right.'

'It may be *Pseudomonas* but it did not come from me. It's not mine! Can't you see? That incompetent clown of a microbiologist has interfered with the cultures!'

'Mr Thelwell, you are being entirely unreasonable,' said Jamieson calmly.

'Unreasonable!' exploded Thelwell. 'Unreasonable, you call it! That man tries to wreck my career and blame all these deaths on me and you call me unreasonable! I knew it! What did I say the last time? I told you Richardson would dream up something to embarrass me. It's a wonder he didn't find bubonic plague in my swab!'

Jamieson found himself becoming angry. Thelwell appeared unable to see beyond some petty feud. His patients seemed to be the last thing on his mind. 'I understand Mrs Edelman is running a temperature and is in some pain this morning,' he said flatly.

'Mrs Edelman?' asked Thelwell absently.

'The patient you operated on yesterday,' said Jamieson harshly.

'What are you suggesting?' hissed Thelwell.

'I am suggesting that she may be infected with the *Pseudomonas*,' said Jamieson. 'I am further suggesting that the evidence currently points to you being the carrier of the infection in this hospital. I must ask you to refrain from operating until this has been thoroughly investigated.'

'Refrain from . . .' repeated Thelwell as though stunned. 'This is ludicrous!'

'It's common sense,' said Jamieson. 'The lab doesn't have the antibiogram results yet and it may be that you are carrying a quite ordinary strain, but until we know for sure I am going to ask the authorities to suspend you if you will not do it voluntarily.'

'Get out!' spat Thelwell. 'Just get out!'

7

Jamieson kept his eyes glued to his swing mirror as he accelerated out of the feeder lane to join the main carriageway south. It felt good to be going home but ever since the accident he felt uneasy about driving on motorways. He slipped into the inside lane and settled there for a bit until he got a feel for how much traffic there was. In past times he would have put his foot to the floor and moved over into the fast lane as quickly as possible. Those days were gone.

After three or four miles he moved out into a gap and accelerated to sixty-five. He did this partly because he had a long way to go, but mainly because it was part of a self-imposed therapy. The accident had actually left him physically afraid of travelling in the outside lane. When he did so he was constantly beset by the image of a vehicle coming towards him and swerving into his path.

As an intelligent and rational person he knew that the likelihood of this happening to him again must be extremely remote. This helped him cope with the fear, but it did not obliterate it. It was still there. It made his mouth dry and forced up his pulse rate whenever he moved out to the right, but it was not so great that he could not live with it, however unpleasant. The more he forced himself to do this, he reckoned, the sooner he would be free of it.

The traffic ahead slowed as it was channelled into a contra-flow system and his speed dropped to a crawl as they all moved forward at the speed of the slowest vehicle ahead. In this instance it was a mobile crane. The break in concentration gave Jamieson a chance to think about other things. He thought back to how Thelwell had behaved when he had told him about the swab result. It alarmed him that a man of such quick temper and volatility could be a surgeon.

After further consideration, Jamieson found himself changing his mind. When he thought about it, a great many of the surgeons he knew, or had known, were volatile characters. Most could be described as extrovert and a few had monstrous egos. But Thelwell was also extremely unpleasant. He wondered how he would behave if and when the lab found that he was carrying the killer strain.

There was, of course, a chance that the *Pseudomonas* strain found on Thelwell's swab might turn out not to be the problem bug, but Jamieson felt that this would be stretching coincidence too far. He would prepare himself for the worst.

As the traffic entered its second mile of walking-pace progress, Jamieson started to consider Thelwell's angry allegations that his swab had been tampered with. Until that moment he had not given the slightest credence to the notion that Richardson could have 'fixed' the swab test. That was surely beyond the bounds of possibility . . . wasn't it? But maybe nothing was beyond the bounds of possibility at Kerr Memorial. In the space of one week he had come to dislike the place intensely.

It was nothing unusual for clashes of personality to occur in medical circles, but they were usually confined to academic jousting, comprising occasional caustic remarks and continual sly innuendo. This rarely developed into open feuding and outright hostility. Things at Kerr Memorial were getting out of hand – or was that an understatement? he wondered. Had they already got completely out of hand? And if that were true, what should he do about it?

There seemed to be no straightforward solution to the problem as far as Jamieson could see. Strictly speaking, Thelwell's bad behaviour did not constitute an offence requiring disciplinary action, certainly nothing that would warrant suspension from duty. He tried to formulate such a charge in his own mind but failed. Thelwell was like an angry driver at the wheel. Nothing had happened yet but the potential for disaster was there, however competent he might be.

If Thelwell was shown to be the carrier of the lethal strain then suspension from duty would be automatic and, with luck, he might return to medicine as a humbler person after a suitable course of treatment to clear up his carrier state. Jamieson suddenly thought that this was always assuming that it could be cleared up. If not, then the bug was so dangerous to surgical patients that Thelwell's days as a surgeon might well be over.

The balance between bacterial infection and disease was a precarious one. Most people carried within them a range of bacteria which had the potential to cause disease, but the body's natural defences were sufficient to cope. If for any reason, however, a person should become debilitated through illness or damage to their immune system the balance would be lost and infection would almost certainly follow. Surgical patients were particularly vulnerable. As soon as the first incision was made the body's first and main line of defence had gone. Sterile gloves and face masks helped protect the patient but if a real killer organism was present in the theatre, they would be little more use than token gestures.

Jamieson sought diversion from that unpleasant thought from the car radio and switched to Classic FM. Vivaldi filled the car and accompanied his acceleration now that the bottle-neck had cleared. As the traffic sorted itself out, an articulated lorry suddenly pulled out in front of him from the inside lane and caused him to brake sharply. He immediately checked his rear view mirror to make sure the car behind him had reacted as well. It had. He could see its driver shaking his head.

As he passed the lorry, Jamieson glanced up at the cab to see the driver lighting a cigarette; he seemed quite oblivious of the near incident he had caused. Jamieson sighed. If only there was some way he could convey to people who had never experienced it just what happens when human flesh gets in the way of colliding metal!

As he thought about it, his subconscious fed the vision of the spreadeagled body of the vanboy into his conscious mind. He began to sweat on his forehead despite the fact that he actually felt a bit cold. He then started to feel light-headed. He pulled over into the inside lane at the first opportunity and brought his speed down to forty as he kept pace with the caravan being towed in front. He concentrated hard on the back of it, examining details in an attempt to block out any more subconscious feedback. An outside observer might have dismissed the incident with the lorry as something that happened a hundred times every day on the country's motorways, but Jamieson was not yet able to be so objective.

As always, he left the motorway on the near side of Canterbury, so that he could enjoy the view of the city as he approached from the west. It was bathed in evening sunshine and the cathedral spire caught the full yellow glow as if it were its heavenly right. He kept glancing up at it as he followed the ring road round to the east to pick up the Dover Road and, shortly after that, the spur leading off to Patrixbourne. As he entered the village he could hear the birds sing. He was back in the peaceful timelessness that he and Sue had come to love so much. Whatever else happened in the world, Patrixbourne would stay the same; it would go on unchanged as it had done since the time of the Romans.

He brought the car off the road and drove up the narrow, gravel drive to the parking space at the rear of the cottage and switched off the engine. At first there was silence in the fading twilight, but as he listened hard he did begin to pick out sounds. Somewhere in the distance a church bell was being rung and somewhere much nearer the intermittent clack of contact between ball and bat told him the local cricket team were practising. It wouldn't be long before the fading light stopped them and they would be off to the pub.

Sue put her arms round Jamieson's neck in the doorway and they kissed.

'Come in before the neighbours start talking,' said Sue.

'Let them.'

'You sound more cheerful,' said Sue. Jamieson agreed and said, 'I think we've found the source of the infection. The consultant surgeon in gynaecology appears to be a carrier.'

'Poor man,' said Sue, 'How is he taking it?'

'Not well,' replied Jamieson.

'What a position to be in,' said Sue.

Jamieson did not argue. He said, 'It's not absolutely certain yet, but the lab will know by tomorrow morning. I'll ring when I get up.'

'I suppose this means that your first job for Sci-Med is now over,' said Sue.

'I suppose it does,' agreed Jamieson. 'Although, to be honest, I didn't do much. I merely suggested that the surgeon concerned send in a routine nasal swab. He had done it before, of course, but he had been using antiseptic cream at the time so the lab test was negative.'

'And you spotted that?' said Sue.

'Well, yes.'

'Then you solved the problem. Sci-Med should be delighted.'

'Maybe they won't sack me just yet,' smiled Jamieson.

'You're too modest,' insisted Sue. 'We must have a small celebration.' She held up a bottle of wine that she took from the fridge in the kitchen. 'What do you say?'

'Why not,' agreed Jamieson.

After dinner Jamieson took off his shoes and lay along the couch, pleased at the feeling of contentment inside him.

'What's Kerr Memorial like?' asked Sue.

'A gloomy place, old buildings, full of people doing their best against the odds. The usual.'

'If the phone call in the morning confirms that the surgeon was to blame, will you have to go back up there?' asked Sue

'Briefly, to tidy things up.'

'Then what?'

'Whatever Sci-Med has in store.'

Sue moved to the couch. She lifted Jamieson's head momentarily to sit down and then replaced it in her lap. 'Did you miss me?' she asked.

'More than I can say.'

'Early night?'

'Early night.'

Jamieson rose first in the morning to make the breakfast. It was a beautiful day and he took the opportunity to stand out in the garden while he waited for the kettle to boil. There was hardly a breath of wind and dew drops hung on spiders' webs in the bushes. A village cat which had been stalking birds scurried away as Jamieson neared the spot, idly kicking a crab apple that had fallen from its tree. He was up at the top of the garden when he heard the telephone ring.

It was John Richardson. He said, 'I thought I'd ring so that I wouldn't have to wait around for you to call me.'

'Good thinking.'

'I'm afraid the strain from Thelwell is the killer strain. It has the same immunity pattern to antibiotics.'

'So that's that,' said Jamieson conclusively.

'Ostensibly,' said Richardson, his voice pregnant with hesitation.

'I don't understand,' said Jamieson. 'You have found the source of the infection. Thelwell was carrying the bug. It all fits. What more conclusive evidence could you hope for?'

'I know that's how it seems,' agreed Richardson, 'but I want to talk to you before we say any more.'

'What about?'

'I'd rather not say on the telephone. Perhaps you could come in to the lab on your return?'

'That won't be until tomorrow evening, unless of course there's some good reason for coming back sooner?'

'Tomorrow evening will be fine. I'll stay behind in the lab until you get here. Any idea what time that will be?'

'About eight.'

'Fine.'

'Who was that?' called Sue from the bedroom.

'John Richardson, the consultant bacteriologist at Kerr Memorial.' said Jamieson thoughtfully. 'The surgeon was carrying the killer strain.'

'So it's all over?'

'I think so,' said Jamieson distantly. 'But Richardson wants to talk to me before he makes the final report.'

Sue dressed and came downstairs. She sensed that Jamieson was troubled about something and asked what it was.

'Richardson,' said Jamieson.

'What about him?'

Jamieson paused while he inserted bread into the toaster then he said, 'It was as if he really didn't believe what he was telling me.'

'You mean he thinks he's made a mistake?' asked Sue.

Jamieson smiled wryly. 'That's what Thelwell would maintain. He thinks that Richardson in some way engineered the whole thing.'

'Good Lord, what a place,' said Sue. 'And what do you believe?' she asked.

'I saw the culture. It was *Pseudomonas*,' said Jamieson. 'He didn't make that up.'

'Then I can't see the problem,' said Sue.

'Neither can I,' confessed Jamieson. 'That's what's bothering me. But if there is one I'll find out tomorrow night.'

The traffic was light on Sunday evening and this, combined with the fact that he had had such an enjoyable weekend, ensured that Jamieson did not lose his temper once on the journey north. He was still in a good mood when he got into his room and unpacked his bag. He would have a coffee before going down to see Richardson, then he would write up his report for Sci-Med. If there was time after that and Richardson had introduced no new problems he would go out for a couple of drinks at a nearby hotel and then have an early night.

As he rounded the corner to cross the courtyard in the direction of the steps leading down to the lab, he saw a figure hurrying along the far side. Jamieson recognised the walk. It was Gordon Thelwell. He wondered what the surgeon was doing in the hospital at this time of night.

Jamieson took extra care on the stone steps to the lab for the light was failing and the nearest wall lamp was faulty. He pushed open the door and fumbled for the light switch before finding it at the third attempt and clicking it on.

He could see a light coming from under John Richardson's door, but when he knocked there was no reply. He tried again and then entered to find the room empty. The desk lamp was on and some papers were lying there. The swivel chair behind the desk had been swung to the right, as if Richardson had just got up from it. Thinking that Richardson had just stepped out for a moment, Jamieson sat down to wait. The minutes passed and Jamieson had to abandon his theory. He left the room to go in search of Richardson.

A quick search of the ground floor failed to reveal any sign of the consultant. Calling out his name did not help either. Jamieson started down the stairs to the basement. He stopped on the third step when he thought he heard something. It sounded like a creaking tree. 'Is anyone there?' he asked. The steady timbre of his voice broke the silence which was breeding a distinct unease in him. There was no reply. Just the creaking sound again. 'Dr Richardson?'

Jamieson reached the bottom of the stairs and was feeling for the next light switch when something hard brushed against his face. He breathed in sharply and stepped backwards, throwing up his hands to push away whatever it was. When he touched it he knew exactly what it was. It was a foot, a human foot wearing a shoe, but it was at face level!

Jamieson's pulse rate soared and he broke out in a sweat as he continued his frantic, flat-handed search for the light switch like a mime artist faced with an imaginary wall. At last he found it and lit up a nightmare. John Richardson was hanging from one of the wooden support beams in the ceiling. A leather strap had bitten deep into his fleshy neck. His eyes bulged out of their sockets and his tongue, blue and distended, lolled out of his mouth at one corner. The creaking sound was being made by his body revolving slowly in response to the positive air flow through the lab.

Jamieson stared at the spectre for some seconds, unable to do anything. He was mesmerised by the sheer horror of Richardson's appearance, his cyanosed complexion and bulbous eyes. Incongruously, the watch on his wrist was still going. In the silence Jamieson could hear its tick and saw the second hand continue its sweep round the face as the dial passed in front of him. He thought about cutting Richardson down but that would be easier said than done. Apart from the physical difficulties involved in doing this, there was no point. The man was very clearly dead; there was no possibility of resuscitation. The police would probably prefer that everything was left exactly as it was.

Jamieson called them from the nearest telephone. When he had done that he asked the operator on duty in the hospital front office to call out both the medical superintendent and the hospital secretary. He did not say why, just that it was very important and that they should come right away. Jamieson replaced the phone and the lab was returned to silence. At times like this he wished that he still smoked. He had given up some five years before, but right now it would have been a real comfort to light up a cigarette.

Jamieson stood in the background while the police photographer took pictures of Richardson from every angle before the corpse was cut down and laid out on the floor. The inspector in charge left the forensic people to their task and came over to Jamieson. 'I understand you found the body,' he said. 'I'm Ryan. Is there some place where we can talk?'

Jamieson nodded and led the way to Richardson's office. He thought that Carew and Crichton would both call in there first when they arrived. When they did he could tell them what had happened.

Jamieson gave Ryan details of how and when he had discovered Richardson's body. He said who and what he was and what he was doing at Kerr Memorial.

'You and me both,' replied the inspector when Jamieson said that he had been investigating the cause of an outbreak which had resulted in the deaths of three women patients at the hospital.

'I beg your pardon?'

'I'm investigating the deaths of a couple of women myself,' said the policeman.

'Oh, the murders? I read in the paper that you were looking for a gang in connection with the latest killing,' said Jamieson.

'They were involved,' said the policeman. 'But they didn't do the actual killing. Our nutter did that.'

'Nutter?'

'A ripper-type,' said Ryan. 'Forensic told us. The woman was badly beaten and mutilated but bits of her were missing just like the first. The ripper copy-cat scenario.'

'God, it sounds awful,' said Jamieson. 'Do you have anything to go on?'

Ryan shook his head and said, 'This is always the worst kind of killer to find. Most murders are domestic, plenty of leads and ready-made suspects. When it's a nutter, it's different. It's odds on he's a loner with no friends or family and no personal connection with the victims. He could have some kind of general obsession, or there may be no motive at all other than the fact that the victims were in the wrong place at the wrong time.'

'I see,' said Jamieson. 'If it's any comfort I thought I had found my killer or rather, he had.' Jamieson gestured with his head to where Richardson had been found. 'Now I'm not at all sure what's going on.'

Carew and Crichton arrived almost together and were shocked at the news. Jamieson noted that both of them immediately assumed that Richardson had committed suicide. 'Why?' asked Jamieson, preempting Ryan's question.

'John has been under a great deal of pressure over this infection problem,' said Carew. 'Much more than he ever showed. It's pretty clear that it just got all too much for him.'

'But a lot of that pressure was relieved yesterday,' said

Jamieson. 'Dr Richardson called me at home. He had proof that Mr Thelwell had been carrying the bug that was causing the infection.'

Carew and Crichton exchanged glances.

'Mr Thelwell did not believe him,' said Carew.

'Worse than that,' said Crichton. 'He insisted that Dr Richardson had deliberately fabricated the result. He insisted that the opinion of another lab be sought.'

'And?'

'The Public Health Service carried out a second swab test on Mr Thelwell on Saturday. He got the result this morning. It was negative. They found no trace of *Pseudomonas* at all.'

'I see,' said Jamieson slowly, still reluctant to believe that Richardson had really falsified the lab test. 'That in itself isn't conclusive,' he said. He mentioned Thelwell's use of antiseptic creams in earlier tests. 'He said it was a habit of his to use it.'

'That's possible, I suppose,' agreed Carew. 'But when I told Dr Richardson this morning about the PHS result he reacted very oddly to say the least.'

'How so?'

'It was almost as if he expected it.'

'I don't understand,' said Jamieson.

'When I told him he turned ashen and had to sit down. Then he said, "It's all my fault."'

'"All my fault"? You mean he confessed to faking the swab test?' asked an astonished Jamieson.

'Not exactly,' replied Carew. 'He seemed somehow to be talking to himself when he said it. When I asked him what he meant he said that he now knew what had been going on and that it would all be over soon.'

'What did he mean?'

'I don't know and he wouldn't say any more. But now it seems quite obvious what he meant, wouldn't you say? He seemed quite ill, poor man.'

'I'm afraid,' said Crichton, 'that all the evidence points to Dr Richardson being responsible for deliberately engineering a positive swab test on Mr Thelwell. I think the pressure of continuing failure to find the cause of the outbreak must have pushed him too far and he saw a way of relieving it. By contaminating Mr Thelwell's swab with the killer strain of *Pseudomonas* he would at once appear to have identified both the cause and the carrier.'

Jamieson noticed that Ryan had a bemused look on his face and caught his eye. 'Is this for real?' whispered Ryan during a lull, while Crichton and Carew carried on a conversation of their own.

'I'm afraid so,' replied Jamieson

'What's happened?' said a voice at the door.

Jamieson turned to see Clive Evans standing there.

'There's been an accident,' replied Carew.

'Dr Richardson is dead. He hanged himself,' said Crichton.

Evans sank down into a chair and shook his head slowly. 'I don't believe it,' he murmured.

'May I ask what brought you here this evening, Doctor?' asked Ryan.

'I'm on call,' said Evans distantly. 'I'm the duty bacteriologist. John was on this afternoon.'

Later on, Ryan and Jamieson sought out Evans and found him working in his own lab. Jamieson had remembered that Evans had been in Richardson's office when Thelwell's swab had arrived. He also remembered that Richardson had delegated the test to Evans. Now he asked him about it.

The Welshman adjusted his spectacles and said, 'That's right, I inoculated the swab into two cultures.'

'Then what?'

'I don't understand,' said Evans.

'What did you do with the cultures? Did you keep them in your lab? Did you put them somewhere else? Did you read the results in the morning? Were you the one who found and identified the *Pseudomonas* in them?'

'No,' replied Evans, looking confused at the line of questioning. 'Dr Richardson said that he wanted to read the tests personally so I put the cultures in the incubator in his lab. He read the results. He found the *Pseudomonas* and made out the report.'

'Do you think it possible that Dr Richardson could have interfered with the cultures you put in the incubator?' asked Jamieson.

'What kind of a question is that?' exclaimed Evans.

'One I have to ask,' replied Jamieson.

'Anything is possible.'

'Could you tell by looking at the culture dishes whether they had been changed or not?' asked Jamieson.

'I suppose so,' said Evans hesitantly. 'I wrote something on the dishes in marker pen.'

'Would you check, please?' said Ryan.

Evans left the room briefly and returned with two plastic dishes. He said, 'These are the cultures from Mr Thelwell's swab.'

'Do they have your markings on them?'

Evans examined both sides of the dishes and said with some obvious reluctance, 'No, they don't.'

'So Dr Richardson could have substituted different cultures for the ones you inoculated?'

'I suppose so,' agreed Evans with a pained expression. 'What the hell is going on?'

'There is a suggestion that Dr Richardson took his own life after faking a culture result in order to implicate Mr Thelwell as being the cause of the recent infection problem in the hospital,' said Jamieson.

'Good God,' said Evans slowly. 'He has been under a lot of strain recently. We all have.'

'You liked Richardson?' asked Ryan.

'Yes,' said Evans.

'But you do think now that he switched the cultures?'

'That's what it seems like.'

'Do you think that he hated Thelwell that much?'

'He certainly didn't like Mr Thelwell, but I don't think it was hatred that motivated him if, in fact, he did what's been suggested. Mr Thelwell blamed Dr Richardson for the lab's failure to identify the source of infection in the hospital. Dr Richardson felt the fault must lie with the surgical team. Maybe he felt pressured into coming up with some "evidence". He was certainly under a great deal of stress.'

'Suicidal stress?'

'Who's to say.'

Jamieson nodded his agreement but he was remembering the furtive figure of Gordon Thelwell hurrying away from the vicinity of the lab just before he arrived. He considered telling Ryan about it but decided not to for the moment.

Jamieson lay on his bed and tried to think calmly and rationally. It was difficult; his mind was cluttered with doubts and suspicions. What had Thelwell been doing near the lab if he had not been to see Richardson? If Richardson really had faked the test results in order to take the pressure off himself and his department, why on earth had he behaved the way he had on the telephone when he himself had seemed to inject doubts about the result? Surely it would have been in his own interest to have made the report seem as conclusive as possible? Instead, it was Richardson who had wanted to delay the final report and talk to him first. What about? Jamieson wondered.

He got up and went over to the the window to look down at the courtyard below. Perhaps it was the darkness or the gloomy buildings that encouraged the thought, but he remembered the parallel that Ryan had drawn between their respective jobs. They were both seeking killers. Ryan was looking for a crazed psychopath while he sought an unfeeling, mindless bacterial killer. His quarry was invisible to the naked eye, a small rod-shaped organism, only three thousandths of a millimetre long, but both were killing women in the city.

Jamieson took out a notebook from his brief case and started to jot down what he already knew. The infection at Kerr Memorial had been caused by a particularly virulent strain of *Pseudomonas* which was impossible to treat. The organism had been isolated from the nasopharynx of the surgeon in charge of the affected unit. That should have been the end of the story, but at Kerr Memorial it seemed more like the beginning.

The bacteriologist who had identified the cause of the outbreak was now dead and the evidence suggested that he had taken his own life after faking the lab result which implicated the surgeon. Where did that leave things? Jamieson was reluctantly left to conclude that he would not now be going home. He was back at square one.

Perhaps it was even worse than that. Things had become even more complicated than when he had started the investigation. The infecting organism itself was becoming a bit of a puzzle, for although it was an everyday sort of germ this particular strain seemed to be unique in terms of its virulence and resistance to treatment. The Sci-Med labs had failed to come up with any explanation for the virulence of the organism, but for some reason the deceased Richardson had been less surprised about that than anyone else. Just what was it that Richardson had realised? And could that knowledge in some way be connected with his death? Jamieson pursed his lips in frustration as he failed to come up with an answer.

Jamieson decided he had better turn his attention to more immediate matters. His first job would be to see Thelwell in the morning and inform him that the ban on his operating was still in force despite his negative result from the Public Health lab. While there was still some doubt over the tests, he would have to insist on three negatives in a row, taken on separate days and under supervision.

'This is ridiculous!' exploded Thelwell. 'The Public Health Service has completely exonerated me. It's quite obvious that Richardson fabricated the result in order to cover up his own incompetence. At least it's obvious to anyone with an IQ greater than that of an earthworm!'

Jamieson ignored the comment. He had come prepared for Thelwell at his worst and had not been disappointed. He was determined to keep his temper. 'Your single negative from PHS is insufficient to clear you and you know it. Several more tests will have to be made and under properly controlled conditions before you can be pronounced free from contamination.'

'Free from contamination!' stormed Thelwell. 'I never was contaminated in the first place! It was that moron Richardson who made everything up!'

'That has yet to be established beyond doubt,' said Jamieson calmly.

Thelwell became almost speechless with anger and frustration. 'The man committed suicide, didn't he? As soon as he was faced with the PHS report he strung himself from the rafters! What more do you want?'

'Two more negative tests from the PHS,' replied Jamieson.

'And meanwhile my lists keep getting longer and longer,' said Thelwell, shaking his head in exasperation.

'Better your lists than the obituary columns.'

'I want it placed on record that I object most strongly to your attitude and interference in my department,' hissed Thelwell through gritted teeth.

'I would have thought that the safety of your patients would have been at least as important to you as it is to me,' said Jamieson.

'What's that supposed to mean?' snapped Thelwell.

Exasperation got the better of Jamieson and he could not refrain from commenting, 'Your enthusiasm for the operating table in the circumstances suggests a certain disregard for the consequences. The source of the outbreak in your department has still not been established. Don't you care about these women?'

The expected outburst did not occur. Instead, Jamieson was treated to the spectacle of Thelwell having some kind of fit. At least that was what it seemed like, for he went quite white and his hands started to tremble violently. It was some time before he could speak. Jamieson waited patiently for the onslaught to begin.

'What right have you to say such a thing?' rasped Thelwell hoarsely.

Jamieson was taken aback by Thelwell's reaction to what

he had said for, even by Thelwell's standards, the result had been dramatic. He had the distinct feeling that Thelwell's exaggerated reaction to any kind of criticism might indicate some underlying clinical disorder. He said, 'Mr Thelwell, this kind of conversation is getting us nowhere. I suggest we talk again after your series of tests and after the police investigation into Dr Richardson's death.'

'What investigation? The man committed suicide.'

'That's for the police to decide when they have gathered all the facts.'

'What facts? What are you suggesting?'

'I'm not suggesting anything, but they will probably want to know why you were seen near the bacteriology lab at eight o'clock last night.'

Thelwell turned so pale that Jamieson thought he must faint. He clutched the edge of the table. 'By whom?' he whispered.

'By me,' replied Jamieson.

'I see – have you told them?'

'Not yet, but I'm going to. I wanted to hear what you had to say first.'

Thelwell hung his head and there was silence in the room for what seemed like an eternity before he spoke again. 'I don't suppose you will believe this, but I just went there to have it out with him about the test. I didn't intend to, but when I was passing the hospital on my way to choir practice, I saw his light on and I called in on him.'

'And?'

'He was dead when I went in, hanging from the beam like a carcase in a butcher's shop.'

'Why didn't you call the police?' asked Jamieson quietly.

'Because of what people would think. Because of what you are thinking now.'

'What I think is not important. It's the police you will have to convince.'

Gordon Thomas Thelwell was questioned by the police for over two hours that same afternoon. He was allowed to go home

shortly after five and Jamieson, who had been waiting for the
outcome at the lab, took a call from Ryan. 'We've let him go,'
said Ryan.

'What convinced you?' asked Jamieson.

'The PM report suggests that it could have been suicide.
There were no other signs of injury and the man had been
under severe stress. It would have been better if he had left
a note, but there we have it. If we don't have a murder, we
can't have a killer.'

'What did you think of Thelwell?' asked Jamieson.

'A weirdo,' replied Ryan. 'If you ask me, Richardson wasn't
the only one suffering from stress in that hospital of yours.
Is there anything else I should know that you haven't told
me?'

'No, nothing.'

Jamieson had a short meeting with Carew to discuss the
re-scheduling of the surgery lists in gynaecology and the
continuing microbiological investigation into the cause of the
outbreak.

'Doctor Evans will be in charge of bacteriology until a locum
consultant is appointed. Phillip Morton will continue to operate
in gynaecology, but only on emergency cases.'

'I've requested that a small team from the Public Health
Department be called in to help with the investigation,' said
Jamieson.

'What exactly will they be doing?' asked Carew.

'Just what Richardson's people have been doing all along,'
replied Jamieson. 'Taking swabs from all the likely places in the
theatres and wards and hoping to get lucky. The more people
we have doing it the better our chances.'

'Do you want to do any more tests on the *Pseudomonas*?' asked
Moira Lippman when Jamieson came into the lab the following
morning.

Jamieson, who had temporarily forgotten about the biochemistry of the organism, thought for a moment and then

decided that he might as well continue the tests. It would give him something to do while he waited to see if the surgical infection problem would re-occur. He said that he would make a start immediately. Moira Lippman smiled and helped him to gown up.

Jamieson found the lab work therapeutic, a brief respite from wrestling with the greater problems of the hospital. He was not so familiar with the protocols involved in setting up the tests that he could perform them without thinking – he had to concentrate on what he was doing and refer to lab manuals where necessary. While he was doing that he could not think about anything else.

In the late afternoon he was interrupted by a call from Thelwell. Jamieson's heart sank when he heard his voice, but the surgeon had calmed down considerably since their last meeting. 'What can I do for you, Mr Thelwell?' he asked.

'I have just had my second negative swab result from the Public Health Service lab,' said Thelwell.

'I'm delighted to hear it,' said Jamieson.

'I would now like to return to my lists,' said Thelwell.

'Three negatives are needed, Mr Thelwell,' said Jamieson, feeling as if he had just lit a fuse.

'This is bureaucratic nonsense and you know it!' declared Thelwell.

'We've already been through this. Three please, Mr Thelwell,' said Jamieson.

Thelwell slammed the phone down.

'And to you too, Mr Thelwell,' said Jamieson under his breath as he replaced the receiver.

8

It was later than he had intended when the man reached the basement flat. He had a lot to do. He salvaged some comfort from the thought that at least he would be indoors and out of the rain. It had been raining heavily for the past six hours and the streets were flooding as storm drains gradually became overloaded. He put down his umbrella and shook the worst of the rain from it before opening and closing it quickly several times to clear away some more. It made the sound of a flight of crows flapping their wings in the darkness.

Before he took off his coat he knelt down in front of an old gas fire and succeeded in lighting it with the third match. The blue flames were interspersed with fans of yellow where the radiants had cracked over the years and the hearth was littered with spent matches. After warming his hands for a moment he hung up his coat on the back of the door and donned his apron, mask and gloves. He switched on the lamp above his work bench. It was a bit early for the next phase of the project but not impossible, he decided. Thinking ahead was the key to success. He brought out a series of small glass vials from the fridge and made a start.

As the hours passed and everything went according to plan he started to relax a little. He was under pressure, thanks to the interference of others, but that just added to the excitement. The greater the danger, the greater the thrill. What idiots people were. But he mustn't become complacent, he cautioned himself. If the second phase was going well then

121

he should be thinking ahead to the third and even the fourth. And then there was the problem of the meddler from outside. A permanent solution might have to be found for him soon, but there was no immediate need for action. He mustn't rush at things. He would give the matter some thought. He got up from the bench and started to put everything away again.

He had taken off his protective clothing and rolled up his sleeves before washing his hands and forearms thoroughly when a knock at the door interrupted him. He froze at the sound and remained absolutely silent as his heartbeat quickened. A beaker of water which was still simmering above the blue flame of a bunsen burner on his work bench sounded uncommonly loud. He hadn't made any mistakes up until now, he told himself. There was no need to panic. It couldn't possibly be the police. There had to be some perfectly innocent explanation.

Perhaps, if he remained quiet and didn't answer the door, whoever it was would go away. He stared at the boiling water and wondered if it could be heard outside the door as the glass beaker jumped again on its gauze support and the water bubbled inside it. Thirty seconds passed before the knock came again and the man swallowed. His mouth had gone dry with nerves but there was still no need to panic. He would answer the door. There had to be a perfectly simple explanation for who was there and why.

He removed the plug from the hand basin and closed the bathroom door behind him as he came out. He took a quick look round the room to ensure that nothing incriminating was in evidence. A box of surgical gloves was still sitting on the table. He moved them out of sight and walked slowly towards the door. He stopped half way and returned to the simmering beaker of water. He removed a jar of instant coffee from a cupboard above the sink and stood it beside the beaker to create a motive for the boiling water. He opened the door to find a woman standing there.

'I'm so sorry to bother you at this late hour but I saw your light on and it's the only one in the street,' she said.

'Yes?' answered the man noncommittally.

'My car has let me down and the phone box on the corner has been vandalised. I wonder if I might possibly use your phone?'

The man stared at her silently for a moment, looking for signs of deceit. Had this bitch been sent for a reason? Was she here to trap him? She had all the signs. Red lips, white teeth, large breasts. Her eyes were blue and they were smiling at him, taunting him, daring him to smile back. He resisted, knowing that any sign of weakness on his part would only escalate her efforts to ensnare him. He could smell her scent. He stiffened as he noticed the swelling on her stomach. She was flaunting her past, but he was ready. 'Of course,' he said. 'Come in.'

The woman entered and the man closed the door behind her, shutting out the sound of the rain.

'Where . . .?' began the woman.

The man pointed to the table where the telephone sat and the woman smiled and brushed lightly past him. He stiffened as her arm made contact with him on the way past. God, she was good this one, much more subtle than the whores, but just as evil. He felt the hardness begin and swallowed as she picked up the receiver. Her back was to him. He could see the line of her underwear through the material of her skirt where it stretched across her buttocks. She moved her weight to the other foot and turned to smile at him while she waited for the number to connect. The smile faltered a little when he did not return it and she turned to face the wall again.

The bitch was beginning to suspect that he was on to her little game and that pleased him. He wanted her to know. He wanted her to be afraid. He walked over to where the beaker of water was simmering.

'Darling? It's me. The bloody car's packed in and I . . .'

The woman's voice changed to a scream as a cascade of boiling water hit the back of her neck. She dropped the phone and slumped to her knees with her hands behind her head, trying to bury her face between her thighs in a futile attempt to escape the agony. She sucked in air in great gulps but found it impossible to scream again. Shock

123

had paralysed her larynx. Too late she tried to cover her face as another container was emptied over her. This time it was cold but within seconds it had turned to fire and acid fumes filled her nostrils. Her eyes became burning embers, as hitherto undreamed-of levels of pain became reality. Her previously unblemished skin started to peel and smoulder. Her lips swelled to twice their normal size and her blistered tongue grew too large for her mouth. She whimpered like a wounded animal as she crawled around the floor looking blindly for a way out of the nightmare.

The man replaced the dangling receiver with its distantly calling voice and smiled thinly for the first time. 'Now I can see what you really look like,' he hissed. 'Now that the powder and the paint have gone I can see the real you. You're ugly! Evil!' He went to the bathroom and came back wearing his apron and carrying his instruments.

The floor was awash with blood and the man now had a corpse to dispose of before morning. Easier said than done. If he could reduce the cadaver to packages of manageable size his options would be wider. The immediate problem lay in the fact that he did not have a saw in the flat. He had knives that would deal with flesh and sinew but not with bones. He could not risk leaving the apartment to go fetch one; he would have to break the bones instead.

The first leg was the worst. He did not know how much pressure to apply and consequently needed three or four attempts before making the break. He changed his technique and pressed a block of wood into service as a fulcrum, placing each limb in turn on the bridge so that a sharp blow from the heel of his right foot made a clean snap.

Sweat was running off him by the time he had the body cut and packed into six plastic sacks. The next question was what to do with them. Burial in some remote place was the obvious solution, but just as he had no call to keep a saw in the basement, likewise he had no reason to have a spade. He had no way of digging a hole even if he could think of a good lonely spot. He considered the alternatives of a river or a canal perhaps, but both had their drawbacks.

Contracting noises were coming from the gas fire which he had switched off. He looked at the scorch marks on the old radiants and thought, Fire! That would be the best solution, not a domestic fireplace but a furnace or, better still, an incinerator.

Lots of places had incinerators, but only two kinds of establishment had incinerators where the discovery of human bones would not cause an immediate outcry. Crematoria and, much more conveniently, hospitals!

First he would have to get his car. He did not normally bring his car to the flat, preferring the anonymity that public transport afforded him. Cars had numbers. A sudden icicle of fear climbed the man's spine. The woman had had a car! That was why she had come to the door in the first place! The police would be looking for her car! Her husband would have contacted them after her phone call had been cut off. How could he have been so stupid as to overlook the car? The woman's words came back to him, 'the only light in the street'.

The man almost sprinted over to the door and switched the light off. He stood in the darkness, his breathing made uneven with threatening panic. Think! he commanded himself. Don't panic. Think! The police did not routinely patrol the street outside. There was an excellent chance that neither they nor anyone else would have had occasion to come into the street and find the abandoned car, but he would have to move it. It was too close for comfort. His next thought was that he couldn't. It had broken down!

Once again the man fought to get a grip on himself as he felt circumstances close in on him. There was a chance that the problem with the car was associated with all the rain they had had in the last few hours. Water in the electrics perhaps? There was only one way to find out. He rummaged through the woman's handbag and found the car keys, noting the Volkswagen emblem on the fob. He put on his coat and then slipped on a fresh pair of surgical gloves. He didn't want to leave any prints on the vehicle. He opened the door slightly. All was quiet outside. The rain had stopped, but gurgling sounds coming from the down pipes on the side of the building said that it had done so only recently.

The car was parked at the far end of the street. It was a dark blue Volkswagen Polo. This pleased him. There had to be thousands like it in the city. He opened the driver's door and undid the bonnet catch. The dirt of the engine told him that it had been some considerable time since anyone else had done so. It was a typical 'second car' that didn't get too much in the way of maintenance, the 'run around' for shopping and taking the kids to school. It had no status value other than to exist, unlike the husband's Cavalier or Sierra, which would shine like the sun and merit instant attention at the slightest cough.

The man removed the distributor cap and cleaned the inside with his handkerchief. He prised the contacts apart and slid a corner of the handkerchief between them to dry them out. He replaced the cap and wiped the plug leads and the main lead from the ignition coil. Satisfied with what he had done, he dropped the bonnet back down and tried the starter. The engine whirred into life and settled down to a stuttering idle.

Things were going well again. His confidence was returning. Perhaps he could now kill two birds with one stone? The car was generally dirty. It was quite difficult to read the registration plates as it was. With a bit more dirt applied to the rear one and a corner snapped off the front one he could risk driving it across town. He wouldn't need to fetch and use his own car at all. He turned the vehicle in a jerky three-point turn, through unfamiliarity with the Polo's clutch, and drove it along to the step leading down to the flat. Checking thoroughly that none of the bags was leaking, the man lined them up by the door and then loaded them quickly and quietly into the back.

At three thirty a.m. a figure clad in white tunic and trousers and wearing a surgical mask and cap wheeled a trolley into the boiler house of Kerr Memorial Hospital. The attendant on duty put down his paper and got up from the table which he shared with an open bag of sandwiches and a half full bottle of milk.

'What do you want then?' he asked suspiciously.

'This lot's for the fiery furnace,' mumbled the figure in white.

'At this time? You know the regulations. The proper containers at the proper time.'

'This is different.'

'What way different?'

'A bad car smash. These bits and pieces are what them upstairs had to take off.'

'So they can wait till morning. Rules is rules.'

'You don't understand. One of the victims had AIDS.'

The boilerman visibly withdrew and scowled. 'I ain't touching them,' he growled, looking at the bags.

'You don't have to,' said the man in white. 'Just open up the door and I'll bung them in.'

The boilerman appeared to hesitate for a moment before relenting and saying, 'You're on.' He led the way through to the furnace room and opened one of the three metal doors that stood side by side. 'Put them in this one,' he said. He stood by as the figure in white, now orange against the glow from the fire, heaved the bags, one by one, into the flames.

'Where did you say this accident was?' asked the boilerman.

'On the ring road.'

'Must have been one hell of a crash if they had to take off all them limbs. Funny I didn't hear anything about it on the radio.'

'I suppose they're not releasing the news until the next of kin have been informed.'

'That'll be it,' agreed the boilerman, accepting the plausible explanation. 'Drive like maniacs, some of these buggers do. Probably pissed out their minds as well. It's the innocent buggers they run in to I feel sorry for. Just goes to show, you never know when your time is coming.'

The man in white looked over his mask at the boilerman, the light from the fire flickering in his eyes. He did not say anything, but there was something about him that made the boilerman feel a little uneasy. Maybe it was the firelight, he told himself. 'Do you want a cup of tea or something?' he asked.

'No thanks. I best be getting along,' said the man. He stepped forward to close the furnace door.

'You can take your mask off now,' said the boilerman.

'What?' asked the figure in white.

'Your mask. You've still got it on.'

'Oh,' replied the man in white with a weak attempt at a laugh. 'It becomes a habit in the unit.'

'What unit's that then?' asked the boilerman.

'The . . . A&E team,' replied the man after a moment's hesitation.

'I could have sworn I knew all the porters in A&E,' said the boilerman, 'but I don't think I've seen you before. You sound a bit posh to be a porter. You're not one of them medical students, are you? Playing at being a worker?'

'No.'

'You'll have to sign this,' said the boilerman, handing over a record sheet. It was clipped to a dog-eared piece of board. A blunt pencil was attached by a length of string. 'Print your name on the left, sign on the right. In between, write down what you put in the fire and who authorised it.'

The man accepted the board and wrote quickly and untidily. He handed it back.

'You've still got your mask on,' said the boilerman as he tried to read what the man had written. He tilted back his head so that he could look through the lower portion of his glasses as he held the paper up to the light. 'I'm beginning to think I've got a personal hygiene problem.' He looked at the man and caught his stare. The mask stayed put. 'I can't read the authoriser's name. What does it say?'

'Dr Mullen.'

'Dr Mullen isn't on duty this evening,' said the boilerman quietly. 'I saw him go off at five.'

Again came the stare over the mask. There was no firelight to blame this time. There was something evil about the look in those eyes. 'Who are you?' whispered the boilerman, taking a step backwards and reaching up for the wall telephone. 'What's your game?'

The fist landed perfectly on the boilerman's chin and the man in white reached out to catch the falling figure before he hit the ground.

He laid out the prostrate man gently and looked about him. He would have to get this exactly right. He was approximately the same height as the boilerman, so he could use himself as a measuring aid. He planted both feet apart on the ground in front of the furnace and measured the distance between his feet and the fire door by stretching out his body and moving himself forward with his hands on the ground. When his head reached the fire door he marked the ground with the toe of his left foot and stood up. Next he laid down a fire rake at the spot he had just marked. Someone his height tripping over the rake at that particular spot would pitch forward and hit his head on the iron door.

The man dragged the unconscious body of the boilerman over in front of the furnace and angled it before the fire door. It would have to be done with one blow. He brought the body up into as near a kneeling position as he could manage and held the head in both hands before bringing it back slowly and then slamming it forwards against the iron door with all the strength he could muster. There was a sickening crack and he felt confident of success. He felt for a carotid pulse and was alarmed to detect a faint beating, but it grew weaker by the second until suddenly it stopped altogether and the boilerman was dead. The man arranged the limbs of the corpse in keeping with a trip over the rake and a subsequent accidental blow to the head on the furnace door. He checked that everything else was in order, collected his trolley and left silently.

There were two police cars parked near the hospital front office when Jamieson left the residency to walk to the microbiology lab on Wednesday morning. He asked Moira Lippman about them when he got in.

129

'You didn't hear about the accident last night?' asked Moira.
'No. Tell me.'

'Archie Trotter, the night-shift man in the boiler house, had a fall and hit his head on the furnace door. He was dead when they found him this morning.'

'Poor man, there seems to be a jinx on this place,' said Jamieson.

'Don't say that,' exclaimed Moira. 'My sister-in-law is being admitted for her operation today.'

'Sorry. I'm sure she'll be okay.'

'How did your tests turn out?' asked Moira, seeing that Jamieson was examining the tubes he had inoculated on Tuesday.

Jamieson shook his head and said thoughtfully, 'I'm not sure. There seem to be a number of unusual results.'

'How unusual?'

'Three of the biochemical tests don't seem to match the text-book response.'

'It's not that unusual to come across the occasional one,' said Moira.

'But three?'

'That's a bit much,' agreed the girl.

'Any ideas?' asked Jamieson.

Moira smiled and said, 'Dare I suggest . . . experimental error?'

'You mean I mucked up the tests?' said Jamieson with a wry smile. 'Maybe you're right. I'm a bit of an amateur at this sort of thing.'

'Would you like me to repeat them for you?' asked Moira. 'Give you a second opinion?'

'You're serious?'

'Of course. It's no trouble, really.'

'You're an angel,' said Jamieson.

'Problems?' asked Clive Evans coming into the lab and seeing the two of them with the test tubes.

Jamieson told him.

'That's nothing to worry about, happens all the time,' said

Evans. 'Sometimes I think if I ever come across a bug that matches the text book in every response I'll give a sherry party for the lab.'

'I thought it was me,' said Jamieson. 'Moira said she'd repeat the tests for me.'

'Relax. I'm sure your tests worked fine. There are lots of atypical strains around.'

'I thought three differences were a bit much, Dr Evans,' said Moira.

'It's not common, I'll grant you, but I have seen it happen before,' replied Evans.

Moira shrugged and silently deferred to Evans' greater experience.

Harry Plenderleith was none too happy about working out his shift in the place where a man had died less than twelve hours before. He did not have to imagine where they had found the body, for there was still a chalk mark on the floor that the police had left and a brown stain in the concrete where the blood had collected in a puddle. It all made him very unsettled and he whistled a lot to cover the fact that he was nervous. He had never liked the dead man. Trotter and he had never seen eye to eye about anything. Now that he was dead the possibility that his spirit was still hovering around played on Plenderleith's imagination as he checked that number two fire had been completely extinguished.

Plenderleith put on his protective face mask and started to rake out the ashes, creating clouds of dust as he did so. He had scarcely begun when the rake caught something heavy and it clattered out into the ash can, making him put down the rake for a moment and reach into the ashes to recover the object. It was a long bone. He dusted it off and examined it by holding it against his person in various ways until he decided that it had come from an upper leg. 'Poor bugger,' he whispered under his breath and resumed raking the floor of the furnace. More bones clattered into the can and Plenderleith grew uneasy. He had come across the occasional bone before when these sealed sacks from surgery had been brought down from the theatres, but this seemed out of all proportion. His unease finally peaked when the last artifact rolled out into the can and lay there in the ash.

Plenderleith didn't make much sense on the phone and the hospital telephonist had to tell him to calm down.

'But there's been a bloody murder, I tell you!'

'Start again, you found some bones while you were cleaning out the furnace?'

'Human remains! That's what they are!'

The telephonist, who had turned aside for a moment to consult with someone, came back on the line and said, 'My supervisor says that that is not unusual. You should have been told about amputation waste when you were given the job.'

'Amputation waste!' exclaimed Plenderleith. 'You mean they amputated this bugger's head?'

'So the fall didn't kill him?' asked Chief Inspector Ryan.

'Only if he fell at eighty miles an hour,' replied the police pathologist.

'What are you saying?'

'The indentation on his head is too deep for an accidental fall but it matches the cast of the fire door, so either someone took the door off its hinges and hit him with it, or else they slammed his head against it to make it look as if it were an accident.'

'Thank you, Doctor,' said the policeman. He was about to say something else when he was interrupted by someone who had come into the room. They spoke in a huddle for a few moments before the policeman said to the pathologist, 'I'm afraid we've got something else for you.'

'Never a dull moment,' replied the man laconically.

'A pile of bones from the furnace our late friend here was tending. A body was cremated in it.'

'Never rains but it pours.'

'The jigsaw puzzle is on its way over.'

Jamieson was still in the lab when he heard that the accidental death of Archie Trotter was being treated as murder. Moira Lippman told him. She had heard the rumours at lunch time in the staff canteen. They had started to fly when a police incident 'room' was set up in the grounds outside the boiler house.

'What about motive?' asked Jamieson.

'That's the really grisly bit,' said Moira. 'There's a story going around that they found some human bones in the incinerator this morning.'

'That doesn't necessarily mean that . . .'

'But it was a whole body.'

Jamieson was shocked. The suggestion of murder in the hospital made him look for a suitable excuse to return to his room and call the switchboard. He got through to Sci-Med in London and told them that he wanted to be kept discreetly informed of all developments in the case. He was assured that the local police would be informed of his interest and instructed accordingly.

Moira was on the phone when Jamieson returned. He heard her sound relieved and thank someone before putting down the receiver. 'I was just checking on my sister-in-law,' she said.

'Everything okay?' Jamieson asked.

'Yes, but she's not sure when they're going to operate yet. There's a bit of a backlog.'

'Where's Dr Evans?'

'He's in Dr Richardson's office,' replied the girl.

Jamieson left Moira Lippman and went along the corridor to climb the stairs up to the ground floor. As he reached the top of the stairs he heard a clap of thunder and paused to look out of one of the corridor windows at the darkening sky. A figure on the other side of the courtyard caught his attention. It was Thelwell. He had just come out of the door that led to the central sterile supply department.

Jamieson frowned as he wondered what a consultant surgeon was doing there. He reflected that this was the second time he had had occasion to wonder this, the first being the night he had seen Thelwell in the vicinity of the lab when Richardson had died. The function of the department was to sterilise dressings and surgical instruments. What possible reason could Thelwell have had for being there? After a couple of minutes' consideration Jamieson decided that he would have to satisfy his curiosity. He would make it his business to find out.

The heavens suddenly opened and rain began to hammer mercilessly against the window, all but obliterating his view of the courtyard outside. He paused in the shelter of the front door and waited until the deluge had stopped. His reasoning that such heavy rain could not last long was proved right when after three minutes the sky started to lighten and the rain eased off sufficiently to let him sprint across the courtyard to the entrance of the central sterile supply department.

He felt the humidity in the atmosphere hit him and saw the moisture condensing on the tiled walls as he opened the front door and walked along the thirty metres or so of corridor that led to a pair of heavy swing doors equipped with brass handles. STERILISING HALL said the sign above them. The humidity increased as Jamieson pushed open one of the doors and turned left as instructed by the arrow. He was forced to run his finger round the inside of his collar as he approached the figures in white.

'Who's in charge here?' he enquired, raising his voice to be heard above the hiss of steam and also to compensate for the fact that the man he was asking was wearing a full-face visor. The man pointed to a green door and Jamieson followed his direction and knocked.

'Come.'

Jamieson entered to find a large, well-built man seated at a desk so small that it seemed to emphasise his bulk. He held a pen in one of his fat podgy hands and was ticking off items on a list. Like the others, he was wearing white cotton trousers and a white surgical tunic top with a vee neck. Dark chest hair reached above the centre of the vee. There was a strong smell of aftershave in the room, not expensive, just strong.

'I understand that you are in charge here?' said Jamieson.

'Who wants to know?' asked the man.

Jamieson explained who he was.

'Charge Nurse Blaney,' said the man, leaning across the desk and offering his hand. Jamieson shook it and noticed how soft and flabby it was.

'How can I help you?'

'Mr Thelwell was here a few minutes ago,' said Jamieson.

'Yes.'

'What did he want?'

Blaney's expression changed to one of suspicion. 'I don't think I can discuss . . .'

Jamieson had been prepared for the response. He interrupted saying, 'If you call Mr Crichton on extension 2631 he will tell you that I have the right to ask these questions.'

'I'll take your word for it,' said Blaney. 'Mr Thelwell likes to collect his own instrument packs.'

Jamieson felt his throat tighten. He had to clear it before asking, 'What exactly does that mean?'

'Mr Thelwell insists on picking up the instruments for his theatre himself.'

'Has he always done this?'

'Just for the past few weeks.'

'He just comes down here and takes away his instrument packs?' asked Jamieson.

'He does more than that,' replied Blaney. 'He likes to monitor the sterilising process.'

'What exactly does he do?' asked Jamieson.

'He checks the temperature and pressure gauges during the autoclave cycle, monitors the graph recorder, waits till the instrument packs come out, then takes them up to his theatre.'

'Did Mr Thelwell say why he does this?' asked Jamieson.

'A safety precaution,' replied Blaney.

'A safety precaution,' repeated Jamieson thoughtfully.

'That's right,' said Blaney. 'Is something wrong?'

'No . . . nothing,' said Jamieson, but his mind was turning cartwheels. The revelation that Thelwell was a link in the chain that brought sterile instruments from the supply department to the theatre was something that he hadn't reckoned on.

'Mr Thelwell is a very conscientious man. He leaves nothing to chance,' said Blaney. 'Even though Dr Evans puts these machines through their paces every week and the graph recorders are always spot on, he likes to see things for himself.'

'Does Mr Thelwell just collect his own instruments?' asked Jamieson, trying to make it sound like a casual enquiry.

'No, he takes all the packs for gynaecology,' replied Blaney. 'There's nothing wrong in that, is there?' he responded aggressively to the frown on Jamieson's face.

Jamieson said that there wasn't, but his mind was working overtime.

'Perhaps you would like to see the routine?' asked Blaney.

Jamieson looked at Blaney, smiled and then said, 'Why not.'

Blaney gave him a conducted tour of the sterilising hall, stopping at intervals to explain things when he thought it necessary.

'Do you always use the same steriliser for the instruments?' asked Jamieson.

Blaney nodded and pointed to one of the autoclaves. 'That one,' he said. 'All sterile supplies for gynaecology go through that one.'

Jamieson looked at the dials on the front. He said, 'What would happen if the steam supply should fail?'

'The machine would reset itself and refuse to proceed with the cycle.'

'What if it should fail half way through a cycle?'

'Same thing. It would reset itself and the graph recorder would show the failure.'

'Is there a manual over-ride?' asked Jamieson.

'I don't understand,' said Blaney.

'Can you convince the machine that it has completed its sterilising cycle when it actually hasn't?'

'But who would ever want to do that?' asked Blaney.

'Can it be done?'

'No,' said Blaney. 'The automatic timer will not start until the temperature has climbed to a pre-set value and if at any time during the cycle the temperature should fall below that value, the timer would reset itself and refuse to start until the temperature had climbed again.'

Jamieson looked at the chart recorder on the front of the machine and said, 'Do you keep these charts?'

'Every one,' said Blaney.

'So if I were to ask you for the chart from the run Mr Thelwell has just been watching you could show it to me?'

'Of course.'

'I'd like to see it,' said Jamieson.

Blaney shrugged and asked Jamieson to wait while he fetched it from his office. He returned with a circular piece of graph paper. 'This is it,' said Blaney. 'Dated and initialled.' He traced the blue line on the paper with his forefinger and said, 'As you can see, it was a normal run. The temperature climbed steadily as the steam entered the machine and at 131 degrees centigrade the timer was triggered.' The finger traced a plateau on the graph. 'The temperature held steady until the timer cut out and here . . .' Blaney's finger began to drop with the blue line, 'is where the steam was shut off and the temperature started to fall.'

'Thank you,' said Jamieson. He made a mental note of the reference number on the graph before asking, 'How often did you say the machine was checked?'

'Dr Evans checks it out every week, sometimes twice.'

'You couldn't ask for more than that,' said Jamieson.

Blaney smiled modestly and said, 'We do our best.'

Jamieson returned to the microbiology department to pursue his original intention of going to see Clive Evans but his mind was now almost totally preoccupied with the fact that Thelwell was removing surgical instruments from the central sterile supply department and holding them in his personal possession before they were used. Why? Why? Why?

He found Evans in what had been John Richardson's office. He was sifting through some papers.

'Just checking up on some overdue lab reports,' said Evans by way of explanation when he saw Jamieson.

'Did you find them?' asked Jamieson.

'Not yet. What can I do for you?'

'I wanted to talk to you about correlating your efforts with the Public Health people so that you don't start getting in each other's way,' said Jamieson.

'When will they come?' asked Evans.

'Tomorrow morning.'

'Perhaps I could have a word with their chap before they start and we can agree on a system.'

'Good idea. I'll bring their people across to the lab when they arrive,' said Jamieson.

'Was there something else?' asked Evans, seeing that Jamieson was lingering on.

'When did you last check the surgical steriliser in CSSD?' asked Jamieson.

Evans looked surprised. 'This morning. Why do you ask?'

'Was it all right?'

'Perfect. It always is. I don't see what you're getting at.'

'This lab has so far failed to find the contaminating organism in the theatres, the wards, the air samples or anything else for that matter. Correct?'

'I'm afraid so,' said Evans.

'As I see it there are only a limited number of ways this infection problem can come about. One is that some person is carrying the infection and passing it on to the patients undetected.'

'Like Thelwell.'

'Like a carrier,' agreed Jamieson. 'Another way would be for the instruments or dressings in theatre to be contaminated.'

'That's impossible,' said Evans. 'They are autoclaved in sealed packs.'

'So the lab never bothers to check them, right?'

'There's no need.'

'You check the machines but you don't check what comes out of them?'

'There's no need,' repeated Evans.

'I want you to carry out a spot check on an instrument pack from the gynaecology theatre.'

'When?'

'I'll tell you when.'

'You're the boss,' said Evans, but he said it in a way that made it plain that he thought what he was being asked to do was a waste of time.

Jamieson understood his point of view but did not tell him about Thelwell having collected the instruments from the central sterile supply department. It would have been too easy for Evans to read his mind and know what he was thinking. For the moment that was too terrible to be voiced out loud. If the instruments were at fault, the contamination must be occurring after they had been sterilised. That meant that it was not accidental. The contamination had been deliberate! Women were not dying of an unfortunate, accidental infection at Kerr Memorial. They were being murdered.

9

The possibility that Gordon Thomas Thelwell might actually be interfering with the sterility of surgical instruments before they were used in theatre was an idea so horrendous that Jamieson had great difficulty in even considering it without his subconscious sending up a stream of objections and telling him that there must be some mistake. Such a thing just could not be. This was the stuff of surreal nightmares, the province of the lunatic asylum. It had to be some wild figment of his imagination born out of his intense dislike of the man, but still the thought would not go away.

Later, as he lay on his bed in the early evening, staring idly up at the ceiling, something inside Jamieson's head kept telling him that he had to consider it. He had to think everything through logically and without emotion. He did not have the right to dismiss anything out of hand, however repellent the notion might be. He should do it coldly and dispassionately. He began the process, feeling that he was starting out on a journey that he had very little heart for.

It was a fact that Thelwell had collected surgical instruments personally from the central sterile supply department. To Jamieson's way of thinking, there could be no valid reason for him to have done so. The man was a consultant surgeon, not a porter, not a theatre orderly but a surgeon. If he had gone to pick them up personally then it could only have been because he had had some strong personal reason for doing so. He had wanted to get his hands on them before they reached the operating theatre. Why? What did he want to do with them? Jamieson knew that the answer would not appear out of the blue. This was something he would have to investigate. The time for thinking was over. It was time to take action.

Jamieson knew the reference numbers that were marked on the packs that Thelwell had collected earlier from the central sterile supply department. He had made a mental note of them when he examined the graphs from their sterilising records. He would go up to the gynaecology department and look for them. But first he had to make sure that Thelwell was no longer around. He checked his watch and saw that it was eight o'clock. The chances were that the surgeon had gone home ages ago, but just in case he called the switchboard and asked them to page Thelwell. After a wait of two minutes the switchboard confirmed that Thelwell was not in the hospital.

Jamieson entered the gynaecology department by the side door, deciding that the fewer people who saw him the better. He did not resort to hiding in corners but did, however, pause at the head of the stairs until a nurse's footsteps had faded into the distance before turning the corner and hurrying quietly along the corridor. The gynaecology theatre was right at the far end. Two swing doors, each with a circular glass window and scrape marks where trolley handles had worn away the paint, led through to an outer chamber where the orderlies brought their patients on operating days. Here they would be handed over to the care of the theatre team.

A vague smell of anaesthetic mingled with a stronger odour of disinfectant as Jamieson entered the main theatre and turned on the lights. The room was instantly bathed in bright, shadowless light. Although the air temperature was at least seventy degrees the stainless steel and ceramic tiling made the room seem cold. The gas cylinders on the anaesthetics trolley, scratched and scarred on their surface through continual re-cycling, seemed incongruous amidst otherwise unblemished metallic perfection. Jamieson rested his hand on a black oxygen cylinder with its white top and looked about him. A metal cupboard caught his eye and he remembered Thelwell telling him on his tour of the department that this was where the instruments were stored.

Jamieson was conscious of the sound of his own heart beating as he crossed the theatre floor and knelt down to open the cupboard. There were six packs of instruments inside. He examined each in turn and checked its number. Packs twelve to seventeen were present. Packs eighteen to twenty-four, the packs that Thelwell had taken from the central sterile supply department earlier in the day, were missing!

Jamieson felt the hairs on the back of his neck rise. Until now he had subconsciously believed that his suspicions were going to be proved unfounded, but the missing instruments were saying otherwise. The theatre suddenly felt colder. The atmosphere was hostile. Suddenly the doors opened and Jamieson dropped the instrument pack he was holding. He turned quickly on his heel to find a orderly standing there. He was wheeling a transporter with two gas cylinders on it.

'All right to change these?' the man asked.

'Of course,' replied Jamieson, feeling embarrassed at being so startled

Jamieson closed the cupboard slowly and put his hand to his forehead to massage it absently with his fingertips as he thought what to do next. It was already clear that Thelwell had not brought the instruments directly to the theatre. What had he done with the missing packs? Again, there was no way that Jamieson was going to to be able to guess the answer. He would have to confront Thelwell face to face and ask him what the hell was going on. He returned to the residency and asked the switchboard for Thelwell's home number.

One of Thelwell's daughters answered. 'Father is out this evening. He has a choir practice. Whom shall I say called?'

'Don't bother. It's not important,' said Jamieson. He replaced the receiver.

Jamieson felt deflated. He had prepared himself for the inevitable confrontation and now it hadn't happened. He had been thwarted by a choir practice. Frustration started to gnaw at his stomach. Thelwell seemed to go to a lot of choir practices, thought Jamieson. St Serf's Church, he remembered, the *Te Deum*. This would not wait until morning, he decided. He would go along to the church and talk to Thelwell when he came out. He had put on his jacket and was about to leave his room when the phone rang.

'Macmillan here.'

'Who?'

'Macmillan . . . Sci-Med, London.'

Jamieson apologised. He was more up-tight than he thought.

'The information you asked for. The bones belonged to one Mary Louise Chapman, reported missing by her husband last night. She was twenty-eight years old and five months pregnant. Forensic identified her from dental records.'

'That was quick,' said Jamieson.

'Reports of missing women have taken on a new dimension in that city at the moment,' said Macmillan. 'All the stops are pulled out.'

'Of course,' said Jamieson. 'But it was still very quick.'

'In truth, the police suspected it might be Mrs Chapman. They found her car parked in a lane at the back of the hospital.'

'I see,' said Jamieson.

'Does this have some direct relevance to your investigation?' asked Macmillan.

The question gave birth to a new nightmarish possibility in Jamieson's head. 'I'm not sure,' he said.

'It sounds as if things up there are not as straightforward as one might have imagined?' said Macmillan.

'That's true,' said Jamieson, hoping that he would get away with not saying any more for the present.

'Need any help?'

'Not yet.'

Jamieson had obtained the address of St Serf's Church from the phone book. The good thing about looking for a church, he mused as he turned off into a leafy avenue west of Harden Road, was that you could see it from a long way off. The spire of St Serf's had guided him for the last half mile, until now when he was faced with having to find a parking space among the Volvos and other quality cars that were lined up outside the church hall. It was that kind of an area, pleasant, comfortable, pretty. The church itself stood in a well-tended graveyard and had Virginia creeper growing along its south wall. At the moment it was green but Jamieson could imagine it turning to red in the autumn and complementing the yellow leaves which would fall from the birch trees by the boundary wall.

In the end, Jamieson found a space some two hundred metres down the road. He was a bit close to the entrance to one of the driveways but not close enough, he reckoned, to constitute a real obstruction so he left the car and started to walk back towards the church. He could hear singing coming from the hall that was tacked on to the side of the main building and he could see lights on inside. He checked his watch. It was five minutes to ten. Maybe they would finish at ten?

Jamieson strolled up one side of the street and down the other. It was a nice evening. The gardens of the large houses had obviously benefited from the soaking they had received earlier in the day and the mixed scent of the flowers was heavy in the still evening air. It made him think of Kent and Sue. He saw that people were beginning to emerge from the church hall and took up a position almost opposite the entrance to wait for Thelwell to emerge.

At first, the pavement outside the church was crowded with groups of people laughing and chattering and Jamieson had to keep his wits about him to avoid missing Thelwell. As the minutes passed and the crowds thinned, Jamieson found himself considering that somehow he had missed him. The slamming doors and starting cars were now becoming less frequent. The avenue was returning to its accustomed peace and quiet and still he had not seen Thelwell come out.

It was another ten minutes before a woman, carrying a bundle of papers under her arm and a key in her mouth, turned round as she emerged and locked the door. Jamieson, feeling bemused but still fairly confident that he had not

144

missed Thelwell among the earlier crowds, approached her
and excused himself.

'I was rather hoping to catch Gordon Thelwell this evening,'
he said pleasantly. 'Could I have missed him?'

'Oh no,' exclaimed the woman. 'Mr Thelwell wasn't here
this evening.'

'Oh,' said Jamieson, working at keeping the surprise off his
face. 'Are you sure?'

'Mr Thelwell hasn't been coming to practice for some time,'
volunteered the woman. 'He's too busy at the hospital these
days, I understand. He's head surgeon at Kerr Memorial
Hospital, you know. They've been having a bit of trouble
with one thing and another.'

'Of course,' replied Jamieson distantly. 'I should have considered that.'

Jamieson sat behind the wheel of his car with another unpleasant discovery to digest. All these choir practices that Thelwell
said he had been going to were a fabrication. A lie. What had
he really been doing on these evenings? Where was he tonight?
Was it relevant to the problem at the hospital?

Jamieson drove round in circles for a while, trying to make
sense of it all before deciding finally to drive to the street where
Thelwell lived. It was now his intention to confront Thelwell
openly with what he had discovered. He parked the car on the
other side of the road some fifty metres along from Thelwell's
house and settled down to wait.

At eleven thirty, his vigil was rewarded. Thelwell's dark
green Volvo estate car turned into the street and Jamieson
prepared to get out of his car. He had expected Thelwell to
park outside his house on the street or at least to get out to open
the gates in front of his drive. It had been his plan to intercept
him on the pavement. But, in the event, Thelwell swung his car
in towards the gates and they opened automatically at the signal
from some device on the car. By the time Jamieson reached the
house the gates had closed again and Thelwell was putting the
car away in the garage.

Light spilled out into the garden from the open front door and Thelwell's wife was framed in the doorway. 'You're late, dear,' Jamieson heard her say.

'The practice went on a bit longer than I thought and then I had a quick drink with Roger Denby,' replied Thelwell.

Thelwell was a very plausible liar, thought Jamieson. He had sounded perfectly natural when answering his wife. He considered whether or not he should confront Thelwell there and then but decided against it. For the moment it was enough to know that Thelwell had been lying to everyone, including his wife. He walked back to his car and drove back to the hospital.

The phone in his room was ringing when Jamieson got in. He hurriedly unlocked the door and rushed over to snatch it from its cradle, feeling certain that the caller would hang up the moment he touched it. It was Sue.

'Where have you been?' she asked. 'I've been trying your number for ages.'

'I had to go out,' said Jamieson without further explanation.

'We've been invited out to dinner on Saturday. I thought I'd better check.'

'Sue, I don't think I can come home this weekend,' said Jamieson.

'Oh . . .' Sue's voice trailed off into silence. 'That's a pity. I had something to tell you.'

'I'm sorry, really I am, but the way things are going I just can't get away. What did you want to tell me?'

'Don't worry. It can wait,' said Sue. 'Take care.'

'You too.'

'Shit,' said Jamieson quietly as he put down the phone. Sue had sounded very disappointed. It was unlike her.

Jamieson was up at seven. He was washed, shaved and out of his room by seven thirty and went to get some breakfast. He was in his little room in the microbiology department by eight. The morning cleaners were emptying waste paper baskets outside in the corridor. They pooled all the waste in a large bin which they wheeled around the department on a small wheeled bogie.

'It's getting so you are afraid to go out at night,' he heard one of them say.

'My Stan won't let me,' declared the other. 'Not after what happened to the Chapman woman. That was less than a quarter of a mile away from where we live!'

'Makes you think, don't it.'

Jamieson continued to listen to their conversation for a few moments before opening the door. One of the cleaners clutched her arms across her chest in fright. 'Oh, my God!' she exclaimed. 'You gave me such a fright. I thought for a moment you were him!'

'Sorry,' said Jamieson. 'How do you know I'm not?'

'Because you're Dr Jamieson,' said the woman.

'Doesn't mean he couldn't be the ripper,' said her companion.

'Suppose not,' said the first woman thoughtfully. 'But you're not, are you?'

'No, I'm not,' Jamieson assured her.

'What are the police doing? That's what I want to know,' exclaimed the other woman angrily.

'Too right. It isn't safe to walk out of your door these nights. Them with their free uniforms and rent allowances.'

'And they retire on a big pension at fifty. My brother-in-law's boy Ronnie joined the police and I know for a fact . . .'

Jamieson withdrew from the conversation and closed his door. He could feel the pulse beating in his temple. The woman saying, 'doesn't mean he couldn't be the ripper,' had rekindled the awful idea that there might be a connection between the deaths in the city and those in the hospital. Thelwell had been interfering in the supply of sterile dressings to the theatre and he had been lying about going to choir practices in the evenings . . .

The enormity of what he was considering kept Jamieson

paralysed in his seat for a few minutes. Could Thelwell not only be deliberately causing the deaths of women patients at the hospital but could he . . . could he possibly be the ripper?

Jamieson started to think in practical terms and that meant obtaining hard evidence. He wondered if the dates of the killings and Thelwell's choir practice night coincided. Perhaps he could find out from St Serf's? He would think about that later. For the moment, his immediate priority was to obtain the surgical listing for the day in gynaecology. He called the theatre sister.

'Mr Morton is operating at ten. Will you be attending?'

Jamieson said that he would and said that on no account was the operation to begin without his being present.

'Very well, Doctor,' replied the sister, souding puzzled.

Jamieson called Blaney in the central sterile supply department and asked about the availability of spare instrument packs for surgery in gynaecology.

'We have about a dozen,' Blaney replied.

'I need three.'

'When?'

'Right now. I'm coming across to collect them.'

As Jamieson was returning with the instruments he saw Clive Evans arrive in the car park and waited for him in the doorway to the lab. 'I want you to come with me to theatre this morning. Does that present any problems?'

'No, I don't think so,' replied Evans. 'Are you going to tell me why?'

'I want you to remove some instrument packs and screen them for bacterial contamination.'

'If you say so,' said Evans. 'These ones too?' he asked seeing what Jamieson was carrying.

'No. These are the ones they are going to use,' said Jamieson. 'They just don't know it yet.' He looked at his watch and added, 'I'll stop by your office in fifteen minutes. We'll go up to gynaecology together.'

*　　*　　*

Jamieson's heart sank when he got to theatre and found Thelwell scrubbing up. Thelwell spoke first. 'I take it there's no objection to my being present as an observer in my own theatre?' he said acidly.

'None,' said Jamieson flatly. 'Provided that your swabs are still negative, you've applied nasal barrier cream, and you don't approach the table directly.'

'My swabs were always negative,' said Thelwell through tight lips. 'But I've used Naseptin as I always did in the past in any case.'

Jamieson joined Thelwell at the basins and started to scrub his hands and forearms. Clive Evans did the same.

'I see we have a member of our esteemed microbiology department present,' sneered Thelwell. 'To what do we owe this honour?'

'I am here at Dr Jamieson's request,' said Evans without emotion.

'Ah yes,' said Thelwell with what for him passed for a smile.

The surgical team of Phillip Morton, an assistant, the anaesthetist, the theatre sister and a junior nurse were waiting when Thelwell, Jamieson and Clive Evans joined them.

'May we begin?' asked Morton.

'Not yet,' said Jamieson. He turned to the theatre sister and asked, 'Sister, will you please show me the instrument packs for this morning's operation.'

The nurse showed Jamieson the packs without comment and he examined the numbers. He had to swallow when he saw that they were different from the numbers on the packs that he had found in the cupboard the night before. These were the ones that had been missing from the cupboard! These were the ones that Thelwell had collected from the central sterile supply department personally! They must have been put into the cupboard at some time during the night. Jamieson went over to the cupboard and looked for the packs that had been in there. They had gone.

Jamieson turned round and said to Morton, 'I want you to

use these instruments this morning.' He nodded to the packs that Evans was holding. 'Dr Evans is going to take the other ones away for analysis.'

'What on earth is going on?' exclaimed Morton.

'Explanations will have to wait,' said Jamieson. 'Please just do as I ask.'

'Very good,' said Morton with a shrug of his shoulders.

'Wait!' interrupted Thelwell. 'Might I remind you all that this is still my department and my theatre. I demand to know what is going on!'

'Call it simply a spot check on surgical instruments,' said Jamieson. 'You have no objection to that have you, Mr Thelwell?'

Jamieson could see the burning anger in Thelwell's eyes over the mask. 'I prefer to be kept informed of these things,' said Thelwell. 'Is that too much to ask?'

'Spot checks wouldn't be spot checks if they were advertised,' said Jamieson.

'May I proceed?' asked Phillip Morton with more than a trace of impatience in his voice.

'Of course,' said Jamieson. 'We are just leaving.'

As Clive Evans reached the door of the theatre he collided with Thelwell who had turned to leave at the same time. The instruments he had been carrying were scattered all over the floor.

'Clumsy oaf!' snorted Thelwell and disappeared through the swing doors. Evans turned to face Jamieson, looking bemused. 'He deliberately barged into me!' he exclaimed.

Jamieson looked at the knives, scalpels and forceps lying all over the floor and sighed in frustration. The tests for sterility would now be useless. Evans began picking up the instruments. 'What do you want done with them?' he asked.

'Return them to CSSD for cleaning and sterilising,' said Jamieson. 'I'm going to have a word with Mr Thelwell.'

Jamieson was furious at what Thelwell had done, but he was also afraid of what it inferred. If Thelwell had deliberately bumped into Evans, it must mean that he had done it to prevent microbiological examination of the instruments. It had been a clever thing to do on the spur of the moment. Quick thinking, clever and devious. Wasn't that how Ryan had listed the hallmarks of the psychopath?

Jamieson found Thelwell in his office opening letters. His secretary had not been in the outer office, so that Jamieson had simply pushed open the door which had not been properly closed. At first Thelwell was unaware that he was standing there. He was obviously still in a temper and it showed in the way he was opening the envelopes with a silver paper knife. He inserted the blade at a corner with momentary precision and then ripped each envelope open with a single upwards slash. Jamieson cleared his throat and Thelwell stopped what he was doing and looked up.

'What do you want?' he snapped. 'Or is it another spot test?' He punctuated the remark with a snort.

Jamieson had to work at keeping the anger he felt under control. He said, 'You have just prevented the examination of the surgical instruments in your theatre by spreading them all over the floor. I think that demands some explanation.'

'What the hell are you talking about?' rasped Thelwell. 'That idiot from microbiology barged right into *me*. A typical Richardson protégé. Now, if you will be so kind, I have things to do.' Thelwell sat down and started to read his mail. He pretended that Jamieson was no longer standing there.

Jamieson said slowly and quietly, 'I want to know exactly what you did with the instruments you collected from CSSD yesterday.' He watched Thelwell carefully for his reaction.

Thelwell stopped reading, settled back in his chair and let out his breath in a long, slow sigh. 'My, we have been busy,' he said.

Jamieson waited for his answer.

'I brought them back here.'

'Where?'

'Here, to my department.'

'Why should a consultant surgeon play at being a hospital porter?' asked Jamieson slowly.

'Because this consultant surgeon cares enough about his patients to monitor the sterilising of the instruments to be used in their operations and then make sure that they are not tampered with before they are used.'

Jamieson found himself taken unawares by the directness of Thelwell's answer. He had to be careful. He wasn't dealing with a fool. Was the man just clever? Or very clever? Clever enough to pretend that he was investigating the very act that he could see he was about to be accused of?

'Tampered with?' said Jamieson.

'It occurred to me that this was a possibility,' said Thelwell.

'I see,' replied Jamieson. He tried to trap Thelwell by saying, 'So yesterday you brought the instruments up to the theatre from CSSD and put them away in the theatre instrument cupboard yourself?'

'Not exactly,' said Thelwell, walking round the trap. 'I kept them locked away in my desk overnight. I put them in theatre this morning shortly before the operation was to start.'

'And the instruments that were already in theatre?'

Thelwell unlocked the cupboard in the left pedestal of his desk and brought out the packs he had substituted. 'I was going to take them back to CSSD for re-sterilising.'

'Have you any reason to believe that instruments have been tampered with?' Jamieson asked.

'Just a precaution,' replied Thelwell. 'But I felt it was warranted. As the same thought has obviously occurred to you, you can hardly argue the point.'

Jamieson remained silent.

Thelwell said, 'I can assure you that the instruments Evans dropped on the floor were absolutely sterile and had been under lock and key here in my office ever since they were removed from the autoclave in CSSD.'

'I see,' said Jamieson. He had not managed to trick Thelwell into lying or saying anything that might not conceivably be true. 'Perhaps we can compromise?'

'On what?'

'On an agreed procedure for sterilising and storing instruments and dressings,' said Jamieson.

'What do you have in mind?'

'I suggest that instruments are not stored in the theatres at all. I suggest that they are collected fresh from CSSD immediately before they are required.'

Thelwell thought for a moment and then said, 'Agreed.'

'I'll take these back down with me,' said Jamieson, nodding to the packs from Thelwell's desk. Thelwell handed them over.

Jamieson returned to his room in the lab after setting up the new procedure for instruments with the central sterile supply department and the administration people. Moira Lippman asked if he had a moment to speak.

'Of course.'

'I repeated your tests on the *Pseudomonas*,' she said.

Jamieson smiled. 'What happened?'

'You were quite right. There were three significant differences in terms of biochemistry. In fact I did some extra tests and found two more.'

'Five?' exclaimed Jamieson.

Moira Lippman nodded. 'Very strange,' she said. 'In fact, one might almost think that . . . No, it's silly.'

'What is?'

'No, really. It isn't worth mentioning.' With that Moira Lippman turned on her heel and left Jamieson alone again.

Jamieson reflected for a moment on how much he hated it when people did that.

The first indication that all was not well in the post-surgical care ward in the gynaecology department came at three thirty when Hugh Crichton called Jamieson and said, 'You did ask to be kept informed of any other surgical infections breaking out in the hospital?'

'Yes.'

'It's beginning to look as if eight women in surgical gynaecology who had their operations within the last ten days have developed fever and signs of wound infection.'

Jamieson closed his eyes for a moment then said, 'Go on.'

'There's not much more to report, really. Samples are on their way down to the lab for bacteriology. I just thought you should know.'

'How are the women?' asked Jamieson.

Crichton cleared his throat nervously before replying, 'They are extremely ill. It all happened very suddenly and their condition has been deteriorating all the time.'

'Thanks for telling me.'

Jamieson put the phone down and cradled his head in his hands for a moment while he thought. More infection and again in Thelwell's unit. If the damned *Pseudomonas* strain was responsible again the whole place would have to be closed down. There was no alternative. He went to talk to Clive Evans.

'I've just heard,' said Evans when Jamieson entered. 'The specimens will be here at any moment.'

'So you will know by tomorrow morning if the *Pseudomonas* is to blame?'

'Tomorrow for sure, but we can do a few microscope slides on the specimens directly. We should be able to get an idea from them.'

'How long?'

'Half an hour.'

'Let me know as soon as you have a result, will you?'

'Of course.'

Jamieson was trying to call Sue for the fourth time that day and still without success when Clive Evans came into the room. Jamieson could see that he had the results of the primary tests. He replaced the receiver.

'I've just had a look at the stained slides,' said Evans.

'And?' asked Jamieson anxiously.

'I don't think it's the *Pseudomonas*.'

'You don't?' exclaimed Jamieson.

'They're gram positive cocci rather than gram negative rods.'

'So what do you think?'

'All the indications at the moment are that it's a *Staphylococcus* infection,' said Evans.

'A different infection?' said Jamieson sounding bemused.

'It seems to be, but we won't know for sure until the morning when the cultures have had time to grow.'

Jamieson turned away, wrestling with the implications of what Evans had said. 'Another outbreak of post-operative infection in the same unit but caused by a completely different bug?' he murmured.

'That's how it looks,' said Evans. He could see that Jamieson was deep in thought so he said, 'If you'll excuse me, I've got things to do.'

'Thanks,' said Jamieson absently.

Jamieson walked over to gynaecology at six thirty. The condition of the infected women had deteriorated and there had been speculation that some of them might actually die before morning if the right antibiotic was not found. The choice of antibiotic treatment had already caused disharmony between Thelwell and his team. They were all agreed that penicillin was proving ineffectual. This was not too surprising because most hospital strains of *Staphylococcus* had become resistant to the drug over the years, but Thelwell's insistence that Cephalosporin should continue to be used despite Morton's argument that it was not having much effect, was causing tight-lipped anger all round. Jamieson intervened to suggest that they treat the women with more than one antibiotic at the same time. After a brief discussion they agreed on a regime of three drugs with close monitoring of the patients' condition, so that the treatment could be altered if it was proving ineffectual.

Jamieson took the ward sister to one side and asked her about the infected patients. 'How many patients do you have in the ward, Sister?'

'Seventeen.'

'And of these only eight have become infected?'

'So far,' said the sister.

'Do the eight have anything in common?' asked Jamieson.

'I don't understand.'

'I'm looking for the reason why eight of the seventeen patients developed wound infections and the other nine didn't. Did they all have their operation on the same day? In the same theatre? Were the operations performed by the same surgeon? That sort of thing.'

'I'll check for you.'

Jamieson followed the woman to the ward duty room and waited while she checked the records. He became aware that his presence at her elbow was making her uncomfortable, so he turned away and looked at some postcards pinned up on the wall. Two were views of sun-splashed beaches in the Mediterranean; the rest were saucy seaside cards almost invariably featuring large bosomed nurses and captions of the 'Blimey Nurse!' sort.

'Only two had their operations on the same day,' said the sister. 'Some operations were carried out by Mr Thelwell, others by Dr Morton. Two were done in gynae, six in the orthopaedic theatre. No obvious common factor.'

'There must be one,' maintained Jamieson. 'If they all became infected at the same time, there must be one.'

'I can't think,' said the sister.

'Nor can I at the moment,' agreed Jamieson, racking his brain. 'But there has to be a common link. There are just too many for it to be chance wound infection with an airborne bug.'

A nurse came into the duty room and apologised for interrupting before saying, 'Sister, it's Mrs Galbraith. She's very ill.'

The ward sister left the room. Jamieson could hear cries of pain coming from the ward. He left and returned to the residency.

As he climbed the stairs Jamieson thought he heard a slight sound on the first landing as if someone were standing there.

He paused but could hear nothing. Normally this would not have merited any consideration at all but his nerves were taut. There was something strange going on in this hospital, maybe even something evil. The knowledge brought fear and suspicion with it. He continued up to the head of the stairs but was cautious about turning the corner. The thought that someone was lurking there had become almost unbearably strong. He made a noise with his feet to suggest that his next step would bring him round the corner and then drew back his right fist. An arm emerged from the shadow and Jamieson prepared to let fly. He only just managed to stop himself in time when he caught a glimpse of the wrist and realised that it was a woman's.

'What the hell!' he exclaimed, grabbing the figure by both wrists and pulling her out of the shadows.

'Steady on!' said Sue. 'Why so jumpy?'

Jamieson was speechless with surprise and dismay at what had almost happened. 'What on earth!' he exclaimed. 'I nearly laid you out.'

'I can think of better welcomes,' said Sue. 'Why so nervous?'

'What are you doing here?' exclaimed Jamieson. 'I've been trying to contact you all day.'

'Do we have to speak on the stairs?'

Jamieson opened his door and they both went inside.

'I was feeling guilty about how I treated you on the phone yesterday so I thought I'd come up and say I was sorry. The people in the gate-house told me where you were staying. I saw you start to cross the courtyard when I came in the front door, so I thought I'd give you a surprise.'

Jamieson shook his head and took her in his arms to hold her close. He was still upset at what had happened. 'You're crazy,' he murmured.

'Some welcome.'

'I'm sorry. It's lovely to see you but . . .'

'Relax. I don't intend getting in the way. I know how busy you must be. I've booked myself into a hotel. I just thought that if you couldn't get away, I would come to you . . . and tell you my news.'

'What news?'

'I'm pregnant. You're going to be a father.'

10

'That's absolutely marvellous!' exclaimed Jamieson, taking Sue in his arms and holding her tightly. He rested his cheek on the top of her head.

'You're sure you're pleased?' asked Sue, sounding slightly vulnerable.

'Pleased? How could you think anything else? I'm absolutely delighted! I can't begin to tell you how glad I am,' said Jamieson, letting Sue go and spreading his hands as if appealing for divine assistance. The look on his face now left Sue in no doubt about how he felt and she broke into a broad grin.

Jamieson saw the look in Sue's eyes and remembered the last time he had seen it. It had been near the end of his time in hospital after the accident, on the day he had realised just what an insufferable fool he had been. He had apologised to Sue for his behaviour. For Sue, it had been the moment when she knew she had got her man back. The change in Jamieson's personality had not been permanent as she had feared in her worst moments. The self-pitying, sarcastic monster she had been putting up with for months had vanished. After Jamieson's apology they had looked at each other without saying anything, but understanding everything. Sue had cried for the first time since the accident but the tears had been of relief and happiness.

There was a knock at the door and Jamieson opened it. He found Clive Evans standing there.

'I thought I heard voices,' said Evans.

159

'Come in,' said Jamieson. 'Meet my wife. I've just had some great news.' Jamieson's face was creased in smiles. 'I'm going to be a father.'

'Congratulations,' said Evans warmly. 'Is this your first child, Mrs Jamieson?' he asked, shaking Sue's hand.

'Call me Sue. Yes it is.'

'What are you hoping for? Boy or girl?'

Sue looked at Jamieson and said, 'Well?'

'Don't care,' said Jamieson, putting his arm round Sue again and squeezing her shoulder. 'Mind you, if it should be a boy and if he should play wing three-quarter for Scotland, I can't honestly say that I'd be terribly disappointed.'

The laughter was cut short when Jamieson noticed the look on Evans' face and he realised that something was wrong. 'Something's the matter?' he said.

Evans nodded. 'I came to tell you that one of the women in ward eight has died and two more are deteriorating fast. The antibiotics aren't working.'

'This is crazy,' said Jamieson. 'Surely we can't have a second infection immune to treatment? Are you sure it's not the *Pseudomonas* again?'

Evans shrugged apologetically and said, 'I can only say what I found on the slide. It definitely looked like a *Staphylococcus* infection. I suppose it's possible that the *Pseudomonas* is still lurking there. We won't know for sure until the morning.'

Jamieson sighed in frustration and said, 'I suppose we'll just have to bite the bullet until then.'

'Fraid so,' agreed Evans.

Jamieson thanked Evans for bringing him the news and showed him out.

'What does he do?' asked Sue.

'Clive Evans? He's the bacteriologist at the moment until they appoint a replacement for Richardson. He has the room next door.'

'It sounds as if your infection problem is getting worse not better,' said Sue.

160

Jamieson nodded and told her about the eight women who had developed infections in the last twelve hours.

'Eight!' exclaimed Sue.

'Within hours of each other.'

'Did they all have their operations on the same day?' asked Sue.

'I thought of that,' said Jamieson. 'No, they didn't, and so far I haven't uncovered any other common factor.'

Sue went through the options that Richardson and the ward sister had already considered and then lapsed into silence for a moment while she tried to think of another idea. Jamieson switched on the kettle to make coffee.

'Why has it taken so long this time for the infection to develop in these women?' Sue asked. 'I seem to remember you saying that the others developed the illness within hours of their operation.'

'They did,' agreed Jamieson. 'But this time Evans thinks it's a different bug.'

'This isn't a hospital,' said Sue. 'It's a septic tank!'

'But it's not,' replied Jamieson.

Sue looked puzzled.

'Everything is spotlessly clean and sterile and no one can find where the contamination is coming from. That's the real problem. It appears to come out of the blue.'

'No ideas at all?'

'One,' replied Jamieson a bit reluctantly.

'Well, I'm waiting.'

'It could be deliberate,' said Jamieson.

Sue looked aghast, as if she couldn't believe her ears. There was a long silence before she whispered, 'You can't be serious.'

'I wish I wasn't,' said Jamieson. 'But if we can't find the source of the infection after all the tests that have been done I have to consider the possibility of deliberate sabotage.'

'But how?' asked Sue, her mind rebelling against the notion. 'Why?'

'At the moment I'm considering the possibility that the

instruments used in surgery have been deliberately interfered with.'

'But that's absolutely awful!' exclaimed Sue. 'Surely there has
to be another explanation? Who in their right mind would do a
thing like that?

'No one in their right mind,' said Jamieson, putting emphasis
on the word 'right'.

'You mean someone mentally deranged? On the staff?' Sue
asked, her eyes wide with horror.

'Frankly I don't know what I mean right now but certain
things need explaining.'

'Like what?'

'Like why does a consultant surgeon take it upon himself
to collect surgical instruments from the sterilising department
and keep them in his office overnight and why does the same
consultant surgeon lie about going to choir practices in the
evenings when he is doing no such thing?'

'You have been busy,' said Sue. 'I take it we are talking
about Mr Thelwell?'

Jamieson nodded.

'Have you tackled him?'

'About the instruments, yes.'

'And?'

'He said he took them to prevent them being interfered
with.'

'Then he thinks the same as you?'

'Or he is doing the interfering,' said Jamieson.

'A surgeon?' exclaimed Sue. 'You think that Mr Thelwell is
infecting his own patients?'

'I said that it's a possibility I'm considering,' replied Jamieson.
'I have to and, apart from anything else, the man clearly has a
problem. He's quite paranoid.'

'But that doesn't necessarily mean that he's psychotic,'
retorted Sue.

'No,' agreed Jamieson. 'But he is a liar. He's been telling
his family that he has been going to choir practices when
he's not.'

'So, he's having an affair,' said Sue. 'I don't see what the missed choir practices have to do with the deaths in the hospital.'

'They haven't,' agreed Jamieson. 'It was the deaths outside the hospital I was thinking about.'

Sue looked at Jamieson for a moment as if he had gone mad. She searched for words but remained speechless for a long moment until finally she managed to protest. 'You can't mean it! You are talking about the murders in the city?'

'He's a surgeon. The police told me that the murders are ripper-type, bits of his victims are cut away.'

'People always consider the possibility of a doctor being involved in ripper-style murders,' said Sue. 'I've never known it to turn out that way.'

'True,' agreed Jamieson, 'but it's something to bear in mind. Apart from that, Thelwell is paranoid and he lies about where he's going in the evenings. He interferes in the supply of sterile instruments to the theatre and the body of the last victim was found in the incinerator of this hospital. Food for thought?'

'Is he still operating?' asked Sue.

'No, I had to suspend him when Richardson found the infecting organism in his swab, but when he gets his final clearance from the Public Health lab there's nothing I can do to stop him.

'If you're really serious about this, can't you have a word with the police?' asked Sue.

'I pointed them in Thelwell's direction over John Richardson's death,' said Jamieson. 'I don't want it to seem as if I'm conducting a personal vendetta against the man. Apart from that, I need something more than suspicions before I go to the police about a consultant surgeon and pillar of the community,' said Richardson.

'But what about these choir practices he says he goes to?' said Sue. 'Where does he really go?'

Jamieson nodded and said, 'That's something I intend to find out very soon.'

'You mean you're going to follow him?' asked an astonished Sue.

'Exactly that. He doesn't know that I know about the choir practice lies. That gives me an edge.'

'You don't think you're taking this detective bit a little far?' said Sue. 'Maybe you should leave this sort of thing to the professionals?'

Jamieson nodded and said, 'I know what you mean, but it's a simple enough thing to follow Thelwell just once to see where he really goes. If I find out anything, I promise I'll hand the whole business over to the police.'

Sue smiled. 'All right,' she said. 'Just once.'

At Hugh Crichton's suggestion, Jamieson and Sue moved their things to a second-floor room in the residency, rather than have Sue move into a hotel room. It was an arrangement they were both delighted with. Clive Evans gave them a hand with their luggage. 'No more heavy lifting for you,' Jamieson said to Sue.

'It's a bit early for that,' smiled Sue.

When they had moved everything upstairs and Evans had left them, Jamieson noticed that Sue had become much more subdued. 'What's up?' he asked.

Sue looked at him and said, 'I suddenly feel ridiculous.'

'Why?'

'It seemed the right thing to do to come here to be with you, but now that I am here I feel like a silly schoolgirl. I should have stayed in Kent.'

'No you shouldn't,' said Jamieson softly. 'It's lovely having you near me. We belong together. But it's not going to be much fun for you. I've got to get to the bottom of this business.'

'Understood,' said Sue.

'Let's go out to dinner,' said Jamieson, patting Sue's stomach gently. 'All three of us.'

They were half way through dinner when Sue suddenly laid down her knife and fork and looked at Jamieson, wide eyed.

'What's wrong?' asked Jamieson.

'The women weren't infected during their operations at all,' said Sue.

'I beg your pardon,' said Jamieson, taken aback at the statement.

'The infected women in the ward,' said Sue. 'They didn't pick up the infection during surgery at all.'

'Go on,' said Jamieson, putting down his knife and fork.

'The infection was caused by something in the post-op ward.'

'It's been cleaned and disinfected,' said Jamieson.

'I didn't mean that.'

'Then what?'

'Their dressings,' said Sue.

'Their dressings?'

'The chances are that the women all had their dressings changed during the same ward round. That's when the infection could have set in. That's why they all developed the illness together. The bug was in the *dressings*.'

'Contaminated dressings?' said Jamieson quietly. 'God, you could be right.' He left the table to ring the hospital from the public phone at the side of the bar. He watched Sue play idly with her cutlery while he waited for the hospital to answer. It seemed to take an age.

'Kerr Memorial,' said the voice.

'Surgical gynaecology,' said Jamieson.

'They're engaged at the moment. Will you hold, caller?'

Jamieson said that he would through gritted teeth. He shrugged as Sue caught his eye.

'Surgical, Sister speaking.'

'This is Dr Jamieson, Sister. I need some information about the application of surgical dressings in the ward.'

'What exactly do you want to know?' asked the nurse.

'Tell me everything. I want to know your routine for changing them. I also want to know when you do it and the order in which they're done. I need to know who does them and how often the routine changes. Everything.'

'Let me see now,' said Sister Roache. 'New patients are

treated on an individual basis, so for them, it could be any time. After a couple of days on the ward patients would have their dressings changed after morning ward rounds, say some time from ten thirty onwards. It would be done consecutively.'

'All of them?'

'Yes.'

'But you have seventeen patients in the ward at present if I remember rightly?' said Jamieson.

'Seventeen, yes.'

Jamieson cursed under his breath. If all of the women had had their dressings changed consecutively why had only eight developed wound infections?

'Size!' whispered Sue who had come across to eavesdrop on the conversation. 'Ask about the size of the dressings!'

'What size of dressings were used in the changes, Sister?' Jamieson waited while she went to check.

There was excitement in Sister Roache's voice when she came back to the phone. 'I think you may have your common factor, Doctor,' she said. 'The eight infected women were given 200mm dressings, the others had various other sizes.'

'Were the 200mm dressings all from the same pack?' asked Jamieson with baited breath.

'It would appear so,' replied the nurse.

'Are there any left from that pack?' asked Jamieson.

'I'd have to check.'

'If there are put them to one side. Don't let anyone near them. I have to get them to the lab.'

'Very good.'

Jamieson put down the phone. 'You were right,' he said to Sue. 'You're a genius. It was the dressings. An unsterile pack of dressings'

'But how did they get to be unsterile?' replied Sue.

Jamieson shook his head as a black cloud swirled around inside his head.

When they got back to the residency, Jamieson immediately went up to the gynaecology department and spoke to the ward sister. She handed him a dressing pack with only two remaining in it. Jamieson was careful not to touch either of them.

'Staff Nurse Telfer says that this was the pack she used,' said the sister. 'She and Student Nurse Bailey applied them.'

Jamieson said that he would take them to the lab and asked about the condition of the infected women.

'Not good. I've never known such a virulent outbreak of wound infection before.'

Jamieson didn't tell her that this was an entirely new infection but he thought about it on the way over to the microbiology department. That two completely different organisms had caused such havoc in the same department only reinforced his growing suspicion that the contamination was not due to a quirk of fate. Something much more sinister was behind it.

Jamieson saw a light on in the microbiology lab and found Moira Lippman there. 'I didn't know you were on call tonight. This is a bit of luck,' said Jamieson.

'What can I do for you?' asked Moira.

Jamieson thought the girl sounded a bit distant but let it pass. He asked her about setting up some microbiological tests on the dressings.

'Of course,' said Moira Lippman. 'Just leave them there. I'll do them in a moment.'

The girl turned back to the bench to continue with the specimen she was dealing with and Jamieson felt compelled to ask, 'Is something wrong?'

Moira Lippman put down the tubes she had been holding and laid her hands flat on the bench in front of her. 'My sister-in-law is one of the infected women,' she said quietly.

'I'm sorry. I didn't realise,' said Jamieson softly. 'How is she?'

'Very ill. They all are.' Moira Lippman swung round in her chair and looked directly at Jamieson. 'There's something crazy going on here,' she said.

'Go on,' said Jamieson.

'It's a *Staphylococcus* infection this time, yet it's behaving in exactly the same way as the *Pseudomonas*. None of the usual antibiotics are having any effect at all. We are having to run a race to find alternative drug combinations. Two highly drug-resistant infections in a row. How can that be?'

'Infections that are resistant to treatment are not unknown,' said Jamieson.

'But two in succession? In the same department? There's something not right about this whole affair.'

'If it's any comfort, I share your disquiet,' said Jamieson. 'I can't say more than that at the moment.'

Moira nodded and shook her head slightly. She returned to what she was doing.

Jamieson left the lab to return to the residency. As he crossed the courtyard he saw two porters emerge from the side door of gynaecology. They were wheeling a covered trolley in the direction of the mortuary.

'Can't you sleep?' whispered Sue.

'I'm sorry. Did I wake you?' replied Jamieson in the dark.

'It's all right. What's on your mind?'

'Something Moira Lippman said when I spoke to her earlier. She said that there was something "not right", to use her expression, about there being two such virulent infections occurring in the same department.'

'You mean the possibility of deliberate contamination has occurred to her too?' asked Sue.

'No, I don't think she was going that far,' said Jamieson. 'Moira was talking purely about the bacteria involved.'

'I don't see what you're getting at,' said Sue.

'How would you go about contaminating surgical instruments if you had to?' asked Jamieson.

'What a question! I suppose I'd break the sterility seal and expose them to the atmosphere for a while. Maybe drop them on the floor. Spit on them? I don't know really. Something like that.'

'And then they would be unsterile?'

'Yes, of course. Wouldn't they?'

'Indeed they would, but just think for a moment. Take it a

step further. What sort of organisms would they be liable to attract?'

'Oh, I think I see what you mean,' said Sue. 'The chances of picking up something really nasty are pretty remote?'

'Exactly. I'm not saying its impossible, but it's not all that likely. If it were, all of us would be sick all of the time. Nasty pathogens are few and far between, thank God.'

'So doing it twice and on two separate occasions would be even more unlikely.'

'Yes,' said Jamieson. 'I think that there's more to it than just breaking the sterile seal on the packs.'

'If the criminal were a carrier of a virulent organism it would be possible for him to contaminate the instruments or dressings from his own secretions,' said Sue.

Jamieson nodded but said, 'Again, the chances of him carrying two deadly organisms are so remote as to be ridiculous. And how would he separate them?'

'I see the problem,' agreed Sue. 'So how did he do it, assuming that there is a "he"? Any ideas?'

'None,' admitted Jamieson.

'You said that you thought Dr Richardson had some notion about the first organism?' said Sue.

'But he never told me what it was,' said Jamieson.

'Maybe he told someone else?'

'Like who?'

'His wife maybe?'

Jamieson turned and kissed Sue on the cheek. 'Now I know why I love you,' he whispered. 'You're totally brilliant.'

Jamieson was surprised to find Moira Lippman in the lab again when he arrived at eight. 'You're back early!' he said.

'I didn't go home. It wasn't worthwhile. There was so much to do last night.'

'You must be exhausted,' said Jamieson.

'I'm okay. I couldn't have slept anyway knowing what Jenny is going through.'

'How is your sister-in-law this morning?' asked Jamieson.

'She's very weak and the new drugs are not having much effect.'

'I'm sorry,' said Jamieson. 'Have you looked at the cultures yet?'

'Dr Evans was right. It's a *Staphylococcus*. It's immune to all the penicillins, even the pen'ase resistant versions. Erythromycin is out as well. But I have come up with something.'

'Really? What?'

'Some months ago the hospital took part in a clinical trial of a new antibiotic from Steadman Pharmaceuticals; it was called Loromycin. I carried out the lab work for the trial and I still had some of the drug sitting in the fridge. I tried it out on the *Staphylococcus* and it worked. The medics could use it if they can get some more from the company.'

'Well done,' said Jamieson. 'Have you told them?'

'I called the ward ten minutes ago. They still have a few dozen injection vials left over from the trial. Mr Morton has started the women on them while Mr Crichton gets in touch with Steadman for further supplies.'

'What a bit of luck,' said Jamieson. 'I only hope it's not too late.'

Moira nodded.

'Did you recover the organism from the dressings?'

Moira Lippman nodded. 'You were right about that. The dressings were heavily contaminated with the *Staphylococcus*. There's no doubt that they were to blame for the outbreak this time.'

Jamieson admitted that the idea had been his wife's.

'She's a doctor, too?' asked Moira.

'A nurse.'

'Smart lady,' said Moira.

'She's here in the hospital,' said Jamieson. 'She arrived yesterday.'

'Not so smart,' said Moira.

Jamieson checked his watch and said that he was going over to the sterilising department to check on the sterilisation record of the dressings. He met Clive Evans coming into the lab as he was going out and told him that he had been right about the infecting organism. Evans nodded and said that the microscope slides had been clear. Jamieson told him that Moira Lippman had been on duty all night and obviously needed some rest.

'I'll send her home,' said Evans.

'Did you know her sister-in-law is one of the infected women?' asked Jamieson.

'No, I didn't,' confessed Evans.

'She's very ill,' added Jamieson. He told Evans about Moira's success in coming up with an effective antibiotic. 'With a bit of luck, we can beat this damned thing after all,' he said.

'We could do with a bit of luck,' said Evans.

'We deserve it,' said Jamieson. Once again Jamieson felt the humidity in the air engulf him like an all-embracing cloud as he walked through the swing doors to the central sterile supply department. It reminded him momentarily of visits to the hairdresser when he was young. Whatever the weather outside, it was always warm and moist inside the little shop in the town. To get to the back shop where the men and boys were dealt with, he had to pass a row of curtain-screened cubicles. Gaps in the curtains had afforded him glimpses of women reclining in complicated chairs while their hair was rinsed in white enamel basins. Others had metal umbrellas over their heads.

Charge Nurse Blaney was in the sterilising hall talking to one of the attendants. He stopped when he saw Jamieson approach and waited for him to draw near. He didn't smile.

'I need some more information,' said Jamieson.

Blaney did not say anything. He just nodded and waited for Jamieson to continue.

'A pack of unsterile dressings reached the post-op ward in gynaecology. Ten 200mm dressings. Here is the reference number.' He handed Blaney a note of the number.

'That's impossible,' said Blaney, shaking his head.

'It happened,' said Jamieson. 'I want to see the recorder chart from the steriliser run.'

Blaney shrugged his shoulders and muttered, 'It won't do

171

you any good.' He went off to his office to return a few moments later with a circular chart in his hand. 'Perfect,' he said. 'See for yourself.'

Jamieson traced the line on the chart and saw that Blaney was right. The steriliser run appeared to have been perfectly normal in every way. 'So it didn't happen here,' he said with a sigh of frustration.

'I told you it was impossible,' said Blaney.

'How are the dressings delivered to the wards?' asked Jamieson.

'A porter takes them up.'

'Always?'

'What do you mean?' asked Blaney.

Jamieson caught the aggression in his voice and knew that his allusion to Thelwell making his own collection had rankled the charge nurse. 'It's a simple enough question.'

The edge to Jamieson's voice put an end to Blaney's own aggression. 'Yes, always,' he said.

'Would it be possible to determine exactly what happened to that dressing pack when it came out of the steriliser?' asked Jamieson.

'Up to a point,' said Blaney.

'Let's do it,' said Jamieson quietly, fixing Blaney with a look that suggested any obstruction on his part might not be such a good idea.

Blaney led the way to his office and started leafing through a pile of papers. He pulled out a yellow sheet of paper and matched it against the chart he still held in his hand and said, 'This is the commissioning form that went with that particular steriliser run. There are three signatures on it. John Hargreaves, because he was the attendant who loaded the dressing packs into the autoclave and who started the run,' Dr Evans, because this was one of the monitored safety check runs; and mine, because I checked the chart afterwards and passed the load fit for distribution to the wards.'

'Then what?' said Jamieson.

Blaney referred to the form again and said, 'The load was

held in the clean store until the following Friday, when it was signed out and taken to gynaecology.'

'By whom?'

'One of the general porters. I don't know who, but the dressings were signed for by Staff Nurse Kelly on arrival in the ward.'

'On the same day?' asked Jamieson.

'Yes.'

So there had been no delay between the dressings leaving the sterilising department their reaching their destination, thought Jamieson. If they had been interfered with, it must have been in the three-day period before they were used when they had been stored on the ward, or alternatively at some time in the two days they had lain in the clean store. The latter was something he had not considered before. Supposing the instruments and dressings had been contaminated before they had even left the sterilising department? The thought chilled him. He looked at Blaney's eyes and saw nothing but sullenness.

'Who looks after the clean stores?' asked Jamieson.

'I do,' said Blaney.

'I'd like to see them.'

Blaney shrugged noncommittally and led Jamieson to a long narrow room filled with free-standing metal racks bearing instrument and dressing packs. There were no windows in the room and above them a fluorescent light tube buzzed intermittently. Blaney stood mutely in the doorway while Jamieson walked up and down the narrow gangways. Jamieson had not expected to find anything amiss. He had merely wanted to observe Blaney's reaction to his being in the store. He was alert for any sign of nervousness, but Blaney remained inscrutable throughout.

'Will that be all?' Blaney asked when Jamieson had finished his inspection.

'For the moment.'

Jamieson obtained Claire Richardson's telephone number from Hugh Crichton and called her just after half past eleven. He said that he would like to have a chat with her if at all possible.

'What about?'

'About your husband.'

There was a short pause, then she said with more than a trace of bitterness in her voice and a slight slurring, 'Now there's a novelty. I got the impression that everyone in that damned place was pretending that John never existed. Apart from Clive Evans and Moira Lippman, no one even turned up at his funeral. Bunch of bastards. John gave twenty years to that damned slum.'

'I'm sorry,' said Jamieson and meant it. He had liked John Richardson.

'What do you want to talk about?'

'I'd rather tell you personally.'

'What the hell,' said Claire Richardson. 'When did you have in mind?'

'Would lunch be out of the question?' asked Jamieson tentatively. To his surprise, he heard her laugh. She said, 'It's quite a long time since anyone asked me to lunch. I accept.'

They arranged to meet at a restaurant in town at one o'clock.

Jamieson had been waiting for only five minutes when Claire Richardson arrived. They shook hands and, despite her smile, he noticed the air of sadness about her. She did not wear her grief like a badge, but her eyes held a remoteness and detachment which told Jamieson that she had not yet come to terms with her loss. There was, however, a basic intelligence and humour about the woman that was evident during the course of the meal and Jamieson decided that he liked her a lot. He guessed that she and John Richardson had been very happy together. They would have been good for each other.

Jamieson had feared that conversation might be difficult but this proved far from the case and he enjoyed the meal from start to finish. When the waiter finally brought coffee Claire lit up a cigarette and said through a puff of smoke, 'Now, what was it you wanted to know?'

'Did John speak to you much about his work?' asked Jamieson.

'He told me everything.'

'Then you know all about the infection problem in gynaecology at Kerr Memorial?'

Claire Richardson threw back her head and gave a humourless laugh. 'Know about it!' she exclaimed. 'I lived through every hellish moment of it with John. The agonies he went through over not tracing the source of infection, his elation when he found Thelwell was carrying the bug and then . . .'

'Then what, Mrs Richardson?' asked Jamieson, leaning forward slightly as a sudden cloak of sadness came over Claire Richardson and she stopped talking.

'I don't know. John began to have doubts. He seemed very troubled and clammed up totally, which was so unlike him. We always shared everything. He locked himself away in his study and then . . . well, you know the rest.'

'He took his own life,' said Jamieson softly.

Claire Richardson's eyes blazed. 'Oh no he didn't!' she hissed. 'Nothing on earth will ever make me believe that.'

'Then what?'

'He was murdered.'

Jamieson was taken aback at the matter of fact way that Claire Richardson had made the assertion. She seemed absolutely certain. 'But why?' he asked quietly.

'I don't know why, damn it!' she replied, delving into her handbag to find a handkerchief and quickly dabbing at her eyes. 'Why do you want to know all this?'

Jamieson pondered for a moment over how much he should tell her, then he said, 'I think your husband found out something about the infection. I think he knew something very important, something he never got round to telling anyone. I feel sure he was going to tell me on the night he died, but I got there too late.'

New life came to Claire Richardson's eyes. 'A motive for

John's murder? Someone killed him to stop him telling you something?' she said.

'Maybe,' agreed Jamieson.

'If you can prove that, I will be forever in your debt,' she said.

'Then I will need your help. I have to find out what it was that your husband found out.'

'But I don't know,' she said raising her hands in a gesture of hopelessness.

'Think! Anything he said at the time when he became withdrawn might be important. Something he wrote down, perhaps? You said he spent a long time in his study. Maybe he left papers lying around?'

'I don't think so,' she said thoughtfully. 'But there was one thing . . .'

'Yes?'

'The night it all started he was pacing up and down in the study. I heard him repeat several times, "No blisters. There were no blisters."'

Jamieson looked blank and Claire Richardson shrugged. She said, 'I know. It doesn't make much sense, but that's what he said.'

'No blisters? No blisters on what? On whom?'

Claire shook her head.

'Think about it,' said Jamieson. 'And have a think about anything else John might have said. If you do come up with anything, give me a call.'

'I will,' said Claire. They shook hands and parted.

Jamieson had started to tell Sue about his meeting with Claire Richardson when the phone rang. It was Clive Evans.

'A second woman has died of the *Staphylococcus* infection, but the others are beginning to respond to Loromycin treatment,' he reported.

'Good,' said Jamieson. 'How's Moira Lippman's sister-in-law?'

'She was the second woman, I'm afraid.'

176

'Damnation.'

'I thought you should know as soon as possible and I couldn't find you in the hospital.'

'I was having lunch with Claire Richardson.'

'Really. How is she?'

'Bearing up is the phrase, I think.'

'I didn't know that you knew her,' said Evans.

'I didn't, but I wanted to talk to her about her husband. I think John Richardson knew something about the infections that he didn't tell anyone. I hoped he might have mentioned something to his wife.'

'And had he?'

'No.'

'Pity. What sort of thing did you have in mind?' asked Evans.

'It's a bit difficult to say, but when I had the *Pseudomonas* analysed at Sci-Med and they told me that it was resistant to all these drugs in its own right, I was very surprised. John Richardson wasn't. It was almost as if that was the result he expected.'

'Strange,' said Evans.

'I suppose he never said anything to you about it?'

'Afraid not.'

Jamieson put down the phone and told Sue about the second death in gnaecology.

'Surely the unit will have to close now?' said Sue.

Jamieson started to pace up and down. He said, 'In theory there is no need. There has been an outbreak of *Staphylococcus* infection. The cause has been identified. Two women have died but we now have the infection under control and there is every chance that the others will get better under Loromycin treatment. Tragic, but one of those things that happens from time to time.'

'But more often in the Kerr Memorial than in any other hospital,' said Sue.

Jamieson nodded silently.

'What can you do about it?' asked Sue quietly.

'Nothing. All I have to go on is the suspicion that some head case is deliberately contaminating dressings and instruments. It's not the sort of thing you start saying without any kind of evidence to back it up.'

'On the other hand, women have been dying,' said Sue. 'Three the first time and now another two.'

'You didn't have to point that out,' said Jamieson.

'I'm sorry,' said Sue. 'I didn't mean to . . .'

'No, I'm the one who is sorry,' said Jamieson, coming over to her and putting his arms round her. 'This place is getting to me. I loathe it. I hate every stone of it, every evil inch.'

'But you're not going to give up. You're going to see it through and then we'll go home to our lovely cottage in Kent and we'll go back to being the people we were.'

'What a lovely thought,' murmured Jamieson, his cheek against Sue's hair.

The telephone rang and startled both of them. It was Claire Richardson. 'You did say I should phone you if I thought of anything that might be useful?'

'Of course.'

'I've been having another look through the things in John's study and I've come across something that John never mentioned at all to me.'

'Really?'

'It's a card with the name of a hospital and a telephone number.'

'A hospital?' Jamieson repeated, feeling deflated.

'Yes. Apparently John was in contact with this hospital the day before he died. I've never heard of it and he certainly didn't say anything about it to me. Do you think it might have some relevance?'

'At this point we can't afford to dismiss anything, Mrs Richardson.'

'Call me Claire.'

'Very well, Claire. Which hospital was it?'

'Costello Court Hospital. It's in a place called Willow Norton in Norfolk. Do you want the phone number?'

Jamieson wrote it down. 'I'll check it out. Many thanks.'

'You will let me know if it's anything important?'

'Of course.'

'Sounds like an old folks' home,' Sue said as Jamieson immediately started to dial the number. She waited patiently while Jamieson made enquiries. 'Well?' she asked as she saw him put down the phone and walk slowly over to the window.

'It's not a home for the old,' said Jamieson. 'It's a mental hospital.'

'Costello Court, a mental hospital?' Sue looked puzzled.

'They don't have a laboratory service there, so Richardson's call couldn't have been anything to do with the job.'

'So why would he be calling a mental hospital?'

'Maybe he had a friend or colleague who worked there?'

'If that was true his wife would have known about it. They told each other everything.'

Jamieson thought for a moment, then said, 'Everyone said the strain was getting to him. Maybe he was going to have himself admitted for a rest before he had a real breakdown.'

'And then decided to kill himself instead?' Sue sounded cynical.

Jamieson acknowledged the incongruity. 'Claire Richardson doesn't believe that her husband did kill himself,' he said.

'It would be difficult for her to do that under any circumstances,' said Sue. 'She was his wife. Suicide is always seen as a betrayal by the people who love you most.'

'I wonder what she would think about the idea of her husband having himself admitted as a patient at Costello Court?'

'Ask her,' said Sue.

'Tomorrow,' said Jamieson.

11

'A psychiatric hospital!' exclaimed Claire Richardson when Jamieson told her on the telephone. 'Why on earth would John contact a psychiatric hospital?'

'That's what we have to find out,' said Jamieson. 'You are sure that your husband never mentioned it, even in passing?'

'Positive.'

'Claire, your husband was under a lot of strain. It did occur to me that he might have considered admitting himself to such a hospital, just for a bit of a rest?' Jamieson could feel the tension that he had created as he waited for Claire Richardson to reply. He sensed that she wanted to shout down the idea but had stopped herself, probably admitting silently that her husband had been under severe stress. In the end, she settled for, 'Without telling me? Never.'

'Then there must have been another reason for his call,' said Richardson diplomatically. Perhaps nothing to do with this affair at all.'

'There must have been.'

Jamieson promised to keep her informed of any new developments and put the phone down. He let out a long sigh and said to Sue, 'Not the brightest thing to have suggested to Claire Richardson.'

'She's very protective of her husband. You can't expect her to be anything else.'

'I suppose not, but maybe she's right. Maybe Richardson did have another reason for contacting Costello Court.'

'Like what?'

Jamieson thought for a moment before saying, 'Maybe he remembered a similar outbreak of infection at another hospital in the past and rang up to compare notes?'

'So you think this mental hospital has a gynaecology unit?' asked Sue.

There had been no trace of sarcasm in Sue's voice, but Jamieson saw the slight smile playing at the corner of her mouth when he looked at her. 'You spotted the flaw in the argument?' he smiled. He tapped his pen against his teeth and then had an idea. 'Maybe Richardson was checking up on a patient?' There was a moment's silence before he looked at Sue and added, 'Or someone who had been a patient!'

Sue saw exactly what Jamieson was getting at. 'Like Thelwell!' she exclaimed.

'Exactly!' replied Jamieson excitedly and looking for the piece of paper with the phone number on it. 'If Thelwell has a history of mental instability, then it's something we should know about.'

'Can you just call and ask the hospital?' asked Sue doubtfully.

'No, I'm not even going to try,' said Jamieson. 'They wouldn't tell me. I'm going to call Macmillan at Sci-Med and ask him to find out for me.'

Macmillan was not available but Miss Roberts took the message and assured him that the information would be relayed to him as soon as they had obtained it.

'Now what?' asked Sue.

'I have to go out this evening,' said Jamieson.

'Where to?'

'It's Thelwell's choir practice night.'

It started to rain as Jamieson sat in his car at the end of the street where Thelwell lived. Every thirty seconds or so he had to activate the windscreen wipers. He checked his watch for the umpteenth time and saw that it was eleven minutes past seven. At fourteen minutes past, Thelwell, shoulders hunched inside a dark raincoat with the collar up, stepped out on to the pavement and closed the garden gate behind him. A few moments later the dark green Volvo moved off towards town.

At first Jamieson thought that Thelwell really did intend going to a choir practice when he found the car in front following a route that would take him to St Serf's. He was relieved when the Volvo passed straight by and continued on towards the city. There was an anxious moment for Jamieson when Thelwell went through an amber light while he himself, travelling some one hundred metres behind, had to stop and wait for the lights to change. He caught up, however, at the next junction. Thelwell was at the head of the queue with a Rover Metro and a Ford Escort behind him. The Escort driver stalled as the lights changed and Jamieson cursed under his breath as he saw Thelwell start to pull well ahead. They were moving into busy traffic. It would be all too easy to lose him in this part of town. The Escort finally moved off, engine over-revving as its driver covered his embarrassment.

A service bus started to move out from the kerb as Jamieson tried to make up lost ground. Unwilling to concede right of way, he held his line and slapped his hand on the horn, praying that the bus driver would back down. He did but not until he had given Jamieson a heart-stopping moment. He snatched a quick glance in the rear view mirror and saw the bus driver make a rude gesture. 'You too,' he muttered, still desperately trying to see round the traffic in front and fearing that he might have lost Thelwell.

The road ahead straightened out and Jamieson's heart sank as he failed to see the Volvo anywhere up ahead. He was rapidly approaching a 'Y' junction and he had no idea which arm to take. If he chose right it would take him round the back of the station and on towards the main shopping centre. If he forked left it would take him down through the red light district . . . The decision was made. He veered left and hoped for a bit of luck. He got it as he cleared a roundabout and momentarily glimpsed an uninterrupted view of the road ahead, for he was in time to see a green Volvo turn left at the foot of the hill. It might not be Thelwell, he cautioned himself, but on the other hand, it just might.

Jamieson slowed and turned left where he thought the Volvo had excited the main road. He could not be sure because, in this area, there was an opening every twenty-five metres or so, leading off into the warren of run-down tenement buildings that lay behind the main thoroughfare. There was no sign of Thelwell's car as he moved slowly along a narrow lane, looking to both sides and checking in the mirror to see that he wasn't holding up traffic behind him. There were a number of bars and restaurants in the lane and many had advertising boards out on the pavement. People were constantly stepping off the pavement to walk round them.

A drunk staggered out from a Greek restaurant, his exit being assisted by a swarthy man wearing a dinner jacket who emerged behind him gesturing angrily. Jamieson had to brake to avoid the drunk who stumbled out in front of him, but he was travelling so slowly that there was no danger of hitting the man. The drunk regarded him with expressionless eyes and then veered to return to the gutter.

Two whores looked at Jamieson's car as he slowed to a halt at an intersection. One smiled, the other put her hand on her hip. They were standing together at the corner of the street. Jamieson assumed that working in pairs was their safety measure. He wondered how effective that would be, but recognised that business would probably go on as usual whatever the risk. Paid holidays and sick leave were unknown to the oldest profession.

Jamieson turned the corner and looked along both sides of the street. There was still no sign of Thelwell's Volvo. He pulled in to the kerb and paused with the engine still running while he thought what to do next. Live jazz music was coming from a bar some fifty metres down the street. He found the tune familiar but the title eluded him. He ran through a few possibilities in his head before remembering that it was Cherokee.

Jamieson was vaguely aware that his action in stopping had been misinterpreted by a black girl wearing a tight white sweater under an open leather jacket and a black woollen mini skirt. She started to cross the road towards him. Through the open window on the driver's side he could hear her thick thighs rubbing together. He smiled thinly and held up his open palm to signify that she was not the object of his desire and the girl retreated with a sullen shrug. Jamieson felt embarrassed by the incident. He found himself wanting to apologise. He was about to move off again when the passenger door of his car was suddenly pulled open and a male voice said languidly, 'Run out of petrol have we, sir?'

The sneer in the voice immediately put Jamieson's back up as had the man's action in opening the car door. Apart from anything else, it had startled him. 'No, we haven't,' he replied, maintaining the plural for the benefit of the man he knew was about to announce himself as a police officer.

The anticipated warrant card was flipped open and the sneering voice continued, 'Then just what are we up to, sir, might I ask?'

Jamieson read the relevant credentials from the card. The man was a detective constable. 'We are working,' said Jamieson, presenting his own ID. '*We* are working for the Sci-Med Monitor and *we* could get very annoyed if some half-arsed detective constable were to fuck up *our* investigation. *We* would like to be alone.'

'Sorry, sir,' replied the constable, his manner changing immediately. 'I thought . . .'

'I know what you thought,' said Jamieson. 'I'm going to be in the area for a while.'

'Very good, sir.'

'Have you seen a green Volvo estate around here?' asked Jamieson.

'Lots,' replied the policeman.

'I wouldn't have thought there would be too many down here,' said Jamieson.

'You'd be surprised,' said the constable. 'Apart from the yuppie evening visitors who come down here to eat and savour the "danger", there are lots of well-heeled folk who actually live down here. It's become trendy to return to the heart of the city ever since Prince Charles said so. The Volvo mob have been moving in in a big way. They live in converted warehouses and mews garages. They need the estate car to take the labradors for a shit up in the park. I sometimes think that the whores round here will soon have daylight running lights.'

Jamieson did not smile. He was thinking about what the man had said. He was considering the possibility that Thelwell might actually have his own flat in the area. That would have distinct advantages for a killer. It would be much more convenient than killing from home. It would be somewhere he could change his clothes, wash, brush up after the event. He wouldn't have to go home with blood-stained clothes and, from what he had heard about the victims, there had been a lot of blood around. It might even make sense on a psychiatric level. Thelwell might be suffering from a split personality. The flat might be a base for his other self, Mr Hyde's place.

Jamieson continued to wind his way through the back streets, finally drawing to a halt when he found a parking place that was being vacated by a white Golf GTi that took off as if it had been entered for Le Mans. He backed into the space and switched off the engine. He rested his arms on the steering wheel and gazed out through the windscreen as he contemplated failure. He smiled wryly as he remembered telling Sue how simple it would be to follow Thelwell. He had been wrong. He had lost him.

The prospect of giving up and returning to the hospital was uppermost in his mind when a green Volvo suddenly crossed at the junction some fifty metres away. It happened so quickly that he did not get a look at the driver. Knowing that it would take a bit of manoeuvring to get his own car out of the small parking space, he jumped out and ran down to the junction to see where the Volvo was heading. It turned left half way down the street. Jamieson debated on going back for his car, but then gambled on the Volvo being near its final destination. He ran down to the intersection where he had last seen it and sneaked a look round the corner. He saw a broad, dark cul-de-sac, the end of which comprised a tall picket fence which fronted a builder's yard. The green Volvo was parked to the left of the gate which carried a notice saying that it was in use twenty-four hours. The car was empty.

The question now was, where had Thelwell gone? Jamieson looked up at the windows on both sides of the street. Thelwell had not had time to walk more than half way back along the lane, he reckoned. That narrowed the choice down to one of four doorways leading to the tenement flats above. As Jamieson considered, he heard the sound of conversation coming up behind him. He looked round. A soldier, obviously very drunk, was being supported by a girl half his size, who was doing her best to keep him upright. They turned into the lane. Jamieson, who had moved back into the shelter of a shop doorway, watched their unsteady progress until they had passed. He was about to move out again when the soldier fell to the ground.

'Oh, my God,' exclaimed his companion in a broad local accent. 'Come on! Wake up! You can't sleep here!' Her voice changed to cajoling when this didn't work. 'Come on, my lovely. Up on your feet! We are going to have a party, remember?'

The soldier gave a drunken giggle, but made no attempt to get up. 'Have a party,' he repeated drunkenly. Then in a sing-song voice he started to chant, 'We're going to have a party . . . we're going to have . . .'

The whore finally lost her temper after failing to get him to his feet for the third time. 'If you think I've carried you all this way to have you flake out on me you've got another think coming, sonny Jim!' she ranted.

Jamieson could see that she was searching through the soldier's pockets. He watched her remove his wallet. 'Put it back!' he hissed from the doorway.

The whore was startled and frightened. 'Who's there?' she demanded shakily. 'Where are you?' She got to her feet and looked about her nervously 'Oh, my God!' she exclaimed, as fear of the unknown got the better of her. She flung the wallet at the soldier and took to her heels.

Jamieson moved the soldier to a sitting position on the pavement and put the man's wallet back in his pocket. He decided that that was the best he could do in the circumstances and continued along the lane. He still had no real idea what he was going to say or do when he found Thelwell, but he suspected that he might have plenty of time to think about it. He found another doorway and decided to wait there until Thelwell reappeared.

After half an hour of moving from doorway to doorway to aid his circulation, Jamieson had a stroke of luck. He saw what he felt sure was Thelwell's silhouette against one of the lighted windows above. He walked over to the relevant building and tried the entrance door.

Another piece of luck; it was unlocked. He slipped inside and closed the door quietly behind him, holding his breath as he released the handle with painstaking slowness.

The stupidity of his action was becoming more and more apparent to him as he put his foot on the first step. He might be about to confront a psychopathic killer with little more than the hope that the man would fall at his feet and confess everything. The thought made him tense all his muscles. He had to be prepared for anything that might happen, but as long as Thelwell did not have a gun or a knife, he should not pose too much of a problem. After all, he, Jamieson, had the element of surprise in his favour. The fact that all the lights in the stairway had suddenly just gone out argued against that.

Jamieson stood stock still in the darkness. He was half way up the third flight of steps and the blackness was so complete that he could almost feel it. He desperately wished that he had a match or cigarette lighter with him. There was a smell of dampness in the stair well and the cold was tangible against his face. Suddenly there was a shuffling noise somewhere above him and he drew in his breath sharply. 'Is that you, Thelwell?' he demanded, annoyed that his voice had developed a slight tremor. Silence. There was a sound on the other side of him, another shuffling of feet. 'Stop playing games, Thelwell!' said Jamieson, sounding a lot more courageous than he felt. Silence.

Jamieson took a step back down the stairs, feeling for the step below with the toe of his right foot. He was trying to move as quietly as possible, but his heart was beating so fast and so hard that he felt sure that it must be audible. He kept his back against the wall to ensure that he could not be surprised from behind. He could not be attacked from the front either, he reasoned, for that was where the banister was and on the other side was a thirty-foot drop into the stairwell. He had the feeling that there was more than one of them in the darkness. They were approaching him from above and from below on the stairs. Nerves pressed him to say something aloud again, but he steeled himself to keep quiet and not give away his own position.

'Hsss,' said a voice above him like a sibilant snake.

'Hsss,' answered another voice from below.

They were playing with him, thought Jamieson. The bastards were playing with him! Fear and fury vied within him as he fought to remain calm. His stalkers could not see him any more than he could see them, he reasoned. Slowly he reached out with his foot again for the next step down, but this time it was pulled away from him with a sudden violent tug. He crashed heavily down on to the stone steps with his cheek taking the brunt of his fall. His head filled with stars and the pain made him cry out loud. A fist smashed into his right kidney making him cry out again as he tried to roll himself into a ball for protection. He swung his fist backwards, hoping to make contact with something, but there was no power behind it and in reply a foot crashed into his stomach taking the breath from him.

'Get his arms!' rasped a voice in the blackness.

Jamieson felt his arms being pinned behind him as he was dragged to his feet and more blows thudded into his body. As he felt himself being pushed against the banister, the thought that they might be about to push him over to almost certain death bred new strength in him. He lashed out with the heel of his right foot and caught one of his attackers below the knee cap. The man yelled out and released his grip on Jamieson's arms, so that Jamieson was able to pull back a bit and turn round. He took a swipe at his other attacker but failed to make any contact, whereas something heavy and hard hit him on the side of the head and the strength drained from his limbs.

'Break the bastard's neck!' Jamieson heard one of the voices say as he struggled to remain conscious.

'We're gonna do this right!' said another voice.

'I'll cut his balls off!' said the first voice again.

Jamieson heard the metallic click of a knife being opened in the blackness. Blind panic fuelled him with enough energy to wrench his right arm free again. He swung his fist with all his might and this time it connected, but only with the wall. Another violent blow to his head snuffed out all consciousness before the pain in his hand had even reached his brain.

Jamieson came round with a blinding headache. He felt as if two hydraulic rams were trying to push his eyes out of their sockets and the merest movement of his head exacerbated the pain to such a point that consciousness threatened to leave him again. In the moments when he could think clearly, those when he lay absolutely stock still and kept his breathing to a minimum, he deduced that his hands were tied behind his back and that he was lying on a rough blanket that was none too clean. There was a smell of stale sweat in the still air and a faint, seminal odour about the room. But at least he was alive. Pop music was being played somewhere in the distance and a young girl's exaggerated laughter drifted up from the street below.

The fact that he was still alive was something that Jamieson found surprising. Come to think of it, he couldn't understand any of it. There had been two attackers and neither of them had been Thelwell. He was quite sure of that. So who had assaulted him and why? Psychopaths didn't have accomplices. It didn't make sense.

189

Jamieson heard footsteps on the stairs and felt afraid. He was facing the wall when he heard the door open behind him. The pain in his head prevented him from turning over; he hadn't moved more than a few centimetres since he had regained consciousness. The light clicked on and he focused on faded green wallpaper. Behind him he heard more than one person come into the room.

'He's still out,' said a voice.

'Turn him over,' rasped a second voice.

A hand gripped Jamieson's shoulder roughly and stars exploded in front of his eyes as he was rolled over on to his back. He grimaced and let out a whispered curse in the form of an appeal to the Almighty.

'He's awake,' said the man at the foot of the bed without any emotion. 'He's conscious.'

Jamieson opened his eyes with pained slowness and looked at the speaker. He was a tall, powerful looking man aged about thirty, dressed in an expensive leather jacket and open-necked shirt which looked as if it might be made of silk. But the expensive clothes could not mask the rough features or the scowl that looked as if it might be permanent. The other man was a full head shorter and dressed in a pinstripe suit which seemed a shade too tight for his expanding waistline. His thin lips were disguised by a bushy, black moustache, which also interrupted a scar line that ran down the left side of his face and turned in to finish in the centre of his chin. Both men had a Mediterranean look about them, although they sounded local.

'Sharon! Get in here!' the tall man called back over his shoulder.

A girl in her mid twenties sidled into the room, her skirt riding high on her thighs. Although still young, her face bore the signs of imminent ageing. Excess make-up could not disguise the early sinking of her cheeks and a hollowing of the eyes. By the time she was thirty even more make-up would turn her into an ugly caricature of the prostitute she was at present.

'Seen him before?' asked the tall man.

The girl examined Jamieson as if he were an inanimate object. 'Don't think so,' she said unsurely. 'Hard to say when you have to see so many in one night.'

Jamieson got the impression that her statement was an accusation and that it was directed at the shorter of the two men. Without looking at her the short man rapped, 'Cut the shit and just answer the questions.'

'Yes, Louis,' replied the girl sullenly but obediently. She looked at Jamieson again and said, 'If this is the bastard, I'd like to . . .' Words failed her and she made a lunge at Jamieson, fingernails bared. Jamieson turned his head to one side, but one of the girl's nails had scratched his face before the tall man pulled her off. He could feel a trickle of blood start to run down his cheek.

'What the hell is going on?' demanded Jamieson through his pain and confusion. His voice was a croak.

'Don't play the innocent with us, you bastard!' snarled the big man. He looked to his shorter companion and said, 'I still think we should settle this our way. Cut him and have done with it.'

Once again Jamieson heard the sound of a flick knife being opened and this time he could see it gleaming in the tall man's hand.

'Why are you doing this? What in God's name is going on? Who are you? What do you want with me?'

Jamieson's questions were ignored. The girl said, 'Ronnie's right. Teach the bastard a lesson. Better still, leave him to me and the girls!'

Jamieson looked at the expression of contempt on the girl's face and was completely bemused. 'What the hell have I ever done to you?' he demanded.

'It's what you might have done, you swine!' snarled the girl, once again trying to get to Jamieson but being constrained.

'It's too late for that,' said the small man.

'Will someone please tell me what's going on?' pleaded Jamieson. The sound of police sirens outside suddenly filled the room and the tall man went over to the window and opened it to look out. Jamieson could hear car doors slamming outside in the street and decided to gamble. He shouted at the top of his voice. 'Help! Police! I'm up here! Help!'

To Jamieson's amazement no one in the room made any move to stop him. The three behaved as if nothing had happened. The tall man closed the window and went to open the front door. The girl and the small man waited patiently until policemen started to pour into the room.

'This is the bastard, officer,' announced the small man as someone wearing an open raincoat made his way through the uniforms. 'Here's your killer.'

Jamieson closed his eyes as everything became clear to him at last. The irony of having been taken for the killer himself did not go well with his headache.

'Looks as if you've had a go at him yourself, Louis,' said the policeman looking at Jamieson's face.

'We had to restrain him, Inspector, nothing more. It took me all my time to stop Sharon here removing his assets, so to speak.'

'There's been an awful mistake,' murmured Jamieson.

'If I had a pound for every time I've heard that before,' said the policeman in a bored voice. He was middle aged, balding, with a short moustache and a world-weary look about him that said that he had seen and heard it all before. He spoke as if Jamieson wasn't there. Jamieson was reminded of certain consultants he had known who discussed patients with colleagues at the patients' bedsides in similar fashion. 'What did you say he was doing, Louis?' the policeman asked.

'He was lurking about the lane, trying doorways, looking up at the windows. The boys have been keeping a look-out for any weirdos in the streets and along comes this one.'

'Very public spirited of you, Louis,' said the policeman. 'But then, this sort of thing is bad for business anyway, eh?'

'Don't know what you mean, Inspector,' said Louis with an air of outraged innocence.

'Of course not.'

Jamieson tried to sit up and two uniformed policemen moved in to restrain him. 'I'm not the killer! My jacket. Look in my jacket. I have identification.'

The inspector nodded to one of the constables and then accepted Jamieson's wallet casually as it was handed to him by the uniformed man. He rifled through the contents until he found the Sci-Med card and then paused before letting out his breath slowly and looking up at the ceiling. 'Sweet Jesus,' he said softly.

Louis and the tall man could sense that something was wrong and began to get nervous. 'He is the killer, isn't he?' asked Louis, anxious for reassurance.

'You pillock!' said the inspector quietly. 'You have just assaulted an officer of the Sci-Med Monitor?

'Does that mean he's a copper?' asked the tall man with a vacant look on his face.

'You could say,' replied the inspector.

'Well, how were we to know?' complained Louis.

'You can ask the judge that,' said the policeman.

'Judge? You mean you are going to charge us?'

'Charge you?' exclaimed the inspector. 'When this hits court they'll probably bang you up and melt the key.'

'Shit!' said Louis. 'You try to help the police like a responsible citizen and . . .'

'Louis, you've been pimping since you were old enough to tell your arse from a hole in the wall. Let's cut out the responsible citizen crap.'

'I don't want to press charges,' said Jamieson, grimacing as he sat up to have his hands released by one of the policemen.

'That's very generous of you, sir,' said the inspector, 'But you'd probably be doing the city a service if you were to rid its streets of this garbage for a while.'

'No,' said Jamieson. 'It was my fault. I should have realised that someone might think what these guys obviously thought.'

'If you're sure, sir?'

Jamieson nodded as he rubbed his wrists painfully.

'Thanks,' said Louis as if the word pained him.

'Yeah thanks,' echoed the tall man. 'No hard feelings, eh?'

'If I can repay you in any way . . .' simpered Sharon.

Jamieson smiled in spite of his pain and the inspector snarled, 'I'll pretend I didn't hear that, Sharon, if you get out of my sight within five seconds.'

Sharon disappeared and two policemen helped Jamieson to his feet. 'We'd best get you to a hospital for a check-up,' said the inspector. 'By the way, what were you doing here in this area?'

'I was looking for the owner of the green Volvo estate down there at the end of the lane.'

'Volvo estate?'

'The green one.'

The policeman came back from the window with a blank look on his face.

Jamieson knew what he was about to say. 'No Volvo, huh?'

'No Volvo, sir.'

It was well after midnight before Jamieson got back to the residency and heard Sue gasp when she saw the state of him. Jamieson sat down slowly in the only armchair and asked her to pour him a drink while he told her what had happened.

'So you didn't even find out what Thelwell was up to?' said Sue. There was a suggestion of 'I told you so' in her voice, but she didn't actually say it.

Jamieson agreed with a shake of the head and said, 'More Clouseau than Poirot.'

Sue smiled as she tended to Jamieson's cuts and bruises.

'But I should be able to find out if Thelwell owns or rents one of the apartments in that block and if he does . . .'

'Then what?' asked Sue suspiciously.

'I'll hand the information over to the police.'

'And if he doesn't?'

'I don't know,' confessed Jamieson.

'Sci-Med called when you were out. Thelwell has never been a patient at Costello Court.'

'The perfect end to a perfect day,' sighed Jamieson, massaging his bruised cheek gently with the tips of his fingers.

'Oh, and Moira Lippman phoned.'

'What did she want?' asked Jamieson.

'She said that she was at the lab and that she wanted to talk to you.'

'She shouldn't be at the lab,' exclaimed Jamieson. 'She was there all last night. She'll make herself ill. What time was that?'

'About eleven.'

Jamieson dialled the lab extension but there was no reply. 'She must have gone home. I hope she's all right. I thought Clive Evans was going to persuade her to take some time off. How did she sound?'

'A bit agitated. I asked if there was anything I could do, but she said she had to speak to you about the result of some tests. Mean anything?'

Jamieson shook his head. 'Maybe I should call her at home.'

Sue looked at her watch and said, 'It's late. Can't it wait until morning?'

'No,' said Jamieson flatly. He flicked through the pages of his diary, though he was hampered by the bandage over the knuckles of his right hand, the aftermath of having swung his fist into the wall. 'Damn, I didn't make a note of her home number. Maybe Clive is still awake.'

Jamieson went downstairs and along the corridor to Clive Evans' room. He could see there was a light under the door and knocked gently.

'What on earth!' exclaimed Evans when he saw the bruising on Jamieson's face.

'It's a long story. What I need right now is Moira Lippman's home number.'

'Of course,' said Evans. 'Come in. Is anything wrong?'

Jamieson told Evans about the message and Evans was surprised. 'Test results?' he exclaimed. 'But she wasn't working today. I sent her home this morning. She'd been up all night and what with the death of her sister-in-law she was just about all in.'

'She must have come into the lab this evening. Sue said that she called from there. Who is on call in the lab this evening?'

'I am,' replied Evans. 'I've just come from there. I must have just missed her.'

'She may have discovered something important.'

'I can't think what. She hasn't had to time to set up any tests this evening and get their results.'

'I think I have to speak to her.'

Evans shrugged and conceded. 'We can call her from here,' he said, picking up the phone.

Jamieson glanced at his watch as they waited for an answer. It was twenty past one. In the quiet of Evans' room he heard the phone being answered. Evans asked to speak to Moira.

'Out? At this time?'

A pause.

'Where did you say?'

Jamieson saw Evans frown as he put the phone down. 'She's out,' said Evans. 'Her flatmate said she went out about an hour ago.'

'Did she say where?' asked Jamieson.

'She went to meet Mr Thelwell.'

Jamieson felt as if someone had just switched on a machine inside his head, one of those engine models you find in museums which have been cut away to expose their workings. Wheels turned and gears meshed, shafts moved up and down, but nothing really happened. Everything just moved. He rubbed his forehead and whispered, 'What on earth . . .'

'This is all very puzzling,' said Evans.

12

Jamieson felt the hairs on the back of his neck start to rise. He was afraid for Moira's safety, but couldn't say as much to Evans without voicing his suspicions out loud. 'What on earth is she doing with Thelwell at this hour?' he said.

Evans shrugged. 'If she couldn't find you and she couldn't find me and it was something important perhaps she called Mr Thelwell,' he suggested.

'I'm going to call him,' said Jamieson picking up the phone.

The phone seemed to ring for ages before it was answered. To Jamieson's surprise, one of Thelwell's daughters answered. The young voice said shakily, 'Yes. What is it?'

'I'd like to speak with your father, please,' said Jamieson, wondering why the girl was up so late.

'You can't,' said the girl.

Jamieson thought he detected a sob in the girl's voice. He frowned and looked at Evans, who was listening in. 'It's very important. Perhaps I could speak to your mother if your father isn't there?'

'No, you can't . . . Mummy's upset. Call back another time.' The phone went dead, leaving Jamieson to exchange puzzled looks with Evans. 'What do you make of that?' he asked.

Evans shrugged and scratched his head. It made a noise like sandpaper on wood. 'Something's obviously happened over at Thelwell's house.'

'I'm going to call Moira's flat again,' said Jamieson. He checked the number in Evans' book and dialled quickly. Once

197

more Moira Lippman's flatmate answered. 'No, she hasn't come back yet. Is something wrong?'

'Frankly, I'm not sure,' replied Jamieson, feeling even more anxious. 'If she returns soon, will you ask her to contact the hospital switchboard and leave a message for Dr Jamieson.'

'I'll do that,' said Moira's flatmate. 'Perhaps you would let me know if you find her first?'

'Of course,' said Jamieson.

'What now?' asked Evans.

Jamieson hesitated for a moment and then said, 'I think I'm going to go round to Thelwell's house.'

'At this time?' exclaimed Evans.

'You said yourself that there's something going on. I have to find out what.'

'I'll come with you,' said Evans, seeing that Jamieson had made up his mind.

It took less than ten minutes to drive through the deserted streets to Latimer Gardens. Jamieson found Thelwell's Volvo parked outside his house. A beige Rover, which Jamieson thought looked vaguely familiar, was parked directly behind it.

Evans said, 'That's Carew's car.'

'Carew? What the hell is he doing here?'

Jamieson drew up behind the Rover and he and Evans walked briskly towards the gate. As they passed the Volvo, Jamieson put his hand on the bonnet and noted that it was cold. Thelwell had been home for some time.

It was Carew who opened the door of the house when they rang. When he got over his surprise at seeing Jamieson and Evans standing there, he said, 'How did you know? I was expecting the police.'

'Police?' asked Jamieson.

'You'd better come in,' said Carew. He put his hand on Jamieson's shoulder to signify that he should wait while he closed the door and then whispered, 'I'm afraid there's been a tragedy.'

Jamieson felt his heart sink.

'What kind of a tragedy?' asked Evans.

'Mr Thelwell is dead.'

Jamieson was stunned. He had been so afraid that he was going to hear some bad news about Moira Lippman that this was the last thing in the world he expected to hear. He waited for Carew to elaborate and had to contain himself while Carew shook his head and looked at the floor in a solemn display of official grief. 'Tragic, tragic,' he muttered. 'A brilliant man. Not always the easiest of men to get along with, I'll admit, but that's often the way of things. Don't you think?'

Jamieson found the question ridiculous, just as he found Carew's apparent need to improvise an obituary for Thelwell ridiculous. Thelwell had been a shit. He had been loathed by almost everyone. There would be plenty time later for platitudes, but right now he wanted some answers. He ignored Carew's question and asked, 'What happened?'

'He took his own life.'

'Thelwell?' exclaimed Jamieson almost involuntarily. 'Committed suicide?'

Carew gave a nervous glance at the door behind him and Jamieson deduced that Thelwell's family must be in the room. He lowered his voice. 'I'm sorry,' he said, 'But Mr Thelwell wasn't the sort I would have thought likely to take his own life.'

'I suppose that goes for me too,' agreed Carew with another exaggerated shake of the head. 'But the poor man did. Who among us can ever know fully what goes on in another man's mind?'

'What happened exactly?' asked Evans, this time in a matter of fact Welsh accent that seemed to ridicule Carew's whispering air of reverence. Carew gave him a distasteful look and addressed Jamieson. 'Marion said that he was very upset when he got back from choir practice this evening. Apparently he went straight to his study and locked the door. She was alarmed some time later when she couldn't get a reply from him and in the end had to enlist the help of a neighbour to break down the door. Mr Thelwell was dead.'

199

'I'd like to see him,' said Jamieson.

Carew looked shocked. 'Is that really necessary? The police are on their way and I really don't think that . . .'

'I'd like to see him,' repeated Jamieson.

'As you wish,' Carew concurred. 'He's upstairs.'

Jamieson and Evans followed the medical superintendent up the green-carpeted stairs to an oak-panelled door that creaked as Carew opened it with obvious reluctance. 'Nothing has been touched,' he said. 'I strongly recommend that we keep it that way until the police have finished their business.' He stepped back in order to allow Jamieson to enter. Evans followed in his wake, attracting another annoyed glance from Carew.

Jamieson was unprepared for the sight that met him and recoiled slightly. For some reason he had expected Thelwell to have killed himself with poison or drugs, but he found the surgeon's body slumped across his desk in a crimson pool of blood. In his right hand he still held the scalpel that he had used to slit his jugular vein. Jamieson remembered how Thelwell had opened his mail with the paper knife and he grimaced slightly. Thelwell's eyes were wide open and they retained in death the sullen anger that he had managed to sustain so persistently in life.

'Ye gods,' said Evans in a whisper. 'Why on earth . . .'

'There was a brief note left for his wife,' said Carew, taking an envelope from his pocket. He handed it to Jamieson.

Jamieson removed the single sheet of blue notepaper from the envelope and opened it. It read, 'My Dear Marion, It's all going to come out and I can't bear the shame. Please try to understand there are some forces inside a man which cannot be denied however strong the will. I tried but have failed, so now I have to pay the price.' The note was signed with the initial 'G'. Jamieson handed it back to Carew who said, 'Most peculiar. Wouldn't you agree?'

Jamieson gave a half nod and asked, 'What did his wife say when she read this?'

'Marion was totally bemused,' replied Carew. 'The poor woman has no idea at all what it means.'

'Poetic in a way,' said Evans, looking at Thelwell's corpse with his head on one side.

'What is?' snapped Carew, still annoyed at Evans' presence.

'That Mr Thelwell should die by his own hand just like Dr Richardson. It's almost as if it were fated for the pair of them. Constantly at loggerheads in life, still locked together in death, you might say.'

Once again, Jamieson was conscious of Evans' Welsh accent. He had often noticed that people under stress exhibited accents that were subdued or absent at other times.

'I see nothing poetic about any of it,' said Carew brusquely. 'This whole infection business has done untold harm to the hospital and its reputation. And now this has to happen.'

Jamieson continued to stare at Thelwell's corpse.

'Do you understand the note?' Carew asked Jamieson.

Jamieson was reluctant to answer. In the end he said, 'I think we'll have to wait for the police to explain it all fully.'

'The police? I don't understand.'

Jamieson looked at Carew, who was still waiting for an explanation, and said, 'If Mr Thelwell had something to hide, a full police investigation could clear up a lot of things.'

Carew looked more bemused than ever. He was unprepared to let the matter rest at that. He said, 'I don't understand what you're getting at. What do you mean, something to hide? What could he have to hide? Apart from his career and his family, Gordon Thelwell had no other interests, except maybe the choir.'

'Mr Thelwell stopped singing with the choir a long time ago. He wasn't at choir practice this evening or any other evening, come to that,' said Jamieson.

Carew's mouth fell open. 'Then where might I ask did he go instead?'

'Tonight he went down to the red light district. Maybe that's what he always did.'

Carew's eyes opened wide. 'Gordon Thelwell?' he exclaimed.

201

'You mean he was consorting with . . . prostitutes?' Carew uttered the word as if it offended him.

'What he was actually doing with or to them is a matter for the police to determine.'

The full implication of what Jamieson meant suddenly dawned on Carew and he rolled his eyes skywards. 'You can't possibly mean . . . the killings? My God! What evidence do you have for this?'

'Very little,' admitted Jamieson. 'But I am certain he wasn't going to any choir practices.'

The police arrived and after due procedure the body of Gordon Thomas Thelwell was removed and taken away in a plain black van to the city mortuary. Jamieson and Evans watched the van drive off in silence and then walked slowly back to their car, leaving Carew to comfort Marion Thelwell and her daughters. As they neared the car, Jamieson suddenly stopped dead in his tracks, prompting Evans to ask what was the matter. Jamieson did not reply. He turned to face the hedge fronting Thelwell's house.

'What is it?' asked Evans.

Once again Jamieson did not reply.

Evans, who had already stepped off the pavement to walk round to the front passenger door, came back and stood beside Jamieson. 'What's wrong?'

'Can you smell something?' asked Jamieson.

Evans sniffed the night air and said, 'Wet leaves? Grass?'

'No. Something else.'

Evans sniffed again. 'Scent,' he said.

'Perfume,' said Jamieson. 'Not just any perfume. Moira Lippman's perfume.'

'Are you sure?'

Jamieson did not reply. He tried to part the hedge with his hands to peer through but found it too dark. 'I'm going back,' he said to Evans.

The two men retraced their steps to the gate of Thelwell's house and turned to make their way along the back of the hedge in the front garden. Jamieson swore as a branch he had failed to see in the darkness caught him on his bruised cheek. 'It's getting stronger,' he said as they approached the circular summer house in the darkest corner of the garden.

'We need some light,' said Evans.

'There's a torch in the car,' replied Jamieson. 'Can you fetch it? It's in the glove compartment.' He handed Evans the car keys.

Evans was back within thirty seconds, using the narrow beam from the torch to pathfind his way along the back of the hedge and negotiate a passage round a rusty hose-reel and broken paving slabs that lay piled up outside the summer house.

Jamieson felt a wave of reluctance and foreboding sweep over him. He put his hand on the door handle and froze for a few moments, feeling the rust on the handle rough on his palm.

'Is it locked?' asked Evans, misconstruing Jamieson's reluctance to turn it.

Jamieson finally turned the handle and the smell of perfume became almost overpowering. He took the torch from Evans and shone the beam on the floor. He saw the pile of sacking . A black handbag lay beside it. It had been flattened by someone standing on it and it was the source of the scent. Broken glass from the perfume bottle protruded from its side.

It was not difficult to discern the shape of a body underneath the sacking. 'My God,' whispered Jamieson as he knelt down to pull back the top sack. A faint haze of hessian and potato dust hung in the torch beam as it lit up a face.

Moira Lippman was practically unrecognisable as the girl Jamieson had known in the lab. He had to turn his head to one side for a moment to gain control of his emotions and suppress the urge to vomit. The instrument of Moira Lippman's death had been a pair of garden shears, but she had not simply been stabbed. She had been systematically mutilated. Her body had been opened up from lower abdomen to throat and a crude attempt had been made to open up her skull. The bloody shears lay beside her.

'The bastard,' whispered Jamieson. 'The absolute bastard.'

'Do you think this is this why Thelwell killed himself?' asked Evans quietly.

'I suppose,' replied Jamieson. 'Come on. We better get the police back here.'

'The swine!' Sue exclaimed when Jamieson told her. 'How could anyone do such a thing!'

'Nutters know no bounds of depravity,' said Jamieson.

'It seems so unsatisfying to blame it all on mental illness,' complained Sue.

'I know what you mean,' said Jamieson. 'It thwarts the desire for revenge.'

'I suppose that's it,' admitted Sue.

'Well, he's dead now and beyond revenge, whatever excuse he might have had to hide behind in life.'

'Does this mean it's over now?'

'I think it does,' said Jamieson.

'You look all in,' said Sue, gently ruffling Jamieson's hair.

'I can't say I will be sorry to leave this place,' said Jamieson.

'Me neither,' agreed Sue. 'You know I felt it as soon as I walked through the hospital gates. It was as if there was something evil about it.'

They both looked out of the window at the dark shadows below. A cat leapt silently from the lid of one of the dustbins to the ground and prowled along the base of the wall opposite. It started to rain.

'What a mess,' whispered Jamieson.

'There was nothing you could have done that would have made it any better,' said Sue comfortingly but, for the moment, Jamieson was beyond reach of consolation. His first assignment for Sci-Med had been a nightmare. Two consultants and a senior technician from the lab had finished up dead along with five patients who had died of their infections.

'All because of one damned lunatic,' murmured Jamieson. He reflected for a moment on the human mind, so often an instrument of wonder with capabilities beyond what any

computer could hope to simulate, but when it turned to evil
. . . Jamieson shivered slightly.

'I don't suppose we will ever know how he managed to
contaminate the instruments and dressings with such horrible
organisms,' said Sue.

'I suppose not,' agreed Jamieson, whose mind was still
reeling from the awful sight of Moira Lippman's body.

'That's a pity,' said Sue. 'I wish we could find out, particularly
in view of what you said the other night about how unlikely it
was that he could have done it by chance.'

'We'll have to content ourselves with the fact that he's
stopped doing it now,' said Jamieson.

Sue gave a slight nod. She asked, 'Did you find out what it
was that Moira wanted to see you about?'

Jamieson shook his head. 'Whatever it was, it died with
her.'

'Do you think it was the same thing that made her go out
at that time of night?'

Jamieson shook his head and said, 'I don't know. I can
check her desk in the morning. Perhaps she wrote something
down.'

'Maybe she found out what you think Dr Richardson found
out. Something about the infections?'

Jamieson had the distinct impression that Sue was trying to
lead him down a particular road. A pointer here, a question
there. He suddenly thought he saw what she was getting
at. He said, 'But if she found out about Thelwell's involvement in the deaths, she wouldn't have gone to see him,
would she?'

'My feelings exactly,' agreed Sue.

'On the other hand,' said Jamieson thoughtfully, 'Thelwell
was responsible for her sister-in-law's death. People do strange
things when matters get personal. She may have gone there,
knowing that Thelwell was the killer.'

'For revenge, you mean?' said Sue. 'Poor girl.'

They fell to silence and Sue looked at her watch. 'Good Lord,
look at the time.'

Jamieson smiled thinly and put his hand round her shoulder. 'Let's turn in.'

There was no sign on her desk or work bench of any discovery which would have made Moira Lippman so anxious to contact either Jamieson or, in the end, Thelwell. Jamieson searched all through her desk drawers and when that proved fruitless he examined all the cultures in the incubators with her writing on them. There was nothing that could not be attributed to the routine work of the lab. He was cursing under his breath when Clive Evans' voice behind him said, 'I've already done that. There's nothing.'

'Strange,' said Jamieson. 'She must have written something down.'

'Maybe she took it with her to see Thelwell,' suggested Evans.

'Ye gods,' said Jamieson', not relishing a second visit to the Thelwell house.

'Will you check?'

Jamieson nodded.

'Want me to come with you?'

'No need,' said Jamieson. He left Evans and telephoned Chief Inspector Ryan to arrange access to the house in Latimer Gardens. He was relieved to be told that Marion Thelwell and her daughters had gone off to stay with relatives for a few days. The forensic people had finished in the house and garden and he would be able to get the keys from the officer stationed at the front of the house to keep the morbidly curious at bay.

The policeman at the gate stiffened when he saw Jamieson approach and moved from one foot to the other. Jamieson sensed that he was preparing to bar his way. He probably thought that he was yet another journalist after some lurid copy to satisfy the insatiable needs of the press. Jamieson showed his ID and said that he had permission from Chief Inspector Ryan to enter the house. The constable checked through the radio clipped to his lapel and after a burst of static Jamieson caught the word 'Affirmative.'

The house was silent, a brooding silence that Jamieson felt was oppressive. It was as if the walls and floors resented his presence there. He climbed the stairs slowly, reluctant to create any noise and feeling like an intruder on private grief. He opened the door to what had been Gordon Thelwell's study and stepped inside.

He found nothing on Thelwell's desk to suggest any contact at all between Moira Lippman and Thelwell. Jamieson looked through the drawers and finally the waste paper basket and again drew a blank. He felt sure that Moira would have had notes. She had told Sue that she wanted to talk about the results of some tests. That meant that there must be lab notes somewhere. Apart from routine procedure it was in the nature of people who worked in labs to keep notes.

Had Thelwell destroyed them? he wondered. He had to acknowledge that this was a possibility, but if he had, how had he done it? He had not left this room. His wife had said so. There was no fireplace and there was no document shredder in the room. He conducted another search but again drew a blank. Maybe Moira hadn't brought them with her, but if they weren't here and they weren't at the lab, where else could they be? Her own flat? Jamieson decided to make that his next port of call. He started to tidy up by putting back the contents of the waste paper basket when suddenly he heard footsteps on the stairs. His first thought was that it must be the policeman. The door opened and Marion Thelwell stood in the doorway. Jamieson felt guilty and embarrassed. He started to apologise by saying that he had understood that the house was going to be empty.

'I had to come back for some things for the girls,' said Marion Thelwell, her voice devoid of emotion. 'Did you find what it was you were looking for?'

Jamieson looked at her dull eyes and the deep lines in her face. It was obvious that she had had no sleep.

'Actually no,' he said softly.

'What was it?'

'When Miss Lippman came to see your husband last night. I think she had some notes, perhaps a lab notebook with her. I was looking for it.'

Marion Thelwell looked long and hard at Jamieson as if he were a stain on the ground and then said slowly and deliberately, 'The Lippman girl phoned Gordon last night and said that she had to speak to him. He did his best to dissuade her, in fact, he told her point blank not to come. But she must have come over anyway, only she never got here.'

'But . . .'

'I repeat, she never got here. She must have been murdered outside somewhere and her body placed in our summer house.'

Jamieson looked at the floor in an attempt to hide the disbelief which he felt sure must show in his face. 'And your husband, Mrs Thelwell? Where was he at the time?' asked Jamieson with as much delicacy as was possible in the circumstances.

'Gordon was locked up in his study, as I've already told the police. He never left the house.'

Jamieson's eyes moved involuntarily to the study window and confirmed that it overlooked the garden. Thelwell could have left the room by the window.

'Can I ask how you know that it was Moira Lippman who called him on the phone?' said Jamieson

'I took the call.'

'And how did you know what was said?'

'I listened in on the extension in the hall,' she answered without a trace of guilt.

Jamieson looked at her without speaking until she felt obliged to elaborate.

'I knew that Gordon had stopped going to choir practices some time ago. I thought there might be another woman, even though I found that hard to believe.'

'Why?' asked Jamieson, detecting an odd note in Marion Thelwell's voice.

She gave a mirthless shrug and said, 'Gordon was never very *physical*, not even in our courting days.'

Jamieson nodded. 'Weren't you ever tempted to find out where your husband went when he went out?' he asked.

'At first I was, but then I became frightened. I decided that I didn't want to know . . .'

Marion Thelwell started to shake with pent-up emotion. Jamieson found the sight alarming for there was absolutely no sound coming from her, just a series of silent shuddering convulsions. He pressed her further. 'Because of the killings in the city?' he asked.

Marion Thelwell continued to shake. She nodded but didn't say any more.

Jamieson put his arm round her and led her to a seat. 'You need a drink,' he said softly. 'Is there anything up here?'

Marion Thelwell indicated with her right hand and Jamieson opened up the bureau. There was a crystal decanter on a silver tray with four glasses. He poured Scotch into one of them and handed it to her. He watched her take a long gulp and said, 'You've been through a lot. You must be absolutely exhausted.'

'That's nothing to what's to come,' replied Marion Thelwell distantly and Jamieson could not disagree. 'It's not so much for myself I worry, but the girls . . . Other children can be terribly cruel. I'll have to take them away somewhere, somewhere where we'll not be known. Start a new life. Isn't that what they say? A new life.' Marion Thelwell put her hand to her head and closed her eyes. There was silence in the room.

Jamieson had difficulty finding Moira Lippman's flat. He had to stop twice and ask for directions before finding the small back street and the number he was looking for. He had half expected to find no one at home, fearing that Moira's flatmate might have gone to work, so he was pleasantly surprised when a voice behind the door replied, 'Who is it?'

'It's Dr Jamieson from Kerr Memorial. I spoke to you on the phone last night.'

'Can you prove who you are?' said the voice.

Jamieson put his ID card through the letter box and waited patiently while the door was unchained and then unlocked. The door opened a few inches and Jamieson could look down at a thin, dark girl in her mid twenties. She had a sallow skin and large hazel eyes which mirrored the apprehension she felt.

Jamieson smiled.

'You can't be too careful,' said the girl, opening the door further and taking off the final restraint to allow Jamieson to enter.

'I thought you might have gone to work,' said Jamieson.

'I couldn't after what happened to Moira,' said the girl. 'Besides, the police wanted to ask me a few things.

'Like what?'

'Like what time Moira got in last night and what time she left. Things like that.'

'Were you here when she got back from the hospital last night?' asked Jamieson.

'Yes I was.'

'Was Moira carrying anything?'

'Only her briefcase. Why do you ask?'

Jamieson, excited by the girl's reply, ignored her question and asked, 'Can I see it, please?'

The girl shook her head. 'Sorry, no.'

'Why not?'

'Because she took it with her when she went out.'

'Are you absolutely sure?' asked Jamieson.

'Absolutely. I watched her take out some papers from it and check them over before putting them back. I remember her actually saying that she had to show them to someone from the hospital. Thelwell, I think she said his name was. Would you like some coffee?'

Jamieson agreed absent-mindedly. If Moira had taken her notes with her, why hadn't he found them in Thelwell's house? What had happened to them? The briefcase hadn't been in the hut with her body and it hadn't been in Thelwell's study, so where the hell was it?

'Penny for them,' said the girl, returning with two mugs of instant coffee.

Jamieson smiled apologetically and said, 'I'm sorry, that was rude of me.' They spoke a little about Moira and agreed what a nice person she had been. Jamieson asked the girl if she was in the same line of work.

'I'm a physiotherapist at the Royal,' replied the girl. 'Bacteria give me the heebie jeebies.'

'So you two wouldn't talk about work much?' said Jamieson.

'Not really, although I did ask her about the infection problem, of course.'

'What did she tell you?'

'That it was caused by bacteria that were very difficult to treat. I can't remember what she called them.'

'Nothing more than that?' asked Jamieson.

'Maybe,' smiled the girl. 'But it probably washed over me. I didn't understand most of it.'

Jamieson smiled and they fell to talking about other things while he finished his coffee. During the lulls in conversation he took note of his surroundings. The flat was clean and tidy, but none of the furniture matched. It was a typical rented furnished flat, the kind he used to live in when he was a student. He drained his cup and took this as his cue to get to his feet. He shook hands with the girl and they said that they would probably see each other at the funeral.

Jamieson sat in the car for a moment before starting the engine. He wondered about the missing briefcase. It was important. Maybe Thelwell had dumped it somewhere outside his house after murdering Moira Lippman. An outside rubbish bin? The garden compost heap? He decided to drive back to Latimer Gardens and check.

'Something in particular you're looking for, sir?' asked the constable as he watched Jamieson empty the rubbish sack outside the kitchen door of the Thelwell house.

'A briefcase.'

The officer gave Jamieson a hand to sift through the refuse and then replace it when they had no luck. They pitchforked their way through the compost heap with the same lack of success.

'What makes you think it's here, sir?' asked the policeman.

'I just hoped it was,' said Jamieson.

The constable gave Jamieson a puzzled look. 'Hoped, sir?'

Jamieson shrugged and said, 'Because if it's not here, it means that someone took it and that means I have to figure out who and why.'

'You're not happy,' said Sue as Jamieson stood with his back to her at the window.

'I'm not happy,' agreed Jamieson.

'Want to talk?'

'I'm uneasy about the whole thing. There's something fundamentally wrong.'

'Explain.'

'First Richardson finds something out about the infection and then commits suicide before telling anyone. Then Moira Lippman finds out something, maybe the same something, and is murdered before she can tell anyone.'

'Thelwell killed them both to keep them quiet,' suggested Sue.

'And then committed suicide himself? Why go to the bother of killing someone to keep them quiet when you are going to kill yourself anyway?'

'The man was deranged.'

'Maybe, but it's all a bit too convenient.'

'I don't follow.'

'There were no papers or notes in Richardson's office to suggest what the theory was he had been working on. None at all.'

'So Thelwell took them,' suggested Sue.

'And now the same thing has happened with Moira Lippman's notes. She gets murdered and now there's no trace of them.'

'Same thing. Thelwell took them.'

'But Thelwell didn't have them. I looked everywhere.'

'Maybe he destroyed them.'

'But how? Marion Thelwell is positive that her husband did not leave his study last night. According to her he did his damnedest to dissuade Moira Lippman from coming round; it was she who insisted. So now we have to believe that Thelwell climbed out of his study window and waited for Moira to arrive. He murdered her in the garden, climbed back into the house, destroyed her notes and her briefcase, God knows how, and then committed suicide. It doesn't make sense.'

'What's the alternative?' asked Sue.

Jamieson turned round and faced her before saying, 'The alternative is that someone else killed Moira and took her notes.'

'Not Thelwell? I don't think I like the sound of that,' said Sue slowly.

Jamieson agreed with a forced smile. He said, 'But maybe you're right. Maybe it was just the irrational behaviour of a lunatic.'

'What are you going to do?'

'Leave it all to the police. For my part I'm going to insist that all instrument packs in storage and all dressing packs in the gynaecology wards are re-sterilised. When that's done I think surgery can resume and I'll report as much to Sci-Med.'

'And then we can go home?'

'Yes,' smiled Jamieson.

'How long?'

'Couple of days.'

'I'm counting the hours.'

'Let's count them in bed.'

213

13

The rain persisted through the night, waking Jamieson, who was a light sleeper at the best of times, with the noise it made against the tall windows of the residency. At seven he gave up trying to sleep and got up. He washed and shaved as quietly as possible to avoid waking Sue, who was still in a deep sleep.

As he emerged from the bathroom holding the towel to his face he looked down at her left profile against the pillow and was filled with affection. He reached out with his hand, intending to trace the back of his fingers down her cheek, but stopped when she moved in her sleep and turned over. He finished patting his face dry and walked over to the window to see if the rain showed any signs of slacking off.

There were large puddles in the courtyard below; they were being pock-marked by falling rain and a heavy grey mist hung over everything. Across the wet cobbles on the other side of the yard Jamieson could see a small group of nurses, huddling inside their red capes as they talked in the shelter of the entrance to the wards. He looked at his watch and saw that it was time for the change-over from night to day shift. It was not hard to guess what they were talking about. By nine o'clock Thelwell's demise would be common knowledge throughout the hospital.

Sue opened her eyes and made a sleepy sound.

'Coffee?' asked Jamieson as he plugged in the electric kettle.

'Please. You're up early!'

'The rain woke me,' said Jamieson.

'And what else?' asked Sue, sensing that something was wrong from the inflection in Jamieson's voice.

Jamieson shook his head in a dismissive gesture and said, 'Oh, just what we were talking about last night. I'm missing something about the whole affair. I keep thinking I should be able to see what it is, but I can't and it's getting to me.'

'Maybe you're too close to it. Maybe you have to step back a little before you can see clearly?'

'Maybe,' agreed Jamieson. 'But I keep thinking that if Richardson realised something about the infections and then Moira Lippman did the same, surely I should be able to see it too.'

'Not necessarily. They were both bacteriologists. You're not,' said Sue.

Jamieson looked at her as if she had just given him an idea. 'Perhaps that's it,' he said, 'I've been assuming that they discovered something about the source or spread of the infection, but maybe it was something about the bugs themselves. Something only an expert would see. That would fit in with Richardson's interest in the Sci-Med tests on the *Pseudomonas*. He wasn't surprised at all at a result that clearly surprised everyone else, but never got round to telling me why. On the other hand, it's difficult to think what could be gained from lab tests on the bugs themselves. I've seen the results of all the tests that were done by Richardson's people. I've carried out some myself and the Sci-Med people have been involved too. At the end of the day we are left with two highly virulent microorganisms which are very difficult to treat and which display some odd biochemical characteristics.'

'How "odd"?' asked Sue.

'The *Pseudomonas* differed from the text-book response it should have shown to several tests,' said Jamieson.

'What can you deduce from that?' asked Sue.

Jamieson shrugged and said, 'It could hardly be regarded as a typical example of its species,' said Jamieson. 'In fact, both bugs were oddballs because of their high resistance to antibiotics.'

'Did you discuss this with anyone?' asked Sue.

'Of course,' replied Jamieson. 'Moira Lippman thought it odd that the *Pseudomonas* should vary from the norm so markedly, but Clive Evans didn't think it too strange.'

'Well, not much to go on there,' said Sue. She sighed and said, 'As you said yourself last night, the main priority is that there should be no more post-operative infections at Kerr Memorial. You've seen to that and now that Thelwell is dead, the matter of how he actually introduced the contamination into the wards and theatres has become more or less academic.'

'Just as long as there are no more deaths,' said Jamieson.

'What are you going to do this morning?'

'Write my report.'

'And then?'

'This afternoon I'll go over to the CSSD and make sure that all the instruments and dressings from the gynaecology department have been re-sterilised.'

'And this evening you can take me out for a meal,' said Sue.

'Good idea,' agreed Jamieson.

Jamieson was well into the substance of his report by eleven o'clock. He had no great love of paper work and, recognising this, had chosen to work in the medical records office where there were no windows to gaze out of, making distraction more difficult to find. One of the clerks brought him a cup of coffee at eleven fifteen and laid it gently down on the desk in front of him. There was also a shortbread finger sitting in the saucer. 'I hope you don't mind me asking,' she said. 'But there's a rumour going about that Mr Thelwell from gynaecology is dead?'

'It's true, I'm afraid,' said Jamieson, wondering if the question was the *quid pro quo* for the biscuit bonus.

'I suppose I should say I'm sorry,' said the girl.

'But?' prompted Jamieson.

'That man gave me the creeps,' said the girl.

'Did you know him?' asked Jamieson.

'Not well,' said the girl, quickly on the defensive as she read an implied accusation into what Jamieson had asked.

216

'You didn't have to know him well. Everyone disliked him. It makes you wonder what goes through the heads of people like that.'

'What do you mean?' asked Jamieson.

'Well, you'd think that they would realise that everyone dislikes them? Can't they sense it? Why don't they do something about it? Or do you think it doesn't matter to them?'

'I'm not at all sure,' said Jamieson. 'Maybe the really unpleasant people don't even notice.'

'But we all need love,' said the girl.

The girl turned on her heel and left Jamieson to consider what she had said. The girl was right about one thing. You did not have to know Thelwell in order to dislike him. He'd been that kind of a man. The point was, what part had natural dislike played in his own judgement of Thelwell? It was always so easy to believe the worst of people you didn't like. You could do it without a second thought, you expected it, you even wanted it to be true, but was that relevant to anything that had happened? he wondered.

The rain stopped and the sky showed every sign of brightening, so Sue decided to take the bus into town, ostensibly to do some shopping. She had no particular reason for going at all, but the idea of crowds and bustle appealed to her. Apart from anything else, it would be an excuse to get away from the forbidding grey confines of the hospital for a while. She looked out one of the back windows from where she could see the turning circle outside the hospital gates that the buses used. There was a double decker sitting there. She saw that the driver was in his cab, reading a newspaper. Sue grabbed her coat and hurried downstairs.

The town was very busy, but because Sue had nothing particular in mind to buy, she could avoid the busier shops and browse at will. She was drawn to the windows of Mothercare and felt good as she looked at all the things that she and Scott would be buying in the near future. She only just resisted the urge to go inside the shop and find some excuse to tell the assistant that she was pregnant. Her hand strayed to her stomach in an unconsciously protective gesture as she made her way across the road and through the pavement throng to the doors of Marks and Spencer.

She lingered a while in the mens' clothing section, admiring some Shetland pullovers and wondering whether or not to buy one for Scott. Her only reservation lay in the fact that he did not like having his clothes chosen for him. He preferred to do his own shopping, although in truth, he hated the very idea of it and usually had to be goaded into it, an early-morning expedition two or three times a year. On the other hand, she felt that she knew Scott's tastes by now. A plain grey pullover would be nice. He would like that. She picked out one his size and held it up in front of her, but as she did so she became aware of a man looking at her from the other side of the counter.

There was something disconcerting about the intensity of his stare. She diverted her eyes but was still very aware of his presence. There was something familiar about him, but at first she could not think what. Then she remembered. The man had been on the same bus on the way down from the hospital. She couldn't remember where he had got on; she had first only noticed him when he had stood on the platform with her as she waited to get off. The recollection made her uneasy. Was it her imagination or was he still staring at her?

As an attractive woman she was used to having men stare at her, but she never encouraged it. She steeled herself to look directly at the man with a contrived cold, blank expression. To her discomfort, the man just stared back and, what was worse, it was not difficult to understand what he was thinking. The look on his face was one of pure hatred.

Sue felt a slight tremor in her hand as she put down the garment she was holding and looked away. She was breathing a little unevenly and something akin to real fear was starting to creep through her. She could feel the blood pounding at her temples and a slight unsteadiness in her legs. This is ridiculous, she told herself. It wasn't as if she were walking through a lonely park on a dark night, for goodness' sake. She was in the middle of a crowded shop at eleven o'clock in the morning. There were people all around her.

She turned her back on the counter and walked away, taking comfort from the number of people she had to squeeze past as she headed for the ladies' clothing section. She wanted to turn round to check if the man had followed her, but something prevented her from doing this. It was as if she feared that this act in itself might precipitate the man's presence.

In the end, she did it surreptitiously. She had to know. She found a coat rack and pretended to examine the garments, using this as a pretext to half turn. As she pulled out the hem of one of the coats to feel the material a hand touched her back and she gasped and felt her body go rigid. 'Excuse me, dear, could I get past?' said a little old woman. She was wearing a flower pot hat and a slightly puzzled look at Sue's rather dramatic reaction. Sue smiled to hide her embarrassment and let the woman past, then she went on pretending to examine the coats. Her head was bent forward but her eyes were kept up to look around her. There was no sign of the man. She let out her breath in a long slow sigh, unaware until then that she had been holding it.

Could that look on the man's face have been her imagination? she wondered, as she went on browsing through the store; try as she might, she could not rid herself of the latent image. Maybe the man suffered from some medical condition? Something that affected the muscles in his face, giving him no control over his expression? Bell's palsy, or something like that. She sought distraction in a row of nightdresses, but had to remind herself that her shape would be changing soon and not in the appropriate direction for these nightdresses. Might as well look at the 'tents' while I'm here, she thought and moved to the maternity section. She discovered a line in long, flowing gowns which she thought attractive or, more correctly, the least unattractive, and idly checked the labels for one her size. As she parted the gowns to extract one she suddenly froze in terror. The man was standing on the other side of the rack, looking through the gap. He was less than a metre away from her and his eyes, behind small circular glasses, burned with loathing.

Sue took an involuntary step backwards and put her hand to her throat to combat a momentary inability to breathe. She found herself trapped against the wall. Sheer terror made her speak, although she had difficulty getting the words out. 'What . . . do you want?' she stammered, trying to look out of the corner of her eye at the same time for the best escape route.

'Revenge,' hissed the man without hesitation. It was as if he had been waiting for Sue to ask.

'What . . . are you talking about? I've never seen you before in my life. There must be some mistake . . .'

'You belong to him and I am going to take you away. See how he likes it when it happens.'

The man made a move towards Sue and she lost all self-control and screamed out loud, closing her eyes and her fists in a defensive gesture.

'Madam! Madam! Whatever's the matter?' asked a solicitous voice in Sue's ear. Sue opened her eyes to find an assistant with her hand on her arm. All around people were staring at her and talking in quiet voices.

'There was a man,' spluttered Sue.

The assistant looked around and so did Sue. There was no man.

'He was just there,' sobbed Sue. 'He said he wanted revenge.'

The words sounded silly and Sue looked at the assistant to see if disbelief would register in her eyes.

'Revenge, madam? Revenge for what?'

'I don't know,' confessed Sue helplessly.

'Perhaps a nice cup of tea would help,' said the assistant gently.

'No, no tea,' said Sue, painfully aware that people were speaking about her. She wanted desperately to be out of the store. 'Perhaps you could call me a taxi?'

'Of course. Why don't you come through here for a moment?'

The assistant led Sue through one of the doors marked STAFF ONLY and sat her down at a desk to wait while she called a taxi. Sue was glad to be out of the public gaze and her breathing started to subside as she regained control of her emotions.

'There will be a taxi here in five to ten minutes,' said the assistant putting down the phone. 'Are you sure you're all right?'

Sue managed a nod and a smile and thanked the assistant for her kindness.

'There are some weird people about these days,' said the assistant. 'I don't know what the country is coming to.'

Sue nodded. She needed no reminding of the fact.

The world had suddenly become a much more hostile place. Sue began to worry about crossing the pavement from the door of the store to the door of the taxi. It arrived within three minutes, its diesel engine ticking over loudly.

'That was quick,' said the assistant. 'If I were you, I'd have a stiff drink when you get home.'

Sue thanked her for her kindness and hurried over to the taxi. She slammed the door behind her and took comfort in the solid thunk it made. 'Kerr Memorial Hospital,' she said and settled back into her seat. Almost subconsciously she checked that the windows were closed.

The cab pulled away from the kerb and started to head for the hospital. Sue looked out at the streets, but did not see much for she was still too upset to concentrate. She could not recall ever having been so frightened before and her heart was pounding even now. Gradually she became aware of normality in the streets they were driving through. People were shopping, men were working, children were playing. She embraced the sights greedily and started to calm down.

As the minutes passed, Sue opened her handbag and took out her purse. She knew that she had enough money for the cab fare, but nerves were making her check all the same. She glanced at the meter and her gaze froze as she realised that it wasn't running. She was mesmerised by the digits; they were stuck on zero. Could the store have paid for the taxi in advance? She had not seen anyone pay the driver.

Apart from that, no one at the store had asked her where she was going.

Inside her head, the store assistant repeated over and over again, 'That was quick . . . That was quick.' Sue faced the awful truth. This cab had not responded to the store's telephone call at all. It had appeared at the door for quite a different reason. Her eyes moved slowly up to look at the driver's mirror. Two burning eyes behind small, round glasses stared back at her.

Panic exploded inside Sue's head and she screamed. 'What do you want with me?' she demanded, banging her fists on the glass partition. The driver did not react. The cab sped on.

The cab was moving too quickly for Sue to attempt to get out, but she clawed at the window winder with one hand while continuing to bang on the glass with the other as she tried to attract outside attention to her plight. The world seemed determined to ignore her. No one looked. No one cared.

'Are you all blind?' she screamed, as frustration and fear rose in her like a spring tide. 'Let me go! Let me go!' she implored the driver. 'There's been some mistake! I don't know you. You don't know me!'

The cab turned into a narrow lane and Sue started to clutch at the door handles again. She was thrown off balance when the driver swung the cab violently across the lane and parked with one side close up against the wall closing off one route of escape. He leapt out to bar the other door and opened it as Sue scrambled up from the floor. In his hand he held a long thin knife. 'One word out of you, just one, understand?' he hissed.

'Sue could only nod.

'Get out!'

She got out and the man put a hand on her shoulder to steer her through a narrow doorway. She was guided along a dark passageway; it smelt of oil and petrol. The hand on her shoulder made her stop while the other one fumbled for a light switch. The light came on and Sue saw that she was in some kind of cellar. The stone walls had been whitewashed at some point in the distant past but now they were green with damp and paint was peeling off.

'In here!' snarled the driver. He opened a wooden door and pushed Sue through. Again she had to wait for the lights to go on before discovering that she was now in a lock-up garage. There was no car, only an oil drum and two wheels with threadbare tyres on them lying flat on the oily floor. There was a black hose hanging up on one wall and a calendar showing a semi-clad girl advertising exhaust systems on another. Her toothy smile seemed to mock Sue.

'You're the killer, aren't you?' she stammered through her fear.

The man did not reply.

Sue's mind was in agony. Scott had been wrong. Thelwell had not been the ripper. The ripper was here with her in this lonely place and no one knew she was here! 'What are you going to do to me?' she asked, as if in response to some subconscious urge to have her fate spelled out.

'Anything I damn well please,' snarled the man. 'Over there. Move!' The man pushed Sue hard in the back and she stumbled and fell headlong to the floor. She grazed her knees and one elbow on the rough concrete. In a trice the man was securing her feet with a length of electrical cable which he brought out from an old chest of drawers in the corner. Sue could sense that the man was enjoying her fear. He seemed to be feeding on it. She stiffened as he put his hand on her knee and watched her reaction. He seemed pleased with the way she responded and slowly moved his hand below her skirt, kneading his fingers into her leg, watching her eyes while he did it.

'Don't! Please don't,' Sue pleaded with tears running down her face, but the hand continued to rise. It stopped when it could go no further, and as she threw her head from side to side in despair, Sue felt a thumb slip inside her underwear and circle her pubic hair. It could only be a matter of seconds before he used the knife.

'For God's sake, stop it!' she screamed.

Instantly the man lashed the back of his free hand across her face. 'Stop the noise, you stupid cow!' he snapped.

Seemingly satisfied with Sue's level of terror, the man resumed tying her up. Her hands were spread out on either side of her and tied to metal rings sunk into the brickwork of the wall. A rope was looped round her waist and again secured through the metal rings.

'Now for the important bit,' breathed the man, as he smoothed out a length of electric cable. He started to weave it in and out of Sue's hair.

Sue sobbed as pain and fear mixed in a hellish cocktail.

The man grunted in satisfaction as he examined his handiwork. 'That should do nicely,' he murmured.

When her hair was tightly tied to the cable at several points the man stretched out the loose end and secured it tightly to something on the wall above Sue's head.

She was in a lot of pain. The man had made sure that the cable was stretched to the limit, so that while the metal rings were holding her arms tightly to the floor her hair was being pulled upwards. She was held completely immobile.

The man looked down at her and seemed pleased. 'In a while your husband will come and collect you,' he said. He knelt down in front of Sue to watch her face fill with confusion. 'And when he does, do you know what will happen?

Sue remained silent, her eyes wide with fear.

'No? Then I'll tell you. His car will break the infra-red beam outside the door and when that happens the garage door will open . . . and when that happens . . .' The man paused to allow Sue to work it out for herself. The man read in her eyes that she had understood. 'That's right,' he said in a whisper. 'The cable is attached to the door motor. Your scalp will be lifted from your head and what's more your husband can watch it happen, then maybe he will know what it feels like. Bastard!'

Sue opened her mouth to scream but the cry was smothered. The man forced a rag into her mouth and then gagged her securely. He got to his feet and checked the cable once more. Seemingly satisfied, he walked over to the door, switched out the light and left. Sue was left alone in fear and darkness.

Jamieson finished his report for Sci-Med and sealed the envelope. He left it for posting and went on up to gynaecology to speak with Phillip Morton, who was now acting head of surgery. They discussed waiting lists and schedules and it was agreed that surgery would restart as soon as soon as the first batches of instruments and dressings were re-cycled through the sterilisers.

'Mr Thelwell's final swab result came back from the Public Health people this morning,' said Morton quietly as Jamieson got up to leave.

'And?' asked Jamieson.

'It was completely negative,' said Morton.

As Jamieson started to descend the stairs outside Morton's office, he heard the phone ring and a moment later the door opened and Phillip Morton called down to him that he had call. Jamieson sprinted back up the stairs. Morton handed him the receiver and left the room, closing the door quietly behind him.

'Hello, Jamieson here.'

'Good.'

Despite the fact that only one word had been spoken, Jamieson did not like the inflection in the voice. He suddenly began to feel uneasy. 'Who is this?' he asked.

'Never mind who it is. I've just spent the morning with your wife, Doctor,' said the sneering voice.

'Really? Who is this?' Jamieson repeated, now feeling desperately afraid that something had happened to Sue.

'She's a very attractive lady.'

Jamieson swallowed. His imagination was running riot. 'Who is this?' he asked, trying to sound calm but having to swallow again, his mouth was so dry.

'Very attractive indeed. Almost irresistible, one might say. At least, I found her irresistible . . . I just couldn't resist her at all . . . So I had her . . .' The voice sniggered.

'Where's Sue? What have you done with her?' demanded Jamieson now at fever pitch.

'Oh, you can have her back now,' said the voice. 'I've finished with her.'

'What do you mean? What have you done to her?' Jamieson almost shouted down the phone.

'I had her, Doctor. I enjoyed her. I screwed her. I fucked her blind. Do you really want all the details? Or maybe you would rather hear them from her, always assuming that you want her back, considering the state she's in.'

Jamieson had to steady himself against the desk. He tried to take a deep breath, but only succeeded in taking a series of short gulps. It was an effort to speak. 'Where is my wife?' he asked in a whisper. 'What have you done with her?'

An address was read out and Jamieson searched for a pen on Morton's desk. He scattered a series of things with his hand as he grabbed at a Biro and wrote on the first thing that came to hand. 'Lock-up number seven, West Side Mews,' he repeated.

'You're a lucky man, Doctor,' continued the voice. 'She's a wonderful screw.'

The phone went dead and Jamieson was almost beside himself with fear and anger. He snatched at the door handle and flung open the door. Morton was nowhere to be seen, so he ran downstairs and asked the first person he met where West Side Mews was. The man, a laundry porter delivering bed linen to the wards, scratched his head and thought for a moment. 'It's off Croxton Road to your left. Second or third opening on your left after you go through the traffic lights at Midgely Road.'

Jamieson ran off without hearing the porter continue, 'Or am I thinking of Weston Mews . . .'

Jamieson swung the car into Weston Mews and thumped both hands down on the steering wheel in temper as he saw the sign. 'Stupid, fucking . . .'

Words failed him. He got out the car and ran towards the first

pedestrian that he saw. It was a postman doing the lunch-time
delivery.

'West Side Mews? That's miles from here, mate,' the man
smiled patiently. 'You want to turn left when you leave here
and . . .'

Jamieson tried to absorb assimilate what he was hearing,
although the rising tide of anguish within him made it difficult.
The postman was taking an age to deliver his directions, but
Jamieson knew it would do no good to shout at him.

'. . . and it's the third opening. You can't miss it.'

The tyres screeched on the road as Jamieson turned the car
without the nicety of a three-point manoeuvre. A dustbin was
sent tumbling as the front of the car bounced up on to the
pavement and hit it a glancing blow. An on-coming car blew its
horn long and loud as he pulled out in front of it, but Jamieson
ignored it, as he did the angry gesture from its driver.

The needle of the speedometer was touching fifty as he
screamed up the outside of a long trail of traffic in third
gear, but then was forced to cut in again when the blazing
headlights of a petrol tanker coming towards him assured him
that its driver was not going to give way.

'Bloody lunatic!' yelled the tanker driver from his window
as he drew level. Jamieson ignored him. He could only think
of Sue and what she must be going through.

'For Christ's sake, move!' hissed Jamieson through gritted
teeth as he saw the traffic lights ahead change to green with no
apparent response from the head of the queue. 'Do you need
a personal fucking invitation?' He craned his neck impatiently
to see what the hold-up was and caught a glimpse of the 'L'
plates on the roof of the car. 'Jesus Christ!' he swore loudly
and slapped his hand down hard on the wheel. He rubbed his
forehead hard with the heel of his right hand in an unconscious
gesture of annoyance with himself. 'For God's sake, get a grip!'
he muttered.

In the moments when blind anger did not obscure his vision
to anything other than Sue's plight, Jamieson began to wonder
why the man had telephoned him at all. Why should a sex

attacker phone the husband? To gloat perhaps? But if that was the case, did not that infer that he was the man's real target and not Sue? Who would do such a thing and why?

As the traffic again slowed to a halt it now occurred to Jamieson for the first time that the call might conceivably have been some kind of awful hoax. He had not checked to see if Sue had gone from the residency. Maybe she was sitting there at this very moment wondering where he was. But if that were the case, why should the man give him an address to go to? Could this be some kind of trick to lure him personally into something? This line of reasoning suddenly became secondary as Jamieson again considered that Sue could be lying bruised and beaten in this lock-up place, alone and terrified. A surge of anger came over Jamieson again as the traffic started to move and he engaged first gear.

He turned left at the junction after Halford's Cycle shop. This was the last of the postman's directions that he could remember. He pulled in to the side and asked a woman pushing a trolley with her shopping basket on it for directions to West Side Mews. The woman shied away from him as he approached. 'It's all right! I only want to ask the way to West Side Mews,' Jamieson assured her, but the woman was not listening. A strange man had accosted her in the street and in this city at the present time, that was enough. She was off.

Jamieson looked for someone else to ask. A teenage boy was coming along the road on a bicycle that was several sizes too large for him. He was standing on the pedals, moving up and down like a fairground horse. Jamieson shouted to him as he drew level. 'Where's West Side Mews, son?'

'Along there on the left, Mister. After the yellow painted shop.'

Jamieson turned left into the lane. The yellow painted shop was a sub post office. There was a telephone booth outside it and it was empty. It would only take a moment to check out the hoax theory. Jamieson called the hospital. There was no reply from his room. He asked for Clive Evans' extension and the call was answered at the first ring.

'Have you seen Sue? Is she in the residency?'

'No, she isn't. I bumped into her earlier this morning. She said she was going into town to do some shopping. I don't think she's back yet.'

'Sweet Jesus,' muttered Jamieson.

'Is something the matter?'

'Sue's been hurt. I want you to get an ambulance and the police to West Side Mews.' Jamieson gave Evans the number and checked that he had taken it down correctly. 'It's urgent!' Jamieson put down the phone and cut off the question that Evans was about to ask. He left the phone booth and decided to leave the car where it was. He ran round the corner on foot and into West Side Mews. Lock-up number seven was the last one in the line.

Jamieson stopped in the middle of the road and stared at the white painted number seven above the garage door. There was no one else in the lane and it was very quiet. He could hear the sound of his own breathing as he began to walk slowly towards the door. There was a window above the garage. Jamieson guessed that it was some kind of loft store room, judging by the junk he could see through the dirty glass. Just below the window he caught sight of the infra-red beam device. It comprised a black, plastic box with a small tube protruding from it at an angle. Jamieson stared at it and wondered. There was nothing unusual about garage door opening devices these days, but you could use beam triggers for a range of other things. Maybe he was being paranoid, but explosions featured among them. He avoided crossing the path of the beam and tried the small door at the side of the garage. It was locked.

There was still no sign of life anywhere and no sound came from inside any of the lock-ups. The awful thought that Sue might be dead was born inside Jamieson's head as he stared at the featureless door in front of him. He stook a step back and threw himself at it. The door did not give, but the splintering sound gave him encouragement. He put his shoulder to the door another two times and it flew back against the wall with a crash.

Silence returned as Jamieson took his first tentative step inside. He was in a narrow corridor that led to a flight of steps leading up to the loft above the garage. Just in front of the steps was a door leading off to the left. It had to lead into the lock-up. Jamieson turned the handle slowly and it opened. It was pitch black inside. He felt along the wall for the light switch and pressed it.

Sue's terror-filled eyes were like saucers above the gag that kept her silent. Jamieson rushed towards her. All he could think of was that he had found her and that she was still alive. Why had the bastard tied her up in the way he had? Why had he tied her hair to the ceiling? He was searching in his trouser pocket for a penknife to cut away the gag from Sue's mouth when he heard the police cars turn into the mews outside.

Jamieson smiled reassurance at Sue but saw that there was something awfully wrong. Her eyes were not registering relief; they were showing absolute terror. Her eyes rolled up to the top of her skull and Jamieson looked at the wall above her head. Her hair was not tied to the ceiling, it was tied to . . . 'Jesus Christ!' yelled Jamieson as the truth dawned on him and the first police car crossed the path of the infral-red beam outside. The door motor whirred into life and Sue's head was jerked hard against the wall. 'No!' he cried, springing to his feet and throwing his arm into the pulley mechanism. Pain exploded inside his head as the flesh of his forearm was drawn into the moving gears and then he blacked out momentarily as the bone jammed hard against the steel pivot and the whole mechanism seized to a halt. Smoke started to rise from the motor and a burning smell filled the garage before the main fuse blew and the lights went out.

Jamieson came round to discover Clive Evans and two police-men trying to free him.

'We'll have to get the Fire Brigade,' said one of the police-men.

'We can do it if you bring that hydraulic jack over here,' said Clive Evans with quiet authority.

'Sue . . .' murmured Jamieson. 'Where's Sue?'

'Your wife is all right, sir,' said one of the policemen gently. 'She passed out, but she's all right.'

The other policeman wheeled the garage trolley jack across the floor as in the distance they heard the siren of an approaching ambulance.

Clive Evans gave instructions for the jack's positioning and then asked the policeman to start pumping the handle. The steel bar trapping Jamieson's arm was prised slowly away from the pulley wheel and Evans released the arm. There were sighs of relief as Jamieson brought his arm down in front of him and they could assess the damage.

'The bone isn't broken,' said Evans, 'but the flesh is a bit of a mess. You're going to have some scars to remember.'

Jamieson ignored his wounded arm, holding it across his stomach as he went to kneel by Sue, whose head was being cradled by one of the other policemen. He could see that that her hair and scalp were undamaged. 'Oh, my love,' he said softly.

'I'll have to deal with that arm,' said Evans standing behind him, and after a few moments Jamieson complied with the hand that was put on his shoulder. He continued to watch Sue as Evans stopped the bleeding in his arm with a make-shift tourniquet. The ambulance arrived and took Jamieson and Sue back to Kerr Memorial.

Sue regained consciousness in the ambulance. Her relief at seeing Jamieson sitting beside her was suddenly eclipsed by the memory of what he had done to save her. 'Your arm!' she whispered. 'Your poor arm!'

'It will be fine,' Jamieson assured her.

Sue looked to Clive Evans for confirmation and Evans concurred.

'Oh, Scott!' Sue exclaimed as emotion overtook her and tears started to flow.

'There, there,' murmured Jamieson. 'You're safe now, Sue. We both are.' He took her hand.

Sue began to shiver. Jamieson felt it begin with a little tremor in her hand, but the shaking began to spread until she could not speak properly and her whole body was trembling. 'That man . . .' she stammered. 'How could anyone . . .' Jamieson tried to hold Sue with one arm, attempting to reassure her, but inside he was hurting. The pain from his arm was getting steadily worse and it was now starting to come in waves, each one stronger than the last, until one finally washed away his consciousness and he slumped backwards into oblivion.

14

'I'm sorry. She's lost the baby,' said Phillip Morton, who had been called in to examine Sue.

Jamieson nodded and looked away. He had no wish to look anyone in the eye when he felt this vulnerable. In his heart he had known what Morton was going to say. He had known from the moment that he had heard someone say that Sue was bleeding. He had only been semi-conscious at the time and lying on a trolley being wheeled into A&E, but snatches of conversation had drifted through to him. Hearing was always the last thing to go and the first to come back.

Now that his pain was under control and his arm had been cleaned up and stitched, he had been sitting waiting with Clive Evans, who had volunteered to keep him company until Morton had completed his examination of Sue. Despite fearing the worst, he had been clinging to a wisp of hope that it had all been some kind of misunderstanding on his part and that everything was going to be all right. Morton snuffed out the candle of hope and Jamieson felt his shoulders sag and his limbs start to feel very heavy.

'I'm sorry,' said Evans, putting his hand on Jamieson's shoulder.

'Bad luck,' said Morton. 'But she's young and strong and there's no reason why . . .'

Jamieson had stopped listening. He knew the routine. He just wanted to be with Sue. 'I'd like to see her now,' he said.

'Of course,' said Morton and stood back to allow Jamieson to pass.

Jamieson opened the door with his left hand; his right arm was bound up in a sling. Sue was lying motionless on the bed, her eyes fixed on the ceiling.

'Hi,' said Jamieson softly. 'How are you feeling?' The words turned to acid in his mouth. He knew exactly how she was feeling, but he had to start somewhere and beginnings demanded words.

Sue continued to stare at the ceiling as if she hadn't heard and then Jamieson saw a tear start to roll down her cheek. She turned her head to look at him. 'I'm sorry,' she whispered. 'I'm so sorry.'

'You idiot!' whispered Jamieson, taking her hand in his, 'You are all that matters. Nothing else.'

'But you wanted the baby so much,' said Sue, the tears now flowing freely.

'There will be others. We've got all the time in the world. Right now you are all that is important. God! I was so relieved to find you alive . . . I can't begin to tell you how worried I was. I was going out of my mind . . .'

Sue put a hand up to his lips and whispered, 'I know, I know.'

They held each other in silence for a moment, happy that the need for words had been overcome and they were truly together again. Sue said, 'I can't seem to stop thinking about what would have happened if you had driven up to the garage instead of walking. I just go through it over and over again. It's a nightmare I just can't seem to escape. Why did you stop down the road from the garage? What made you do that?'

Jamieson stroked her hair. 'You can thank a traffic jam for that. It gave me time to think.'

'Tell me,' said Sue.

Jamieson told her about his initial panic-stricken dash to what had turned out to be the wrong address and then how he had started to consider the motives behind the phone call, including the possibility of a cruel hoax. 'So I stopped at the phone box round the corner from the garages and called the hospital to check if you were still there. Evans told me that you had gone into town earlier, so I asked him to call the police. When I came out of the phone box I was so close to the lane that I left the car where it was and ran round on foot.'

'Thank God,' said Sue.

'I'll second that,' said Jamieson.

'Scott?'

'Yes?'

'What did the man say on the phone?'

'A lot of sick nonsense.'

'What exactly?' asked Sue.

Jamieson told her.

'That was untrue, you know?'

Jamieson squeezed her shoulder.

'I don't want you thinking that I lost the baby because of anything he did to me like that. He didn't touch me in that way. I think I lost the baby because he just scared me so much. It sounds silly now that you're here and I'm all safe and warm, but at the time . . . I thought he was the killer, the man who cut up those women. I never knew I could be so frightened.'

Jamieson soothed Sue as she started to shake again. When she had calmed down he said softly, 'Clive tells me that the police are waiting downstairs to talk to you if you feel up to it.'

Sue made a face.

'If you can't face it tonight I can tell them that, but the sooner they set about with finding that lunatic the better, so anything you can tell them . . .'

'Can you stay with me?'

'We could make that a condition,' said Jamieson.

'All right. I'll see them now. Correction, we'll see them now.'

The two police officers seemed decent, sympathetic individuals, but Jamieson still felt it necessary to remind them of what Sue had been through and to go easy with her.

'We do understand, sir,' the inspector reassured him. 'We'll be as brief as we possibly can.'

Sue told them about the man in the store and the subsequent train of events.

'You say that he said he wanted revenge?' asked the inspector.

'That's what he said.'

'But he didn't say for what or give any indication?'

'No.'

'And you say you have never seen this man before?'

'No. Apart from on the bus down.'

The policemen looked at each other. 'The bus down?' asked the inspector.

'Yes, he was on the same bus into town. He got off where I did,' said Sue, as if this had been an irrelevant detail.

'You didn't say anything about that earlier,' said Jamieson.

'Didn't I? Sorry.'

'Mrs Jamieson, this is very important. Did you happen to notice where this man got on the bus?' asked the inspector.

Sue shook her head and apologised. 'No, I didn't.'

'Did you look out the bus window on the way into town, Mrs Jamieson?'

'Yes, I did.'

'But you don't recall seeing this man get on the bus?'

'No.'

'Is it possible that he was on the bus when you got on?'

'But I got on here at the hospital,' said Sue. 'It's the terminus.'

'So it is,' agreed the policeman. 'Were there any people sitting on the bus when you got on?'

'Quite a few.'

'Is it possible that he was among them?'

'I suppose so,' said Sue. 'I didn't pay much attention to the people sitting inside when I got on. I just went straight upstairs.'

'Thank you, Mrs Jamieson.

Jamieson saw what the police had been getting at. The man had not just suddenly appeared at the store down town. He had followed Sue and, what was more, it seemed likely that he had done so from the hospital.

'There's something else,' said Sue.

'Go on, Mrs Jamieson.'

'He was wearing a disguise,' said Sue.

'A disguise?'

'His hair was a wig. I saw that when he was close to me at the garage and his moustache was false. It had started to come adrift at one of the corners.'

The inspector continued his recap. 'He was a large man, heavily built.'

Sue nodded.

'If you forget about the hair and the moustache, can you think of any man you've come across recently who has that build?'

Sue shook her head and said, 'I've been thinking about that a lot but no, I can't think of anyone. I hardly know anyone in this city!' she added.

'And you, sir?' the policeman asked Jamieson. 'Does that description mean anything to you?'

'Not off-hand,' said Jamieson with a shake of the head.

'Strange,' said the inspector. 'It's pretty clear this man was not our celebrated ripper. He wasn't too interested in your wife at all, apart from using her as a tool to get at you. For some reason he wanted to get at you very badly, sir. Can you think why anyone should feel that way?'

'No, Inspector. I can't.'

Phillip Morton came in to the room and insisted that the interview come to an end. Sue had to sleep. The policemen didn't argue. They thanked Sue and Jamieson for their co-operation and left. Jamieson had a few moments alone with Sue before he too left the room and returned to the residency with Clive Evans.

'You look as if you could do with a drink,' said Evans.

'I could do with ten,' replied Jamieson.

'We could go out?'

Jamieson did not need much persuasion. 'Good idea,' he said.

Jamieson had downed two large whiskies before he noticed that Evans was drinking only orange juice. 'You don't drink?' he asked.

'Nothing stronger than this,' replied Evans, tapping his glass, 'a legacy of Chapel days in the valleys.'

Jamieson smiled. 'Very wise.' He drained his own glass.

'Let me get you another,' said Evans.

'Not if you're not drinking,' protested Jamieson, but Evans ordered a whisky for him anyway. 'You have had one hell of a day. Call it medicinal. Half our patients do.'

Jamieson accepted the drink and admitted to himself that the whisky was doing him good. He had been under almost unbearable stress for the past few hours and now, for the first time, he felt himself start to unwind.

'What are your plans now?' asked Evans.

'When Sue feels better we'll go back to Kent and have some time off together. Ideally, I'd like to take her away on holiday somewhere. We'll see. Either way we should be gone by the end of the week and I can't say I'll be sorry to see the back of this place.'

'The hospital or the city?'

'Both.'

'I can understand that,' said Evans. 'You have not had the easiest of times.'

'None of us has in this mess.'

'Well, it's over now,' said Evans.

'Thank God,' said Jamieson. 'Damn, I meant to check on the re-sterilising of the instruments and dressings from gynaecology.'

'It's all right, I did it. Every single item has been autoclaved and returned under fresh seal.'

'Thanks,' said Jamieson. 'I wish you would let me buy you a drink.'

'You can send me some strawberries from Kent when the season arrives,' said Evans.

'That's a promise.'

Surgery resumed in the gynaecology department of Kerr Memorial on Wednesday of Jamieson's third week there with a full operating schedule designed to make inroads into the waiting list. There were no post-operative problems at the end of the day or on the following two days and by the time Jamieson and Sue came to leave the hospital on Saturday morning everything seemed to be back to normal. Hugh Crichton saw them off and wished them well and, holding a document case over his head with one hand to ward off the rain, he held the driver's door open for Sue to get in. Jamieson's arm, although out of the sling, had not recovered sufficiently for him to undertake the strain of a long drive.

Jamieson looked back as they drove through the hospital gates and then over at Sue. 'Feel good to be going?' he asked.

'Do you really need an answer to that?' said Sue.

As they sped south on the motorway Sue said, 'Have you had any more thoughts about the man in the wig?'

'A lot of thoughts but no answers,' replied Jamieson. 'You?'

Sue paused while she concentrated on finding a suitable moment to pull out and overtake the lorry in front. When they were safely past she said, 'I think he was homosexual.'

'What makes you say that?'

'He put his hand up my skirt at one point.'

'And that makes him homosexual?'

'He did it to frighten me – and he did – but I could see from the look in his eyes that he got no kick out of it. He could have been twisting my wrist.'

'Maybe you should tell the police that.'

'It's not exactly evidence, is it? And maybe it's not even important. It doesn't help to explain why he hates you or why he wanted to hurt you so badly.'

'I suppose not.'

'Does it worry you?'

'Of course,' said Jamieson. 'Particularly because I don't understand it. I can't imagine what I could possibly have done to make someone feel that way about me and yet, someone obviously does.'

They lapsed into silence for a few minutes until Sue asked, 'When will you go to see the Sci-Med people?'

'I'll go into London on Monday, if that's all right with you? The sooner I make my report the better.'

'Of course.'

The weather was clear and bright on Sunday morning, permitting Jamieson and Sue to enjoy their planned walk. It had been raining overnight and they enjoyed the smell of wet leaves as they walked along the lanes, arms wound round each other. They timed it so that they would be in the village of Bridge around lunch time to enjoy a meal at their favourite pub. But despite their conscious attempts at restoring normality to their lives, it was becoming apparent to both of them that this was going to take time. The nightmare of Kerr Memorial Hospital was not going to fade away readily.

Their conversation, once punctuated by comfortable silences, was now the subject of awkward ones, when one of them knew that the other had strayed off to brood on some happening of the past few weeks. At one point Jamieson had to admit that thoughts of the man who had abducted Sue were haunting him. 'You know what worries me most?' he said. 'It's the fact that the reason this man hates me so much must be in some way tied up with the events at the hospital. I hardly met anyone at all outside the hospital, apart from a couple of Italian waiters when I went out to eat – and the tip wasn't that bad.'

Sue smiled at Jamieson's attempt to lighten the conversation, but it fell flat. 'But surely no one could possibly blame you for the deaths at the hospital,' said Sue.

'I hope not,' said Jamieson. 'But maybe someone thinks I should have been able to do more. I should have been able to clear the matter up sooner and they blame me for the death of their wife or daughter?'

'Doesn't sound plausible,' said Sue, shaking her head decisively, and Jamieson had to agree.

'You don't think he might still try to get at you, do you?' asked Sue with a worried note in her voice.

'No, of course not,' said Jamieson. He met Sue's gaze and saw an accusation in her eyes. 'All right,' he said. 'The truth is I have no idea; he may do; there's no way of predicting anything unless we know what we're dealing with.'

'That's more like it,' said Sue. 'Don't bullshit me.'

'Dr Jamieson is here for his debriefing,' said Miss Roberts into the machine at her elbow. A disembodied voice replied, 'Send him up.'

'It's all right, I remember,' said Jamieson, turning to head for the lift.

'No, that's not allowed,' said Miss Roberts, loudly at first to stop Jamieson and then more apologetically, 'Visitors must be accompanied at all times in the Ministry. It's a rule.'

Jamieson acceded with a smile and waited for the uniformed man to escort him. They exchanged pleasantries in the lift about the weather and Jamieson learned that Mr Jackson had spent his summer holiday in Torquay. The weather had been 'mixed'.

'Good to see you,' said Macmillan when Jamieson entered the room.

Jamieson shook hands with him, using his left hand, and did the same with Armour and Foreman.

'I haven't done that since I was in the Boy Scouts,' joked Armour.

'You had a bit of a rough time up north, I understand,' said Macmillan.

'My wife had a rougher one,' said Jamieson.

'A nasty business,' said Foreman, and the other two concurred with nods and sympathy.

'Still no idea why he wanted to get at you?' asked Foreman.

'No, but my feeling is that it had something to do with the affair at the hospital. It must have done.'

'Why?' asked Armour.

'Apart from the fact that I hardly met anyone outside the hospital, I think that there was more to the infection problem than I managed to find out. There were lots of loose ends not tied up. I suspect some of them were quite important.'

'But the circumstantial evidence against the man Thelwell was very strong, even if the confession in his suicide note was a bit vague.' said Macmillan. 'I agree,' said Jamieson. 'But I still worry.'

Macmillan gave a wry smile and said, 'We have to be pragmatic about it. If the infection problem at Kerr Memorial has been cleared up, our job is done and that's an end to it.'

Armour said, 'Again, it's only circumstantial, but perhaps I might just add that there has been no new murder in the city in the last ten days.'

'We may never know the whole story,' said Macmillan, 'but I repeat, if Kerr Memorial's problem has ceased to exist with the death of this man Thelwell then that is good enough for us.'

'Very good, sir,' said Jamieson.

Macmillan got to his feet and Jamieson took this as his cue to do likewise. 'I'm sorry your first assignment for Sci-Med turned out to be so demanding and traumatic for you, Doctor. You must have a little break before we think about asking you to help us with anything else.'

'Some time alone with my wife would be nice,' replied Jamieson. 'I think I owe her some attention.'

'Of course,' said Macmillan. 'By the way,' he held out a brown envelope, 'This is the report you asked for from the Sci-Med lab. You had left Leeds before we could get it to you.'

Jamieson was puzzled. He said, 'I only asked for one lab report and I got that.' He took the report out of the open envelope, one handed, and read it. It was an analytical report an the *Staphylococcus* that had caused the second outbreak cf post-operative infection at Kerr Memorial. 'Strange,' he muttered. 'I don't remember asking for this.' He looked at the photocopy of the request that was stapled to the report and saw who had. It was signed M. Lippman, pp Dr S. Jamieson. Moira Lippman had sent cultures of the organism and made the request.

'Mystery cleared up?' asked Armour.

'Yes, thank you,' said Jamieson, still puzzled but not wanting to discuss it further. He put the report in his pocket.

'We'll be in touch,' said Macmillan.

Jamieson had more than two hours to wait for a train that would stop at Bekesbourne Halt, the tiny station within a mile of his home at Patrixbourne. He didn't mind because he was in no hurry and it gave him time to consider why Moira Lippman had made the request to the Sci-Med lab. Had she just been anticipating that he himself would want such an analysis? After all, he had sent the *Pseudomonas* there. Or did she have a good reason of her own? Something to do with what she had found out? Jamieson found the notion exciting, but there was no point in trying to decipher the report in his pocket in the dirt and damp of a railway station. He would wait until he was at home and had all his reference books to hand.

'How did it go?' asked Sue.

'All right. They're happy as long as the infection problem is over.'

'As you said yourself, it's a matter of priorities,' said Sue.

'What have you been doing with yourself?' asked Jamieson.

'Cleaning!' said Sue. 'We've been away so long that the house is filthy.'

'You shouldn't be doing that just yet,' said Jamieson softly. 'It's too soon after . . .'

Sue stiffened as he touched her and half turned away. 'It's over and done with and I'm fine,' she said in a tone that brooked no further discussion. She turned and walked through to the kitchen to put the kettle on. 'Why didn't you tell me the police were watching the house?'

Jamieson was taken aback. He considered pretending that

he did not know what she was talking about but capitulated instead. 'I'm sorry,' he said. 'I suppose I didn't want to alarm you. I just thought it might be a good idea if someone kept an eye on you today when I was away in London and you were here on your own. I arranged it through Sci-Med.'

'Next time tell me,' said Sue sharply. 'Agreed?'

'Agreed,' said Jamieson sheepishly.

'If that man at the end of the lane this morning had not looked so much like a policeman I might have thought he was . . . someone else entirely.'

'Oh God, I didn't even consider that,' said Jamieson. 'I'm so sorry. It was thoughtless of me.'

Sue dropped the teaspoon she had been holding and put her hand up to her face.

Jamieson came up behind her and put his arm around her. He sensed that Sue was still under great strain.

She recovered quickly and continued making the coffee. 'Tell me all about today,' she said as she led the way back to the sitting room, carrying the coffee cups on a tray.

'There was one strange thing,' said Jamieson. He told Sue about Moira Lippman's request for a Sci-Med analysis.

'And she didn't say anything to you?' said Sue

'She used my name but she never mentioned it.'

'What did the report say?'

'I brought it home with me. I'll have to work on it.'

'Does this mean you're going to spend the evening upstairs?' asked Sue.

'A little while,' said Jamieson. He kissed her hair. 'Won't be too long. I promise.'

Jamieson paused to look out of the study window at the willow tree in the garden. He always thought that it looked best at dusk, its branches drooping to touch the lawn as if weary from a long day's work. The trees on the far side of the cricket field were silhouetted against the evening sky. Jamieson drew the curtains, switched on the desk lamp and sat down.

Moira Lippman had asked for a full biochemical analysis on

the *Staphylococcus* organism and this had been carried out by the Sci-Med people. Some of the tests had been duplicated, for they had already been done at Kerr Memorial by Moira herself. A summary of the results said that the bug was a coagulase positive *Staphylococcus*, highly pathogenic to man and resistant to many of the branded therapeutic agents tested. If it had not been for the fact that Moira Lippman had remembered about the Loromycin trial and the fact that the drug had subsequently been found to be effective against the bug, as many as eight women at Kerr Memorial might have died. Unfortunately for two of them, Loromycin treatment had come along too late to save them. Ironically, the second one had been Moira's sister-in-law.

Jamieson read through the list of biochemical results and decided that he needed help in deciphering what they all meant. He got down his copy of Bergey's *Manual of Determinative Bacteriology* from the shelf above the desk and looked up *Staphylococcus* in the index. It had been a while since the book had been opened. It had collected a thick film of dust along its top. Jamieson blew as much of it away as possible before opening it at the index. He turned to the tables giving the information he needed and copied out the normal values for the biochemical tests listed in the report.

As he compared them with the results from the Sci-Med lab he began to see discrepancies and by the time he had finished he had discovered that four of the lab results did not agree with Bergey's idea of how a standard *Staphylococcus* should behave.

'Just like the *Pseudomonas*, he muttered. Was this what Moira Lippman had wanted to talk about? What did it mean?

'Scott! It's half past ten,' came Sue's voice from downstairs 'You promised!'

Jamieson automatically looked at his watch. He hadn't realised how time had been passing. 'Coming,' he replied. He closed the book slowly and put it back up on its shelf. The report was telling him something. He couldn't quite put his

finger on it yet, but it must have something to do with this
constant deviation of the bugs from text-book values. As
he cleared away his notes he decided that he would have
to give the matter some more thought. For the moment, it
could wait.

Eight days passed before Jamieson heard from Sci-Med again.
Sue and he had been out for the evening and the telephone
was ringing when they got back to the cottage just after
eleven.

'Jamieson here.'

'Ah, got you at last. Macmillan here.'

Jamieson looked at the clock on the wall. If Macmillan were
calling him at this time, something must be wrong.

'Trouble, I'm afraid,' said Macmillan.

Jamieson experienced a sinking feeling in his stomach. He
had come to know that when the smooth velvety tones of
the establishment actually used words like 'trouble' it almost
invariably meant something a good deal worse.

'What's happened?'

'There's been another outbreak of post-operative infection at
Kerr Memorial. In gynaecology again.'

Jamieson closed his eyes as the words drilled through him,
destroying all the good effects of the evening. He felt the energy
drain from him as if a tap had been opened. 'Go on,' he said.
The words were hoarse; he had to clear his throat before he
could say any more.

'It's bad, I'm afraid. Five women are affected at the moment.'

'And the cause?'

'The bug hasn't been identified yet, but Phillip Morton with
some impromptu detective work has narrowed the possibilities
down to a batch of saline drip packs. The lab is analysing them
right now.'

'I'll get back up there,' said Jamieson. 'In the meantime
there's something I'd like you to organise with the Sci-Med
lab.'

'Go on.'

'I want them to get their hands on as many unauthorised antibiotics as possible.'

'Unauthorised?' exclaimed Macmillan.

'Yes, drugs that the pharmaceutical companies have not yet got a license for.'

'But why?'

'I think we can expect that there will be a treatment problem with this outbreak just like last time and the time before. The bug will be immune to standard drug treatment. If it's the *Staphylococcus* we can use Loromycin again, but if it's the *Pseudomonas* we still have a problem – unless your people have come up with anything in the meantime?

'Not that I've heard,' said Macmillan. 'I think we rather thought that it was all over.'

'I'd like the Sci-Med lab to test both bugs against drugs that weren't commercially available before. There's a chance some of them may be effective, just like Loromycin turned out to be. We'll be taking a risk using unlicensed antibiotics and you'll have to square it with the authorities, but I think the circumstances warrant it.'

'Absolutely,' said Macmillan. 'I'll tell them.' Macmillan paused before saying, 'Look here, if you feel that you'd rather not get involved again . . . I mean, with your wife and all that, we'll quite understand here at Sci-Med.'

'I'll be returning to Leeds in the morning,' said Jamieson curtly.

Sue was standing looking at him when he put the phone down. 'I heard the last bit,' she said quietly.

'It's not over yet at Kerr Memorial. I have to see it through, Sue. I can't leave it like this.'

'I understand,' she assured him. 'What's happened?'

Jamieson told her.

'But how?'

Jamieson shook his head and said, 'I don't know, but I'm going to find out, if it's the last thing I do.'

Sue saw the look on Jamieson's face. She simply said, 'Of course.'

'I think it might be best if you were to go stay with your father for a few days,' said Jamieson.

'No,' said Sue flatly.

'What?'

'I said no. I'm coming with you.'

'This is crazy! I mean, after what you went through last time . . .'

'Stop treating me like "the little woman", will you! I'm not an object you hide in a cupboard, I'm your wife! It's our problem, not just yours. I'm coming.'

It was Jamieson's turn to concede that there was no room for argument.

There was a small crowd of people at the gates of Kerr Memorial when Jamieson and Sue arrived at eleven the following morning. Jamieson could see that some of them were carrying cameras and had the look of the press about them.

'Looks like it's really hit the fan this time,' he said as they waited for the gateman to come over and inspect his ID card.

'I thought you'd left, sir?'

'So did I.'

The gateman moved the crowd back with difficulty and opened the gate so that Jamieson could proceed. Sue felt uncomfortable with so many people looking in at her through the window. She felt like an inanimate object in a glass case and said so.

'We'd better let Crichton know that we've arrived,' said Jamieson as he brought the car to a halt outside the administrative block.

'I'll wait,' said Sue.

Jamieson got out of the car and swung the door shut with one hand before running up the steps of the main office building two at a time. His feet squeaked on the newly polished linoleum as he made his way along the corridor to Crichton's office and knocked on the door.

'Who is it?' came the voice from inside. There was a slight

note of surprise in the tone and Jamieson knew that this was because he had short circuited the receptionist and secretary to come to the side door of Crichton's office.

'Jamieson,' he replied, looking round the door. 'I just popped in to say that I'm back.'

Crichton indicated that he should come in and sit down and then returned to his telephone conversation.

'I'm sorry we have no further comment to make at this time,' said Crichton. 'No nothing!' He put the phone down and rapped his fingers on the desk in frustration.

'Problems?'

Crichton raised his eyes and said, 'I'll say. One woman has died so far in this latest outbreak and the other four are gravely ill. The newspapers have got hold of it and are howling for someone to blame. The Conservative group on the council are blaming bad management for falling standards of hygiene in the hospital. The Labour group are blaming government cuts and understaffing for the problem. Either way this office seems to be the front line.'

'Has the lab report on the saline come through yet?'

'Yes, half an hour ago.'

'Is it the *Pseudomonas* or the *Staphylococcus* this time?' asked Jamieson.

'Neither,' replied Crichton.

'I don't understand,' said Jamieson.

'I'm not sure I do either,' said Crichton, adopting a pained expression. 'But the lab says that once again it is an entirely different organism.'

'A third bug!' exclaimed Jamieson. 'This is getting absolutely ridiculous.'

'The outside world agrees – and by the way, the outside world is baying at the gates . . .'

'I saw them on the way in,' said Jamieson.

'To them, the hospital is a cesspool of infection and we, the staff, are all doing our best to cover it up.'

'Surgery in gynaecology has been halted?'

'Of course.'

Crichton's telephone rang again and Jamieson got to his feet to leave. 'See you later,' he whispered as Crichton picked up the receiver.

Jamieson and Sue settled in to their old room in the residency. They didn't say much, for both were feeling depressed at being back. There was a knock on the door and Jamieson opened it to find Clive Evans standing there.

'I saw your car,' said Evans, scratching his head as he came in.

'So it has started all over again?' said Jamieson.

"Fraid so and worse than ever.'

'Any ideas?'

'We know that the saline drip bottles were the source of the outbreak this time. Mr Morton worked that out and thank God he did before even more women were infected.'

'Crichton tells me that it's yet another bug?'

'That's right. It's a *Proteus* this time and . . .'

'Don't tell me. It's resistant to antibiotics just like the other two organisms?'

'I'm afraid so,' agreed Evans.

'Antibiotic synergism tests?'

'They are under way. Nothing yet.'

'Get some off to Sci-Med, will you. They are going to work on it too.'

'Very well.'

'Have you had full biochemistry done on the bug?' asked Jamieson.

'Not yet. There hasn't been time.'

'Sci-Med will do that too. Get the bug to them as quickly as possible and then we can have a look at all three reports.'

'Three?' asked Evans.

'Oh yes, I didn't tell you. Moira Lippman had the *Staphylococcus* analysed by the Sci-Med lab. I think that that's what she wanted to speak to us about before she died.'

'Really?' said Evans. 'What did the report say?'

'There are several discrepancies between the actual report

and how the book says a *Staphylococcus* should behave, just like there was in the case of the other bug.'

'Did your people have any comment to make about that?' asked Evans.

'I haven't asked them yet. I was lulled into believing that this business was over. But if we get the same sort of report this time there must be something in it. Something we've been missing.'

'If you like I could drive over to the county lab and ask them to carry out the tests on the latest bug? It might be quicker,' said Evans. 'We'd save a day.'

'Good idea,' said Jamieson. 'But do both. I want Sci-Med to work on the treatment angle. I'm going to be busy here tracing the history of that batch of saline and trying to find out how it got contaminated. Will you be all right on your own, Sue?'

'Of course. Is there anything I can do to help?'

'I don't think so at the moment,' said Jamieson. 'How about you, Clive? Need any help?'

'I'll call you if I think of anything,' said Evans. 'Thanks.'

15

Evans and Jamieson left Sue and walked over to the lab together, Evans to phone the county lab to alert them about the samples he would be bringing over and Jamieson to start work down in his old room.

'I've collected all the information I thought you might need about the contaminated saline,' said Evans as they reached the steps leading down to the microbiology department. 'I've left it on your desk, but I don't think you'll find anything there. I've already been through it pretty thoroughly. If there's anything else you need, just ask one of the technicians.'

Jamieson closed the door of the small room and took off his jacket. He sat down slowly on the swivel chair and felt depression settle on his shoulders like a lead collar. He had returned to the realms of a bad dream. There was a closed cardboard file lying on the desk in front of him; he flipped it open. He knew that he would have to examine all the files pertaining to the contaminated saline as a matter of routine, but there was such a feeling of *deja vu* about it. He knew very well that all the paperwork would be perfectly in order, just as it always had been in the past.

An hour later Jamieson was proved right. The sterilisation procedures had apparently been faultless; all the proper checks had been performed and there was no obvious way that the saline could have become contaminated with anything at all, let alone a deadly new organism. This particular batch of saline had been delivered directly to the gynaecology department and, of course, there could have been no interception by Thelwell this time. Despite all this, the saline had been contaminated and one woman had already died because of it.

In a search for alternative theories, Jamieson considered the possibility that the saline had been interfered with while it had lain in storage in gynaecology. Was it even conceivable that the contaminated saline had been some awful legacy from Thelwell? Could he have infected it before he died? It had simply not been used at the time? Jamieson checked the dates of sterilisation and delivery to the department. It gave him a clear answer. It was not possible. Thelwell had already been dead for two days when the saline was sterilised and delivered to gynaecology. If it had been contaminated in the stores, Thelwell had certainly not done it.

Jamieson turned his attention to the preliminary report on the new infection and decided that he needed to find out more about the organism. He went into one of the neighbouring labs and asked one of the technicians for some reference literature. The man reached up to the book shelf behind him and brought down a copy of McLennan's *Microbiology in Medicine*. 'You'll probably find all you want to know in here,' he said, handing it over.

'I'll bring it right back,' said Jamieson.

'No hurry.'

Jamieson checked the index and flicked through the pages to find what he was looking for.

'PROTEUS: A gram negative, non lactose fermenting organism often found in sewage, soil and manure. Commonly implicated in urinary tract infections but also found in other, often more serious, infections. Named after the Greek sea god, Proteus, because of a tendency to display a variety of changing cultural characteristics.'

The section went on to list the cultural and biochemical details of the organism. This was followed by a section on the treatment of the organism. Four antibiotics of choice were listed. Jamieson noted that the current hospital strain had already been shown to be immune to all of them. He was trying to recall what he knew about Proteus in Greek mythology when his bleeper went off; it was Chief Inspector Ryan.

'I heard you were back,' said Ryan. 'Perhaps I could have a word?'

'Of course,' replied Jamieson. 'I'll be in the lab for a while yet. Come on over.'

Ryan arrived within fifteen minutes and the two men shook hands and exchanged pleasantries. 'How's the investigation been going?' Jamieson enquired.

The policeman shrugged and said, 'If you mean have we been able to pin the ripper murders on Thelwell posthumously, the answer is no. We still don't have one single piece of evidence to link him conclusively with the killings. It's all circumstantial. But I understand you've got problems, too?'

'The post-operative infections have started up again and we don't know why,' said Jamieson.

'And it can't have anything to do with Gordon Thomas Thelwell this time?' said Ryan.

'No,' replied Jamieson. 'That fact has not escaped me. Did you have any luck with the dates of Thelwell's choir practice nights?'

'We didn't come up with a perfect match of dates,' said Ryan. 'One of the murders was committed on a night when Thelwell did not have a practice, but on the other hand he *was* out of the house.'

'Did you manage to trace his movements?'

'We did,' said Ryan. 'He was attending a function in the city, some Rotary Club function.'

'And?'

'He did attend,' said Ryan.

'So he couldn't have carried out the killing on that night?' said Jamieson.

Ryan sighed and said, 'Unfortunately, we can't say that for sure. It would have been possible for him to slip away long enough to do it. The venue was within range of the murder location. Thirty minutes' absence would have been sufficient. It's all a bit inconclusive.'

I take it Thelwell did not own or rent a flat in the building I followed him to in the city?'

The policeman shook his head, 'Unfortunately not. We checked out all seven apartments, interviewed their owners and tenants, but there was no connection with Thelwell that we could establish. I would have told you sooner, but we had to wait for one of the owners to return from abroad to be sure. I just got the report this morning.' Ryan illustrated his point by showing Jamieson a folded piece of paper. 'The bottom line is that no one admits to having known Thelwell.'

'Pity,' said Jamieson. 'So we still have no idea what he was doing down there that night?'

'None.'

'What are your feelings?' asked Jamieson.

'About Thelwell? I'm not sure. I think the truth is that we're waiting to see if the killings have stopped.'

'Like the infections,' said Jamieson with a wry smile.

'Quite so,' agreed Ryan. 'And look what happened.'

'But if he wasn't the killer, why did he do himself in and what was his suicide note all about?

'You're right,' agreed Ryan. 'It's difficult to think anything else. Even his own wife had her doubts about what he was up to.'

'But if there should happen to be another killing . . .' said Jamieson.

'Then we're dealing with a psychopath and he'll be a police nightmare to hunt down. He'll probably have no form and no discernible motive, apart from some vague nonsense that makes sense only to him. By nature these killers tend to be loners, so there's no family or friends to shop them. And above all else, they are clever.'

'Clever?'

'They are cunning and devious; they enjoy what they see as a contest, a game, a battle of wits. Ironically, it's that that usually leads to their downfall. They become too arrogant; they get over-confident, push their luck too far and that's when they slip up and we get them. But waiting for that to happen stretches everyone's nerves to breaking point.'

'I believe it,' said Jamieson.

'I would have thought that, if it was someone other than Thelwell, we would have had a note by now, but there's been nothing as yet.'

'What sort of note?'

'Psychos like to have a dialogue with the police. They like to give little hints and clues so that we can get closer, but not too close of course. They get some kind of kick out of it. It adds excitement to the game.'

'I hope you get him soon,' said Jamieson.

'We'll get him all right,' said Ryan. 'But I wouldn't like my salary to ride on it being soon. There could be a lot more heartache in this city before that happens.'

'What about the other nutter?' asked Jamieson.

'The other one?'

'The man who kidnapped my wife?'

Ryan said, 'No joy there either. It looks like a one-off and we don't even have a motive for the crime. Have you come up with anything yourself?'

Jamieson shook his head. 'Sue came back up with me,' he added.

'I didn't realise that,' said Ryan, his face showing surprise. 'Would you like an eye kept on her?'

'Unobtrusively,' said Jamieson.

'I'll see to it.'

Jamieson made a mental note to tell Sue and shook hands with Ryan as the policeman got up to go.

Jamieson was pondering what he should do next when a piece of paper lying on the end of his desk caught his eye. He remembered Ryan putting it down there after he had taken it out of his pocket. Jamieson picked it up and read it. He recalled now what Ryan had said it was. It was the transcript of an interview with the last of the apartment owners to be questioned, the one who had been abroad.

The woman's apartment had been unoccupied for the entire month she had been abroad in Tenerife. There was nothing remarkable in that or in any of the answers, but Jamieson found his heart thumping and his skin prickling as he read the name of the owner at the end of the report. It said, Jennifer Blaney!

It was too much of a coincidence, Jamieson decided. Blaney was not that common a name. There just had to be a connection between Jennifer Blaney and Charge Nurse Blaney who ran the central sterile supply department at Kerr Memorial. Jamieson thought about Blaney and with each passing moment he felt he was coming closer to some terrible truth. Blaney had been hostile to him when he had enquired about Thelwell's interest in the sterilising department, but he had assumed at the time that it was just professional resentment on Blaney's part. He had not considered that there might be some kind of relationship between Blaney and Thelwell. It still seemed rather incongruous, but then he was familiar only with the public persona of both men.

Jamieson was musing about it when another thought brought ice to his spine. Blaney was a large, well built man. The man who had abducted Sue answered that description.

Jamieson's pulse rate started to rise as he saw how certain facts might fit together. If there had been some 'association' between Blaney and Thelwell, however unlikely this might seem, then it was just possible that Blaney might hold him personally responsible for Thelwell's death. If this was so, he had uncovered a possible motive for Sue's kidnapping. Revenge, the man had said. An eye for an eye. A tooth for a tooth. A lover for a lover?

Jamieson called the front office and asked for Chief Inspector Ryan. He was told that Ryan had just left. He put down the receiver and rested his hand on it while he thought it through. Adrenalin was coursing through his veins and a maelstrom of ideas and motives was swirling inside his head as he saw himself on the very brink of solving the whole affair.

Blaney was in charge of the central sterile supply department. That gave him every opportunity to interfere with sterilised packs of instruments, dressings or whatever. Maybe he was a willing accomplice to Thelwell? That would explain how the dressings and the saline could have been contaminated after apparently having been properly sterilised. Blaney could have contaminated the packs before distribution to the wards! Or maybe it was just Blaney all the time? Maybe Thelwell had had nothing whatever to do with the infections!

Jamieson's mind was running on overdrive. He needed something to slow him down and he found it when he tried to work out how Blaney could have obtained the deadly organisms to carry out the contaminating procedures? Jamieson's theory ground to a halt as he failed to solve this part of the puzzle. But there was one thing for sure, he had some questions for Mr Blaney to answer and if it should turn out that Blaney was responsible for what had happened to Sue, there was a personal score to settle.

Jamieson knew that he was doing the wrong thing in tackling Blaney on his own. He knew that emotional involvement was not a sensible basis for action and what he should be doing was waiting for Ryan to turn up, so that he could be presented with all the facts. Despite all this, he found the personal motive too strong. He got up from his desk, put on his jacket and set off for the central sterile supply department.

Jamieson marched towards the department with cold determination. He thought about what Sue had suffered and of the baby they both had lost. He had no real idea what he was going to say to Blaney, but this did not make him alter his pace at all. He pushed open both swing doors and entered the steamy heat of the approach corridor.

The preparation benches where the attendants packed instruments were deserted. Jamieson looked at his watch and saw that it was lunch time. Perhaps Blaney would be out at lunch, too. He walked past the row of gleaming sterilisers and up to the door of Blaney's office. He pushed open the door.

Blaney was sitting there, eating sandwiches. He stopped as he saw Jamieson, a sandwich suspended in mid air between his desk and his mouth. His eyes displayed a mixture of disbelief and surprise as he saw Jamieson standing there. 'Yes?'

Jamieson just stared at Blaney. He was picturing him with a wig and false moustache. He looked at the fat podgy hands that had tied Sue's hair to the door motor.

'What do you want?' stammered Blaney.

Jamieson could read the guilt on Blaney's face and he felt the anger rise inside him. 'You bastard!' he said with cold deliberation.

Blaney had started to get up slowly from his chair and back away but there was nowhere for him to go. 'What are you talking about?' he said, as he looked out of the corner of his eyes for an escape route.

'It's over, Blaney. But before the police can have you I want a piece of you for what you did to Sue.'

Blaney stopped all pretence of innocence. His bottom lip quivered. 'You killed Gordon Thelwell!' he accused, 'You drove him to it! You hounded him until he took his own life. You killed him! You are responsible! He meant everything to me and you took him away. You deserved to suffer! You deserved to go through what I went through.'

Fired by his own rhetoric, Blaney threw the contents of the coffee cup he was holding directly into Jamieson's face.

The coffee was not very hot but the liquid temporarily blinded Jamieson. Blaney took the opportunity to rush past him to the door. Jamieson stuck out his foot and Blaney crashed headlong out of the door into the sterilising hall. But by the time Jamieson had cleared his eyes and could see properly again, Blaney was back up on his feet and had picked up a steel dish full of instruments lying in antiseptic solution.

Jamieson put up his hands to protect himself as a hail of scalpels and forceps flew through the air towards him. Several small cuts opened up on the backs of his hands and on his scalp, but he ignored them as he again moved towards Blaney. He stopped when he saw that Blaney had picked up a post-mortem knife. Jamieson found himself mesmerised by the long blade which swept out from the black, bone handle held tightly in Blaney's fist.

The fact that Jamieson had stopped in his tracks gave Blaney a surge of confidence. He gave a half smile and sneered, 'Come on then, Dr bloody smart-arse Jamieson. What are you waiting for? Changed our tune, have we?'

Jamieson had indeed changed his tune. The folly of his angry, headstrong action in confronting Blaney alone had now come home to roost. He stared at the razor sharp blade in Blaney's hand, a blade that was no stranger to the insides of a human being.

'Who did it, Blaney?' he croaked. 'Who contaminated the instruments and the dressings and the saline? You? Or was it Thelwell? Maybe it was both of you? You sick bastard!'

A look of puzzlement crossed Blaney's face. 'What the hell are you talking about?' he demanded.

'Is that how you two got your kicks? A couple of old queens against a world of women, eh?'

'You're mad,' said Blaney. He lunged at Jamieson with the knife. It was the angry reaction that Jamieson had been goading him into. Jamieson side-stepped smartly and grabbed at Blaney's knife arm as he lost balance. He twisted Blaney's arm up his back, but Blaney remained upright as Jamieson tried to loosen his grip on the knife.

Jamieson was concentrating too hard on the knife to be prepared for Blaney's sudden drop to the floor. With his centre of gravity undermined, it was all too easy for Blaney to tumble Jamieson over his shoulder and send him sliding across the tiles to crash into a table by the wall. The table was knocked over and steel dishes fell to the floor as Jamieson struggled to regain orientation.

Jamieson recovered in time to see Blaney rush towards him, knife held aloft, his eyes betraying an anger beyond reason. In a desperate last ditch attempt to protect himself, Jamieson raised both feet and caught Blaney in mid lunge. The charge nurse's momentum took him clean over Jamieson's head and he hit his skull against the tiled wall with a sickening crack.

Jamieson lay still for a moment recovering his breath. There was no question of Blaney still being a threat. After such a blow to his head, the nurse must certainly be unconscious, if not dead. Jamieson got to his feet slowly and went over to where Blaney lay. He felt for a pulse and found one with ease; it was strong and regular. 'You've got a head like a rock, Blaney,' he said to the unconscious man as he tied his hands behind his back using lengths of gauze. Satisfied that Blaney was secure for the moment, he called the police.

Jamieson reckoned that he had at least five minutes before the police arrived, probably a bit more. He looked down at where Blaney lay and felt frustrated. There were so many things he wanted to know, things he felt that Blaney could tell him, if only he were conscious. The steel dishes lying on the floor decided him. He filled one with cold water and threw it in Blaney's face. Blaney did not stir, so Jamieson repeated the operation until he did.

As Blaney uttered the first groans of consciousness, Jamieson started to question him. 'Come on Blaney, how did you do it? How did you contaminate the instruments and dressings?'

Blaney put a hand to his head and looked around him groggily. Jamieson repeated the question.

'Don't be ridiculous,' groaned Blaney. 'That was nothing to do with me.'

'You mean it was Thelwell?'

'You stupid bastard. Is that what you think? You think that Gordon and I murdered the patients?' Blaney snorted and gave a humourless guffaw. 'Christ, you must be desperate for an idea!'

'You gave all the instruments for gynaecology to Thelwell, instead of having them sent to the wards by a porter. Why?'

'You know why, damn it! Gordon told you. He was worried about the possibility of the instruments being interfered with, so he collected them immediately after they had been sterilised for safe keeping until such times as they were required.'

'Or until he had contaminated them with deadly bacteria,' said Jamieson.

'Deadly bacteria!' snorted Blaney. 'Where the hell would Gordon get deadly bacteria from? He was a surgeon, for Christ's sake!'

Jamieson avoided a question he could not answer. 'Tell me about Thelwell's missed choir practices.'

'Gordon and I used to meet once a week. It was all we could risk without arousing suspicion. We used to drive out to a hotel, but when my sister went abroad on holiday I "borrowed" the key to her flat and we used that for the month she was away.'

'Why did Thelwell kill himself if it wasn't because of the murders?' asked Jamieson.

'Because he thought it was all going to come out about us! When you followed him to my sister's place, he thought it was inevitable.'

'How did he know I followed him there?' asked Jamieson.

'We both heard you in the stairway that night. You called out his name. He was convinced that you knew everything about us, but you didn't.'

'No, I didn't,' agreed Jamieson.

'There was just no way a man like Gordon could have faced the scandal and ridicule. He was a very sensitive man, you know.'

'Really, said Jamieson drily.

The mist faded from Blaney's eyes and they turned to flint. 'Yes, you bastard! Nobody really understood him!' Blaney struggled at his bonds but to no avail; the police had arrived.

Blaney was formally charged and taken away, in the first instance to have X-rays taken of his head injuries. Chief Inspector Ryan stayed behind to talk to Jamieson.

'Well, that's one mystery solved,' said Ryan. 'At least we know now why your wife was attacked and once we've had a chat with Mr Blaney we might be able to clear up some other things.'

Jamieson nodded, but he was deeply troubled.

'Is something the matter?' asked Ryan, conscious of the fact that Jamieson was not sharing his euphoria.

'Before you arrived, I talked to Blaney about Thelwell's involvement in the hospital deaths,' said Jamieson. 'Blaney maintains that neither he nor Thelwell had anything to do with them.'

'Well, he would wouldn't he?' said Ryan.

Jamieson looked at Ryan and said, 'Yes, but the trouble is, I believe him. He says that Thelwell killed himself because he thought I was going to destroy his reputation by publicising his homosexual affair with Blaney. He thought I knew . . .'

Jamieson lingered on alone in the central sterile supply department. He heard Ryan's car drive off as he sat down slowly at the desk beside the autoclaves and idly sifted through a pile of recorder charts. Much as he disliked Blaney, he had to admit that what the charge nurse had said sounded like the truth. But if neither Blaney nor Thelwell had been involved in spreading the infection – and Thelwell had actually been guarding the instruments as he maintained – how could they have possibly become infected? Unless, of course, they had never been sterilised in the first place? But that was ridiculous. He himself had seen the recorder chart from the steriliser run on the day Thelwell had collected the instruments and all the others for that matter.

Jamieson got up and walked towards the autoclave. He stood in front of the silent steel machine that Blaney had confirmed was the one used for gynaecology supplies. Not only had the chart record been spot on, but Clive Evans had carried out the weekly test on the machine just before the run. Jamieson walked slowly up the side of the machine to the supply pipes at the back and ran his hand idly over the smooth copper pipework.

There was some extra pipework on this machine to facilitate the insertion of test thermocouples for monitoring the conditions inside the sterilising chamber. Jamieson traced the pipes and then noticed several smaller ones which led back into the machine. He was puzzled for a moment because he could see no obvious reason for them. He stared at them for a full minute, then looked around for a screwdriver to remove the side panel of the machine. He found what he was looking for in a drawer marked, TOOLS.

With the metal shield removed, Jamieson could see that the small pipes ran along the outside of the sterilising chamber and were connected to the gauges at the front of the machine. But why? Why should it be necessary to reflect the readings on the monitoring equipment on the gauges on the front of the machine? Jamieson felt the blood start to pound in his ears as he retraced the pipes once more and followed the logic of the valves.

He found himself transfixed by the sight of two red valves in the left upper quadrant. Surely he must be wrong. He followed the circuit again and reached the same frightening conclusion. On this machine it was possible to isolate the sterilising chamber from its supply lines and still have the readings of pressure and temperature in the pipes at the back of the machine appear on the gauges and the chart recorder at the front. The chamber thermometer could read one hundred and thirty one degrees centigrade while the steriliser remained stone cold.

'Christ Almighty,' whispered Jamieson, as he saw how it had been done. The instruments and dressings had been contaminated before they had gone into the steriliser, then they had gone through a dummy run before being distributed. Blaney had been right when he had asked how he or Thelwell could have got hold of deadly bacteria. It would have taken a specialist for that . . . Jamieson felt a slight tremor run through his body at his last thought. What kind of specialist was he talking about? A microbiologist! He would have to be a microbiologist! A man or woman who would know how to handle bacteria and viruses with confidence, grow them, manipulate them . . . mutate them!

There had been three key players in this affair with that

kind of ability and two of them were dead, John Richardson and Moira Lippman. That left the third, Clive Evans!

The pieces suddenly seemed to fit like some hellish jigsaw puzzle. Richardson and Moira had been killed because their specialist knowledge had led them to the truth about the contaminating organisms. Sue had suggested as much. Evans was not only in the front line of the lab investigation, he was responsible for monitoring the sterilisers!

Evans had come to the central sterile supply department, ostensibly to test the machines, but in reality to contaminate their contents! It had been Clive Evans all along! Evans was the killer!

Jamieson's head reeled as he recognised how Evans had so expertly diverted suspicion towards the hapless Thelwell. It had been Evans who had faked the result of Thelwell's test swabs, knowing what this would do to the already strained relationship between Thelwell and Richardson. It had been Evans who had been responsible for dropping the instruments on to the floor up in theatre, but he had made it look like Thelwell's fault. Clever . . . but mad, completely mad.

The thought reminded Jamieson of Costello Court, the mental hospital that John Richardson had been in touch with before his death. He picked up the phone and asked for Sci-Med's number in London.

'I have to have the following information fast! I repeat fast! Was a Clive Evans ever a patient at Costello Court Hospital and if so why? I need to know all the case details. Call me back on . . .' He gave his extension number at the hospital.

It took twelve minutes for Sci-Med to return the call. It was Macmillan himself.

'I have just gone out on a limb for this, Jamieson. You had better have a good reason for wanting this information.'

'I have.'

'Dr Clive Linton Evans was a patient at Costello Court Hospital from July third last year to March fourteenth this year after suffering a severe mental breakdown. The breakdown followed his contracting an incurable venereal disease from a prostitute. It was thought that he might not work again, but an altruistic consultant at one of the northern hospitals took him under his wing and elected to oversee him through a period of rehabilitation. Apparently, medical opinion at Costello Court was bitterly divided over the Evans case. One psychiatrist on Evans' review panel even went so far as to suggest that Evans might be conning them all. The word "psychopath" was mentioned, but this doctor was overruled. I take it you have come across Dr Evans?'

'He's on the staff,' said Jamieson.

'My God!' said Macmillan. 'And do you think . . .'

'I know and I've just found out how he's been doing it. I'd better ring off and contact the police.'

'Is there anything we can help you with?'

Jamieson was about to say no when he had another thought and asked, 'Who was *Proteus* in Greek mythology?'

'Good Lord,' exclaimed Macmillan. 'Let me see . . . the sea god who changed his form at will, if my memory serves me right.'

'That's exactly what I wanted to know,' said Jamieson and put down the phone. He could hear himself breathe in the silence as the awfulness of Evans' crime tested his own credibility to the limit. The current *Proteus* infection was a sick joke! Evans had been changing the infection at will! He had been deliberately engineering the bacteria before using them to contaminate dressings and equipment bound for the wards. He had been mutating them so that they would be resistant to treatment. Using a strain of *Proteus* for the latest outbreak and its inherent allusion to a Greek god in its name had been sheer arrogance, just like Ryan had said, the arrogance of a complete psychopathic lunatic!

The full meaning of the earlier biochemical test results now became clear to Jamieson. The bugs had differed from the text-book values so drastically because they had been artificially mutated! Evans had deliberately induced genetic changes in the bacteria. He had done it to make them more virulent and virtually untreatable, but the procedure would have induced many other mutations in the bugs at the same time. This is what Richardson and, later, Moira Lippman must have deduced!

Jamieson finally reached Ryan. 'Can you come back to CSSD at Kerr Memorial? It's urgent.'

16

Ryan was back within ten minutes and Jamieson told him everything. He showed him what he had discovered about the plumbing at the back of the steriliser. Jamieson had left the side shielding off the machine, so that Ryan could trace the pipes with his hand as it was pointed out to him what would happen when the wheel valves were altered.

'The mad bastard,' murmured Ryan.

Jamieson told Ryan about the report from Costello Court.

'Then why the hell didn't they keep him under lock and key?' said Ryan angrily. 'Surely if there was the slightest doubt about his mental state they should have erred on the side of caution?'

'For what it's worth, I agree,' said Jamieson.

'We seem to spend half our time hunting people who shouldn't be on the streets in the first place!'

'Medical opinion was divided in Evans' case,' said Jamieson

Ryan's look said what he thought of medical opinion. 'And so the bugger ends up in charge of a hospital lab! I ask you! Kerr Memorial is an equal opportunity employer! Being a psychopath is no drawback!'

Jamieson could not find it in his heart to offer up any defence of the system. He understood and shared Ryan's anger.

'Can all the contaminated material be traced back to this machine?' asked Ryan.

Jamieson nodded and said, 'I checked that while I was

waiting for you to arrive. The instruments, the dressings and the contaminated saline were all sterilised in this machine and in each case immediately after Evans had carried out "testing" of the machine.'

'Well, that's it then,' said Ryan.

'Not quite everything,' said Jamieson. He told Ryan about the genetically altered bacteria. 'I don't know where or how he did it, but I'd like to find out.'

'How do you go about inducing mutations in bacteria?' asked Ryan.

'There are several ways. You can treat them with chemicals or you can irradiate them with X-rays or ultra-violet light. It's really not that difficult . . .' Jamieson suddenly stopped in mid sentence and exclaimed, 'No blisters!'

'Pardon?'

John Richardson's wife told me that just before her husband died he seemed very troubled. She heard him repeat over and over to himself, "No blisters." He was talking about Evans' arm!'

'I'm sorry. You've lost me.'

'When I first came here, I had an accident involving an electric heater in my bathroom, although now, I wonder if it was an accident. Evans had the room next to mine and it's possible he set the whole thing up. At the time, Evans appeared on the scene as my rescuer and later I saw that he had a burn mark on his arm. I assumed that he had got it "helping" me and pointed this out to John Richardson. But there were no blisters! Just a red mark. It was actually a radiation burn! Richardson must have worked out that the infections were being caused by mutant bacteria and then realised the significance of the mark on Evans' arm.'

'So he confronted Evans and Evans murdered him,' said Ryan, getting up. 'Is Evans in the lab just now?'

'No, he went up to the county lab. He won't be back for another hour or so.'

Ryan thought for a moment and then said, 'There's no

point in putting out an alert for him. Nothing has happened to make him suspicious. We'll wait till he returns and then grab him.'

'I want to have a look round his lab and office to see if I can find a clue to the radiation source,' said Jamieson.

'I'll get more of our people down here,' said Ryan.

The technician who had loaned Jamieson his diagnostic bacteriology book came into Evans' lab while he was rummaging through one of the cupboards.

'Is there something I can help you with?' he asked, his tone hovering on accusation.

'Is there an ultra-violet lamp anywhere in the lab?' Jamieson asked.

'No, why?'

'How about an X-ray source?'

'No.'

'Is there a spare key to the office that Dr Evans uses?'

'There's a sub-master key in the office.'

'Get it, will you.'

'Are you sure you should be doing this?' the technician asked as Jamieson opened up Evans' office and started to work his way through the drawers and cupboards.

'I'm dead certain,' replied Jamieson and added, 'You can help if you like. We're looking for any radiation source, but probably a UV lamp.'

The technician shrugged his shoulders and started to open up cupboard doors.

Ten minutes later Jamieson admitted defeat and sat down in Evans' chair. 'Nothing, damn it,' he said.

'Nothing,' agreed the technician, closing up the last of the cupboards.

'What the hell did he do with it?' murmured Jamieson.

The technician stayed silent. Jamieson opened the desk drawer and was about to close it again when he noticed a small brown bottle lying on top of an old domestic electricity bill. He picked it up, expecting it to be Aspirin, and read the label. N-Nitrosoguanidine, it said. He read it out and asked, 'What would you use this for?'

'We wouldn't,' replied the technician. 'But be careful how you handle it. It's a powerful mutagen.'

'That was the answer to my next question,' said Jamieson. 'But we still haven't found the radiation source.'

'Would you like me to continue the search in the other labs?'

'I'd be grateful. If you find anything, let me know at once, would you? I'll be in the residency.'

'What should I say when Dr Evans returns?'

'He won't be returning.'

Jamieson ran up the steps to his room and was disappointed to find no one there. There was a note lying on the coffee table. Jamieson turned deathly pale when he read it. It said: 'Have gone with Clive to the county lab. See you later. Love, Sue.'

Jamieson fought hard to keep a grip on himself. There was no need to worry, he told himself; Clive Evans had no idea that they were on to him. There was no conceivable reason why Evans should do anything to harm Sue and draw attention to himself. The fact that Sue had gone off in the company of a psychopathic killer with a particular hatred of women was no cause for alarm. The hell it wasn't! A knot of fear settled in Jamieson's stomach as he flew down the stairs and rushed back to the central sterile supply department to tell Ryan.

'Take it easy!' soothed Ryan, who started telling him all the things he had been telling himself.

'I want him picked up!' said Jamieson. 'Now!'

'If police cars should suddenly appear in his mirrors and start chasing him, your wife will be in a lot more danger than she is now,' maintained Ryan.

Jamieson had to concede the point, but he was in no mood for common sense. He wanted action. He was like a cat on hot bricks.

'I'll tell you what,' said Ryan. 'Call the county lab and if Evans is still there ask to speak to your wife. You can get her to make some excuse for not accepting a lift back. Say you have to go out there yourself and you will bring her back.'

'Good idea,' said Jamieson. He snatched at the phone and asked the operator for the county lab. He looked at Ryan and drummed his fingers impatiently on the desk while he waited.

'County Laboratories.'

'This is Dr Jamieson at Kerr Memorial Hospital. Are Dr Evans and my wife still with you?'

'Pardon?' said the voice.

'Dr Evans was bringing some bacterial cultures over to you for analysis. He made the arrangement this morning by telephone. I wondered if he might still be there.'

'One moment, please.'

'What's the problem?' whispered Ryan.

'I don't know,' shrugged Jamieson. But inside, he felt ill. He heard the receiver at the other end being picked up.

'We have no record of Dr Evans having contacted us,' said the voice.

Jamieson felt his head swim. 'Are you quite sure?' he croaked.

'Quite.'

'So he's not been there?'

'No.'

Jamieson put down the phone and couldn't speak for a moment.

'What is it?' demanded Ryan. 'What's happened?'

'Evans isn't there. He never was. He didn't call them. He never intended going there. He must have known I was getting close and now he's got Sue!'

'Okay,' said Ryan. 'I'll put out an APB for them. Don't worry. We'll find them.' Ryan swung into action, leaving Jamieson to slump down in a chair as he faced another personal nightmare. Where would Evans have taken her? What was he doing to her? He did not have an answer for the first question, but his mind filled with agony when he thought about the second.

He tried to think logically and assess what he had learned

about Evans so far in the hope that it might provide him with some clue, but he only succeeded in becoming more and more anxious. He failed to come up with any idea at all. He was almost at his wits' end when he did realise that there was one thing he knew. The search for the radiation source in the microbiology lab had proved fruitless, so that must mean that Evans had carried out his lab work on the bacteria somewhere else! He must have alternative premises somewhere in the city! He had to find out where!

He ran back to the lab to ask the technicians if they knew of any such place. He drew a blank. As far as they knew, Evans lived in the residency. No one was aware of him having any other address.

'I didn't come across a UV lamp anywhere else in the lab,' said the technician who had helped him search earlier.

Jamieson nodded.

'Shall I put this back?' The technician held up the small brown bottle that Jamieson had found in Evans' drawer.

Jamieson nodded absent-mindedly, but the technician's question conjured up a memory of the bottle. He saw it again lying on its side in the drawer on top of . . . an electricity bill! Why would Evans have an electricity bill when he lived in the hospital residency?

Jamieson leapt to his feet and chased along the corridor. He burst into Evans' room and brushed past the startled technician to yank open the desk drawer and pull out the bill. It was addressed to Evans at a place in the city.

As they drove through city streets, Sue fell silent as she recalled her terrifying drive in the taxi. She looked at the busy entrance to Marks and Spencers and felt a shiver climb her spine.

'Cold?' asked Evans, leaning across to adjust the heater levers on the dash.

'Not really,' replied Sue. 'Someone must have walked over my grave.'

'Strange expression that,' said Evans.

'Mmm.'

'Any idea where it comes from?'

'Afraid not.'

'Let's talk of graves, of worms and epitaphs.'

'What?'

'Shakespeare. Richard the Second.'

'Oh,' said Sue.

'I hope you don't mind if we take a short detour. I want to pick something up at my flat.'

'Not at all. I didn't realise you had a flat?'

'It's more of a studio really.'

'You're an artist?' asked Sue.

'I like to pretend I am.'

'How interesting,' said Sue.

The car slowed and turned off the main road to glide slowly through back streets and come to a halt.

'I have the basement flat here,' said Evans.

'The basement?' exclaimed Sue. 'I thought artists needed lots of light?'

Evans looked at Sue in silence for a moment and then said, 'We have to use what we can afford.'

'Of course,' smiled Sue.

'Perhaps you would like to see some of my humble efforts?'

'I'd love to, Clive,' said Sue. 'I have the greatest admiration for anyone who can draw or paint.'

'They're not very good, I'm afraid.'

'I'm sure you're just being modest.'

Evans led the way down the stone steps and Sue waited while he fiddled with the locks on the door and finally got it open. The air inside seemed cold and damp and for a fleeting moment Sue felt apprehensive without knowing why. She stepped inside.

What little light there was inside was suddenly dimmed by Evans closing the door behind them. 'I'll have to switch on the electricity at the mains,' he said.

'I'll open the curtains, shall I?' said Sue, making a move towards the heavy drapes.

'No. Don't do that,' said Evans behind her. His voice

had changed. It was quiet now, authoritative and somehow different.

Sue turned round as the lights were turned on and saw Evans leaning against the door looking at her. 'I don't understand,' she said. 'Where are the paintings?'

'There are no paintings,' said Evans in a flat, even voice.

Sue looked at Evans and saw that his eyes had changed too. They seemed to be made of grey, expressionless glass and she could hear him breathing. He was making a hissing sound as air was sucked in and expelled again through clenched teeth.

'Is this some kind of tasteless joke?' she asked, but fear was already beginning to gnaw at her stomach.

'No joke,' whispered Evans. 'It's all deadly serious.'

Sue made a move towards the door, but Evans shifted slightly to bar her way.

'Let me out of here!' demanded Sue. Fear had put a tremor into her voice.

'You are not going anywhere,' continued the voice. 'First I'll deal with you and then I'll deal with your interfering clod of a husband. He's getting to be too much of a nuisance.'

'Interfering? Interfering in what?'

'My work, that's what,' said Evans his voice rising in volume for the first time.

Sue was terrified by the change coming over Evans. His eyes were suddenly filled with unreasoning hatred and his voice took on the timbre of a religious zealot. She felt sick with fear. 'What do you mean, "Your work"?' she stammered.

'I mean ridding this city of female filth, cleaning up the pestilence that they spread. You all look fine on the outside, but it's just a front. Inside you are filthy! Dirty and filthy!'

Sue screamed as Evans came towards her. She moved backwards, feeling out behind her for obstacles with an outstretched hand, but not daring to take her eyes away from the madman who was coming towards her. She half stumbled as her leg caught the edge of a table and hastily altered course to avoid it.

'Whore!' hissed Evans. 'There is no escape!'

Sue moved in unison with Evans, trying to keep the table between herself and him, but could see it was only a short-term ploy.

Evans could see that too and with a sweep of his foot he cleared away the obstruction. He lunged towards Sue and in her haste to escape him she stumbled backwards and crashed to the floor. She tried to scramble to her feet using the handle of the fridge to help her to her feet, but the magnetic catch on the door released and she fell once more to the floor as the the fridge door swung open. The illuminated interior seemed strangely compelling in the gloom of the basement room. Sue saw what lay inside and her imagination refused to contemplate any more horror. She passed out.

She came to as if waking from a bad dream, only to find that she was part of a living nightmare. She was lying on wood-framed camp bed with her hands and feet securely bound. Something had been stuffed into her mouth and a handkerchief used to keep it in place. As she moved her head she felt the wad of material in her mouth move a little further towards the back of her throat, threatening to induce the gag response. Suddenly fearful that she would choke, she moved her head again in an effort to stop her airway becoming blocked. The terror she felt was working against her by increasing the demand for oxygen to supply the blood that was rushing through her veins. She could hear the rapid thump of a pulse in her ears. Her movement on the camp bed brought Evans to her side.

From where Sue lay, Evans appeared to be seven feet tall. He was wearing a long rubber apron and in his hand he held a surgical knife.

'Awake? Good. It's important that you are conscious at the moment of your cleansing, the instant when the evil is excised from your corrupt body.'

Sue's eyes grew wide with terror as Evans bent down and started to cut away her clothing. She saw his eyes linger on her breasts. He seemed to be engaged in some deep inner struggle. Sweat began to appear along his upper lip and his pocked skin became deathly pale. He was muttering something under his breath. His hands moved to hover near her breasts, but then were withdrawn while he looked up to the ceiling as if for guidance. He started to remove the rest of her clothes.

As she threw her head back in anguish, Sue again caused the rag in her mouth to move backwards, threatening to make her retch. If that happened while she was gagged, she would inhale her own vomit and die of asphyxiation. When assessed coldly and dispassionately that might have been preferable to what Evans had in store for her, but there is nothing cold or dispassionate about the desire to cling on to life. Sue jerked her head forward violently in a desperate attempt to clear the obstruction.

Suddenly, fists pounded on the outside door. 'Sue? Are you in there?' demanded Jamieson's voice from the other side of the door.

Evans straightened up and stood there silently, his eyes filled with uncertainty, the knife still raised in his hand. Sue still fought desperately for air.

'Sue! Evans! Can you hear me?'

Evans stood like a statue until the footsteps started to recede up the steps outside. The knife in his hand slowly started to descend as he relaxed. It cut an invisible line through the air. He turned to look at Sue again, his pock-marked face a mask of venom. 'So he knows!' he hissed. 'The interfering idiot knows, but he's too late!'

Sue stopped breathing altogether as she saw the knife in Evans' hand move towards her. Her silent scream was interrupted by a tremendous crash of broken glass as the window was kicked in. The sound continued as several more kicks were applied to remove all the glass from the frame. Evans left Sue and ran across the room in time to meet Jamieson coming in through the opening. He swung the knife and caught Jamieson on the left shoulder, opening up a cut from which blood welled up and soaked his jacket, but no muscular damage had been done.

The two men circled each other, Evans making regular gestures with the knife to keep Jamieson at bay.

'You mad bastard!' whispered Jamieson. 'You crazy mad bastard!'

'You don't understand,' insisted Evans. 'She's evil. They're all evil. You've just been blinded to it by her looks. She'll destroy you in the end.'

Jamieson shook his head in disbelief at the deranged man he saw before him. He risked a quick glance at Sue and was so alarmed at the colour of her complexion, which was becoming blue through asphyxiation, that his concentration was broken. The excitement and panic brought on by watching the fight between Evans and her husband had made the rag in her mouth move backwards into her throat.

Evans took full advantage of Jamieson's lapse. He picked up the ultra-violet lamp that had been sitting on his work bench and threw it at Jamieson. It caught Jamieson high on the temple and sent him crashing to the floor in a haze of pain.

Jamieson was aware of Evans coming towards him. He groped desperately for anything near him on the floor that could be used as a weapon against the madman. His hand closed round a long shard of glass that had fallen from the broken window.

At the very moment that Evans threw himself at him, Jamieson brought the jagged shard round in front of him and held it firmly upright with both hands. The full weight of Evans' body came down on it and a look of stunned surprise appeared on his face. His body went completely rigid for a moment and then slowly relaxed into death.

Jamieson was pinned to the floor by the weight of Evans' body. He was desperate to get to Sue, but it seemed to take an eternity to free himself from the sprawling corpse on top of him. With a final desperate shove he managed it and staggered to Sue's assistance. She was unconscious and badly cyanosed when he cut away the handkerchief and pulled the gag out of her mouth. He felt for a pulse and failed to find one. In desperation he started to blow air gently down into her lungs. There was no response.

He was still engaged in mouth-to-mouth resuscitation when the police arrived and Chief Inspector Ryan entered the flat. Ryan took in the situation and radioed for an ambulance before doing anything else. He approached the table and stood quietly at Jamieson's side. 'The ambulance is on its way. How is she?' he asked quietly. Jamieson shook his head as if to dismiss the question and continued as if he were in another world. In the background a policeman threw up as he opened the fridge.

Sue coughed and Jamieson paused, thinking it the most beautiful sound he had ever heard. He exchanged glances with Ryan and his cheek muscles started to quiver as he watched Sue begin to breathe again on her own. After a few minutes she opened her eyes. She appeared to look at Jamieson but then closed them again. Ryan knew as well as Jamieson that there was a danger of brain damage, depending on how long Sue had been without oxygen.

'It's over, my darling,' Jamieson whispered. 'You're safe now. No one is ever going to hurt you again.'

There was an agonising pause before Sue said, 'I seem to have heard that somewhere before.'

Jamieson let out his breath in a long sigh and Ryan smiled at him. Sue was going to be all right.

'It is, my darling,' said Jamieson. 'We're going home.'

Two days later, Jamieson and Sue left Kerr Memorial for the last time. Maybe it was the fact that the sun was shining, but it seemed to both of them that the hospital had become a friendlier place. Phillip Morton was the last to come down and say good-bye to them and with him he brought the news that the four remaining *Proteus* patients were responding well to one of the antibiotics sent up by the Sci-Med labs. They were expected to make a full recovery

As they drove out through the gates, neither Sue nor Jamieson felt inclined to look back. Sue clicked on the car radio in time to hear a government spokesman assure his interviewer that screening procedures for hospital staff were entirely adequate and there was no cause for public alarm. Jamieson reached out and switched it off again.